UNDER FIRE

THE FIREFIGHTERS OF STATION FIVE

JO DAVIS

A SIGNET ECLIPSE BOOK

SIGNET ECLIPSE
Published by New American Library, a division of
Penguin Group (USA) Inc., 375 Hudson Street,
New York, New York 10014, USA
Penguin Group (Canada), 90 Eglinton Avenue East, Suite 700, Toronto,
Ontario M4P 2Y3, Canada (a division of Pearson Penguin Canada Inc.)
Penguin Books Ltd., 80 Strand, London WC2R 0RL, England
Penguin Ireland, 25 St. Stephen's Green, Dublin 2,
Ireland (a division of Penguin Books Ltd.)
Penguin Group (Australia), 250 Camberwell Road, Camberwell, Victoria 3124,
Australia (a division of Pearson Australia Group Pty. Ltd.)
Penguin Books India Pvt. Ltd., 11 Community Centre, Panchsheel Park,
New Delhi - 110 017, India
Penguin Group (NZ), 67 Apollo Drive, Rosedale, North Shore 0632,
New Zealand (a division of Pearson New Zealand Ltd.)
Penguin Books (South Africa) (Pty.) Ltd., 24 Sturdee Avenue,
Rosebank, Johannesburg 2196, South Africa

Penguin Books Ltd., Registered Offices:
80 Strand, London WC2R 0RL, England

First published by Signet Eclipse, an imprint of New American Library,
a division of Penguin Group (USA) Inc.

First Printing, May 2009
10 9 8 7 6 5 4 3 2 1

Copyright © Jo Davis, 2009
All rights reserved

SIGNET ECLIPSE and logo are trademarks of Penguin Group (USA) Inc.

Printed in the United States of America

For my husband, Paul, my headstrong alpha male with a mushy heart of gold. You are the light of my life, my muse, my hero. We've come a long way, baby. May the next eighteen years hold as many wonderful surprises.

ACKNOWLEDGMENTS

As always, my heartfelt thanks to:

My husband and children, for their steadfast support, and for smiling when I'm on deadline and declaring that ordering pizza for the third time this week is a great idea.

Roberta Brown, my agent, miracle worker, and friend.

Tracy Bernstein, my fabulous editor; Angela Januzzi, my awesome publicist; the art and marketing departments and all of the folks at NAL who work hard behind the scenes. You guys rock.

Tracy Garrett and Suzanne Welsh, the best critique partners and friends a girl could ask for.

The Foxes, without whom I cannot imagine getting through a single day. I'd always wanted a sister, and now I have nine.

Captain Steve Deutsch and the C-shift firefighters, for their wisdom and inspiration.

Note: Any mistakes I've made or liberties I've taken for story-line purposes are completely my own.

1

The back end of the SUV filled Zack Knight's windshield before his exhausted brain jolted to awareness, screaming the belated message to slam on his brakes.

Too late, he jammed his foot hard to the floorboard. Only a split second to realize he wasn't going to be able to stop on the rain-slickened pavement, for his stomach to plunge to his toes. One heartbeat to curse his stupid mental lapse and recognize the very real irony of a firefighter/paramedic causing a traffic accident.

A brief, muffled squeal of tires sounded in his ears. His classic 1967 Mustang was low to the ground and built like a sleek silver bullet, and the car hydroplaned right into the tail of the SUV with slightly less force than a shot from a gun.

A loud, sickening crunch of metal, and the bone-jarring impact was over before he could blink. Just like that. One millisecond of inattention. On the job, he'd seen the tragic results often enough.

Fortunately he was alive and seemingly unhurt, if a little dazed and breathless.

Mortification cut through the shock. Good God, he'd just rear-ended someone! "Oh, Jesus."

Unfastening his seat belt, he glanced behind him to

check for oncoming traffic in the left-hand lane, then threw open his door and slid out. Taking a couple of steps, he grimaced in pain. The impact had wrenched his back and neck. Not too bad right now, but by tomorrow he'd be damned sore. Putting aside his discomfort, he limped to the driver's side of the SUV he hit. The sight that greeted him made his heart lurch. A woman sat behind the wheel, face buried in her hands, expression hidden by long honey brown hair.

"Ma'am?" She didn't move, so he knocked on the window, his pulse jackhammering. "Ma'am, are you all right?"

Slowly, she lowered her hands, raised her head, turned to peer at him . . . and the world did a funny little flip.

Wow. The lady had a lovely oval face that would make angels weep. Frigging supermodel drop-dead gorgeous. She opened her door and he stepped back to accommodate her, nervous and embarrassed. On top of everything, he'd never been good at relating to women on any level—pathetic, but true—and now he had to keep from staring like an idiot at the goddess standing in front of him.

A visibly upset, wide-eyed, long-legged goddess wearing black leather pants and high-heeled boots, a snazzy black leather coat, and a fuzzy red sweater underneath. Oh, *wow.*

And, holy shit, those eyes! Golden and dark-edged around her irises, like a jungle cat's. Exotic. For a brief second, he allowed himself to wonder what it might be like to just throw in the towel and let himself get eaten.

Shaking himself from his stupor, he held out a hand. "God, are you okay? I'm *so* sorry. I—"

"Don't they *stop* at red lights where you're from, Forrest Gump?"

Ouch. No doubt she wouldn't believe the man who'd just plowed into her backside—now, *there* was a double entendre he didn't need—possessed a so-called genius IQ of 150.

"Like I said, I'm sorry. I'm Zack Knight, and I'm a firefighter and paramedic. Would you sit in your truck and let me check your vitals?" Oh, Christ. He'd like to check a helluva lot more than the lady's pulse, if the stirring in his poor, neglected groin was any indication.

She laughed, a bold, brassy sound, and plenty jaded. Like life was one big, unfunny joke after another, usually on her. Zack knew the feeling well.

Her smile was breathtaking, wide and full of straight white teeth, dispelling the notion she was the frightened victim he'd first thought. No, this woman was capable of handling anything, and probably had. Twice.

"My vitals. Right. Like you haven't done enough already? Thanks, sugar lump, but I'll take my chances. Let's see the damage."

She walked to the rear of her SUV, a sporty red Explorer with the bumper and hatch door buckled inward at the bottom, the paint scratched. And wasn't his insurance agent going to be ecstatic? This ought to do wonders for his premium, which he couldn't afford in the first place.

Even the Mustang, built in an era when manufacturers didn't use plastic soda bottles for bumpers, had sustained a mangled grille and buckled hood. Hundreds, if not thousands of dollars down the drain. Zack swayed a little, feeling sick.

Heaving a deep breath, he tugged his wallet from the back pocket of his regulation blue pants and removed one of his cards. He forced himself to meet her amber gaze squarely.

"This has my work and cell phone numbers on it. I'll call the police so they can make a report, and write my insurance information on the back while we're waiting. Sound okay?"

She nodded. "Fine."

"Are you sure you're all right? I really think you should go get examined." He ought to do the same, but wouldn't. He had to get his ass to the station, pronto, before the captain served it to him roasted on a platter.

Her mouth tightened. "Let's just get on with it, hotshot. It's colder than a well digger's butt out here and the rain is getting harder." Tucking a damp strand of hair behind her ear, she started to turn.

"Wait. What's your name?"

Arching a brow, she gave him a penetrating look, as though deciding whether to grace him with the information. For the first time, he realized how very tall she was. In the heels, she topped his six feet by an inch or so. Without them, she'd still almost match his height.

Sensual lips curving upward, she stuck out a slender hand tipped with bloodred nails. "Corrine Shannon, exotic dancer. Cori, if you like."

Shit, yeah, I like.

Her throaty voice flooded his mind with naughty images of her lips nibbling down his naked body in the dark—

Whoa. Down, boy. He cleared his throat and clasped her hand. "That's nice. Company or p-private?" Immediately, he wanted to slice off his tongue. What the hell had made him blurt such a stupid question?

"Private. I work birthdays, anniversaries, bachelor parties . . . whatever. Thursdays through Saturdays, six p.m. to two a.m." The smile became knowing, feral. Her tawny eyes sparkled as she reached out, pushed his gold wire-rimmed glasses higher on his nose, then trailed a long nail down his cheek. "Don't sweat it, fireboy. You can't afford me."

His eyes widened. "I—I didn't mean . . . I wasn't—"

Cori turned on her elegant heel, strode back to her vehicle, and climbed in, leaving him with his mouth hanging open, the memory of her touch scorching his skin. Until he reminded himself the woman was an admitted pro. Seduction came naturally to her, probably meant nothing more than bigger tips. And his experience with women was sadly lacking.

Just as he turned to walk off, she leaned out her open door. "Listen . . . are *you* all right?"

The soft question, posed with genuine concern and without a trace of her earlier attitude, almost did him in.

He managed a weak smile that felt lopsided on his face. "Yeah, I'm good."

She frowned. "You don't look so good, Zack Knight."

Which made today like any other.

"I'll be fine, but thanks."

The extralong forty-eight-hour double shift ahead seemed an impossible feat. And when the looming bad weather finally hit, their emergency calls would more than triple. A wave of sheer exhaustion swamped him anew, with no relief on the horizon. Discouraged, he returned to the Mustang and used his cell phone to call the police. Next, he phoned the station and spoke to Eve Marshall, the station's only female firefighter, and his closest friend.

"Zack, you're almost an hour late! Sean's in a shitty mood, my friend, and this doesn't help. Where are you?"

"I was in an accident, Evie. The police—"

"Oh, shit! Are you hurt?"

"No, no. Just a fender bender." To the tune of about a hundred wrenched muscles and a few thousand in damages to the vehicles, but he left that part out.

Eve sighed in relief. "Thank God."

"Tell the captain I'll be there as soon as I can, will you?"

"Huh. I'll try, but he's been holed up in his office since we came on shift, barking at everyone who sticks their nose in, including Six-Pack. We heard them yelling at each other earlier. It got real nasty."

Zack closed his eyes. Lieutenant Howard "Six-Pack" Paxton and Captain Sean Tanner were tight, the best of friends. Over the years, they'd been through hell and back together, and more than anyone, Howard had been struggling to see his friend through a horrible personal downslide. Six-Pack was as patient as they came, a solid rock of a guy. If those two were tearing strips off each other, Zack could only imagine the joyful reception he'd get later.

"Wonderful. If he asks, just let him know I'm coming. Tell Six-Pack, too."

"Sure thing. Glad you're okay, buddy," she said warmly.

Her obvious concern helped, just a little, and he smiled in spite of the crappy morning. "Thanks."

Settling in to wait for the police, he ran a hand through his short, wet hair.

Lightning flashed across the sky, stretched a bony white finger to the ground in the distance. A clap of thunder followed, promising that the steady freezing rain would gather in velocity for the fierce winter storm the forecasters had been predicting. The light and sound show was beyond strange for January.

He shivered; whether from the chill gripping his

soaked body or from the eerie disquiet an approaching storm always evoked in him, he couldn't say.

The cop, when he finally deigned to show, proved to be a bored, sarcastic prick. In Zack's experience, working closely with the police at traffic accidents and various emergencies, most cops were cool, if somewhat rough around the edges. This one wasn't. Zack's lucky day, all around.

Jerk or not, he took down the pertinent information about the accident with efficiency, and handed Ms. Shannon the promised card Zack provided with his insurance information written on it. Of course, the cop couldn't resist a parting jab or two as he returned to conclude business.

"Nice car. A classic. In a bit too much of a hurry in dangerous weather?"

Zack made an effort to sound respectful instead of annoyed. "I wasn't speeding."

The cop arched a brow. "In a 'sixty-seven Mustang? Right."

"You don't believe me." Big surprise.

"People yank my weenie all day, Mr. Knight. I got no reason to think you're any different, fire department or not." He held out a small yellow card and tapped a beefy finger at eight digits he'd written on top.

"This is the number of my traffic report. Give that to your insurance rep when you call. Bada-bing, you're set. Try not to pulverize anyone else, will ya?"

Biting back a retort, Zack tucked the card into a pocket inside his coat to protect it from the persistent rain, which had ramped up to a downpour. He was so cold and miserable, his face had gone numb. His chest felt heavy and his body ached as though he'd been beaten with hammers, and not just because of the wreck. Worse, he was now so late for A-shift that the captain would definitely chew his ass, spit it out, then devise some wicked method of punishment. Fantastic.

"Oh, by the way," the cop said, rubbing his chin. "You got any business east of town, stay away from the Sugarland Bridge. I heard the Cumberland is swelling by the hour, and they're sayin' what with the runoff from the melting sleet we've had all week, the storm will have the river overflowin' the banks by this afternoon. Hope you boys don't get any calls out there."

Zack nodded, somewhat revising his opinion of the man in light of his genuine concern. "Me, too. I appreciate the advice."

The cop jogged to his cruiser and jumped in. After the man drove away, Zack contemplated the wisdom of apologizing to Cori Shannon one more time, making sure she'd be fine before he left.

She settled the matter by giving him a quick wave good-bye out her window, then rolling it up and pulling carefully into the morning traffic. So much for chivalry. With a weary sigh, he followed suit, dreading the imminent confrontation with Tanner.

Whatever he'd been expecting, the reality turned out to be much, much worse. Stiff, shivering, and saturated to the bone, he squished inside, leaving puddles in his wake through the station's TV room. Where was everyone? He prayed he'd get the chance to grab his extra navy pants and Sugarland FD polo shirt from his bedside locker and change before facing the captain's wrath.

Voices drifted from the kitchen, along with the rich aroma of fresh coffee. God bless Six-Pack for insisting they stock an excellent Starbucks blend. He couldn't wait to get his hands wrapped around a hot mug. If only he could stop shaking enough to hold it steady. Nerves had set in, and the full import of how bad the wreck might've been left him rattled.

In the kitchen, he found Six-Pack leaning his rear against the counter, arms crossed over his massive chest, talking in a quiet, somber tone to Eve. With his short, spiky brown hair bleached blond at the tips, his towering height, and his buff physique, Zack always thought Howard resembled an action-movie star. He and Eve were dressed in the same navy pants and polo shirt that were required on duty, except his friends' clothes were nice and dry.

"Hey, guys." They turned to him and he attempted a smile, but it wouldn't materialize.

Six-Pack pushed off the counter and crossed to him in three strides, Eve on his heels, worry etched on his rugged face. The lieutenant laid a big hand on Zack's shoulder, pinning him with serious brown eyes.

"Eve said you were fine. You don't look fine to me."

"Nah, not even a scratch. Where's Tanner?" He looked around warily.

Eve scowled. "Forget Sean for a minute. I'm not talking about bumps and bruises at the moment, my friend. You've been walking around here like a zombie for weeks. Next thing I know, you've bred that car you're so meticulous about with someone else's. What's going on with you?"

He shrugged, going for nonchalant. "I've been working a lot of doubles. Somebody has to fill in for Val on B-shift while his leg is healing. Might as well be me."

Because he desperately needed the extra money, and none of his friends knew why. After Darius Knight's stroke landed him in a nursing home last year, discovery of the staggering gambling debt the old man owed to Joaquin Delacruz, a dangerous Atlantic City hotel and casino mogul, shocked Zack to the core. What followed ensured a succession of sleepless nights.

Delacruz's cold promise of bodily harm if he didn't recoup his money launched Zack into a sick, dizzying slide into hell. He'd gone to the police and the FBI, who ceased to give a shit upon learning the debt was legal. Delacruz knew how to play the game. Threats weren't actions, so the authorities' hands were tied. Fine. Zack could take care of himself and if his own safety were the only issue, he would've told Delacruz to shove it.

But his father was completely incapacitated, in a coma and helpless to defend himself. Zack just didn't have it in him not to care what happened to his own father . . . even if the sentiment had never been returned.

Delacruz had ruined Zack in record time.

His beloved home, gone. The life savings he'd built for his own future, gone. The Mustang, his pride and joy, he'd held on to by his fingertips.

He'd never recover from the financial blow, not to mention the physical one. God, he was so tired, most days he couldn't remember his name, and the team had started to notice. This morning's wreck had been a mere symptom of a much larger problem. They'd watch him like hawks now, ready to intervene if he started to sink.

They had no idea how easy giving up would be.

Twenty-six years old, flat broke, and at the mercy of dangerous criminals. How do you like those apples, genius?

Eve took his hand, her bronzed, angular face scrunching into a frown. Striking pale blue eyes regarded her friend with affection. "Zack, you're freezing! Are you sure you're all right? You look ready to pass out."

"I'm fine. I just want to get out of these cl—"

"Knight! Where the holy hell have you been?"

The captain stepped into the kitchen from the hall-way leading to the office and sleeping quarters. Tanner's hard face was thunderous, startling green eyes snapping with fury.

Ah, fuck.

Cori Shannon squinted through the windshield at the sleet, fighting the steering wheel in the pissy weather. The wipers slapped to the rhythm of an Aerosmith tune as Steven Tyler shagged somebody in the elevator, the old guy getting more action than a team of Navy SEALs on shore leave. Which normally would've lifted her spirits, the rockin' beat and the mental image of someone going after what they wanted, and getting it.

Dammit, she'd missed her morning class. And right before a big exam, too. Now she'd have to make time she didn't have in her already-insane schedule later today to get two estimates to have her truck fixed, get a rental, deal with insurance. All because that guy frickin' fell asleep at the wheel. What was his name?

Zack. The firefighter.

The cutie with the laser blue peepers hiding behind those conservative wire-rimmed glasses. Tall, lean, and fit. He'd been young, twentysomething, with soft, coal black hair tumbling over his forehead and framing a kind face. Okay, a *gorgeous* face with a delicious body to match.

In truth, she hadn't been able to take her eyes off the way his rain-splattered shirt clung to the hard muscles of his chest. Had feasted on the sight of his wet pants plas-tered to his long legs and tight, perfect rear end.

Oh, he was a very sexy man all right, but . . . there'd been something vulnerable in his gaze. Something deep and sad that drew her, made her want to take him in her arms and hold him.

Because, shit, she recognized herself in his lost expression. Crazy, but for one split second, she'd fought the impulse to grab his hand and say, "Hey, let's blow this place. Jump in and we'll get the hell gone."

Funny thing was, the man looked like he might've taken her up on the offer.

Not that she would've made it, much as the idea had merit. "You're an upstanding citizen nowadays, Corrine, my girl," she muttered to herself. "No more disastrous decisions for you."

She shivered. Alexander Gunter was dead, and she'd come damned close to paying the ultimate price for giving up her dreams the first time around the block. For marrying a man wearing the guise of a savior before she discovered the ruthless jackal underneath.

Done and gone. She was so near the realization of her dream, she could taste success. In spite of the crappy start to her day, happiness curled through her belly. May graduation was a mere four months away. By God, she'd done it! A position at Sterling Medical Center, Sugarland's new hospital, was already hers.

In a few months, once the last of her school bills were paid off and she started drawing a regular check from her new job, she'd start repaying her oldest brother in earnest for his latest "gift." Her brother's presents came with too many strings. She hated owing him and he knew it.

All her debts would be history.

Best of all, she'd say so long to exotic dancing for good.

Despite her distaste at using her body to achieve an end, the money was fantastic and immediate, and had served two purposes. One, excavating her life from the nightmare that was her marriage to Alex. Two, proving to her brother that she could take care of herself, despite his being royally pissed at her method.

Brows furrowed, she wondered why on earth she'd deliberately given Zack Knight a skewed impression of herself. Why hadn't she just told him she was in nursing school? A bit of defiance rearing its ugly head, she supposed. Alex would've killed her had he lived to discover how she was paying for her education, if not for defying his edict in the first place.

Yeah, a secret, perverse part of her had wanted to see how Zack would react to news that would have most men panting in anticipation—however incorrect—of an easy screw.

Not this one. The memory of his blue eyes widening in innocence at the disclosure of her *profession* caused a weird ache in the region of her heart. No guy could possibly be so sweet and naive in this day and age.

What a refreshing change.

Rot in hell, Alex.

A crack of lightning and drumroll of thunder made Cori jump, startling her attention back to the road. The sleet drove against the windshield in sheets, lowering visibility to almost nil. Clenching the steering wheel in a white-knuckle grip, she made up her mind to pull over at the first opportunity and wait until the weather let up. Maybe park at a fast-food restaurant, sip a cup of coffee to ward off the chill. She'd already missed her class, so what did it matter?

Problem was, there weren't any good places in sight to

stop. The Sugarland Bridge loomed ahead, a ghostly specter enshrouded in gray. The morning had grown so dark she could hardly tell where the sky ended and the river burgeoning underneath the bridge began.

Easing off the gas, she suppressed a nervous shudder. Heights scared the shit out of her, always had. Couple that fear with a seventy-year-old bridge the county should've replaced years ago, rising water, and a fierce storm, and you had a real bladder buster.

Glancing in the rearview mirror, she noticed a pair of headlights approaching from behind. The deluge might be distorting things, but it seemed the lights were approaching far too fast for the treacherous conditions.

Starting over the bridge, she tensed, attention divided between driving carefully and the idiot who was indeed gaining rapidly on her tail. What fool needed to be in such a hurry in terrible weather like this?

The driver was closing the gap between them at an alarming clip, rushing up until the glare from the headlights filled her back end. The jerk didn't try to pass, but rode her tail no more than a few feet back. Too dangerous and freaky for words. Cori held steady, determined to pull off to the shoulder on the other side and let the car go around her. Just a bit farther and—

A muffled pop sounded a split second before Cori realized her SUV had blown a tire. The vehicle skidded to the right, and, panicking, she jerked the wheel in the opposite direction, overcorrecting.

On a clear day, in dry conditions, she would've been able to straighten the vehicle without mishap. But not on what might well be the last day of her life.

Crossing the oncoming lane, she saw the opposite guardrail approach at a terrifying speed. In knee-jerk reaction, she stomped hard on the brake, sending the Explorer into a skid there was no stopping. Too late.

Cori screamed as the SUV rocketed into the guardrail. A deafening explosion of glass and grinding metal drowned out all else. The air bag deployed in her face, saving her from slamming into the steering column or windshield, but the crash jarred every bone in her body. The awful tearing of metal that seemed to go on forever lasted only seconds.

She sat stunned, unable to move, taking stock.

Pain? Not yet. After the shock wore off, most definitely.

Dizzy? Oh, yeah. Her head spun. The vehicle, which seemed to be tilted nose down, rocked like a child's see-saw. Christ, she must've really shaken her brain to be rewarded with that kind of action. At least the glaring headlights were gone.

Frowning, she turned her head to look out her driver's window, wincing at a stab of pain in her temple. *What do you know?* The jerk hadn't even stopped. Unlike the rocking.

Oh, no. The motion wasn't from dizziness.

Hands shaking, she pushed the deflating air bag out of her face and peered out the shattered front windshield. Terror numbed her entire body like a shot of Novocain.

"Oh God, oh shit . . ."

Her Explorer tottered just a few feet above the swollen, angry Cumberland River.

Nothing between her and a watery grave except the hand of God.

2

The captain crossed to the group, his lean-hipped stride reminding Zack of a panther preparing to rip him to shreds.

Eve looked at Zack. "Sorry, bud. I tried to explain, but he wouldn't listen."

Tanner's gaze briefly touched hers. "And as I reminded you, you're not his mother. Let Wonder Boy make his own excuses." To Zack, he said, "This is the fourth time you've been late this month. Start talking."

Heat crept up Zack's neck, but he stood his ground. "Does it really make a difference? You've known me for four years, Cap. In all that time, those are the only instances I've ever been late. I'm sorry; it won't happen again."

"Says the slacker who didn't roll the hoses properly or clean the bathroom last month when his turn rolled around," the captain fired back.

"That's not the whole story. I asked Salvatore to—"

"Not to mention taking a week off while Six-Pack was in the hospital recovering from a fucking near-fatal gunshot wound. Your selfishness spread the whole team thin."

Goddamn. Like he'd had a choice? "Clay covered my shifts—"

"And you failed to clean the quint before going off B-shift on Wednesday, and Clay, covering your ass yet again, washed it and got the fucking mud off by himself."

Zack stared at Tanner, who took a step closer, getting in his grill. "I left early with the stomach flu—"

"Where's your part of the grocery money? You still owe from last month, and the others are sick of fronting you. Either pay up or don't eat."

Zack wanted to die. Wished hell would open under his feet and finish the job. Did the captain think so little of him to believe he'd take what he hadn't paid for? Hadn't the man noticed he'd been brown-bagging it with peanut butter and bologna for weeks, when he ate at all?

He wouldn't defend himself again. Not under pain of torture.

Eve, bristling with anger, hands fisted on her hips, had no such problem. "Hang on just a damned minute, Tanner! Zack hasn't—"

"I'll bring the money tomorrow." Where he'd get it was another problem, but he'd cough up the cash somehow.

"Right."

"Are you calling me a *liar*?" Incredulous, Zack gaped at the captain.

"If the shoe fits."

"Slacker" was bad enough. Of all the things he'd been called, "liar" was the worst. And in front of half the team, no less. This wasn't the man he'd admired for so long. He stilled, unwilling to show how much the words hurt. "Why don't we t-take this to your office?"

"Why don't you tell me why you're almost two hours late, goddammit?" Tanner shouted.

"I had a wr-wreck on the way here, sir. I rear-ended

another vehicle, but no one was hurt. S-satisfied?" Damn, he wished he could stop his teeth from chattering. The last thing he wanted was to appear cowed in front of Tanner, but he was so freaking *cold*.

Tanner stared at him a long moment, his gaze frigid. "Nobody was hurt *this time*, so that makes it all right?"

"Sean," Six-Pack warned.

Ah, shit. He'd unwittingly pushed a major hot button with the captain. How to defuse it?

"No, sir. Just stating the facts. The accident was my fault, but it was minor and the lady and I are both okay." He spread his hands, attempting to make a lighthearted joke. "I'm here now and ready to get to work, unless you'd like to spank me and send me to time-out."

The joke backfired. Tanner grabbed a fistful of the front of Zack's soggy shirt and slammed him backward into the kitchen cabinets. "You worthless little shit. You can look in my face and make light of the fact that you could've killed an innocent woman?"

Horrified, Six-Pack leapt forward and hauled the captain backward, forcing himself between his two friends. "Sean, Jesus Christ!"

Zack shook his head, heart in his mouth. "No, I—"

Tanner lunged again, oblivious to Six-Pack holding him back. "What if she had a husband and kids who loved her? She might've been dead and that would be on your conscience forever! Your fault!"

Zack's mouth worked, but his voice deserted him. Six-Pack had no such problem. He yanked the captain off Zack, then pushed the center of Tanner's chest hard, sending him backward a couple of steps.

"Shut up, dammit! Zack's accident was nothing like the one that took Blair and the kids. You're way off the deep end. Calm down and apologize to Knight before I go over your head and report you to the battalion chief, and don't think for one fucking minute I won't do it."

Tanner glared at Six-Pack, panting like a trapped animal. Zack and Eve glanced at each other, stunned. Hard to say which was more shocking—Howard dropping the f-bomb, his having the balls to publicly refer to how Tanner's family died, or his very real threat to make a report. Because the lieutenant meant every word, no doubt.

Tanner shifted his stare to Zack and held it a long moment, making a visible effort to gain control. The madness faded, but there was no warmth. And certainly no respect.

"I apologize for grabbing you. Anything you screw up outside work is none of my business, unless you get arrested. On the job is a different story. I won't yield on that point. If you can't pull your weight around the station, I'll find an FAO who can."

Somehow, Zack found his voice. "Y-you'd strip my rank?"

As fire apparatus operator, the man responsible for driving and maintaining the quint, the city's largest and best-equipped engine, he possessed a hard-earned status second only to that of the captain and lieutenant. Most firefighters would kill for the job he loved. One more blow, the one that might finish him. He'd never survive the pay cut, and besides the Mustang, his job was the sole bright spot left in his existence.

"Don't give me any more reasons to consider it, and we won't have a problem," the captain muttered. "Now that you've graced us with your presence, find something useful to do."

Sean spun on his heel and stalked toward the bay, leaving a vacuum of uncomfortable silence in his wake. Eve stared after him, a rare, undisguised look of wretched worry on her striking face—the look a woman gives a man, not that of a teammate for her captain.

Too bad for her, nursing an attraction to a man with a broken heart. *Can you spell "doomed"?* Not only her but the whole team if she didn't get a grip. A disaster in the making.

Zack felt ill. Literally. The aches and chills were getting worse by the minute, heat radiating off his face. His body was strangely hot underneath the freezing clothes, too. Great. And he didn't dare go home sick after the horrible scene with the captain.

He sent his friends a wan smile. "Well, that was fun. Where are Tommy and Julian?"

Six-Pack snorted. "Hiding out in their bunks like the lily-livered cowards they are." His brown gaze softened in sympathy. "Hey, don't worry about Sean. You know he didn't mean any of the stuff he said. He's not himself. His son's nineteenth birthday is—or would've been—next week. Doesn't give him the right to rag on you, but I'm just saying."

"Ah, Jesus." Zack sighed, hurting for Tanner in spite of the awful things his friend had said. Things he didn't really mean, because of the terrible pain he lived with every day. It must be agonizing for the captain to see his best friend happily married to his new wife, Kat, and contemplating a family of his own.

"Why don't you get out of those wet clothes? After you change, I'm going to check you out, since you didn't go to the hospital," Eve scolded.

"Don't worry about m—" Whatever else Zack had been about to say was interrupted by three loud tones over the new intercom system. Everyone went silent, straining to hear the call over the roll of thunder and pops of lightning rattling the windows.

As the computerized female voice relayed the emergency, the ball of dread resting in his gut since the storm began morphed into real fear. A driver had swerved out of control and plowed through a guardrail in the storm.

The SUV was hanging off the Sugarland Bridge, a hairbreadth from plunging into the rising river.

A-shift had worked some tough scenes over the years, had walked the razor's edge in some gut-wrenching situations. But as Zack drove the quint past the police barricade and neared the bridge's summit, Tanner let loose a few creative curses while Zack gaped in silence. God Almighty, this one was a real bitch.

Tanner directed the situation from his seat in the front next to Zack. At the moment, the captain was all business, their earlier unpleasantness on hold. "We'll wrap the chain around something solid, like the opposite guardrail or bridge support, then hook it to the rear axle of the SUV, try to stabilize the vehicle. Extract the driver through the back hatch."

"Yes, sir." Zack frowned as the teetering Explorer came into view. Recognition dawned, hitting his gut like a fist. "Sonofabitch."

Tanner snapped his sharp gaze to his FAO's face. "What?"

"That's her. The lady I hit on the way to work."

"Keep your head in the game, kid. That doesn't necessarily mean anything."

Zack's thoughts mirrored Tanner's. The woman might've been more injured than Zack previously believed. She could have passed out. Or perhaps she was rattled from being hit, and a moment of inattention resulted in her current predicament. Either way, the idea he might be responsible for a woman's life literally hanging in the balance, even inadvertently, filled him with dread.

If what happened to Cori Shannon was his fault, Tanner wouldn't have to fire him. He'd be finished.

Pulling the hat low over his eyes, Zack threw open the door and swung down from the quint, wincing at the pain in his stiffening muscles. The wind howled with frightening strength, the forceful gusts threatening to sweep man and machine right off the structure and into hell. Rain pummeled his body in icy sheets, soaking him to the skin once more and chilling him to the bone despite the thick coat, pants, and hat.

And in spite of the rising fever he hadn't told anyone about. Zack trembled so hard there was no way Tanner hadn't noticed, but the stubborn jerk never acknowledged it. He was hot and cold by turns, limbs weighing a ton. Once Ms. Shannon was safe and the situation put behind them, he'd collapse on his bunk at the station. He doubted he'd be able to drive to his crappy apartment even if he wanted to.

Opening a side compartment on the quint, he and Tanner wrestled out a thick, industrial-strength chain while Eve and Tommy Skyler ran over to the Explorer. Six-Pack and Julian Salvatore hopped out of the ambulance and jogged toward Zack and Tanner.

"Get this wrapped around the guardrail over there," Tanner shouted at Salvatore above the thunder and lightning. "Hurry!"

After shooting the captain a grim look that spoke volumes, Salvatore nodded. Handling metal, being surrounded by the stuff in a storm, exposed on an open bridge, was a necessary risk with potentially deadly consequences. Of all the dangerous battles they waged upon occasion, Mother Nature was the most formidable opponent. Some guys didn't face her and go home to tell the story.

As Skyler helped Salvatore, Zack hurried to the side of the Explorer, watching his footing. The driver's door was positioned over open space, muddy water swirling only feet below them. To see Cori, he had to lean forward carefully without touching the vehicle and upsetting it, or losing his balance in the wind and falling off the bridge. With the added weight of his gear, he'd sink like a stone.

He knocked on the window as hard as he dared. "Ma'am? Ms. Shannon?" Slowly, she turned her head to peer at him through the rain-splattered glass. "Sugarland Fire Department. Are you hurt?"

"Hit my head," she called back, voice barely audible above the storm's racket. "Nothing's broken."

Thank God for that. A concussion, most likely, but she might also have some internal injuries. He tried to sound encouraging. "All right, that's good. Listen, I promise we're gonna get you out of there. Sit tight while we secure the back end, and then we'll bring you out through the rear. Okay?"

After a pause, she nodded.

"That's my girl. I'm going around to the back and—"

"No! Don't leave me!" she wailed, shaking her head.

"I'm not leaving you, Cori. You have my word." He put a thread of steel into his voice, using her first name on purpose. The calm assurance, the familiarity—firefighters employed these to keep a victim from wigging out. "I'm not going anywhere except through the back to meet you."

"Promise?" Cori pushed a wet strand of brown hair from her eyes. Even through the sleet, he could see the tension and fear etched on her white face.

Cori was terrified. Depending on him. In that moment, Zack's problems, the sickness threatening to topple him, vanished. His whole world shrank to a laser point of purpose. Nothing mattered except keeping his promise, getting her to safety.

"Absolutely. Just give me a few seconds."

"O-okay."

As Zack hurried to the back end of the vehicle, he wondered if she'd recognized him. Probably not, with the storm obscuring her vision and the hat shielding his face. If she was in shock, she might not even consider how he knew her name.

Skyler and Salvatore had secured the chain to the rear axle by the large hook on one end. The other end, they'd wrapped several times around the guardrail on the opposite side of the bridge to take out as much slack as possible.

Salvatore waved a hand at the makeshift support. "I don't like this," he said in his clipped Spanish accent, which always grew more pronounced under stress. "The guardrail can't take the deadweight if she shifts."

"It's what we've got to work with." The captain jabbed a finger at Howard. "Six-Pack, you're the heaviest. Your weight will help hold it steady while you take her—"

"No." That single, sharp command from Zack got the attention of the entire team. Including Tanner, who gaped at him. "I promised Ms. Shannon I'd go in and get her, and I'm not about to break my word. She's hanging by a thread, and we need her calm."

Tanner's face darkened with anger violent enough to rival the storm. "Knight, did you hear what I—"

"I heard, Cap, and I'm still going in. Ms. Shannon doesn't have time for us to stand around arguing about it." Dismissing Tanner, he turned to Skyler, the youngest team member. "Tommy, get the hatch."

Skyler stared at him, pale eyes wide, jaw slack. To his credit, he turned and twisted the knob, opening the rear entry without argument. The door gave easily, despite being bent from the earlier wreck. Had to be done anyway, so Zack hoped Skyler wouldn't catch hell later. His own job, however, was probably toast.

"What's this? Look!" Crouched by the right rear tire, which was suspended a couple of feet off the ground, Eve pointed to the tread.

"Tire blew," Six-Pack observed. "That's what sent her into the skid."

"Not just a blown tire. A bullet hole." Crouching by Eve, Salvatore poked a finger at the rubber about an inch from the rim. "Where I come from, I ought to know. *Madre de Dios.* Skyler, get a police officer to come take a look."

Skyler jogged down the bridge, toward the barricade. Another wave of heat and cold swamped Zack, and he had to concentrate hard not to let his weakness show. A bullet. Jesus Christ, someone shot out her tire! Who would do such a malicious thing?

"Let's push the vehicle down, get the back tires on the ground," Tanner said. He positioned himself on the right corner of the vehicle, leaning just inside the hatch, Six-Pack on the left. The two men braced their hands on the lip, above the bumper. "Slow and easy."

When the rear tires met pavement, the captain nodded at Zack. Carefully, Zack popped a latch on Tanner's side and let down the rear bench seat to clear the path somewhat. Cori moving from the driver's spot and climbing over the console would be the tricky part.

Pushing his hat back, he crawled inside. On his hands and knees, inch by inch. "Cori? You still with me up there?"

"Hurry!" Long gone was the cocky attitude of their earlier meeting.

His heart lurched in response to her terror. "I'm here, but you're going to have to meet me halfway."

"Nooo! If I move, we'll fall!"

"If you don't, we'll fall anyway. You want me to get you out, right?"

"Yes, but I can't—"

"You *can*. Listen to me. Unbuckle your seat belt. Do it now."

She did, taking the strap off her shoulder. "Okay. Now what?"

"Good. Turn your body to your right, nice and slow, so you can see me." Leather squeaked as she followed his direction, scooting around in the seat. Bracing a trembling hand on the console, she got her first good look at him. Instantly, her eyes widened in recognition.

"You!"

He tried a reassuring smile. "Must be kismet, huh? Don't worry. In spite of earlier evidence to the contrary, you're in good hands."

She let out a shaky laugh that didn't quite hide her fear. "So you're not a *complete* dipstick. Nice to know, Zack."

He grinned at her, glad she had some sass left, even if the barb was directed at his head. That meant she was thinking clearly and would help him get her out of this mess.

A groan of metal reached his ears from somewhere be-hind him, and a ripe curse from Salvatore.

"Move it, amigo! She's not gonna hold for long!"

Amigo? Since when? Salvatore couldn't stand him, so he and Cori must be in deep shit. A trickle of sweat streaked down Zack's fevered cheek as he inched for-ward. Reached out a hand. "Cori, climb over the con-sole."

"Zack—"

"If you don't, we're both going to die, because I'm not leaving without you. I promised."

She glanced at his outstretched hand. Read the truth on his face. He'd willingly give his life for hers. His resolve seemed to fortify her own, and she heaved a deep breath.

"All right. Here I come." Wiggling a bit, she crept forward, squeezing between the seats. One hand over the other.

"Easy does it. Just a little more."

The truck gave a sudden lurch, nose dipping down-ward. Cori shrieked, grabbed for him, and missed. Metal squealed, the noise deafening as the truck slid, tearing the undercarriage. He didn't have to look to know the guard-rail was giving way. Or that Sean and Howard were no longer holding down the tailgate. The SUV tilted toward the swollen river at a crazy angle.

With nothing to stop him, the momentum sent him into the back of the seats. Sweet Jesus. If he went over, he'd crash into Cori and send them both toppling through the shattered front windshield.

The vehicle shuddered and stopped.

"Zack, get out of there, dammit!" the captain bellowed. "Grab her and go!"

Leaning over the row of seats, he reached for Cori once more. "Now or never."

Bracing her booted feet against the back of the driver's seat, Cori pushed herself toward him in one last-ditch effort, beautiful face totally focused. Determined. When she grabbed for his hand this time, she didn't miss.

Zack pulled Cori over the seat, practically threw her toward the open hatch. Bracing himself underneath her, he cupped her ass and shoved her hard toward his team. Toward freedom.

Several pairs of hands hauled her to safety, and he exhaled in relief. Cori was out. Following behind, he scrambled toward the opening. His fingers wrapped around the lip and he hauled himself up—

Just as the guardrail holding the chain gave way.

A terrible rending of metal filled the air. Lightning split the sky and thunder rolled as the rail snapped. The chain whipped, the backlash popping like a gunshot. A blow slammed into his head with the force of a shotgun blast, and he flew backward from the impact.

"Zack, *nooo*!"

Shouts, screaming. Drowned by the storm as the truck slid free of its perch. He tumbled with it, falling, falling. Saw the bridge disappear.

The rear door banged shut as the SUV hit the river, hard, and rolled. He crashed around in the interior, along for the ride, and thought, *Well, shit. There goes my brand-new glasses. Will insurance cover a new pair?*

Ice-cold water rushed in, filling the cabin. Dragging at the heavy protective clothing that would serve as his shroud if he didn't get out. Before the water closed over his head, he managed to suck in a deep breath.

The Explorer lurched once more, the sideways motion

ending in a jarring halt as though it was butting up against something in the current. One of the bridge supports?

Zack's head, the entire right side of his face, throbbed with intense agony even shock and the freezing water couldn't blot out. Disoriented, he groped for a window or door handle.

Which way out? Where? Nothing but pitch-blackness.

He searched, running his hand along the interior. Leather. A seat, but which one? The cumbersome gear weighed him down and must come off, but his need to reach freedom pushed him dangerously close to panic. *Stay calm. Find the windshield, exit through the busted glass, then discard the coat.* He shoved forward, hands out, but he was swimming blind. Totally turned around. Instead, he found a side window, the edge of a door.

Zack yanked on the handle, pushed. The door wouldn't budge, and panic knifed his chest. Swiveling in the opposite direction, he tried for another escape route. Seconds passed, maybe half a minute. His chances slipping away. He found another door, but by now his lungs burned. He needed air.

He located a different handle. Pulled, pushed. Kicked the glass. All to no avail.

His lungs screamed, his futile efforts to free himself slowing. As reality hit, horror electrified his brain.

He wasn't getting out of this alive.

Two hours ago, he'd actually entertained giving up. Now he wanted desperately to live. Get involved with life again. To find out who'd taken a shot at Cori Shannon, and why. Maybe get to know her and . . . what?

But fate had stolen those options from him.

Please, God, I don't want to die! Help me. . . .

Precious air exploded from his lungs. Unable to stop

the inevitable, he sucked in great gulps of brackish water. Clawed at the glass, the door. No use.

His limbs grew heavy, refused to function any longer. His struggles ceased, the fight over. Consciousness began to fade, along with the pain.

Besides his team, who would mourn his loss?

Nobody. Not even his father.

You're a disappointment, boy. Wasting the superior intelligence God gave you on a city job, going nowhere.

If he could, he'd laugh at the irony. His father had been right after all. And he couldn't even blame his own tragic end on the old fucker's debt to his dangerous friends.

No time for regrets. No more fear. Only a strange lightness in his body as he finally accepted, let go.

Zack smiled inside, raised a gloved middle finger in defiance.

Get seven hundred fifty thousand dollars out of that, assholes.

When he drifted into the gentle embrace of death, all he felt was relief.

3

A tall firefighter yelled, "Zack, nooo!" He had the name TANNER printed across the back of his coat in reflective lettering. The grief and rage in his voice—and the others' voices, as well—went through Cori like an arctic blast.

Tanner started to yell orders. One of the team ran for the huge red engine, jumped inside, and started it. He pulled up near where her Explorer had gone over, and she wondered what they planned to do.

Cori rushed to the mangled opening in the guardrail, stared in horror at the sight of her SUV sinking into the Cumberland River. With Zack Knight trapped inside. "Oh, my God!"

"Please, stay back. In fact, why don't you step over to the ambulance with me and I'll check you out?"

Frowning, Cori glanced around to see a lady firefighter gripping the sleeve of her leather coat, expression grim. She shrugged out of the woman's grasp. "You're kidding, right? Do I look like I'm unconscious and drowning to you? Did you see how hard that chain hit Zack in the face?"

"They're going to get him out," the woman replied, striving for calm. But her voice wobbled, betrayed the upset she tried to hide. "I'm Eve Marshall. Right now my job is to attend to you."

"Look, Eve, I appreciate that, but I'm a nurse." Or she would be in four months . . . a graduation that wouldn't be in her future if not for Zack's sacrifice. "I got a bump on the head and I'm shook-up, but Zack's going to need you more."

Eve paused, then nodded. "All right. You're welcome to go sit in the ambulance, where it's dry, or—"

"I'll stay out of the way." Cori gestured to a mountain of a man donning a harness with a thick rope attached to it. He'd stripped off his fire department hat, coat, pants, and boots, leaving him in a navy polo shirt and trousers. Two others were checking every square inch of the straps. "Is he going in?"

Eve turned and heaved a deep breath, eyes darkening with worry. "Yes. That's Lieutenant Paxton. We can all lift or carry a person if necessary, but he's the strongest in a situation like this."

Cori studied the giant, hard and popping with muscle. The man looked like he could bench-press a truck, which meant he had a chance of rescuing Zack. Maybe a better-than-average chance. The ferocity of the storm had abated somewhat, and although the Cumberland was swollen to overflowing the banks, it wasn't a swift-moving river.

Please, let him get Zack out. Alive.

In those couple of seconds, skidding for the guardrail, she'd felt completely helpless. Alone, terrified and at the mercy of fate. Zack must've felt that way when he went over the side.

Tears sprang to her eyes as she watched them lower Lieutenant Paxton the few feet to the river. Her head knew the accident wasn't her fault, but her heart wasn't listening. If either of these men was hurt, she'd never be able to live with herself.

Leaning over as far as she dared, craning her neck, she noted the metallic red of her Explorer just below the water's surface. From here, she couldn't tell whether she was looking at the side or the roof, but the vehicle was jammed against one of the bridge columns. She prayed the vehicle would stay put.

Paxton went in right next to the submerged SUV, tugged on the rope. They gave him slack and he dove, disappearing into the murk. How long had Zack been under at that point? Less than one minute?

The bridge might've been deserted, the only sound the dying wind and soft patter of sleet. No one spoke; no one moved. The tension and fear were palpable as everyone waited, practically hanging over the edge, gazes glued to the water. Next to the firefighters, Cori saw two cops she hadn't noticed before. They seemed nervous, too.

A minute passed. Longer.

The lieutenant surfaced, but had no one in his grasp. He took a deep breath and dove again.

Another minute. The strain mounted in the anxious group. Cori glanced at them to see a Hispanic firefighter tug a gold cross from beneath his coat, clutch it in his palm. No one else noticed, but she saw the handsome man bow his head, lips moving in silent prayer. His entreaty lasted only a few seconds; then he crossed himself, hid the necklace, and resumed his vigil.

Touched, Cori ached with the need to cry. That one act, witnessing a man's prayer for his missing comrade, and these people became *real*. These were Zack's friends, sick with fear. They knew there was a good chance by now that he wouldn't make it.

"Please," she whispered, crossing herself, as well. "Get him out."

How long since the vehicle went under? Four or five minutes? Too long, even if Zack held his breath for the first couple of minutes.

Another squad car pulled up. A cop got out and shuffled over, joining the first two. "The firefighter still under?"

"Yeah," one muttered, sounding glum. "Looking more like a recovery than a rescue."

Oh, God! She refused to believe that. Zack Knight couldn't pay with his life for saving hers. *Don't let it be true.*

Paxton's head broke the surface again—along with the burden in his arms. The lieutenant nodded, and a collective burst of relief from the group was quickly replaced by greater anxiety as they began to haul the men out of the water.

Paxton had both arms wrapped around Zack's chest, holding the man's back against his front. The lieutenant gritted his teeth, neck corded, every muscle straining with his friend's limp, sodden weight.

To Cori, it seemed to take forever for the team to bring the two men up and onto the bridge. In reality, mere seconds passed. Paxton released his burden to the care of his comrades and rolled to his knees, coughing, broad chest heaving from exertion as he watched.

Tanner and the Hispanic man—Salvatore, the lettering on his coat revealed—laid Zack flat on his back. Eve ran for the ambulance, and a fourth firefighter crouched close at hand, letting Tanner and Salvatore take over. The three cops hovered several feet away, obviously wanting to assist, but out of their element. At the moment, no one paid Cori any attention.

Salvatore checked Zack's neck for a pulse. Shook his head. "Nothing."

Tanner ripped open Zack's coat and Salvatore started chest compressions. Heart in her throat, she wobbled forward on shaking legs. Stared down at the man who'd saved her life.

Black hair was plastered to his skull, his fire hat and glasses gone. His sculpted lips were blue. Long, thick, spiky lashes curled against pale cheeks. The right side of his face bore a raw, scraped imprint where the chain had struck, from his hairline, across his cheek and jaw. He'd have a nasty, swollen bruise for weeks, possibly some broken bones—if he survived.

Eve returned, rolling a gurney with a plastic backboard and a portable defibrillator unit on top.

"Come on, Knight." Salvatore pumped his chest furiously. "Goddammit, don't do this. *Breathe*, you little shit!"

Nothing little about Zack. He was six feet of lean, graceful male. The glasses hadn't detracted from his appearance, but without them, his good looks were even more noticeable. He'd been blessed with high cheekbones, a sharp blade of a nose leading to full, sensual lips. A strong jaw. His was a kind face, and she prayed he'd open those laser blue eyes and smile at her again.

Salvatore paused long enough for them to quickly slide the backboard under Zack's body. Cori wondered at this, until Eve grabbed the defibrillator from the gurney and placed it on the ground next to Salvatore. Of course.

They couldn't afford to waste precious seconds getting Zack settled into the ambulance before jump-starting his heart. With the rain, however, there was a chance of electric current zapping whoever handled the patient. The backboard would keep Zack grounded so this shouldn't present a danger to anyone else.

Eve handed Salvatore a small pair of scissors, and he cut Zack's shirt in two up the front, parted the material. Next, he wiped his friend's chest with the torn edge of the shirt and stuck two pads to his skin, one over his heart and the other to the side of the left pectoral. Wires ran from each pad to the defib box. Cori had seen these new units before, hands-free types that were slowly replacing the traditional paddles used to deliver the shock to the patient.

"Clear," Eve said.

Salvatore pushed a button on the unit. Zack's body jolted, then lay unmoving. Eve noted the readout and shook her head. No dice.

"Again." Her mouth flattened into a thin line.

Another jolt. But the shocks weren't working. Belatedly, it occurred to Cori that the blow to his temple might've killed him outright. That he'd never had a chance at all.

"Again." Wetness rolled down Eve's cheeks that had nothing to do with the melting sleet. Her face reflected the entire team's anguish as the third try met with no success.

No movement. No life.

"Julian, it's been too long," the lieutenant said quietly, laying a big hand on Salvatore's shoulder. His eyes were red-rimmed, his voice breaking. "He's gone. I'll call time of death." The other man shrugged off his touch.

"No! *Dios*, not yet."

"Y-you can't give up! Please . . ." Cori stood riveted in stunned horror. *God, this man drowned saving my life. He's dead.*

Tanner wiped a shaking hand down his face. "Howard's right. There's not—"

"Wait!" Eve shouted. "We've got a faint pulse. Let's get his lungs clear, get him breathing."

Salvatore pushed upward on Zack's diaphragm, shoving the water from his lungs. Murky liquid gushed from between his bluish lips several times, but Salvatore's efforts went unanswered.

Paxton, who'd removed the harness, leaned forward. "Come on, buddy, breathe."

Salvatore spat a vicious curse in Spanish, flung aside his hat. Helpless anger twisted his features, but his attention never wavered from their fallen brother. Moving positions, he tilted Zack's head back, pinched his nose, and placed his mouth over the other man's. Gave a couple of puffs of air, sat back.

Nothing. *"Dios mío."* He bent, gave two more.

Zack's chest heaved once. Twice.

His body jerked, and he vomited the river. Coughed a couple of times, and lay immobile. Much too still.

"That's it, my friend, hang on," Eve whispered, smoothing back his raven hair.

There were no joyous cries, no relieved faces. He wasn't responding as they'd hoped. Cori knew the survival rate on revived drowning victims wasn't good, and during nursing school, she'd known a handful of them to come into the ER during her required rotations. More than half hadn't made it. Knight wasn't out of the woods by a long shot.

"He's breathing, but his pulse is too weak," Tanner said as he and Salvatore lifted the backboard and Zack onto the gurney. "Salvatore, you're the acting FAO."

A ripple of shock seemed to bolt through the assembled group at this announcement, but they recovered quickly. Cori wondered what on earth an FAO was and guessed the title used to belong to Zack. Poor man.

"Six-Pack, ride in my place on the quint. I'm going with Knight, and Eve's driving. Let's get him rolling! Go, go!"

"Sterling's the closest," Eve said, expression tense. She looked at Cori. "I recommend you get checked at the hospital. You can go with one of the officers and make your statement, or we can transport you in the ambulance with Knight, but we can't just leave you stranded here."

"I'll ride with Zack," she replied firmly. At Sterling, she could keep tabs on the man's condition through the doctors and nurses she'd soon be working with. A nobrainer.

"Could get rough."

Meaning, her rescuer could still die. The emotional consequences didn't bear thinking about. "Rough is what I do best." The woman had no idea.

Zack was strapped in, ready to go. Eve and Tanner quickly slid the gurney into the waiting ambulance. The others sprinted for the quint, where they'd follow Knight to the emergency room. The cops and another engine company would handle the remaining mess out here.

Tanner climbed in the back of the ambulance. Cori scrambled in after him, taking the opposite seat. Eve slammed the back doors shut, and Cori winced inwardly at the ominous sound.

As the vehicle began to move, Tanner laid a hand on Zack's shoulder. Sorrow and regret swam in his green eyes. "I'm sorry, Zack," he said hoarsely. "Please forgive me."

Cori's throat burned as she lowered her gaze so the man wouldn't see how his words affected her. What had happened between them for Zack to forgive?

She studied her rescuer's pale face, painfully aware of

the faint blip of his heartbeat on the monitor. Fighting for his life.

The ultimate price of selfless courage.

This morning, Zack had been a stranger. A nuisance who'd caused her an inconvenience. Now he was a hero.

No. A man like Zack was a hero every day of his life. She'd just been too blind to notice.

Oh, God, she had some apologizing of her own to do.

She only prayed he lived to hear it.

Eyes closed, coat wrapped tightly around her body, Cori huddled in a corner of the ER's waiting room, trying to stave off an unearthly chill from more than just her wet clothing.

"She's so upset," Eve murmured quietly to her companion in the opposite corner of the room.

But not quietly enough. Cori knew she should sit up, let them know their conversation wasn't private, but she was too tired and heartsick to care.

Salvatore snorted. "You would be, too, if the cops claimed some asshole tried to murder you."

Possible attempted murder. The police officer's stunning, impossible words returned with a vengeance. Made her curl into a tighter ball, wishing she could disappear.

God help them all if her brother found out.

"Allegedly. Could've been random."

"Either way, the deal sucks."

"You're so eloquent, Salvatore." Cori pictured the woman rolling her eyes.

Ignoring the gibe, Salvatore sighed. "We should tell her what the doc reported about Zack. No point in her waiting around if she's not going to get to see him anytime soon."

News of Zack roused her to sit up and look around. The other firefighters were haunting the hallway off the waiting room. She blinked at the approaching pair. Their faces were solemn, guarded. Salvatore spoke first.

"Ms. Shannon—"

"Cori, please."

He nodded. "Cori. I'm Julian. We know you've been waiting for word about Zack, so we wanted to let you know what the doctor said. He's stable, but hasn't regained consciousness."

"He's got brain activity," Eve said, trying to sound positive. "We won't know whether he sustained brain damage or the extent until he wakes up."

Their grim expressions mirrored the curl of dread in Cori's gut. Her rescuer, reduced to a vegetable. The tragic loss didn't bear consideration.

"What about his head?" The blow he took to his face wasn't a concern to be taken lightly.

"His skull isn't cracked, but his cheekbone is," Julian said. "There's swelling and deep bruising, but that will heal fine. The real threat is a bad case of pneumonia clogging his lungs."

"What! How'd he get sick so fast?" A ripple of fear went through her. People of all ages died of pneumonia. But the infection could swiftly overcome a victim of a near drowning.

Julian ran a hand through his black hair. "Zack was already ill and kept it from everyone."

Cori sat up straighter. "Zack could still die." A conclusion, not a question.

A flash of pain darkened his eyes. "We're hoping for the best. He's on massive doses of antibiotics and being monitored closely. His chances are good."

"I know. I'm a nurse . . . or I will be in May. Thanks to your friend." Her lips trembled and she brushed at an escaped tear, but held it together.

Julian tried to sound reassuring, bless him. "I'm sure you'll be a good one, and you'll get your chance to thank Zack. In the meantime, why don't you go home and get some rest? You know the drill. He won't be allowed visitors for a while yet."

"No, I'll wait a bit longer, see if there are any new developments. I appreciate your concern, and for filling me in on his condition."

The pair in front of her knew a firm dismissal when they heard one. Cori hadn't grown up in a house full of stubborn, overbearing brothers to learn nothing.

Julian's lips curved into a small smile. "No problem. We—"

The crackle of his and Eve's radios interrupted the conversation. The dispatcher relayed another traffic accident, the freezing rain taking its toll, and getting worse.

"Here's my card," he said, digging one out of his breast pocket. "My cell phone's listed. If you hear something before we get back, would you—"

"You got it," Cori replied, snatching the card. "Go on."

"Thank you."

He and Eve hurried for the exit, joining Tanner and the others. In two seconds, they were gone.

Cori stared at the nearly empty waiting room, discomfited by the tomblike silence left in the wake of their departure. The picture was no longer complete and she couldn't help but wonder at the sudden sense of loss. As though she'd sort of bonded with them over Zack's near tragedy, and now she was alone to endure the unnerving wait.

Alone. Her brows furrowed. Where was Zack's family?

None of the firefighters had mentioned anyone, but his loved ones were probably rushing to get here and worried sick about him.

"Corrine? How's your head?"

Startled from her musings, Cori looked up at the young Asian doctor she'd seen speaking with the firefighters a couple of times since Zack had been brought in. She'd worked with him on rotation, though she didn't know him well. He hadn't treated her, but his colleague had obviously filled him in.

"Tylenol saves the day." She gave him a weak smile.

"Any dizziness? Blurred vision?"

"No, I'm fine. I've got a hard head." She didn't want to talk about herself. "I know I'm not family, but . . . can you tell me how Zack is doing? The man saved my life," she added when the doctor hesitated.

Just when she thought he wasn't going to answer, he did, with some reluctance. "Mr. Knight is in ICU, still critical. He can have one visitor at a time, but I see his friends had to leave. Would you like to sit with him?"

"Yes! I would, very much." Glancing around, she frowned. "I don't want to intrude on his family's time with him. Surely there's *someone* here by now?"

"No, there isn't. There won't be." The doctor's eyes filled with compassion—and regret. "I understand Knight doesn't have any family."

Zack wanted to stay dead, but nobody would let him.

No matter how hard he strained toward oblivion in a desperate bid to escape the fire licking his entire body, the awful, suffocating pressure on his chest, they—whoever *they* were—pulled him back from the edge.

Let me go. God, please, make them let me go.

God wasn't listening. Neither were *they*.

Stick a fork in good ole Zack, 'cause he was done. He refused to survive this hell one more second. Somehow, he'd find a way out—

"Zack? Can you hear me?"

Miraculously, the chaos in his brain quieted. Her voice again. Low, throaty, and lovely. Familiar. Who was she?

The woman didn't want him to leave this world, and his lack of cooperation was getting to her. Every time she spoke, her emotions battered his resolve. Worry, frustration . . . guilt.

And he should care, why? Who was she to him?

"Come on, fireboy," she pleaded, soft as a caress. "You can't die on me. I've weathered a lot of crap, but not this. I can't do it. I'm the one who's supposed to be dead, not you. Zack, *please*."

Aw, fuck. That gurgling sound was his plan for a graceful swan song going down the toilet.

Damsels in distress had always been his downfall—in this case, literally, it would seem. Christ. He couldn't wrap his mind around what had happened, but apparently, he was neck deep in some badass shit.

"I'm sorry I was rude to you—even though you hit me."

Appalled, he scrambled to make sense of that. He'd never hit anyone in his life, especially a woman!

"I mean, you *did* save my bacon. Went a tad over-board, too, if you ask me." She gave a tremulous laugh. "No pun intended. Work with me here, will you?"

Saved her life . . .

He struggled to remember. Caught flashes of water. Freezing cold. *Can't breathe.*

The not-breathing part wasn't just a memory, either. An elephant must be parked on his chest. Matched nicely with his screaming muscles and throbbing head.

God Almighty, why couldn't he just—

Soft sniffles interrupted his black thoughts. Muffled sounds of . . . weeping.

Damn, she was crying.

Over me? Curiosity finally won over self-pity. He wasn't going to die anytime soon—oh, goody—so he might as well try to put an end to the waterworks and the red-hot poker French-frying his brain cells.

And the odd stab in the center of his chest that had nothing to do with illness.

Zack licked his lips. "Hey." Unfortunately, the word emerged as a great imitation of a cat hawking up a hair ball. All he managed to accomplish was possibly rupturing a lung in the ensuing fit of coughing.

"Zack? Easy, there. You're going to be all right."

The warm hand on his arm and the slender fingers stroking his hair went a long way toward bringing him back to the living. Nice.

The band around his chest loosened and he made an attempt to open his eyes. Success took a couple of tries, but then, he had the best of motivators. He *really* wanted to get a good look at his guardian angel. Blinking to clear his vision, he wondered why his eyeballs felt like they were coated with sand.

Turning his head, he peered at the woman sitting beside him. Slowly, her blurry image came into better focus, though still a little fuzzy around the edges. Where were his glasses?

That fleeting concern quickly gave way to amazement as he recognized the amber-eyed beauty with the honey brown hair. Yeah, even with her eyes red-rimmed and her hair disheveled, the lady was a knockout.

"Cori? What . . ." He swallowed hard, fighting off another bout of coughing as he stared at her.

"Thank God, you're awake! You're in the hospital, Zack. You sure know how to scare your friends, you know that? *Everyone* has been waiting for you to come around. Hang on, I'm going to get Dr. Chu."

"Wait—"

Cori hurried out the door before Zack could protest. Her sudden departure left him feeling cut adrift in a sea of confusion. Would she come back? He hoped so. Her touch had been . . . more than comforting. Deeper, somehow.

The doctor bustled in, beaming and exclaiming how lucky Zack was after drowning, then almost succumbing to pneumonia. *What?* Christ, no wonder he felt like dog crap.

Dr. Chu's brisk questions as the man gave him a thorough exam put Zack's own on hold. There was a tense moment when Zack had difficulty recalling his occupation and the president's name, but the doctor's satisfaction returned when he croaked the correct answers.

Zack would be just fine in a few days, Chu declared, then sped out after promising to stop by later. The whole visit lasted maybe two minutes.

Gradually, Zack's muddled brain cleared. He stared at the ceiling, the silence getting to him a little. If "everyone" had been so worried, where were they? Funny, solitude never used to bother him so much.

As though in answer to his thoughts, the door opened and Cori returned. And damn, she looked gorgeous in a pair of snug jeans and a blue sweater. Smiling, she resumed her spot at his side and his heart gave an odd leap. Like it might've been beating, but hadn't really been *alive* before she came back.

"Dr. Chu says you're on the mend," she said.

"Looks that way." He tried to return the smile, but, God, his face—his whole head—was killing him. "What happened to me?"

Her expression sobered. "Do you remember rescuing me from my Explorer? The damned thing fell off the bridge and into the river with you inside. You . . . almost died."

Everything came back in a rush. The call, the storm. Cori's vehicle hanging off the bridge. His determination to get her out alive, whatever the cost.

The cost had been quite high—but he'd do it again.

"How did they get me out?" His voice was barely more than a whisper, but even that slight noise skewered his skull. He wished she'd stroke his hair again.

"Lieutenant Paxton went in and pulled you out," she said with no little awe. "Then Julian did CPR forever and finally got you back, and just in time, too. We all thought you were a goner."

So did I. "That was . . . today?"

Cori shook her head. "Three days ago. We've been taking turns sitting with you, but you've been really out of it. Pneumonia—which I'm told you'd neglected to get diagnosed, by the way—and drowning don't exactly make a healthy combo."

"Yeah, Dr. Chu enlightened me. In my defense, I thought I just had a bad cold, and I need the overtime." He groaned. "Why does my face feel like it hit a brick wall? It hurts just to talk."

"I'm not surprised. You're lucky you didn't lose all your teeth, or worse. The chain snapped and bashed you upside the head. Cracked your cheekbone."

Fan-frickin'-tastic. So much for hoping to retain a thimbleful of cool in front of this woman. His head must look like a purple and blue lopsided pumpkin. But he took some comfort in the fact that she'd been staring at him for three days and hadn't been scared off.

Three days. Holy Christ, that meant . . .

"My team is working today?" There. Nice and casual.

Cori graced him with another million-volt smile. "Yes, thank goodness. They've been driving the doctors and nurses crazy! I tried to call Julian on his cell phone while Dr. Chu was with you and give them the great news, but there was no answer. I'll try again when I leave."

"Thanks. Did, um, any of them happen to mention who's covering for me?" *Please, let it be Six-Pack or Eve.*

She patted his arm in sympathy. "Don't worry. Julian is driving the quint while you're out sick. He said if you woke up before they got back, to tell you he's glad you're okay and that everything's under control."

"I'll bet he did." God, he wanted to laugh. Cry. Hit something.

She gave him a funny look, as though trying to decipher his sarcasm. "In fact, that's pretty much the message they all gave me to pass along. I'm sure they'll drop by as soon as they can."

"Okay. Thanks."

His trip to hell was now complete. Salvatore had been eyeing the coveted FAO's position for a while now, and Tanner had gift wrapped and handed it to the man with a shiny bow. The one man on the team with whom Zack's tension ran the highest, save for Tanner himself.

Yeah, he didn't need a freaking telescope to read that particular writing on the wall.

His spirits sank. *What the hell will I do now?*

"Hey, what's wrong?" Her gorgeous face scrunched into a worried frown.

"Nothing." *Except that I'm broke, and soon to be jobless. Wanna elope?*

She sighed. "Cheer up, fireboy. At least nobody tried to kill you."

"Really, would you please stop calling me ... *kill* you?" His muddled brain caught up to his mouth. "Your tire! God, how could I have forgotten? Do the police know who shot it?"

"Not a clue, and neither do I."

Something about the soft way she said it, how her tawny eyes darted briefly to the side, made him wonder.

What secrets was Cori hiding behind that firecracker of a personality?

"It was probably random," he said, trying to reassure her. "Or maybe even an accident. The shot could've come from the forest along the river." Unlikely, given the angle and the bad weather, but stranger things had happened.

"Maybe. It's just . . . no, never mind."

Reaching for her hand resting on the mattress, he curled his fingers over hers. "Go ahead, spill it. I'm a friend. Or I'd like to be."

She looked at him from under her lashes, her gaze haunted. "I'd like that, too, Zack. I have friends, but to be honest, most of them do more talking than listening."

"I'm all ears, beautiful." He felt his face heat at how easily the endearment had slipped past his lips. Jesus.

"This is going to make me sound like a nut. The cops didn't take me seriously, even after my car was shot at."

"You're stalling."

Cori heaved a deep breath and looked him straight in the eye.

"Zack, I think someone is watching me."

4

Cori shifted self-consciously, studying Zack's expression of wary surprise. Yeah, it sounded just as kooky as it had when she'd told the police yesterday.

"Watching, as in a creepy feeling, or as in the infamous pet bunny boiling on a stove?"

Cori's face heated. "We're not talking *Fatal Attraction* at this point, but it's more than just a creepy feeling. For starters, I've seen the same white van everywhere I've been for the past three days." She held up a hand. "Don't say it. The police already pointed out that I might be 'overly jumpy' after being shot at. Imagine."

"I wasn't going to say that. You don't strike me as the nervous type."

"Oh. Thanks."

"Did you get a look at the driver?"

"No, the windows were tinted dark and the vehicle's been too far away. When I came out of the bank yesterday, it was parked across the street and I couldn't even tell if anyone was inside. That's when I finally phoned the officer who took the report on my so-called accident. I told him about the van and the other stuff, and he pretty much gave me the hysterical-little-woman crap and blew me off."

Zack frowned. "What else has happened?"

"Noises outside at night. Crunching sounds near my bedroom window, a metallic bang as though someone dropped a bucket. A scrape on the porch. Nerve-racking but not directly threatening."

"Do you live in town?"

She sighed, knowing where this was going. "On the outskirts. The house is set back in the trees and the neighbors are spread out."

"Cori, I'm not trying to patronize you, but Tennessee is overrun with all sorts of wildlife, especially deer. At night, they'll come right up to the house and get into everything."

"I know. Listen to me," she said, waving him off with a smile that didn't squelch the inner disquiet. "I shouldn't have bothered you with this. You're tired and I have to run."

Disappointment flashed in his blue eyes. Then his expression smoothed into calm acceptance. "Already? Well, thanks for coming by and keeping me company. Don't be a stranger, huh?"

Her insides lit in a warm glow as she stood. Zack didn't want her to leave! She squeezed his fingers. "I can come back tomorrow, if you want. If you don't, no problem. I wear big-girl panties now, so I can take the rejection."

This earned her a lopsided grin. "No comment on the panties, on the grounds that it may incriminate me. Come back tonight?"

"Can't, sugar. Got a bachelor-party gig in Nashville."

His grin faded some—whether from the reminder of her exotic dancing or from not being able to see her tonight, she wished she knew.

"Okay. Tomorrow, then. I'll see if I can fit you in."

"Cute." Leaning over, she gave him a brief kiss on his dark-stubbled cheek. A peck she meant only as a friendly good-bye but somehow felt like something more. His heat, his nearness, pulled at her, and she straightened quickly. "Hang tight and you'll feel better fast. You'll see."

He gazed at her from beneath a fringe of black lashes. "Can I have that in writing?"

"Hey, chin up. Keep improving and you'll be out of here by the day after tomorrow."

"How do you know that?"

Oops. "I keep my ears open. Now rest."

"Like I have a choice," he muttered, looking like a sullen little boy.

Lips curved into a smile, she turned to leave. "Bye, Zack."

"Cori?"

She paused and glanced over her shoulder. "Yeah?"

"Be careful in Nashville tonight. Watch your surroundings."

Zack's concern both chilled and warmed her at the same time. With his huge blue eyes and black hair tousled against his pillow, even with the vivid bruise on his pale face, he looked so impossibly sexy, warmth won out.

No sneer of derision for her job, no attempts to sway her to pursue a better line of work. Just honest worry for her safety.

The man was a cool drink of water in the desert.

"Will do."

Damn, she didn't want to leave. And, for the first time in a very long while, fervently wished she were headed anywhere else except to take off her clothes for yet another drunken bachelor party.

You don't have to, the nagging little voice tempted her. *You could dip into the till, pay off the rest of that pesky school loan. Who'd care?*

No. Over her dead, stinking corpse.

Besides, her debts were almost paid. She'd emerge with her pride intact.

Tomorrow, she'd tell Zack the truth.

Well, at least the part about her nursing job. The rest she'd buried with Alex's dead body two years ago.

Those horrible days were behind her, and she wasn't dredging them up for anyone.

Not even Zack Knight.

Lionel hunched over his mop, silently cursing the subtle stench of piss and vomit combined with ammonia. Using the considerable skill born of poverty, honed on the blade of hunger, he schooled his features to reveal nothing. To give those around him the comfortable illusion of what they expected to see.

No one ever noticed a janitor.

Sheep, his brother had liked to call the hapless people who fell prey to their schemes. Dumb animals to be herded to figurative slaughter, the wool and meat turned for profit, the carcass discarded.

Never one to forget how easily the cruel fist of fate crushed the complacent, how quickly all was lost, Lionel had always disagreed. The human psyche was a wonderful wellspring of untapped emotions, ripe for exploration. Exploitation.

Consumption.

People wanted to believe their lives weren't small and insignificant. That they mattered, could be more than they were, safe and loved. A few well-placed kindnesses, whispered caresses, and their bodies, souls, and wealth belonged to Lionel.

Lonely businesspeople. Overworked doctors, lawyers, politicians with everything to lose. Lovers who eagerly surrendered all to him, received the sexual adventure they craved. For a price.

Now he'd reel in the biggest prize of all.

Lionel usually worked alone these days, but he'd been unable to resist this new proposition. Especially after listening to what the man had to say, when the sly manipulator finally caught up with him, that was. Lionel had been indisposed, courtesy of an eighteen-month stay in Huntsville State Penitentiary. He and his new "partner" finalized their plans right under the ignorant noses of the armed guards.

Sure, his partner could've sought someone else to carry out the deed and not wasted months locating Lionel. But no one else quite matched Lionel in skill or motivation. The opportunity to exact justice on the hot bitch made the pot of honey extra sweet.

So Lionel mopped, sweating in stupid goddamned coveralls the pallid shade of a dead body, putting up with the stink of Sterling's ICU in order to study his latest target from beneath the brim of a battered baseball cap. Months of planning with his annoying business cohort, poised to bear fruit.

Corrine Shannon. A wet dream in fuck-me designer jeans and high-heeled boots. As though sensing his scrutiny, she glanced in his direction as she exited the firefighter's room before striding briskly down the hallway, tight ass swinging.

A chameleon who adapted to suit his purposes, Lionel wasn't worried. She'd never dream of connecting the grizzled janitor swiping up urine with the enigmatic, urbane friend from her favorite coffee shop. And she'd certainly never know the man he'd been—until he chose to reveal the truth.

His secret was secure. Soon, he'd make his next move. A gorgeous former jet-setter like Cori had to be bored out of her mind in the boring vanilla community of Sugarland. She needed a concerned friend, a confidant. An exciting lover.

Lionel would provide all three . . . with a heaping dose of revenge as the coup de grâce.

Anger boiled in his gut. Lust in his groin.

Lionel's hands tightened around the mop handle as he thought of Cori's upset over her rescuer. A man named Zack Knight. Hadn't been difficult to ascertain the situation with all the firefighters and cops hanging around shaking their heads, looking as though the world were ending. Since the shot Lionel had taken at her tire was intended only to frighten her, he supposed he ought to thank the poor bastard for salvaging his scheme.

Recalling the earlier call from his partner, his lips thinned into a grim line. The man had been pissed enough to shit monkeys.

"What in the goddamned hell was *that*? Do you have any idea how much creative maneuvering and string pulling I had to do in order to keep your little fiasco quiet on my end?"

"It didn't go quite as planned."

"No fucking shit! You're supposed to kill her *after* you seduce the information from her, you idiot!"

"I'll be more careful next time." If he could, he'd shoot the sonofabitch.

"You'd damned well better."

"You know, this whole operation would be expedited more efficiently if I simply took the slut and forced her to give us what we need. Screw this seduction bullshit."

"And that would be exactly the wrong move. Cori would dig her heels in and die before telling us jack. We play this my way," he'd said coldly.

And look where that had gotten them.

Fine. If Cori became too attached to Knight, the man's only thanks would be swift elimination.

Lionel pushed the mop faster, working down the adjacent corridor. He'd been here too long and someone might get suspicious.

Returning the mop to the janitor's bucket, he cast a furtive look around and, seeing no one, stepped into the men's restroom. Quickly, he shed the borrowed coveralls and ball cap, stuffing them into the garbage. He shook out his dyed blond hair, which fell in artful array to the shoulders of his black sweater. Designer jeans hugged lean hips and long thighs, cupped his sex.

Not bad, he thought dispassionately, studying his reflection. He had never been homely, but now? He was nearly as beautiful as Cori. The idea made him smile, even though the total package was nothing more than a tool of a necessary trade.

A vehicle to the ultimate payback.

Caution, however. He wanted Cori all to himself, without interference. From his partner or anyone else. Straightening his shoulders, Lionel prepared himself to take another significant risk.

The traitorous bitch was about to discover she needed a ride home.

How convenient for them both.

Zack looked up, eyes widening in surprise as Julian strode into the room. "Lost?"

Julian moved to his bedside, extending his hand. "Heard the great news, man. We just finished a call, thought we'd stop by. The guys are in the waiting room at the end of the hall. I saw your lady outside and she said she'd been trying to call me. How're you feeling?"

He glanced at the offered hand and up at Julian's earnest expression again before accepting it with a half smile. Either the man really cared, or those were some good drugs. "Like my face caught on fire and someone put it out with a brick," he said, his roughened voice little more than a whisper. "Pretty awful, huh?"

Careful of the IV, Julian clasped his hand briefly, then let it go, sitting in the chair beside the bed. Wincing, he studied the bruised and abraded side of Zack's swollen face. "Nah, it's not so bad. Besides, chicks dig a knight in shining armor. Get it?"

Zack snorted, then grimaced in pain. "Don't make me laugh, asshole. Hurts too damned much."

"Sorry. So this is what I have to do to get a pretty *chica*? Seems like a lot of trouble. What do you think?"

"That you're full of shit. You have a different *chica* for every night of the week."

"Yeah, sucks to be me." Julian smirked, but Zack narrowed his eyes, thinking it seemed a little forced. "Anyway, we're not talking about my love life. What gives with the luscious Ms. Shannon?"

"Nothing. A little bonding between victim and rescuer, maybe some subconscious, misplaced feelings of guilt on her part over my accident, whatever. Now that she's seen I'll be okay, it'll pass. Happens all the time." He hoped not, but wasn't about to get warm and cozy with Jules, of all people.

"I don't know, man. That's not the vibe I was getting from her these past few days when we didn't know if you'd make it. She practically camped here, bullying the doctors and nurses to keep us informed, sitting by your side when we couldn't. Seems like more than—"

"Drop it, Salvatore. I don't want to talk about Cori."

Not with you hung in the air between them. Appearing stung and determined not to let it show, Julian changed the subject. "All right. Well . . . work has been busy."

"I'll bet." The unspoken accusation resounded in his soft tone. Shit, now things were getting awkward.

Heaving a sigh, Julian straightened in his chair. "Okay, listen good. I'm not after your job, Knight. I don't want it, not like this." He held up a hand, cutting off Zack's protest.

"I mean, sure, I want to be FAO one day. But even you can't believe I'm a big enough prick to walk over your corpse to get it."

Zack frowned. "Julian—"

"I'm not willing to settle for what I haven't earned, and I'll put in for a transfer before I let Tanner screw me over with the team and alienate me any more than I already am."

Zack knew he was staring at the other man as though he'd started speaking in tongues, but he couldn't help it. Jules had a conscience. Who knew? "I don't—"

"Whatever you think, I'm really glad you're going to be okay. Get well and get the hell out of here. We need you. I'll send in Eve or Six-Pack next."

He stood, heading for a quick escape.

"Hey, wait!" Julian stopped, glanced over his shoulder. "Thanks for saving my ass. For . . . everything."

"Forget it, geek. Had to do it over, I'd throw you back in the river."

Well, it was a start.

5

The Explorer was a total loss, and now this.

Cori slapped a hand on the steering wheel of her rental in frustration. "Arrrgh! Stupid piece of shit!"

Normally, she wouldn't lose her temper over a trivial matter out of her control. For example, the egg-shaped scrap heap the rental company stuck her with failing to start. This week, however, had been a *teensy* bit hard on her blood pressure.

A knock on her window nearly sent her into cardiac arrest.

"Cori?"

Splaying a hand over her pounding heart, she exhaled a whoosh of breath, trying to squash the spurt of annoyance at being surprised. She *hated* surprises, and holy macaroni if this week hadn't been chock-full of them. Pasting on a smile, she got out of the car to greet Tony Banning, an artist whom she'd met several months ago at the local coffee bar where she and some of the other nursing students liked to hang out.

"Tony! What brings you here? Not a sick friend or relative, I hope."

Delight shining in his dark eyes, Tony stepped up to her, skimmed a palm down the sleeve of her sweater, and zeroed in for a kiss. Quickly, she turned her head so he landed a harmless buss on the cheek. A maneuver she'd had to use more than once lately with him.

"No, no, nothing like that," he said, apparently undaunted by his intended target avoiding full lip service. "Actually, I was looking for you. I called you at home and stopped by the coffee shop first. Then it occurred to me that you might've been scheduled for rotation."

"No, not today. I was just visiting someone."

Eyeing his tall, lean form from head to toe, Cori thought for the millionth time what a shame it was that Tony's going to the trouble to seek her out didn't affect her the way it would most women.

From his windblown, shoulder-length golden hair— cue Fabio posing in front of a wind tunnel—taut chest, slim hips, and long thighs, Tony was melt-your-panties gorgeous. He had money, if his taste in clothes and his black Viper were any indication, he was attentive, and his interest in Cori had progressed past mere friendship. He'd been sending off signals for months now, though he hadn't pushed much. Until recently.

Cori's friends thought she was nuts to keep him at arm's length. Maybe she was, but unfortunately for Tony, he reminded her far too much of the world she'd left behind.

Too fast, too slick. The sex and money too easy.

That lifestyle had nearly destroyed her once. Over her dead body would she invite disaster again. Whether it was unfair to Tony or not, she'd listen to her instincts.

"Um, Cori, darling?"

She blinked at him. "I'm sorry; what did you say?"

He gave her an indulgent smile. "I asked if you'd like to have dinner tonight. There's a new restaurant in Nashville off Broadway—"

"I can't. I have a dancing gig tonight. Tomorrow night, too," she added before he could ask. "Fridays and Saturdays are my busiest nights; you know that."

Deflated, he sighed, mouth pulling down in disappointment. "Coffee after your Tuesday class as usual, then?"

"Wouldn't miss it." Gesturing to her rental car, she steered him off the topic of their nonexistent dating life. "Know anything about cars? This one seems to have kicked the bucket."

"Wish I did," he said, shaking his head ruefully. "I'd be glad to give you a lift home, though."

Drat. "No, that's okay. I can call E-Z Rental and have Donnie Wayne send someone over."

"Really, I don't mind." Face lighting, he snapped his fingers. "How about I drive you to the rental company? That way you won't have to stand out here waiting for God knows how long before those yokels show. You can secure another car and be on your way."

She had to admit, while she didn't appreciate Tony calling them "yokels," his offer was preferable to waiting. Donnie Wayne Tuttle, the owner of E-Z, who *did* remind her suspiciously of Larry the Cable Guy, would take ages to get someone here. Still, she got the impression Tony was more interested in finding an excuse to be alone with her than in helping out.

"Well, if you're sure you don't mind . . ."

"Not at all! Shall we?"

She retrieved her purse and keys from the car. Linking her arm through his, Tony steered her to the Viper parked on the next row. Instead of opening her door, he simply let her go, went around to the driver's side, and slid in. Another tiny, but telling, black mark against her friend as potential lover material. Call her silly, but she was really an old-fashioned girl at heart when it came to the mating game.

The Viper roared to life, settling into a low purr under her bottom. Tony revved the engine a couple of times, and Cori suppressed a smirk. Poor man had obviously deluded himself into believing she'd be impressed by his expensive rolling phallic symbol, and she wasn't insensitive enough to spoil his fantasy.

Real class was on the inside.

Like a man willing to die for you.

Steering deftly from the parking lot, Tony cut her a brief, searching look. "You've been a tough lady to reach. You never did say why."

Was he kidding? "Don't you read the paper or watch the local news? I was almost *killed.*"

"Of course, I know! Why do you think I've been so concerned?" He pulled to a stop at a red light and arched a brow. "But you look fine to me. Radiant, in fact. Could your rescuer have anything to do with that glow? I wonder. I assume that's why you're spending so much of your time off at the hospital."

He stated it like an accusation. Cori felt herself bristling in irritation. Her budding relationship with Zack wasn't anyone's biz, especially not that of someone who was only a casual friend. She tried to envision Tony hanging off a bridge, risking his life to save hers, and couldn't picture him mussing one perfect, golden hair on his head.

"If I'm glowing, it's because I'm happy to be alive," she said evenly. "I owe Zack more than you can imagine."

"Yes, I suppose you do." The light turned green and he gave his attention back to the road.

Cori gaped at him in disbelief for a moment, then faced forward in disgust. Really, what had she expected? An undignified, weepy show of gratitude for her safety and well-being?

She gazed out the window at the sunny January day, hardly listening as Tony prattled on about his sculptures and an upcoming showing at a small gallery.

Was Zack resting comfortably? Had his nurses begun his breathing treatments? Damn, she should've checked before she left. What if he relapsed? In his weakened condition, he might not survive another round with pneumonia.

If she hurried, she'd have a few minutes to drop by the hospital before her job tonight. He'd asked her to come, so it wasn't as though she were pushing herself on the man. Nothing wrong with making certain he was being taken care of.

"Here you are." Tony pulled to a stop in front of the only rental place in town, just off the square. He put the car in park, letting the engine idle as he scooted around in his seat to face her.

Brushing his knuckles lightly along her jaw, he leaned so close she caught a nice whiff of expensive cologne. "Why the silent treatment? Darling, please don't be angry with me." His long blond hair tickled her cheek as he fitted his lips over hers.

After the initial shock of contact, Cori realized she wasn't surprised by the kiss. Not really. Especially not after he'd shown some jealousy over her visits with Zack. She could've pulled away—probably should've—but curiosity got the better of her judgment, in spite of her annoyance with Tony. She couldn't help wondering whether her girlfriends were right.

By keeping Tony at a distance, was she truly missing out?

Relaxing, she opened herself to the kiss, angling her head for better access. He groaned, spearing her lips with his tongue, invading with his moist heat. Devouring her mouth.

The tingling began, welcome and long denied. Tightening her nipples, inciting the warmth at the apex of her thighs. Her response wasn't totally unexpected. Tony was a seducer of the first order, and she'd been too long without a man's touch. Without passion. She needed to be held, to feel a man's strength pressing down on her body, his hardness sliding into her.

I don't have to wait. She buried her fingers in his hair, pressing closer, deepening the kiss. So easy to let him follow her home. She had no doubt he'd be fantastic in bed. Within the hour, they could be naked. Slick with sweat. Tangled in her sheets.

She didn't love him, found it difficult to even like him some days, but tender feelings had nothing to do with hot, blistering sex.

Because that was all it would be. A hard, pounding, break-the-headboard fuck.

Sex, not lovemaking.

A kind, handsome face with huge blue eyes and framed by rumpled black hair ghosted into her mind. His beautiful, genuine smile, filled with hope.

Come back tonight?

The memory was a bucket of icy water dousing her blind lust in an instant. She still ached to be held and touched, but not by Tony. She didn't want an empty encounter that would leave her lonelier and more dissatisfied than before.

The next man she invited into her bed would be the last. The one who'd make sweet love to her for the rest of their lives. Cherish her as much as she did him.

Tony wasn't that man.

Placing a palm on his chest, she pushed him back, breaking the kiss. The heat of his arousal radiated off him in waves, his heartbeat thudding under her fingers even through his sweater. The raw hunger in his dark eyes left no question about what his answer would be if she issued the invitation.

His fingers trailed down her throat. "I knew you'd taste just like honey. I'll bet you're sweet everywhere."

Oh, God. She might not want *him* specifically, but her body reacted all the same.

Time to escape. Giving him a smile she hoped wasn't as fake as it felt, she grabbed his hand before it could complete its journey into the vee of her sweater. "Not too subtle, are you?"

"Why waste energy better spent on more pleasurable things?"

"True, but my life doesn't lend itself much to indulging right now." She reached for the door handle. "See you Tuesday?"

He wasn't so easily deterred. "You enjoyed our kiss as much as I did. Don't try to deny it, Cori."

"All right, I did, but—"

"We'd be good together," he said, lids heavy. "Come home with me. Just for an hour or two."

Anxiety balled in her stomach, the urge to get away suddenly very strong. "I'll admit I considered it. But I'm not ready to take that step at this point, with you or anyone." Okay, the "or anyone" part wasn't quite true. Tony, however, did not need to know that.

His gaze chilled and Cori suppressed a shiver. Had it been her imagination, or had something dark and ugly slithered through his eyes for a second?

The fleeting impression vanished as he nodded, his expression serious. "I'm willing to wait. When you're ready, I'll be here."

"Thank you."

Seizing her opportunity, she scrambled out of the Viper and slammed the door, giving him a wave. He drove off without so much as a nod in her direction, leaving her standing in front of the E-Z Rental. . . . He hadn't even waited to make sure they switched out her car with no hassle.

She frowned after the Viper's disappearing taillights, bothered. Yes, she'd wanted to put space between them. Was, in fact, relieved to see him go. But a true friend and gentleman would've gone inside, put her safety above his disappointment over not getting her into bed.

A real man, her dream lover, would've stayed with her no matter what.

A man who bore a helluva resemblance to a raven-haired firefighter with stunning blue eyes.

Arguably, Zack's return to the living was good news.

The bad news? Tanner was on the way to his room.

Funny how that knowledge didn't feel so very different from when he'd plummeted over the side of the bridge.

Nothing to do but lie here and wait for the impact. Zack hadn't yet been moved from the ICU with its strict visitor's rules, or the others would've accompanied the captain to provide a buffer between them. As humiliating as the dressing-down in front of Eve and Six-Pack had been, the idea of facing Tanner alone had him a little freaked. He wasn't afraid of the man by any means, but he wasn't exactly in shape for another bout in the ring, either.

Over the past few hours, his battered body had come to vivid life by painful degrees. His head pounded, his muscles ached, and his chest burned with every rattling breath. He was so frigging miserable he couldn't sleep, yet being awake was sheer torture—especially the disgusting breathing treatments to unclog his lungs. The pain meds that provided a couple of hours of blessed fog weren't nearly enough.

A fifth of Jack might do the trick.

The door opened and Tanner walked in without knocking. Which didn't surprise Zack. What did was the hesitance in the captain's green eyes. Even before the tragedy that had claimed his family, Tanner had been a hard man. Fair, but tough. The type of man who strode boldly through life without remorse for his unbending attitude, viewing the world in black-and-white.

Today, Tanner had grooves of stress cut deep around his mouth and silver in the dark brown hair at his temples . . . and his world had dissolved into a palette of murky gray.

Zack shoved down a wave of sympathy. "Cap."

Tanner stood over his fallen man, hands in the pockets of his regulation trousers, electing not to waste time mincing words. "Knight. All the shit I said the other day, I was wrong." His mouth tightened. "Can you forgive me for being such a fuckhead?"

In spite of himself, Zack choked a hoarse laugh. "You could've just said it with Hallmark. Sir."

One corner of Tanner's lips tugged upward. A thin crack in the veneer. "Didn't get by the store this week."

Zack let the silence stretch for a minute, and considered his next words carefully. Holding the captain's gaze, he continued. "Forgive, sure. Forget? That'll take a while."

"You want your pound of flesh, I won't fight you. I'll get written up or suspended, maybe both."

"And what would that solve?" If Tanner got suspended, he'd go home and drink himself to death. Maybe he even wanted to. No way would Zack be a party to a good man's destruction simply to assuage his hurt feelings.

"Probably nothing, but it's your call. I'm not asking for leniency just because I'm apologizing."

"Are you? Apologizing, I mean."

"Yes. I'm sorry, Zack. More than you'll ever know." His voice was rife with sincere regret.

Zack was only human. The part of him that was still hurt and humiliated by their run-in wanted retribution, no matter how messy. The more insistent part of him wanted the team to regain its cohesiveness. These guys were his brothers, his only family.

Destroying Tanner would finish them as a team.

Hadn't the captain—*all* of them—been through enough?

"I accept, and I recommend we put this behind us," Zack said quietly. For one second, he could've sworn Tanner swayed on his feet.

"Thank you." He stepped closer, gripped Zack on the shoulder. "For what it's worth, I'm goddamned glad you're all right."

Zack managed a smile. "Me, too, Cap."

"I'll come by again soon and we'll talk. Get some rest."

It wasn't until after Tanner left that Zack realized the captain had never addressed the touchy issue of appointing Salvatore as acting FAO.

And whether Zack would ever recover the position.

A noise jangled near his head, startling a curse from his lips. Why did hospital phones need to be set loud enough to make a person's brain bleed? Groaning, he rolled to his side and reached for the receiver with his free hand—the one without the IV—and brought it to his ear.

"Hello?"

"Mr. Knight. Back from the dead, are you?"

The clipped, cultured voice, dripping with feigned cordiality, curdled his bone marrow.

Oh, God. Not Delacruz. Not now. "How did you know where to find me?" No need to ask why the man had bothered. At least the rusty croak from his illness masked the fear and strain behind the question.

"With a minimum of difficulty. Your landlady seemed to think something horrid must've befallen you, and there you are."

His landlady! Dammit, he'd forgotten that his rent was long overdue. And now, as far as she was concerned, Zack had gone AWOL. *Shit!*

Delacruz chuckled as he went on. "And I'd thought perhaps you were avoiding me by not answering your cell phone."

The bastard's smug tone grated. "Considering the damned thing is sitting on the bottom of the Cumberland River? No. Besides, if I want you to fuck off, I'll tell you straight up. Like now, for instance."

"That's what I admire about you," Delacruz said smoothly. "Such indomitable spirit. I like you, Zack."

"You don't like anything but money. Which, FYI, I don't fucking have any more of."

"Oh, where there's a will and all that." He paused. "I assume your old man is resting comfortably in the nursing home?"

The veiled threat shredded Zack's forced calm, fired his anger. Darius Knight had been a lousy father in his day, a selfish motherfucker, but was now just a pitiful shell of a man. His father deserved to face his debts, the trouble he'd caused. He did *not* deserve to be murdered for them.

Zack held the receiver in a death grip. "You stay away from my father, you sonofabitch. Or I'll kill you."

Delacruz laughed. "Noble as well as spirited, even after all he's done to you. 'The gods visit the sins of the fathers upon the children,'" he quoted. "Exodus 20:5."

"Euripides, 484 through 406 BC." *Bastard.*

"I stand corrected," he said in amusement. "My faith in you is restored."

Zack closed his eyes against the pounding in his head. "What the hell are you talking about?"

"I mean that an intelligent young man such as yourself will have no problem solving the dilemma of how to come up with another fifty-thousand-dollar installment, let's say, two weeks from today. I'm feeling generous, in light of your accident."

Zack's hands started to shake. He wondered whether suppressed rage would cause him to stroke out like his father. "You're pissing into the wind, Delacruz. I'm not a magician."

"But you *are* a genius. Be a problem solver, Zack. I'll expect good news in two weeks."

Their connection was ended with a *click*. For a few seconds, Zack sat with the receiver pressed against his ear, the pressure building in his chest, white-hot and unstoppable.

Fifty thousand. Two weeks.

They'll kill my father.

And when Delacruz decides I'm tapped out, they'll kill me.

Too much. It was all too much and he couldn't take this on top of everything else. Was helpless to stem the tide of resentment and rage sweeping every nerve ending, devastating the iron-willed control he'd held on to by a slim thread for so long.

A roar erupted from his throat as he rolled, scooped the base of the phone from the bedside table. With all his strength, he hurled the entire unit. It smacked the wall opposite his bed with a satisfying crunch, clattered to the floor in pieces.

The destruction wasn't nearly enough. He glanced around wildly, but there wasn't anything else to wreck. Moaning, he clasped his head in his hands, the agony overwhelming. Any second, his brain would ooze out his ears.

"Oh, God." *What am I going to do?*

Two nurses burst into his room, one after the other.

"Mr. Knight! What happened? Are you all right?"

Was she serious? "No. My head—"

"Jee-zus, Mary, and Joseph!" The second nurse fisted her hands on her wide hips as she eyed the defunct phone. "You gonna hafta pay for that, baby."

Of course he would. And for some reason, that struck him as suddenly, incredibly funny.

Zack started to laugh. Couldn't help it. He laughed

until he began to gasp and wheeze, while the first nurse fussed at him in vain to be still. Seemed he'd dislodged his IV and his hand was bleeding. He must look like he'd gone completely off his rocker. With any luck, he finally had.

The first nurse—DEE, her name tag read—grabbed his shoulders, pushed him firmly onto his back. "Shawna, get me one milligram of Ativan." To Zack, she ordered, "Mr. Knight, you have to calm down. Your blood pressure is sky-high and you've injured yourself."

Ativan? Shit! If they plugged him with that stuff, he'd be drooling like an infant for the next twenty-four hours.

He tried to compose himself and remain still while Dee cleaned his throbbing hand and readjusted the IV, but it was impossible. His ragged gasps for air came between bouts of the miserable coughing strangling his lungs. Black spots began to dance in his vision and his head spun.

Christ, he couldn't breathe.

"What's going on? Zack!"

From nowhere, Cori appeared at his other side. A gift from heaven. Without hesitating, she took his uninjured hand, brought it to her cheek. "Easy, let them help you. Breathe slowly, honey."

Zack squeezed her fingers as Shawna returned, holding a syringe aloft. "Please," he rasped. "Don't."

"Hi, Shawna. Ativan? Sounds like our hero's been a bad boy," Cori said, worry coloring her attempt at wry humor.

"You know it, girlfriend." Shawna pursed her lips and arched a brow. "I think the man wants to relapse. Crazy fool, throwin' shit around."

"Hmm. Guess you'd better cool it, unless you prefer to be comatose for the next twenty-four to forty-eight hours, hot stuff."

Zack blinked up at Cori. These two knew each other? And how the devil would Cori know about the effects of Ativan?

All three women looked at him in question. He did his best to appear contrite as he wheezed an apology. "I'm sorry. I'm calm now, I promise."

From their dubious expressions, they didn't buy the lie. God, he didn't want to be out of it for another day.

Dee glanced at the monitor. "BP's coming down. I don't know. What do you think?" She looked to Shawna, who gave Zack a scary, I'm-not-taking-your-crap smile.

"That I'm gonna send Mr. Knight to la-la land if he so much as twitches the wrong way again." She sounded terribly disappointed at the lost opportunity.

"No twitching," he croaked. "Honest."

Dee shrugged. "You're being moved to a regular room as soon as they have one ready, so you won't be our problem. How easy you want the rest of your stay to be is up to you."

"A regular room? Does that mean I can go home soon?"

"Keep improving and I'd guess the day after tomorrow."

Thank God. He needed out of here. To crawl into a hole and never emerge again.

Eyes narrowed, Shawna waved the capped end of the needle at Zack. "Until then, mind your manners." She turned to Cori. "I'll leave Conan in your hands. Got a feelin' he'll appreciate your company more than mine."

She sailed out, Dee trailing behind. Conan, huh? From

mild-mannered firefighter to barbarian. Jesus, they'd nearly tranked him like a rampaging elephant.

Cori took a seat beside him, amber gaze shadowed with concern. "Tell me what happened."

"I received a rather . . . upsetting phone call. Didn't handle it well."

"Care to talk about it?"

Hey, sure! I'm gonna get murdered by mobsters!

"No." Hurt flashed across her face, and he winced. "I mean I *can't*. This is something I have to deal with alone, and the less anyone else knows about it, the better."

"Sounds heavy."

"You have no idea."

She paused, studying him as though she could read all his secrets. "Okay. Just know I'm here when you're ready to unload."

"Thanks," he said quietly. Drinking in her lovely face and fall of hair the color of dark honey, he sought to distract himself from his troubles.

Her loose tresses tumbled past the shoulders of her dark overcoat. Underneath the coat, he caught a glimpse of a glittery, low-cut red dress. His gaze traveled down her graceful neck to the swell of her generous breasts. So much golden skin, the dress barely covering nipples he'd love to taste.

"You look beautiful."

"Thank you."

Her big, white smile blasted him with a double shot of desire. Awakened his slumbering libido. She was sex incarnate, a treat he'd never sampled. He wondered if she'd believe his innocence, then reminded himself it didn't make any difference. Even if he wasn't a disaster zone, Cori was way out of his league.

The steely fist around Zack's lungs began to loosen and he sank into the pillows, exhausted. Sick at heart.

He decided to give her an out. "Don't you have to work a party tonight? You're going to be late."

"Do I look like I care? For you, they can wait."

His breath caught and any reply he might've made was stopped by the lump in his throat. No one had ever put him first.

No one.

As he struggled to hold his emotions in check, she leaned into him. Like a dying man, he reveled in the soothing caress on his brow, his cheek. Her breast brushing his arm, the sweet scent of something light and floral on her skin. Lulled by the wondrous sensations chasing off the stress of the day, he yawned.

"I'm so tired." Well, one part of him wasn't convinced that resting seemed like much fun. The one woman he'd ever reacted to so strongly, and he couldn't do a damned thing about it.

"Sleep, Zack," she whispered. "Everything will be all right, you'll see. I'll be right here."

He sighed, turned his face into her touch. The soft promise, her nearness, skittered down his belly to his groin, stroked his balls and cock as he imagined her gentle hands would.

An intimacy he'd longed for . . . and never experienced.

He'd fought so hard day after day since this whole nightmare began, only to find himself stripped down to nothing. He might've quit once and for all. If not for Cori.

For the first time in his life, someone special was at his side. Not just one of his friends, but a woman who was interested in him as a man. Encouraging him to hang on one more day. To believe.

He was sick of just existing. He wanted so badly to be needed. To be the other half of someone's soul. Hers alone. If he had a chance with Cori, he'd take it.

She'll run once she knows the truth. Then you'll be worse off than before, broken and bleeding out in the dirt.

Maybe. But she'd be here when he awoke. For now, it was enough. As the weight of exhaustion pulled him under, he held on to her words.

God help him, that promise was all he had left.

6

In Zack's newly assigned private room, Cori watched over him while he slept. Hours after she should've shown at the bachelor party, she sat by his side, just checking the steady rise and fall of his chest. Making certain he was really okay.

Nothing else mattered. Certainly not the money she'd lost tonight, or the drunken groping she hadn't been forced to endure. No, her only concern was the awful scene she'd walked in on earlier this evening. The anguish in Zack's blue eyes, the defeat.

And how that emotion changed to something entirely different the moment he realized she was there.

She studied his handsome profile, so peaceful in sleep. Absent were the lines of strain around his eyes and mouth that evidenced worry no man his age should know. He looked like a young prince, waiting for the kiss of his princess to awaken him from a wicked spell. "Sleeping Beauty" in reverse.

Maybe not so far from the truth.

"I have to go," she whispered, bending to kiss his uninjured cheek. He didn't stir. "See you tomorrow."

She hated to leave him, but he was out, most likely for the night. Her own bed was calling and she had to be up earlier than normal if she wanted to run her Saturday morning errands and get back here at a decent time to visit Zack.

Okay, truth: She didn't give a crap about the errands. She just wanted to see Zack again.

On the way home, she couldn't stop thinking about him. What made this man, of all the guys who'd shown a interest in her, so special? Lots of men had that sweet, heroic Clark Kent thing going on. Didn't they?

Nope. And they weren't Zack, either.

Be honest, Corrine. If he hadn't nearly died saving your life, he's exactly the sort of quiet, unassuming guy you'd never have given a second glance.

A few days ago, Zack was just a jerk who'd rear-ended her SUV in a moment of inattention.

Because he was ill and battling exhaustion from working much too hard. She'd noticed that he was an attractive man, and that something seemed to be wrong besides his distress over their fender bender, but her own annoyance had been more important.

Which made her every bit as self-absorbed as Tony. The admission shamed her.

Disturbed by the comparison, Cori turned down her driveway and reached for the garage-door opener—only to remember the device had taken a nice long soak in the river with her Explorer. Insurance had declared the vehicle a total loss, but wouldn't cover the cost of replacing the items inside. She needed to find out how to get a new opener, but just hadn't made time to do it yet.

"Dammit."

And of course, it was scary-dark out here, turning her little country jewel of a house into a setting straight out of *Friday the 13th.*

"This is where the too-stupid-to-live heroine gets out of the car and walks to the front door in total ignorance that her spine is about to get ripped out and eaten for a midnight snack," she muttered, putting the vehicle into park.

Terrific. Palming her keys and shouldering her purse strap, she stepped out of the car. The night was freezing, her breath frosting in the air, or so she imagined. The darkness closed around her, a suffocating cloak hiding every frightening creature her mind conjured.

And silent. Much too silent, except for the quiet rattling of bare branches in the chilly wind. Skeletal fingers swaying in the moonlight.

She made a beeline for the porch, not running, but not letting grass grow under her shoes, either. Beady eyes drilled the spot between her shoulder blades, an unseen threat coiled to pounce. Every ridiculous childhood fear spurring her legs to pump faster, the boogeyman you can't see always more terrifying than reality.

Halfway up the steps, Cori discovered how wrong she was.

To her right, a shadow moved. She froze on a strangled gasp, keys outstretched in her hand. Stared into the gloom, straining to make out the shape . . . and then wished she hadn't.

There, by the porch swing. The silhouette of a man. All in black, featureless. Like a manifestation from hell, straight from her nightmares to something corporeal.

And deadly.

Scrambling backward, she found her voice. Screamed loud enough to wake the county, but knew there weren't any neighbors close enough to come to her rescue, even if they'd heard.

Her heels slipped on the steps and she lost her balance, tumbling, landing hard on her back. Without hesitating, she rolled to her hands and knees, pushed up, and ran. As fast as she could in the damned dress and high-heeled shoes, wishing they were sneakers and jeans.

Fumbling with the car keys, she hit the automatic unlock button. Prayed she'd make it inside before he got her.

Flinging open the door, she threw herself in, hit the locks. "Oh, God, please . . ."

Heart jackhammering in her throat, she scanned the front yard frantically. The porch.

Nothing.

No man in pursuit. No ominous shadow moving for the car. But she wasn't taking any risks. "I *know* what I saw."

Hands shaking, she jammed the keys in the ignition, slammed the car in reverse. Tore a path across the dirt-and-gravel driveway and through a corner of the lawn, taking out a hedge in her haste to escape.

She was a mile down the road before realizing she'd lost her purse in the yard, and gave a hysterical laugh. Let the bastard have it. The color and style would match his black ninja ensemble.

Where to go? Not to Tony's, for sure. Playing the hero would give his ego a boost it didn't need, and she didn't want to send him the wrong message about where things stood. Especially since she wasn't going home tonight.

Waking Zack when he was recovering and couldn't help was out of the question. He'd just lose sleep for nothing.

Joaquin? Good God, she really must be shaken to even consider phoning her brother. He'd go berserk.

That left her best girlfriend, Shea Ford. A fellow nursing student Cori had met at the coffee shop a couple of years ago through her buddies, the self-dubbed Latte Ladies, Shea was solid gold. A true-blue soul who wouldn't hesitate to welcome a friend after midnight and listen with concern to her insane ramblings of being watched.

Stalked.

An incredible, impossible word, overused in society to the point of being clichéd. Easy to forget the moment a person flipped off the evening news, as long as it was someone else's problem.

And Cori no longer had any doubts; that was what was happening.

Why?

Fifteen minutes later, she knocked on the door of Shea's apartment. Stood shivering, teeth chattering, as she waited. After two of the longest minutes on record, her friend opened the door, lustrous, curly brown hair flying wildly around her small, surprised face.

"Cori! What on earth—"

With a sob, she flung herself into Shea's arms. Locking up, Shea guided Cori to the sofa and sat with an arm around her shoulders as she bawled out the story in fits and starts. Her friend knew about the bridge accident and Zack's heroic rescue, but not about the bullet in Cori's tire. Nor the sinister turn this week had taken.

"Oh, sweetie." Shea hugged Cori's shoulders. "Why didn't you tell me what was going on? Have you talked to the police?"

Cori snorted a watery laugh, taking the tissue her friend offered. "For all the good it did. They did a great job of humoring the crazy, paranoid lady."

Her friend straightened with a *humph* of annoyance.

"Well, they'll have to listen now, won't they?" Pushing off the sofa, she marched for the phone.

"Don't count on it."

Shea returned, thrusting the handset at her. "You need to have them check out your place. Make the call, or I will."

Shea was right, but she dreaded facing their condescending, big-he-man-with-badge attitudes again. After making the call and explaining the incident to the dispatcher, she let Shea fuss over her, grateful for the hot chocolate and companionship.

Officer Boley was a vast improvement over her last experience with the cops. He took down the pertinent information while making the appropriate noises of empathy—even if skepticism showed in his eyes. Suited Cori fine. At least he wasn't a jackass, and he attempted to comfort her by relating that two officers had gone out to her house to look around.

"So you didn't get a good look at this guy?" he asked again, flipping his small notebook closed.

"No. I only saw a figure. I think he was dressed all in black." She hated the way police tended to ask the same questions several times, as though the complainant was either lying or stupid. Repeating that she didn't actually see the intruder's features certainly made her story sound iffy, and pissed her off.

"And you lost your purse in the front yard after you fell and then ran." His thoughtful gaze bored into hers.

"Yes, exactly."

"Well, that's something."

Before Cori could ask what he meant, the radio on the officer's belt squawked loudly in the tiny space, causing her to jump.

"Hey, Dennis?"

Boley pressed the button on the microphone attached to the collar of his coat. "Go ahead."

"We got nothin' here. Doors and windows are all secure, house is locked up tighter'n my ex-wife's—"

"Copy that," Boley interrupted, rolling his eyes at the two women as if to say, *See what I have to put up with?* "What about Ms. Shannon's purse?"

"Nope, sorry. There ain't a purse here anywhere. If her unwelcome visitor grabbed and dumped it, he didn't dump it on the property."

Boley glanced at Cori. "Most thieves will rifle through the contents, then dump the purse somewhere else. Yours might still turn up."

Sure. Minus her money and plastic. Groaning, she rubbed her tired eyes. Now she'd be up the rest of the night calling hotline numbers to cancel her credit cards.

Could've been much worse.

I could've been canceled instead.

And now she had some sort of tangible proof— however thin—of her claim. Somebody was stalking her, and he'd just gotten across his first real message.

Anytime he chose, the bastard could get to her.

Officer Boley prepared to make his escape. "Don't blame you if you'd rather stay with your friend tonight, but I'm reasonably sure it's safe for you to return home when you're up to it. Surprised a would-be burglar, most likely. He'll head for easier pickings now; don't worry."

If that theory helped the cop sleep like a baby at night, bully for him.

She'd worked so damned hard these past couple of years to finish her aborted schooling, set her life on the right path. Someone wanted to take everything away. Again.

And Cori's best and only suspect was moldering in his grave.

Cori wasn't there when he awoke, after all. Didn't show.

Which made Saturday the longest frigging day of Zack's life.

He flipped through channels on the wall-mounted TV. Flipped through a sports magazine Eve brought him this morning, unable to read the small print without his damned glasses. Nearly flipping lost his mind watching the slow crawl of the hour hand, the day lengthening to evening.

And watching the door, pulse leaping in excitement each time someone entered, only to see another nurse breezing in to poke and prod him.

Walking the halls provided his only distraction. This morning, the nurses had declared he needed to get vertical, and he could've leapt with joy. Figuratively, that was.

The reality was slow and painful. Until Zack had pushed out of bed, he hadn't gotten the full effect of just how battered his body was from his ordeal. Smiling grimly to himself, he imagined looking like an old man shuffling down the corridor, rolling his IV along, trying to keep his bare ass covered.

The high point of his day? A shower.

Hoo-yaa. Are we havin' fun yet?

As the sun sank, so did his spirits. Dark, ugly thoughts crept in despite his effort to shake them. Too many hours alone. Thinking. Why had he been spared? What was the point?

He'd lost everything. Drowning, same as in the river, except going under for good was taking too fucking long.

Poison for the soul.

The phone's loud ring blasted the horrible direction of his musings, and he glanced at the clock. Just past eight.

He snatched the receiver, not daring to hope. "Hello?"

"Zack, it's Cori. I'm *so* sorry I didn't make it to see you today."

Her breathy voice poured over his skin, sank deep, curling warm fingers around his lonely heart. "Hey, no problem. It's been so busy here, people in and out, I've hardly had a minute to myself, you know?" He forced a chuckle past his tight throat, glancing around the empty, silent room.

"Oh. Well, that's good, then," she said, sounding distracted. "Anyway, I had sort of a terrible night and slept until after noon. Then I had some stuff to take care of today—"

"Cori, you don't have to explain." Oh, God. The brush-off, already?

"I will, just not over the phone. Believe me, I really wanted to come see you." A pause. "Did . . . did you miss me?"

Zack closed his eyes, his traitorous cock happily answering her tentative question. Praise Jesus she couldn't see. "Yes. You don't know how much." He heard the smile in her reply.

"Good. I thought about you all day, wondering how you were. Are you feeling better?"

Funny, Eve had asked him the very same question this morning, but it hadn't made him feel as though he'd float off the bed. "Yeah. I think they're springing me tomorrow."

"Oh, that's great! Say, do you need a ride home?"

Zack opened his eyes and blinked. How he was going

to get home hadn't even occurred to him—not that he was in a hurry to go back to his run-down apartment. Or for Cori to see the disgusting slum he called home. Christ.

Quickly, he sorted through his options. He didn't have money for a cab. Eve had mentioned going to her mother's for Sunday dinner. Six-Pack and Kat were house hunting. Skyler would probably be nursing a hangover. Tanner or Salvatore? Forget it.

"Zack?"

"Um, yes. I think I'll need a lift. But only if you don't mind."

"My pleasure. Do you have clothes?"

"What?"

She laughed. "Clothes. Unless you'd planned to be wheeled out naked?"

Only if I'm naked with you. "Right. I guess being arrested for indecent exposure might be overkill for this week, huh?" This time they laughed together, and damn, it felt good.

"What do you need? Jeans and T-shirt? A jacket?"

"And, um . . ." His face heated.

"Undies, socks, and tennis shoes?"

He blew out a breath, trying to hide the embarrassment in his voice. "That would be great, thanks. All I have are the uniform pants I was wearing, along with my wallet and keys. My shirt was destroyed and my shoes got lost."

"Since I don't have the key to your place or know where you live, I'll run by Wal-Mart in the morning before I pick you up. It'll be easier."

"I'll pay you back." *As soon as I sell a kidney.*

"No sweat. You can take me to dinner sometime," she suggested.

Zack's mouth went dry and the waving banner at his

crotch saluted the plan. Yes! He'd take this woman out, even if he had to rob a bank first. And steal a car. "It's a date, gorgeous. Cori, thank you."

"Oh, don't thank me yet. I'm an evil, scheming siren with an ulterior motive."

"Which is?"

"Why, to lead you down the path of temptation and into unimaginable sin. What else?" An air kiss smooched in his ear. "Good night, fireboy."

The soft click barely registered. Zack lay there, a stupid grin spreading across his face, his throbbing dick making a respectable-sized tent in the sheets. God, what sweet agony. If he weren't afraid a nurse would get an eyeful, he'd take the problem in hand.

One phone call from Cori Shannon, and the world seemed a much brighter place than it had ten minutes ago.

She hadn't forgotten him, or blown him off. His room was still stark and empty, but he was no longer alone.

A strange sensation unfurled in his chest, overpowering the desolation he'd learned to take for granted. Driving back his fears. Stronger than hope.

Zack couldn't be certain, but it felt very much like . . . happiness.

It wasn't until he began to drift off to sleep that he recalled Cori saying she'd had a bad night. Something had upset her and ruined her Saturday. Had she seen the van again? Received a threatening note or phone call?

Worrying over Cori's safety, his own predicament forgotten, he tossed for the rest of the night.

"You can't be serious."

Slack-jawed, Zack lifted the offending item from the Wal-Mart bag as though he held a plastic explosive.

Cori stifled a giggle. "They're *cheerful*. If anyone needs cheering up, it's you."

"These can be seen from deep space."

"Real men wear pink."

And, boy, were those boxers pink. Electric pink—with bright yellow happy faces all over them. One smiley, larger than the rest, graced the front escape hatch, a strategically placed tongue sticking from between its lips.

"I am *not* wearing these."

She shrugged, enjoying herself. "Guess you'll have to go commando."

Zack curled his lip. "That's gross. Not to mention unsanitary."

"Goodness! Are you always so straitlaced? Live dangerously, fireboy. Unless you don't have what it takes."

His blue gaze snapped to hers. A slow smile curved his sensual mouth. "All right. Score one for you—this time. Just remember what they say about payback."

"Ooh!" She gave a little shiver. "Promises, promises."

Without warning, he leaned close. Reached out, brushing his knuckles down one cheek. She felt his heat blistering through the thin gown, and not due to fever. His scent, a mixture of soap and earthy male, teased her nose. Brought every female cell to rigid attention, puckering her nipples. Made her long to crawl inside him, learn what would cause him to lose control. Lose himself in *her*.

But those wondrous new feelings were nothing compared with his kiss.

Just a simple kiss. A brush of his lips against hers. A tentative exploration, silently asking permission. She slid a hand behind his neck in answer, playing with the thick hair at his nape. Loving the cool, silky black strands between her fingers.

Encouraged, Zack groaned, giving her a bit of tongue. The gentlest of touches. A hint of toothpaste and spicy man. The slight contact sizzled a fiery path straight to her womb. Gathered there in a delicious ball of swirling, crackling energy. Blazed to her clenching sex.

Wet. God, he'd dampened her panties with nothing more than a vanilla kiss. Needy for more. For *him*. Tony's kiss couldn't begin to compare with something so honest. Pure.

Zack's arousal was like a separate, living entity calling to her. Demanding only one response. She wished they were anywhere but here, free to taste and touch at leisure. She wished—

Zack broke the kiss and tipped up her chin, running his thumb over her plump bottom lip. His lids were heavy, eyes dark with a reflection of her own thoughts.

"Be careful," he murmured huskily. "A gorgeous woman who loves to live dangerously should know I'm a man who's damned sick of being good. One day you might wish you'd let this sleeping dog lie."

Momentarily rendered speechless, Cori could only stare as Zack pushed off the bed and walked stiffly into the small bathroom, sack in hand. An invitation and a warning in the same breath. How could any red-blooded female resist?

She couldn't. A fact that became shockingly clear the instant Zack stepped, fully dressed, from the bathroom.

Sweet leaping Jesus. He's . . . beautiful.

There was truly not a more perfect word to describe Zack. She'd never seen him in street clothes and—*Oh my*—he'd just redefined her opinion of exactly how a man should look.

At just over six feet, he was built like a runner: a man who kept in shape, but didn't bulk up too much. His body was long, lean, and toned, roped with just the perfect amount of muscle, though she doubted she'd be able to span his biceps with both hands.

His chest stretched the confines of his dark blue T-shirt, a sculpted work of art. His stomach was so flat and hard, you could probably bounce a quarter off his abs. A trim waist, jeans hanging low on his hips, long thighs. The soft denim cupped a sizable bulge at his crotch, leaving no doubt that her attraction was returned tenfold.

All told, the man was a feast begging to be devoured.

And he'd all but challenged her to grab a fork.

"Let me guess. These radioactive boxers are making me glow like Las Vegas at midnight."

The amusement in his tone jerked her attention back to his face. His eyes were dancing in mirth. And something else a helluva lot darker. Hungrier.

"You, um, look . . . nice. Really great," she added, feeling thrown off her groove. His sexy smile hit her like a fist to the gut.

"A definite improvement over hospital haute couture, don't you think? Damn, I feel almost human."

Well, she certainly hadn't been referring to the clothing. He couldn't possibly be that innocent. Could he?

Any reply hovering on her lips was lost as Dr. Chu bustled in, handing Zack two prescriptions and issuing stern orders to continue the breathing treatments as an outpatient for at least another week. His directive to lay off work for at least two weeks and obtain written clearance to return to the station was met with silence on Zack's part, his earlier humor evaporating. By the set of his jaw, Cori knew Zack had no intention of complying with that part of the doctor's rules if he could figure a way around it.

A nurse pushed Zack out to the curb in a wheelchair, per hospital policy, while Cori brought her car around. Zack slid into the passenger's seat and they were on the road. Glancing at him, Cori thought how surreal it was to have him sitting next to her. Her rescuer, with whom she'd already faced down death and won.

Because of his courage.

"Tell me something about yourself," she said, turning west like he'd instructed, toward Clarksville.

"Like what?"

"I don't know. Favorite food? Pet peeve?"

"Hmm. Okay, I love baby back ribs. I'd kill for a rack of those smothered with Jack Daniel's barbecue sauce right now." His stomach rumbled and she grinned.

"Obviously. We'll have to do something about that. What else?"

"I hate pasta."

"That's not normal."

"I know. But it's slimy. Blech." He thought for a few seconds. "That's not nearly as strange as my pet peeve; I don't like clowns."

Cori laughed out loud, struggling to keep her attention on the road. "That's just weird, Zack. *Clowns?*"

"As a kid, they seriously freaked me out." He sighed. "Why doesn't anyone but me think there's something creepy about a grown man dressing in a clown suit and makeup? I mean, remember John Wayne Gacy?"

Goose bumps broke out on Cori's arms. "Point taken."

"Your turn."

"All right. Pizza rocks. Hate liver. There's something

really disgusting about eating an organ that used to filter bile."

"Well, thanks a million for that image."

"You're welcome. Let's see, pet peeves. I have a few. Ten weenies in a package, but only eight buns. Okay, that's only a figurative reference, but you get the drift. Stupid concepts bug me."

"Then I'll be careful not to reveal any dumb ideas around you," he said wryly. "What about your family? Do they live around here?"

"I have three obnoxious, overbearing older brothers. Which is why they live on the East Coast and I live here."

"Ah. Overprotective, are they?"

Cori rolled her eyes. "They almost drove me insane after our mother died, especially my oldest brother. He kept his thumb squashed down on me so hard, I did something unbelievably stupid to get out from under his iron rule."

"Which was?"

"I got married." She glanced at Zack to see how he'd absorbed that tidbit. He simply nodded, a sage expression on his face.

"It didn't work out," he guessed.

"No."

Zack's eyes narrowed. "Does your ex still bother you?"

"Hardly." She swallowed hard, weighing the wisdom of opening the door on the awful pain. The guilt. Once she did, there was no turning back. "My oldest brother killed him," she said, her voice almost inaudible.

He sucked in a sharp breath. "Jesus Christ. You mean like . . ."

"In my defense. Alex had beaten me nearly to death and my brother caught him in the act. The grand jury chose not to indict." Cori gripped the steering wheel tighter to hide the shakes. Zack was the only other person besides Shea with whom Cori had ever shared the darkest period in her life. Because sharing it also meant lying to those she'd come to care about, and it hurt too badly to do it.

"You know, that story is one best told over a long evening involving lots of alcohol," she said.

"Understood. And as you said to me, when you're ready to talk, I'm here."

Unexpected tears rushed to her eyes. This man wore his kindness as easily as his clothing. And, oh, God, she could get addicted to the whole package that was Zack Knight.

"Thanks." She sniffed and cleared her throat. "What about you? Where's your family?"

The instant the words left her mouth, she inwardly cursed herself for being an idiot. But there was no taking them back without revealing what she already knew.

"My father is in a nursing home," he said, surprising her. "He suffered a stroke last year and is basically a vegetable. He has waking periods, but he's like an infant. Has to be fed, diapered."

"Oh, Zack, I'm so sorry. What about your mother?"

He shrugged. "I never knew her. My father had lots of women in his heyday. One of them literally left me on his doorstep. Tests proved I was his, and he raised me by himself. Turn here."

His voice was tense, controlled, as though giving a highly edited version of the story. Much like hers. She could hardly blame him for not wanting to open a vein.

Cori made the turn into a low-income neighborhood, each home more dilapidated than the last. Minutes later, as she pulled into his apartment complex, she blinked in astonishment, striving to keep the dismay from showing on her face. How could Zack—anyone—live in a dump like this?

A sagging roof that should've been replaced a decade ago and was missing a ton of shingles. Overgrown hedges that covered first-floor windows. Most of the windows visible on all three floors lacked screens, and many were broken or cracked.

The sidewalk was buckled and faded toys littered the muddy areas where grass refused to grow. Cigarette butts were strewn everywhere. Peeling paint that might have been any color at one time curled and flaked, like a skin disease with no cure.

A group of older teens wearing hooded sweatshirts lurked between two buildings, oblivious to the miserable cold. A wad of green and a small packet exchanged hands.

This wretched, filthy hellhole was not where someone wanted to be caught after sundown.

Expression closed, Zack pointed to a building on the far end, next to the complex's office. "Park over there. I'm on the second floor."

She did, and they got out, hunching their shoulders against the freezing wind and light mist that had started moments ago. Zack started to cough, and she worried about him being out in this weather, in his condition. Did his apartment have enough heat? If not, he'd find himself right back in the hospital.

"You don't have to come up." Clearing his throat, he studied the ground as they walked. The words were underscored with steel, and a touch of fierce pride.

He didn't want her to see the inside of his apartment,

and she hurt for him. She didn't care what his place looked like; she cared about Zack. But now wasn't the time to press the issue.

"I'll just walk you to the door, if that's okay. I've got to run." She didn't, but the lie gave him a way to salvage his pride.

His shoulders relaxed. "Sure. I'll call you later?"

"I'd be disappointed if you didn't, handsome."

He smiled, ducked his head.

The smile vanished as they reached the second-floor landing. She followed him along the breezeway, wondering what on earth had him all tense when she'd just managed to lighten his mood.

He halted, and she nearly bumped into his back. "This is your pad, huh?"

Zack went dead still. She moved to his side, a chill of dread washing through her. His face paled and he stared at the door. Swaying on his feet, he plucked off a square of pink paper that had been taped to the surface.

He stared at the paper for several long moments, in shock.

His hoarse voice emerged as a whisper.

"No. I don't live here anymore."

7

Zack crushed the eviction notice in his hand. He wasn't surprised. Had known this was coming, in fact. But he hadn't planned on a witness to his latest humiliation.

Hadn't planned on Cori.

He turned his back to the wall and leaned against it, buried his face in his hands. The paper fluttered to the concrete.

Broke *and* homeless. God, what a pathetic joke.

Think, genius. What now? Where will you go?

"What . . ."

A paper rustled, and he lowered his hands to see Cori holding the notice, jaw dropping in astonishment.

"They're kicking *you* out? No way!"

If she only knew. "Seems you have to pay them to live here. How picky is that?"

"But—they let drug dealers stay here," Cori sputtered, indignant.

"Drug dealers have money. Hey, maybe those punks will set me up with a side job?" He laughed at his own pitiful joke, which ended in a round of coughing. Better than crying, though.

Scowling, she crushed the slip, tossed it over her

shoulder. "Dammit, this isn't right! Didn't they even give you a grace period?"

Zack hung his head. "I'm two and a half months behind. When I couldn't pay on January the first, the manager gave me an extension until the fifteenth. Which I missed, because I was in the hospital." Not that it made a difference. He was living on borrowed time, no money in his checking account.

"Oh."

One blow after another. Could it get any worse?

She straightened her spine with purpose, pinning him with her amber gaze. "Do you have a place to stay?"

"I . . ." His face heated. Yeah, things could definitely get worse.

"Well, you do now. You're staying with me."

He bit back a bitter retort. Didn't every self-respecting man love to be bailed out of trouble by the woman he'd die to call his own?

Might as well slice his balls off and let her use them for fuzzy dice on her rearview mirror.

"I appreciate the offer, but I can't impose on you."

"What? Like you have a better option?" Arching a slim brow, she crossed her arms over her chest. Zack tried not to stare at how the position hiked up her bosom as she went on. "Who are you going to call? Your buddies at the station? You want them all here, in your business, making sympathetic noises until you puke?"

Which Cori hadn't done, to his immense relief. He studied her, rubbing his aching chest. God, she was right. Firefighters were a brotherhood. If one was in trouble, they banded together. One phone call and word of Zack's problems would spread like wildfire. The only man he trusted to keep this on the down-low was Six-Pack, and he wasn't about to intrude on the lieutenant's newly wedded bliss.

But he couldn't accept. The words wouldn't form.

Cori sighed. "Okay. The truth is, my motives aren't completely altruistic. As wimpy as this sounds, I'd feel better having a man staying with me right now."

"Because of the weird van sightings and the noises at night? I really don't think you have anything to worry about." She shook her head, eyes liquid. Her fear ground into his gut like jagged glass and he straightened, gripping her shoulders. "Something else *did* happen Friday night. Tell me."

Her lips trembled. "When I got home from visiting you, it was late. When I stepped onto the porch, a man was waiting for me."

"Sonofabitch," he gasped, cupping her sweet face. "Are you all right? Did he hurt you?"

"No. I ran, but he didn't chase me. I'm fine."

Cori wasn't "fine." A bad night, she'd said. In his worst nightmare, he'd never expected her to be targeted by a stalker. He couldn't imagine her terror, and a knot of cold rage began to form in his stomach.

"What did the police say?" Gently, he stroked her smooth cheeks with his thumbs, needing to touch her. Reassure himself that she was okay.

"That I'd probably surprised a burglar and scared him off before he had a chance to break in." She gave a watery laugh. "I haven't been home since."

"Where have you been sleeping? A hotel?"

"My friend Shea loaned me her sofa. She sent her brother to my house yesterday for a change of clothes. I'm going home today."

Zack frowned. "Who's her brother?" He didn't like the

idea of a strange man poking through her house. "How do you know he's not the one behind all of this?"

She smiled at his protective tone. "Shane Ford is a homicide detective with the Sugarland PD. I doubt he's our creep. They're twins. Shea and Shane. Cute, huh?"

"If your friend's brother is a cop, can't he do something? Put some pressure on his buddies to investigate?"

"Homicide, hell-oo. I'm not Shane's problem until *after* I'm dead."

"Jesus, that's not funny. Come here." What he knew about women could fit inside a speck of DNA, but he figured frightened women needed comforting. Especially this one. By him.

Zack pulled her into his arms and she went willingly. He tucked her head against his shoulder and she burrowed inside his coat. Warm and soft. Breasts crushed against his chest, hands clutching his back. Breath fanning against his collarbone. All woman.

All mine.

And just like that, the universe rearranged itself. Nothing was more important than Cori, sheltered in his arms. Nobody had the right to frighten her. No man would touch her while his heart still beat in his chest.

Emotions surged, wild and confusing, filling the vast emptiness. Like a hurricane, the onslaught shook his foundations, almost painful in its intensity. And in the wake of that foreign invasion, something dark and dangerous. Ugly.

The desire to wrap his hands around the throat of the person responsible for causing her pain, and squeeze the life from his worthless body.

Cori tipped her face up and he brought his mouth down on hers. There was nothing tentative about his kiss and from the way she melted into him, she didn't seem to mind. Groaning, ignoring the throb in his bruised face, he drank her like a man dying of thirst. Plunged his tongue into her moist heat the way he'd love to slide his cock between her thighs. Brand her with his touch, give her what he'd never given another woman. Ruin her for another man.

Mine.

She broke the kiss, eyes dancing with humor. Fear abated. "I'll take that as a yes?"

"I forgot the question."

"You'll stay with me?"

He tightened his arms around her. Kissed the tip of her nose. "Yes." Another brush of lips. "Yes."

"Good. Let's grab your things and make tracks. It's cold out here."

"Best idea I've ever heard."

But his key no longer fit the lock. Not surprising, but definitely frustrating. Zack offered Cori his arm and they walked to the office together, the one place he'd hoped to avoid. He started to cough again and it made his lungs burn. His head ached and he felt dizzy. Funny, he'd been pretty darned revved while kissing the stuffing out of Cori. If only his tired body would cooperate with his libido.

In the dingy little office, the manager stared at Zack from across her ancient desk for about three seconds before bursting into harsh, gravelly laughter that shook her skinny frame and revealed a mouthful of yellowed teeth.

"You want your shit? By all means, take it." Apparently enjoying this, she pointed to a cardboard box beside her desk.

His hands clenched into fists at his sides. "Where's the rest?"

"Sold to cover your back rent," she said, blowing a stream of cigarette smoke in the general direction of his face. "Saved your uniforms, a few toiletries, and some papers that looked important."

"How kind of you." *Do not strangle her.*

"Have a nice life, kid."

Not trusting himself to say another word, he hefted the box and walked out. He ought to be grateful the vile old biddy had saved his work clothes. God knew he didn't need to give Tanner another reason to gnaw on his ass.

Cori opened the trunk and he stashed the box inside. They slid into the car and fastened their seat belts. Cori shot him a glance as she fired the engine. "Holy crap, there was a freaking *bullet hole* in the wall behind that woman's head!"

"Too bad they missed," he muttered, then felt bad for saying it. That miserable old woman probably had it ten times rougher than Zack on his worst day.

"What?"

"Nothing." He smiled, feeling strangely liberated.

"Anyway, I hope you don't mind my saying so, but I'm glad I'm not leaving you here." She made a face.

"To tell you the truth, I'm *very* cool with letting the cockroaches have this place. Can't wait to be gone." *With you.*

Okay. Maybe this was one of those Big Signs from Above like you read about. Destiny and all that woo-woo shit. Chicken poop to chicken soup. Right?

The drive was nice, her company wonderful. But as they neared Sugarland, the greasy knot in his stomach returned, becoming heavier with every mile. When Cori turned onto Neptune Road and headed deeper into the rural countryside, Zack started to feel a little queasy.

Cori had said she lived on the outskirts of Sugarland, just not exactly where. Of all the dozens of roads in Cheatham County, why this one?

"Wait until you see my place," she said, warming to the topic. His companion's excitement visibly escalated as his sense of doom grew, and she chattered on, unaware.

"It's so beautiful and peaceful out here—well, aside from my unexpected visitor the other night. The house sits off the road about fifty yards, and it has this great deck out back that overlooks the woods and a pretty creek. Someone put a salt block at the base of a tree close to the water, and the deer gather there almost every morning and evening. If I'm real quiet, I can slip outside, drink my coffee, and watch them."

Zack went numb. All over. "Sounds . . . fantastic."

"Oh, you have no idea!"

Yeah, he thought he might. When she slowed and turned down the long, winding drive, he averted his face. Stared out the window so she wouldn't see the anguish struggling to escape the compressed little knot in his chest. Sure, Delacruz had immediately sold his house for a tidy profit. In the back of his mind, Zack had known. But why did the buyer have to be Cori? The sucker punch was almost too much.

This could not be happening, yet here he was, come full circle. In that moment he felt like a ghost. A spectator in his own life, invisible to everyone around him.

Except Cori. He glanced at her, and the happiness radiating from her stilled the turmoil. His need to protect her—to preserve that glow—surged again. Hell, she'd been upset enough when he'd nearly bought the farm saving her life. No matter how painful it was keeping the truth locked inside, she must not find out.

Zack didn't need the pity. And Cori didn't deserve the misplaced guilt.

"Isn't it wonderful?" She parked in front of the garage and shut off the ignition.

Zack summoned all the enthusiasm he could muster. "I'll say. How long have you lived here?" Of course, he knew the answer.

"Just a few weeks. Sure beats the tiny apartment I had in town. Why don't we put your stuff inside, and then I'll give you the grand tour?"

Boy, he must've done something to piss off the gods. "Great."

They got out and Zack retrieved his worldly possessions from her trunk. Gritting his teeth, he followed her onto the porch and waited as she unlocked the door.

Slowly, he followed her inside. Paused to drink in the haven he'd never thought to see again. The soothing earth tones that had succumbed to a more feminine flair along the lines of rugs, curtains, and a couple of floral arrangements. The familiar fresh scent of lemon oil and wood.

Home.

"Zack? Are you feeling all right?"

"Um, yes. I'm fine. Where should I put this?" He jiggled the cardboard box in his hands.

"Just sit it there, in the entry. We'll get you settled in a bit." She frowned and he belatedly realized he hadn't complimented her home, something most people do automatically.

He set the box on the floor, then straightened, gesturing to the large, open space as though finally noticing. "Oh, wow. Awesome place you've got here."

Cori bit her lip, appearing troubled for a second. He

must've imagined it, because her expression cleared and the contentment returned. "Thanks. The previous owner must've put a lot of sweat into updating it." Reaching out, she ran a palm lovingly over the polished oak stair rail. The one he'd spent hours shaping, sanding, and polishing with loving care.

"The custom woodwork and cabinetry throughout the house is incredible. You don't get that quality of craftsmanship from a tract builder."

No, you don't.

"I'm thinking he might've designed and made it all in the shop out back," she went on. "There are saws, sanders, umpteen kinds of wood and stains, and I don't know what else. Probably enough to build an ark. Can't believe it was all left behind."

"What will you do with it?"

"I don't know. Sell the equipment and clean it out, I suppose. Just haven't gotten motivated yet."

A shard of pain knifed his gut. "I see."

"Say, are you any good with woodworking?"

"Fair," he lied. He'd practically lived for the texture of rough wood in his hands. For taking raw, discarded material and creating something new and shiny.

Her pretty face became animated as she warmed to her idea. "You could use the shop if you'd like. Someone might as well make use of all that great stuff."

"Oh, I don't know—"

"You could make something for *me*. If you wanted."

Aw, hell. How was he supposed to look into those sparkling, tawny eyes and say no? God help him if he had a houseful of little girls someday. "Did you have something special in mind?"

She grinned, obviously pleased. "Surprise me. Care for

something to drink while we take a walk? If you're up to it, that is."

"Sounds good, on both counts. I've been cooped up for too long." And not just because of the accident. He loved the outdoors and used to jog along Neptune Road on his days off, or simply go for a long stroll, enjoying the countryside. His most recent abode hadn't exactly been conducive to outdoor activity. At least not the legal kind.

Zack trailed her into the kitchen and parked his butt on the counter while she fished in the fridge. "Got a beer?"

"Yep. Beer, wine, and soda." She peered over her shoulder. "You really shouldn't drink while you're taking antibiotics."

"I know." He stuck out his lower lip in an exaggerated pout. "Just one?"

"Shame on you." Turning, she arched a brow, waggling a can of diet soda. "This is better for you."

"Yuck. Total carcinogen city. Beer is all-natural and *way* more nutritious. Besides, I deserve one after the week I've had."

With an unladylike snort, she replaced the can and took out two longnecks, twisted the top off one, and handed it to him. "As a paramedic, you know that alcohol suppresses the body's ability to effectively process—"

"There you go again." Zack took a swig of his brew.

"There I go doing what?"

"Spouting off like a medical textbook. You sit around and watch the health channel all day or something?"

"When have I said anything medical?"

He gazed at her innocent expression, curious. "You were talking about Ativan with that nurse who almost sedated me. You knew your stuff—and you knew the nurse, too. I'd almost forgotten."

She took a long draw of her beer, and he couldn't help but eye the graceful column of her throat as she drank. Her plump lips hugging the bottle's opening the way he'd love them wrapped around—

"Busted," she said, wiping her mouth. "I *do* read medical textbooks. All the time."

"For kicks? And *I'm* weird, huh?"

"I can think of more titillating things to do for fun than reading." Her mischievous smirk, and the implication of her words, almost gave him blue balls. Before he could respond, she lowered a double whammy. "I study the books for my classes."

He blinked, his brain still stuck on titillating endeavors. "You're taking classes?"

"Don't sound so surprised, hot stuff. Exotic dancers *can* go to school, you know." Advancing on him, she poked him in the chest with her beer bottle. "In fact, dancing is what allows most of the girls I know to pay their tuition. Many of them are going for an education."

God, for a guy with a so-called genius IQ, he was a total dumbass when it came to women. Why hadn't it occurred to him that a smart, fiery babe like Cori had more going on than showing off her smokin' bod? "Like you?"

"Like me. I graduate from nursing school in May." Her beaming smile warmed him like a solar flare.

"Oh, wow! Major congrats, beautiful." He pulled her into a bear hug, and loved how she burrowed her face into the curve of his neck, the tickle of her hair against his cheek. Her arms snaked around his waist under his coat, and he thought what a lucky man he was to hold her twice in one day. And on the heels of that . . .

With most of her income funneled into books and tuition, how on earth had she afforded to buy his property?

None of his business. The idea took him places he'd rather not go, so he shoved it aside. Nothing could be allowed to spoil this. Having a woman's body—this woman's—against his was as close to heaven as he'd ever come.

Being dead for several minutes notwithstanding.

And even then, there had been no fabled brilliant light. No sense of belonging at last. Of real peace.

"That's quite an accomplishment, working so hard to put yourself through school. I'm proud of you," he said, kissing her temple. Immediately, he felt sheepish. Cori wasn't his, and didn't need his approval. Might not even appreciate it.

"Nobody's ever told me that before. Not even my brothers." She tipped her face up to his, her lashes wet, mouth trembling. "You don't know how much it means to me, hearing someone validate my efforts. Thank you."

Ah, God. Tears. He was *so* toasted. "Actually, I have a very good idea."

"Hmm. You're lucky you had your father to guide you in finding the right path. To encourage you."

"That's not what I meant."

Pulling back, she frowned at him, hesitant. "But when you mentioned your father raising you . . ."

"You pictured a Norman Rockwell painting of a doting all-American dad, teaching his boy to play wide receiver?" The question came out sharper than he intended, colored with bitterness. "My father was a self-important bastard. He never—" *Loved me.*

Whoa, TMI. Too late, the words died in his throat. Didn't matter that he'd managed to strangle them. Whether they were unspoken or not, Cori heard the truth that still had the power to make him bleed.

"I'm sorry," she said quietly, searching his face with tentative fingers. His lips. "Seems we have even more in common than I believed."

Sweet Christ, he couldn't gaze into her lovely eyes, so full of compassion, and not fall. Fast. Hard.

Nothing had ever felt so right as Cori in his arms. When he'd first held and kissed her . . . it was as though her lips moving against his had awakened his soul from a twenty-six-year sleep. He'd known her mere days.

Had known her forever.

"Why don't we take that walk?" Clasping his hand, she led him outside, onto the deck.

For a moment they stood enjoying the view in companionable silence. The small creek bisected the gentle slope of the land, and the woods on the other side were broken only by a trail leading up the opposite slope. His—*no, Cori's*—property ended about thirty yards beyond the tree line, bordering hundreds of acres of undeveloped, pristine Tennessee valley.

Her nearness and the welcome sight kept the yawning emptiness at bay as they used the steps at the side of the deck and struck out for the creek. The day was chilly but sunny and the dead, brown grass crunched under their shoes. The water was swollen from the runoff of all the freezing rain last week, though the depth wouldn't reach his knees.

They drew up short on the bank, simply listening for a moment to the gurgle of the stream flowing over the rocks. Cori linked one arm around his and pointed to a wooden plank laid across a narrow section of the creek.

"I slipped and fell in not long ago crossing that thing. You should've seen me on my butt, soaking wet and madder than a spitting cat."

Zack's gaze snapped to hers. "Were you hurt?" Dammit, he'd meant to come up with something better than that old board long ago.

She grimaced, wrinkling her cute nose. "Just my pride, and trust me, I've got plenty of padding to protect the rest."

Oh, he'd love to test that claim.

His leggy goddess wasn't a bag of bones by any stretch. Nope, she put the "voom" in "vavoooom". He wondered whether her ass would fill his hands, soft and pillowy, as he plunged his cock deep inside her.

While she screamed his name.

Leapin' Jesus. Glad his coat hid his rather volatile reaction to the naughty direction of his thoughts for about the third time today, he nodded his head toward the plank. "Shall we brave the raging rapids?"

"Sure. But we won't go far. You don't need to get winded and have a relapse," she said crisply.

"Bossy nurses." In truth, he liked being fussed over. A whole damned lot.

He took the lead this time, treading the board carefully. The wood was slippery, the stream lapping over the surface when it would normally be out of the water. When he reached the middle, he held out his hand for her. "Slowly."

She grasped his hand and they crossed without incident. As they walked toward the path leading up the slope and into the woods, Zack was disturbed by the idea of Cori out here alone. Isolated. What if she'd hit her head on a rock when she slipped? A person could drown in less than an inch of water. Didn't have to be like what had happened to him when her Explorer went into the Cumberland.

As they started up the trail, he glanced back at the creek and the makeshift crossing. Far up on the rise, near the road, a glimpse of metal through the trees drew his eye. A car? Too far off to tell, especially without his glasses. He returned his attention to the creek.

Surprise me.

An idea that had been simmering in the back of his mind since he'd bought the place more than a year ago bloomed into full, living color.

A grin teased his lips, excitement charging his tired body. It would take weeks of planning and hard work in his old shop, but he'd surprise her all right.

And maybe—just *maybe*—by then, he'd find a way to convince Cori that she couldn't live without him.

About a mile away on a curve in Neptune Road, Lionel gripped the van's steering wheel and seethed. Hand in hand, the couple disappeared over the ridge and were swallowed by the trees. Out for a nice, carefree hike.

"Goddammit," he hissed. The firefighter was in the picture now. Possibly intended to stay.

Unexpected. Unfortunate—for Zack Knight.

This changed everything.

They needed to stop dicking around with their scheme and just take the bitch outright. If his stupid shit partner had listened, they wouldn't have this extra fucking complication to deal with. Correction—*Lionel* wouldn't have to deal with it while Mr. Worship My Cock gave orders from his throne on the mountaintop.

No, if they'd done it Lionel's way, he'd already have everything that should've belonged to him before Corrine hightailed it and hid in Podunk, USA. He'd own her by now, body and soul.

For what she'd done, the whore would submit to his will in every delicious way. Then he'd break her.

Surprise, asshole, change of plans. He could taste his soon-to-be ex-partner's impotent rage, too late to stop Lionel from gaining all the power. Arrogant sonofabitch to believe he was running the show. That he had equal rights to the spoils.

Oh, he'd play along for a bit longer. But only until he'd worked out his next move and how to accomplish it with a minimum of fanfare. Cori's rescuer was about to discover that meeting her was the unluckiest day of his life. Choosing to hang around, the worst mistake he'd ever made.

His very last mistake.

8

Zack was coughing when they reached the house again, his face pale. Worried, Cori led him into the living room, rubbed her hands together to warm them, and felt his forehead. He blinked at her, his blue eyes tired.

"Verdict, Nurse Ratched?"

"Your ass is going to bed for a nap," she scolded. "I can't believe I fell for your bull, pretending to be fine when you're about to keel over! Upstairs. *Now.*"

"Yes, ma'am."

His lips curved into a slight smile and she suspected he was humoring her, but she didn't care as long as the fool rested. She didn't blame him for itching to be outdoors after lying in the hospital for almost a week, but their trek had been too much, too soon.

In the foyer, he retrieved his box of belongings and followed her upstairs to the guest bedroom. She stepped inside and gestured to the open, airy space. "You'll stay in here, across the hall from me. The bed isn't made up because you're my first real guest. I'll take care of that while you take a shower," she said, pointing to the adjoining bathroom. When he didn't immediately respond, she glanced at him to see him staring at his surroundings, the oddest expression on his face. "Zack?"

"Oh . . . a shower. Right. I took one at the hospital," he murmured, his voice strange. Distant.

"All the more reason to take another. A person can leave the hospital with more germs than when they entered. Besides, you need to get warm and stand under the steam for a while. Loosen the gunk in your lungs."

He sighed. "Okay. Sure."

What on earth was wrong with him? Before they'd come inside, he'd seemed to be enjoying himself. She couldn't think of anything she'd said or done to change that.

"Make yourself at home and I'll bring you a bar of soap and some shampoo." She snapped her fingers. "Oh, I almost forgot. There's another Wal-Mart sack in the car with more underwear, socks, a couple of T-shirts, pajama bottoms, and a pair of sweats. I'd picked up some extra things in case what I got didn't fit, but those will hold you until we go shopping."

"More happy-face boxers?" His lips twitched in humor, whatever had been bothering him banished.

"SpongeBob and lipstick kisses."

"You're an evil woman."

"Anytime you want a true demonstration, let me know, hot stuff." She paused, giving him a teasing grin. "I'll get that soap now."

Cori turned and sauntered out, but not before she caught the hungry look in his eyes. Pure, blue fire. Tempted beyond endurance, ready to call her dare.

He didn't. She wasn't sure whether to be relieved. If she didn't know for a fact that their attraction was mutual, she'd feel like an idiot for blatantly hitting on him. He might not have responded out loud, but the sizable bulge in his jeans said plenty.

Heartened, she went out to the car and snagged the Wal-Mart bag, then fetched the soap and shampoo from her bathroom. She returned to find him gazing out the window, his expression so sad a lump formed in her throat. She knew how difficult it was to start over after your life had been decimated, knew firsthand the hurt he held inside.

"Here you go," she said.

Jerking his head around, he smiled. Hid his pain as she suspected he always did, beneath a layer of sunshine. "Thanks. I really appreciate this."

Oh, she wanted more than his appreciation. Scary territory. "Forget it. Everybody requires a hand at some point. If it weren't for Shea, I wouldn't have made it when I first arrived in Sugarland."

"Yeah, well . . ." He forked his fingers through his black hair, floundering. A crack in the plastic veneer.

Good. "Look, this sucks, Zack. You don't have to pretend otherwise, not with me."

"My situation sucks, but being here with *you* doesn't." A small curve of the lips. Genuine, no shadows.

"Ditto. So get over yourself before I'm forced to trank you after all." She shooed him toward the bathroom. "Go on. You'll feel tons better once you're warm and rested."

Grinning, he shrugged out of his coat, tossed it onto the bed, and went without argument. He pulled the door to, leaving it cracked open about an inch. Rustling, followed by the telltale sound of his zipper, sent her into retreat mode, for all her bravado.

Maybe the stinker had left the door cracked as an answering dare?

Humming, she took his coat and hung it with hers in the hall closet downstairs. In the kitchen, she dug in the freezer for something nutritious to fix for dinner. Fire-fighters were extremely fit as a rule—Zack's hunk-a-licious teammates all prime examples of melt-your-panties goodness—but fireboy hadn't been taking care of himself. Nothing brought that home like seeing the dung heap where he'd been living.

He needs a friend to care, to give him a swift kick in his very fine butt and propel him right out of the dol-drums, she mused, removing a package of chicken breasts and setting it on the counter. *Might as well be me.*

His strange behavior worried her. There was something else eating at him besides discomfort over accepting her help. Something big. She could still see him lying in his hospital bed, panting like a trapped animal, the phone in pieces on the floor. Who'd upset him so badly?

Not his father. He'd said the man was basically an in-fant. Then who? The unsmiling Captain Tanner? A col-lection agency? Protective anger boiled in her blood. Whoever it was had better stay clear of Zack. When it came to protecting her own, she was her father's daughter in more ways than one. Leaving that role behind didn't mean she wouldn't assume it again if necessary. Even to defend her brothers—arrogant bastards, every one.

But they were *her* arrogant bastards. She'd not forget that Joaquin had paid a high price on her behalf.

Closing the door on a past best left dead, she returned her thoughts to Zack. In the shower. Naked. Mmm.

And drat, wouldn't you know, she'd forgotten to give him towels. *Admit it. You did that on purpose.* At least subconsciously.

Abandoning the makings of dinner, she hurried up-stairs, grabbing a small stack of towels and washcloths from her closet. As an afterthought, she also grabbed a small bottle of ibuprofen. They hadn't filled his prescriptions yet—something else she needed to do while he napped—and his headaches must still border on monstrous. In his room, the splashing of water as Zack moved around drew her like a magnet. She crept to the door, feeling naughty. A little guilty, too.

Not guilty enough to keep her from peeking, however. Just a teensy glimpse; then she'd leave the towels and medicine on the bathroom counter and scram.

A low moan sent her heart skittering against her backbone. Not a moan of mental or physical distress, but an oh-my-God-I'm-gonna-die-if-I-don't-come moan. Unmistakable, tweaking her nipples to eraser points as surely as ghostly fingers.

Peering through the opening, her eyes widened and she gasped, thankful he couldn't hear—and that the glass shower stall wasn't completely fogged over. Watching was *so* wrong and she ought to leave, but the delicious view had her thumping the angel of good conscience off her shoulder.

Zack leaned against the tiled wall, dark head tilted back, eyes closed, inky lashes spiking across his cheeks. The spray hit the center of his chest, sluicing over toned muscle and tawny skin, slicking the light mat of black hair. Streamed a trail down the dark line bisecting his flat belly, past his navel, and between his spread legs.

Where his big hand worked his cock in a slow, sure rhythm. Up to the plump cap and down, down to the base. Squeezing as his hips arched, heavy balls high and taut. Lost in a sea of pleasure. Up and down again. A bit faster, stroking, seeking the little death. Completely uninhibited.

Raw and powerful.

Mother of God, she'd never seen a more magnificent man.

Cori's breath hitched. Her legs shook and her clit throbbed in tempo to his motions. She longed to be the one putting sheer ecstasy on his handsome face, his lips parted, eyes closed. Had a crazy notion to burst in and join him in the shower. Finish him properly, in a way guaranteed to rocket him into space.

She stayed put, unwilling to spoil the moment. Simply drank in the beauty of this man's innate sexuality, hidden perhaps even from himself.

He pumped in earnest now, body tight, the muscles of his neck and chest cording with his efforts. "Ahh, God . . . fuck, yeah. Fuck me, ride me," he groaned. "Cori . . ."

His unguarded, impassioned words torched the aching flesh between her thighs. He stiffened with a cry, shuddering, thick jets of cum spurting in furious arcs, dribbling over his fist, quickly washed away by the shower spray.

He sagged against the tile, releasing his still-hard cock. A soft, muffled curse escaped his lips as he opened his eyes. Cori ducked backward out of sight, pulse hammering in her throat. Dumping the towels and pill bottle on the corner of the dresser, she fled, hoping her foray into voyeurism hadn't been discovered.

In the kitchen, she stared at the package of chicken, trying to force herself to concentrate on how to prepare it for dinner. Instead, she replayed her name on his lips as he'd come. Fantasized about him plunging inside her when he did, filling her, hot and deep. Her entire body trembled and ached for the release he'd just enjoyed.

Jeez Louise, they'd been alone for only a couple of hours and were already hotter for each other than a forest fire in July. Things were moving too fast. She had to get a handle on the blaze before they got hurt.

Zack wasn't the only one with secrets lying in wait to destroy them both.

The sobering thought cooled her libido, but not much. Not nearly enough. She'd wanted him before, but after the scorching shower scene, she knew she'd never rest until he was hers. Every scrumptious inch.

Risk versus reward. No perfect answer.

Except for one.

When Zack wore that expression of rapture on his sexy mug again, she'd be the woman who'd put it there.

Zack dripped water across the linoleum and returned to the bath mat to dry off, wondering when Cori had left the towels and ibuprofen.

Wondering whether she'd seen.

He hated jerking off. Always had. There was nothing lonelier than pretending to love and be loved in return. But this time it had been different.

Cori had been watching. He was ninety-nine percent certain of it. Leaning against the wall, fisting his cock, he'd been overcome by the strangest prickle. Another presence. He'd opened his eyes the slightest bit, and could've sworn he'd detected a furtive movement just outside the door. Maybe he'd been wrong.

Didn't matter. The idea of Cori observing him as he stroked his cock, her earlier dare returned in kind, made him so freaking hot it had stolen his breath. He'd never come so hard.

Over the past few years, the desire to lose the last of his innocence, to bury himself in the soft heat of a woman, had become a bearable ache. Achieving the ultimate gratification had never seemed worth the risk of opening himself to the sting of ridicule. To more rejection—the one sure to finish him.

Zack wasn't like Skyler or Salvatore. He'd never be able to give his body without giving his heart and soul. So he'd become a pro at deflecting the few invitations cast in his direction, usually when the gang hung out at the Waterin' Hole. He'd resisted lush temptation, his ardor quickly chilled by the knowledge that any one of those bar bunnies would've just as gladly gone home with one of his teammates. A couple had.

Now he was profoundly grateful for his resistance. The one gift he had left to give a woman was himself. Untouched by another. Corny as that sounded, it meant everything to him.

Would it mean the same to Cori? Was he living in a dreamworld to entertain the idea of her wanting him?

Get over yourself. Good advice. Hanging the towel on the rack by the tub, he popped three ibuprofen, then went into the bedroom to dress. Christ, his cracked cheekbone was killing him again, the pain radiating through his entire skull. Thank God the swelling in his face had subsided to almost normal, even if the bruise had transformed from dark purple to an interesting array of greens and yellows.

As he fished inside the Wal-Mart bag, he had to laugh. Shaking his head, he donned the lipstick-kiss boxers, which conjured a fantasy of Cori's pretty lips all over the area in question. *Way to torture yourself, idiot.* Next, he pulled on a pair of gray cotton sweats and a navy T-shirt.

He wasn't sleepy, but decided to at least attempt to obey her orders and stretched out carefully on the bed. God, it felt heavenly to sink his sore muscles into a comfortable mattress instead of a hospital bed, or the ratty old one from his apartment, tossed on the hard floor. To smell clean, fresh sheets rather than decay and despair.

So damned good to be home . . .

"Zack?"

Gentle fingers. Caressing his cheek, smoothing his hair. Nice.

"Wake up, sleepyhead."

"Mmm?" Try as he might to stay wrapped in his warm cocoon, he began to emerge. A fresh, herbal scent teased his nose, mixed with the natural fragrance of a woman. Cori's special blend. He blinked his eyes open to see her sitting on the bed beside him. Giving her a groggy smile, he took a moment just to savor her.

Somehow, the afternoon had become evening, the room bathed in shadow. The bedside lamp cast a luminous glow over hair the color of dark honey, spilling over her shoulders. She'd changed into a white V-neck T-shirt and lavender warm-up pants. She studied him with tiger eyes, a soft smile on her beautiful face. For him.

And she hadn't stopped stroking his hair, which was more than fine.

"The prince awakes," she said, a note of affection in her voice. "About time, too, or you won't sleep tonight."

With her in bed across the hall, his imagination running wild, he doubted he would anyway, but refrained from saying so. "How long have I been out?"

"Three hours. It's a little after six. Are you hungry?"

"Yeah, I am." He sniffed, belatedly noting the tantalizing aroma wafting from downstairs. "God, what smells so good?"

"Stuffed chicken breasts with wild rice, green beans, salad, and rolls."

His mouth watered, his brain distracted for once from devouring Cori instead. "Wow, that sounds fantastic!" He sat up and his head swam, the awful pain resuming a steady, pounding cadence.

"Easy there."

She helped him sit up, and he swung his legs over the side of the bed, letting himself get oriented. "Thanks."

"How's your head?" Leaning close, she peered at his bruise.

"Well, I don't feel like I'm going to throw up anymore when the headache burrows into my brain cells. Good news, huh?"

She ignored his sarcasm. "It is. Did you take some of the ibuprofen?"

"Yes, ma'am, three of them. Right before I conked out."

"Too soon for more. Let's wait another hour or so. Here, I went into town and had your prescriptions filled. Take your antibiotics and cough medicine—then we'll eat."

"Thanks. You didn't have to do that for me." He was touched.

"You're welcome. It's no biggie." Reaching past him to the nightstand, she lifted a brown prescription bottle, uncapped it, and shook out a pill large enough to choke a horse. "One every eight hours. There's your water."

Resisting the urge to make a face, he took the capsule, retrieved the glass from the nightstand, and washed it down. He was sick of medication, but not the extra personal care. "I don't need any cough medicine."

"Oh, yes, you do. You've been hacking off and on ever since you went to sleep. Down the hatch."

With that, she handed him a medicine-dose cup already

brimming with gold liquid that no doubt tasted like lighter fluid.

"You're a bossy nurse," he complained, without any real heat.

She beamed, apparently taking it as a compliment. "I'm good at my job."

"No argument there." Curling his lip, he drained the cup like a shot of whiskey. God knew it sure burned like one. "Christ, that's terrible."

"Like they say, if it tastes good, it's not good for you."

"*You're* good for me . . . and I happen to know you definitely taste good," he said, and kissed her lightly on the cheek. He might've felt stupid making the admission aloud, if not for her body melting against his. Her quiet sigh of contentment as she rested her head on his chest, hand over his heart.

"You're good for me, too."

His arm went around her and they stayed put for a few minutes, holding each other, the fragile new bond strengthening even more. However, something had been nagging him since their walk, a detail his mind had filed away as unimportant at the time. He broke the silence first, pulling back to kiss her forehead.

"Did you happen to notice anything while we were out walking? Something out of place?"

She thought a moment, shook her head. "No. Why?"

"I glimpsed what might've been a vehicle parked up on the curve of Neptune Road, but it was so far away I couldn't see much except a sliver of the side through the trees. When we came back, it was gone."

Cori's eyes widened. "You couldn't tell whether it was a car, truck, or van? Did you see a man?"

"I'm sorry, honey. I couldn't tell." Taking her hand, he

kissed the soft skin of her palm and tried to be reassuring. "I didn't think much of it before and it's probably nothing. But considering the intruder who surprised you, we need to keep our eyes and ears open. I know you have classes and I can't be with you every second, but I'd feel better if you're out alone as little as possible. Wouldn't hurt for you to check in with me periodically, too."

"Of course, you're right. I'll be careful and keep my cell phone handy, too."

She looked so worried, he felt bad for upsetting her when she'd gone to the trouble to make dinner. He smiled, hoping to recapture the happy mood.

"Let's eat. I don't want your excellent meal to get cold."

"I *am* hungry."

"Go ahead. I'll be right there."

He made a quick pit stop in the bathroom to brush his teeth—pointless when they were about to eat, but he hated the aftertaste of cough syrup—and headed downstairs.

In the entry to the formal dining room he'd never once used, Zack stared in humbled awe at the table she'd set for them. The lights were dimmed, two long candles gracing the center of an array of fragrant dishes. She stood near the head of the table where two places were set, fairly vibrating with anticipation.

To his absolute horror, his eyes stung. And filled. Totally uncool, and as he looked away, he hoped she didn't notice.

Which she did, of course, and mistook his reaction.

"Is—is something wrong? You said you hated pasta, but I thought you'd like chicken and—oh, no. I went overboard, didn't I? With the candles and the romantic setting and—"

"Cori." He strode toward her.

"I can move us to the breakfast nook or—"

"Corrine." Her mouth snapped shut as he reached her and cupped her face in his palms. "I love everything. It looks fantastic. It's just that . . . nobody's ever done this for me before."

"Oh." Her eyes widened, expression softening. "No one's ever made dinner for you?"

"Just for me? Special, like this? No."

He saw the significance of that statement hit her, and spread like sunshine through her whole body.

"Then I'm glad to be your first."

"Beautiful, you have no idea."

"What?"

Tilting Cori's chin up, he distracted her with a kiss that left him wishing they'd skip the meal. But she'd gone to so much trouble, no way would he disappoint her. Releasing her, he pulled out her chair, relieved he'd gotten himself together.

"You're supposed to be at the head of the table," she protested.

"Nope. You're the chef, and that makes you the boss." He took the seat next to her, and her eyes twinkled.

"You don't think I'm bossy enough already? You called me a 'bossy nurse.'"

"Maybe I've discovered I have a serious thing for take-charge, alpha females."

"Intriguing," she teased, steepling her fingers. "And are you a take-charge alpha male?"

Oh, no. He wasn't very good at this innuendo thing. But what did he have to lose? Might as well up the ante. He was enjoying himself too damned much not to. He shot her a heated look that dipped to the swell of her breasts, lingered on the pucker of her braless nipples against the fabric of her shirt, and rose back to her surprised face.

"Guess that depends on the situation."

"Maybe you're a switch." She grinned, obviously into their little game.

"A switch?"

"A man who takes pleasure in receiving with as much enthusiasm as he dishes out."

At that, little Zack awoke from his nap. Holy shit, she was determined to kill him. Death by eternal erection.

"A possibility worth exploring, I'd say." He congratulated himself on managing to sound smooth and collected instead of croaking like a frog.

"Chicken?" She started serving food on their plates as though she hadn't a care in the world.

The she-devil knew she had him by the short and curlies. He'd heard from the guys that women were better at this sort of premating dance, were able to hold out for a long frigging time, and guessed it must be true.

He tucked into his dinner, groaning in bliss at the burst of flavors on his tongue. "This is wonderful. Where did you learn to cook?"

She lifted one shoulder in a casual shrug, though her face flushed with delight. "I used to spend hours in the kitchen with our cook back home, helping her, mostly because it kept me under my brothers' radar. None of them would be caught dead in a so-called woman's domain."

He barked a laugh. "Woman's domain? They'd starve to death at the fire station—if one of the guys didn't beat the crap out of them first." Her brothers sounded like a bunch of spoiled pansies. He'd love to see one of them prepare a meal for six starving men, then rush to a call and run straight into a burning building.

"That's right—firemen are rumored to be excellent in the kitchen." She leaned forward with interest. "Is it true?"

"For the most part, though some of us are better than others. I hold my own, but Six-Pack doesn't just cook—he creates culinary masterpieces. On the other hand, Tommy's not allowed to heat anything except hot dogs right now. He's learning, though."

"You talk about them as if they're your family."

"Those guys are the closest I've ever had to one, and I consider myself fortunate. Anyway, *your* tutoring sure paid off. I haven't eaten so well in ages." A huge understatement. He paused, taking a swallow of his iced tea, thinking it was time to reroute the subject. "You mentioned home. Where's that?"

"Here, in Sugarland," she said firmly. "The family estate outside Atlantic City could never be mistaken for anyone's idea of a home. Well, except for my brothers. They like it well enough, especially Rafael. Another roll?"

Atlantic City. His gut cramped, food turning a somersault in his belly, and he suddenly felt cold to the bone. Had to be a coincidence. Shoving aside the chill, he forced the issue from his mind.

"Sure." He took the bread, aware she was trying to change the subject. She didn't want to discuss her family or former life, but hey, his own upbringing hadn't exactly been an episode of *Family Ties*. He decided to nudge a bit more. "About Rafael, you were saying?"

"He's the youngest of my brothers—well, technically my half brother, the result of my father's affair with his personal assistant. He's just as hard and uncompromising as the others, though. Really embraced the whole 'family honor' thing. Nothing like the zeal of a convert, huh?"

"And he lives with your family? That's kind of . . . unusual, isn't it, considering the circumstances?"

She gave a rueful laugh. "I suppose so. He was raised at first by his mother, but came to live with us when he was ten, after she killed herself. Oh, he was such a sad little boy. He'd just lost his mother and barely knew our father. It was a huge adjustment for everyone, especially Rafael, but we all did our best to make him feel welcome, even Mother. I don't think he ever got over our father not being there for him during his formative years, though."

Dumped on his father's doorstep. Yeah, he could relate. "How does your father feel about Rafael?" he couldn't stop himself from asking.

"Treated him about as coldly as he did the rest of us, I guess. I don't know. Our father wasn't an open man and he died rather suddenly about ten years ago."

"I'm sorry. Illness?"

"He was murdered. An unidentified intruder walked into his office and blew his brains out." She chewed a piece of chicken calmly. "He didn't have many mourners."

Apparently not. He scrambled for the right thing to say, but she put him out of his misery.

"Mother died four years ago of breast cancer. Said she'd outlive us all, and I think we were all rather shocked when she didn't." This time, she blinked furiously, pushing the green beans around on her plate. "The one and only instance I ever knew her to fail at something she'd set her mind to."

Zack laid his hand over hers. "You loved her."

"Yes. She was my rock and when she passed . . . I couldn't stand living alone with my brothers. They were overbearing and impossible before, but afterward the oldest in particular took it upon himself to run my life."

"How so?"

"Pressuring me to attend boring society functions, telling me what to wear, how to act, how to live. Pushing me to date pedigreed men with his stamp of approval, of which Alex had neither."

"So you married the guy, fleeing for higher ground," he prompted.

"I was immature and stupid. I'd made it halfway through nursing school—which everyone in my family assured me was a waste of time—but then I quit because my attentions being focused on something I enjoyed made my husband unhappy."

"You were in love."

"I thought so, until he started beating me."

His fingers curled around hers, squeezing in encouragement. "How often did this happen?" he asked softly, recalling that the vicious asshole had nearly killed her. Too bad he was already dead, because Zack would very much enjoy strangling him. The violence of his thoughts scared him.

"The first year he got his kicks by verbal abuse, but soon it wasn't enough. Every time he hit me, he'd go overboard making up and life would be great for a while. Each subsequent beating got worse. I hid it from my brothers because I knew they'd gut him like a pig and wind up in prison. My husband watched my every move and controlled the finances, so I didn't know where to go. It didn't stop until the night Alex . . . died."

"Do you want to talk about it? I'll fetch you something stronger than tea if you'd like."

"No. I hope you understand."

"Of course." She looked so forlorn, his heart turned over. This wasn't the sassy stick of dynamite he'd rear-ended in his car. The image of a brutal monster trying to douse her fire forever made Zack postal. Best to move the topic along. "Then you moved to Sugarland?"

Her expression brightened. "I had no clue where I intended to go. I just packed my SUV to the gills and headed west. I fell in love with Tennessee on sight, though Nashville was too big and touristy for what I wanted. I drove a little farther west, and here I am, finishing nursing school."

"Lucky me."

"I'm the lucky one to have met you, Zack. You're kind and gentle, and you'd never harm another person. You have a dangerous job and you save lives," she said, gazing at him as if he were some sort of superhero. "You saved me, literally."

Jesus. Good thing she couldn't read his mind. There was nothing *kind* or *gentle* about what he'd do to anyone else who attempted to harm her. "Don't put me on too high a pedestal, baby. The fall might break my neck."

"Nah, you'd bounce." Pushing aside her plate, she eyed him from under long, dusky lashes. "Your turn. Spill it all."

"Me? Nothing to tell."

"Uh-uh. Not fair."

"Okay, um . . . I once read Stephen King's *It*. Worst mistake I ever made. Didn't sleep for a month."

She arched a brow. "Because of your deep-seated fear of clowns."

"Yep. King's the *man*. Scarred me for life. When we work an accident, I still won't stand next to a storm drain."

Her lips twitched, but she squelched the grin, giving him a mock scowl. "Oh, come on, you big weenie. Give me the real scoop."

"Did you seriously just call me a weenie?"

"I did." Her droll stare said, *So what are you gonna do about it?*

He thought for a minute, considering the risk of sharing his most painful secret. More painful than how he'd become broke. Why not? Cori had been honest with him about a terrible period in her life.

"All right. When I was a kid, I was the short, fat nerd everybody lived to torment. Made straight A's without cracking a book. I . . . I have a genius IQ."

"Wow, that's cool! I mean, the IQ part, not getting picked on." Cori bit her lip, blushing.

He gave her a reassuring smile. "Don't worry; most people have the same reaction. I appreciate my gifts now more than I used to."

"But being the outsider made your life hell as a child, I'll bet."

"Yeah. I wanted friends so badly, but the guys were always tripping or pushing me, knocking my books out of my hands, or calling me names like 'faggot.' Whatever you can think of, they did it to me at least once. That wasn't really the worst part, though." Taking a breath, he went on, amazed the memories hurt to this day.

"My father wasn't a loving man. He believed in doing right by raising his only son, but resented the hell out of my presence. Nothing about me was ever good enough for him. But even the worst fathers defend their kids from bullies, right?"

"Most do," she said quietly. "Even Dad took up for us, hard as he was."

"Well, there came a day when I finally worked up the courage to tell my father what the other boys were doing to me. He said, 'If they think you're a fat, useless queer, then you probably are.'"

This was obviously not what she'd expected to hear, and her face fell. "Oh, Zack."

"You'll be glad to know I exacted my revenge by using his computer to hack into the FBI's database."

Her eyes rounded. "You did not!"

"Two badass-looking men in suits knocked on our door less than twenty-four hours later. Dear old Dad almost got arrested until I got worried about who'd take care of me while he was in prison, and confessed. I was only twelve, so they scared the crap out of me and left."

Cori giggled.

"Long story short, I made it all the way through high school intact, even lost weight and got in shape, made a few friends. But I never again counted on anyone except myself—until I joined the fire department. My father never forgave me for not attending a fancy college like MIT and becoming an astronaut or a scientist who'd develop a weapon of mass destruction."

"Why didn't you?"

"If you're thinking it was to spite him, you'd be wrong. The answer is a lot less complicated." He smiled. "Most little boys get over playing with fire trucks. I never did."

Her nose wrinkled in the way women do when they fuss over a cute puppy or kitty. "Aww. That's about the sweetest thing I've ever heard."

"Then consider this: I've never been more glad I made the choices I have . . . because every one of them helped lead me to you."

9

Cori sniffed. Picked at her paper napkin. *Don't cry, dammit! Don't you dare.*

She loathed weepy, wimpy women. Even while married to Alex, she'd never been one to snivel, her smart mouth earning swift retribution more often than not.

And now? All her remaining defenses blown apart by the power of one good man.

Zack's smile faded. "Did I say something wrong?"

"No! Quite the opposite." Oh, hell. Snatching up the napkin, she dabbed at the moisture threatening to spill. "Do you stay awake at night thinking up wonderful lines to snare all your women, or does the boyish charm come naturally?"

"Only if the woman is you," he replied with total sincerity.

Her trembling hand clutched the mangled napkin tight against her breast. "You don't really know me."

"Not true. I know you're strong and brave, ambitious, determined. You're also funny and warm. You're a survivor. And . . . you're perfect to me."

The connection between them sizzled and popped, smoking like grease in a frying pan. About two seconds from igniting.

"You're blind without your glasses, poor man."

"I see just fine."

God, she could drown in those brilliant blue eyes, framed by thick, sinful black lashes, and go down willingly. He smelled so good, a blend of fresh herbal soap and the natural spice of male. His navy T-shirt hugged the contours of his solid chest, emphasized his flat belly and lean waist.

Her fingers itched to explore underneath the material, to learn whether his skin was as supple and sleek as it had appeared in the shower. To feel his muscles flexing and bunching while he . . .

Shoving to her feet, she waved a hand at the dishes. "Why don't you go relax in the living room while I clear this away?" Too intense. If she didn't put some distance between them, she'd poof into a pile of ash.

Zack, however, thwarted her escape. "I have a better idea. Since you cooked, why don't *you* go relax while I put everything away? Then I'll build us a fire."

"Terrific on the fire; no can do on the cleanup. You're still sick, buddy." Gathering their plates and utensils, she went into the kitchen to rinse them and start loading the dishwasher. Zack trailed her, carrying an armload of leftovers.

"I'm used to doing for myself. I didn't come here so you'd have to wait on me hand and foot. Besides, I'm feeling a lot better." A rattling cough ruined the assertion.

"So I see." Straightening from the dishwasher, she narrowed her eyes at Zack as he walked directly to the pantry, swung open the door, and reached for a box of plastic wrap resting in the holder mounted inside. Just like he'd known exactly where to find it.

Turning, he caught her frown and froze, giving her a

sheepish grin. "Educated guess. Lots of people keep stuff like this in the pantry."

"Oh. Right." But he hadn't even hesitated. As though . . . resuming her task, she shook her head. Jeez, the man possessed a genius IQ; he could certainly hunt down a box of Glad.

Zack finished bringing in the dishes, covered and stored the remaining food in the fridge. Working together in comfortable silence—Cori stealing glances at how nicely her companion's sweats contoured his tight ass—they were done in minutes.

"I didn't have what I needed to make dessert," she said, wiping her hands on a towel. "Hot chocolate?"

"With marshmallows?" he asked hopefully.

"If that's your pleasure."

"Are you kidding? There's nothing better on a cold night. I have a terrible sweet tooth."

The way he said it, all low and rumbly, gazing at her from beneath his lashes, indicated he might be referring to tasting more than just hot chocolate.

Wishful thinking, Corrine. The man just got out of the hospital, for Pete's sake!

"Well, we'll just have to make sure and satisfy it, won't we?" She could swear his pupils dilated. "Um, why don't I fix the cocoa while you start the fire? There's plenty of wood stacked outside by the deck."

"Deal."

Ogling his awesome retreating backside, she blew out a breath. Mercy, living in such close proximity to Mr. Rev My Fire Engine would be the death of her!

Humming to herself, she heated the milk in a pan the old-fashioned way—cocoa nuked using tap water ought to be outlawed—and poured the steaming froth into two heavy mugs with the chocolate. Last, the requested marshmallows. By the time she carried their mugs into the living room, Zack had a cheery blaze dancing in the wide brick fireplace.

He'd left the lights off, and the room was bathed in a romantic amber glow. He'd arranged a few of the sofa's throw pillows on the floor and sat in front of the hearth, staring into the flames, hands hooked around one cocked knee. In that brief, unguarded moment, the poor guy looked exhausted. And something more, a wistfulness she couldn't put her finger on.

But that didn't stop his face from lighting up when he noticed her joining him. "Hey, beautiful." Carefully taking the hot mug from her, he blew on the top, then took a cautious sip. "Oh, man, that's awesome. I can't remember the last time I had hot chocolate. I'm glad it's one of those treats a person never outgrows."

"Me, too." She placed her mug on the hearth and sat next to him on the pillows, shooting him a sidelong glance. "Where were you just now, when I came in?"

"Lost in space, I guess. Long day." Deftly, he diverted the subject. "So, what's your schedule like during the week with your classes and hospital rotations?"

"I have class all day Mondays and Fridays, with tests and evaluations on Fridays. Tuesdays through Thursdays, I have morning classes and clinicals at Sterling in the afternoon, working in the ER with my friend Shea—no pay for me yet because I'm a student."

"Sounds tough."

"In all, it's not too bad now that graduation is on the horizon. I'm usually home by six, but that will change once I get my real shifts." Picking up her mug, she took a drink, observing the interesting hesitance, the trepidation in his expression.

"What about your dancing? Are you booked every single Thursday through Saturday night? Could be hell on a girl's social life."

Setting down her mug, she barely suppressed a triumphant smirk at his transparent fishing expedition. "I'm nearly done with school, so I've been able to taper off my engagements quite a bit. This coming weekend, for example, I'm booked only on Friday night for a bachelor-party gig, doing the whole bursting-out-of-a-cake-wearing-pasties-and-a-thong thing." His scowl was so fierce, she couldn't help but giggle.

"What?"

"The look on your face!" She laughed harder, which only made him grumpier.

"What's so freakin' funny? You've got some creep bothering you and you're just gonna continue to prance around for a bunch of horny, drunken shitheads, showing your—your—" His cheeks reddened.

"Boobs?" she supplied helpfully.

"Yes, dammit!"

"They're just boobs, Zack, not mysterious oracles of divine truth," she managed around fits of laughter. He looked as if he'd swallowed a hair ball. "I'll be careful. I always have someone walk me to my car afterward. And I'll have you know that horny, drunken patrons tip very generously. Most of them are actually pretty harmless."

"Dandy, but if you insist on doing this, you're not going by yourself."

"Fine, just don't be mad."

"I'm not. Just . . . concerned."

Nope, he was irked, but she wisely decided against correcting him. "You can't escort me every weekend, though. You'll be cleared to go back to work in another week or so, and then what?"

"I'll get one of the guys from B- or C-shift to take you if I have to. Dammit to hell."

"What now?"

"Station Five doesn't have any butt-ugly guys," he muttered.

Enjoying this, she scooted close and leaned into him, raking one manicured nail down his chest. "Why, Mr. Knight. Are you saying you'd be jealous to entrust my care to one of them? Hmm, fireboy?"

The blue fire returned, the heat blazing just as intensely as the flames in the fireplace. Purposefully, he set his mug on the hearth next to hers. "Yes, goddammit."

Faster than she could blink, she found herself wrapped in his arms, breasts crushed against his chest. His mouth came down on hers, and his tongue swept past the seam of her lips. Stroked inside, licking, exploring behind her teeth, the roof of her mouth. Ooh, he tasted fabulous, like dark chocolate and marshmallows. A sweet, sugary treat, and, beneath the heady flavor, all man.

But even his essence was nothing compared with the delicious weight of him as he pushed her into the pillows, onto her back. Pressed his body over hers, entwined their legs together, his hard length settled intimately at the juncture of her thighs. She loved the friction of his erection riding her clit, no less pleasurable because of their clothing.

As he kissed her deeply, Cori splayed her fingers across his back, reveling in the feel of his strength surrounding her. He felt so right here, like this, her entire body hummed and rejoiced in recognition. As though every cell in her being had been waiting only for him, for a lifetime. Crazy.

Her hands went roaming underneath his shirt, trailing the indention of his spine to his shoulders. His back was smooth and warm, muscles flexing lazily at her fingertips. "Off. Take your shirt off."

She tugged at the offending material, needing him closer. No barriers between them. Chuckling, he helped her get the shirt over his head, and she tossed it aside. Immediately, she skimmed her palms over his solid pecs, fascinated by the light dusting of springy dark hair. The tight brown male nipples peaking under the brush of her thumbs, gooseflesh rising on his skin.

Yeah, she liked knowing she could reduce him to a quivering mass.

And she had a feeling his wicked side, once unleashed, would be a thing of beauty to behold.

"Jesus." He groaned, his sensual lips curving upward. "Your turn. They're just boobs, remember?"

His teasing tone, colored with a hint of challenge, suggested he didn't really expect her to return the favor. Kinda cute, too, the flush on his face, like the look of a little boy who'd just said something very naughty but refused to take it back.

Exactly how innocent was Zack?

"You want my shirt off? Hmm?"

"I—you don't have to—"

"Remove it yourself, hot stuff."

If only she had a camera. His expression was priceless. Not quite believing, desperate to know she wasn't kidding. In answer to his unspoken question, she let her arms go lax at her sides, and nodded.

Zack rolled to the side, his body half atop hers, and swallowed hard. She couldn't fathom why a hottie like him would be so nervous, but thought it was sweet the way his hand trembled as it brushed her belly. Lifted the material and began the upward slide.

And then she was bared to him, nipples puckering as she arched her back, allowing him to work off the shirt. He pitched it next to his, but his hot gaze never left her breasts. Propping himself on one elbow, he let his fingers drift across her collarbone. Lower, to the swell of her breasts, hesitating.

The only way to describe the emotion in his blue eyes was . . . awestruck. As though he'd been gifted with a treasure he wasn't certain he deserved.

But he desired the treasure badly—the proof throbbed against her hip.

"Go ahead, Zack. Touch me," she whispered.

Apparently afraid she'd break, he carefully brushed one pert nipple. Even that tentative caress shot a jolt of liquid heat to her sex.

"Harder. Pinch them."

"I don't want to hurt you."

"You won't." Had he never done this before? Zack was young, several years her junior, but surely—

Thinking became impossible as he rolled the nipple between his thumb and forefinger. Plucked with just the right amount of pressure, skirting the edge of wicked pain she'd missed. Shooting tiny pinpoints of delight throughout her body. He pulled and pinched, first one, then the other.

"Oh! Zack . . ." Reaching to him, she pulled his head down, burying her fingers in the silky hair at his nape.

No hesitation now. He suckled one peak like a man

who'd just found religion. Reverently, and with great purpose. His warm mouth drew on her flesh, tongue laving. Swirling.

"More," she gasped.

He raised his head, black hair falling into hungry eyes. "Tell me, baby. What do you need?"

The words threaded around her heart. She hadn't been with many men, but none of the few she'd slept with had bothered to ask that simple, wonderful question. Smiling, she grasped the waistband of her jogging pants.

"Help me off with these."

She lifted her hips and in short order, her pants and underwear joined their growing pile. Zack knelt beside her and sucked in an appreciative breath, smoothing a hand over her tummy.

"My God, you're beautiful."

She shook her head. "Thank you, but—"

"Shh. Tell me how to please you, what you like." His hand slid lower, toward the golden brown triangle at the apex of her thighs.

She spread her legs, and the sensuality of being completely exposed to him slid into her blood like a drug. This man wanted her as no one ever had, for the joy of giving to them both.

"I'll do better," she said. "I'll show you."

Slowly, enjoying him watching with feral intensity, she slid her hand down. Across her stomach. Downward, her fingers sliding through the curls. Transfixed, he didn't seem to breathe as she began to massage her aching clit in lazy circles. Round and round, then dipping one finger into her channel. Sliding in and out, spreading the moisture all over her sex.

"Let me," he rasped.

At her nod, he moved to kneel between her thighs. Grabbing a small pillow, he pushed it under her hips, opening her. Making her more vulnerable, though she knew he'd never hurt her.

Resting one hand on her upper thigh, he ghosted a touch the length of her slit. "So pretty."

With the pad of one finger, he rubbed her clit as he'd seen her do. Gently circling, with increasing confidence, probably because of the helpless little moans escaping her lips. Zack's touch. Like no other man's, unfurling a deep desire to lose herself. To let go.

"Like that, sweetheart?"

"Yes!"

Growing bolder, he slid two fingers between her slick folds. Grazing the sensitized nub, pushing deeper. Sinking into her channel. Working them in, slow and easy, and out again. In and out. Fucking her with his hand until she was dripping wet, writhing, nearly out of her mind.

"Zack, please!"

"Finish you, like this? Tell me, honey."

"No, with your mouth! Please, I need . . ."

His hand withdrew and she wondered, for a brief moment, if he'd be like the others. Ignore her pleas and whip out his cock, pound away without particular finesse, much less finishing the decadent feast he'd begun.

She needn't have worried. Zack stretched out full-length on his stomach . . . and fastened his mouth to her sex. His hot, lovely mouth and wet, seeking tongue an instrument of heavenly torture. He licked the bare lips, then tunneled between them, tongue-fucking her into mindless oblivion.

But when he latched on to her clit, dining like a man born to eat a woman, she was a goner. Fisting her hands in his hair, she bucked. Lost to the tidal wave of glorious, shattering orgasms.

"Oh, God! Zack, yes! Don't stop!"

One after another, the tremors shook her, until at last she lay spent. Limp as a noodle and breathing hard.

And more satisfied than she'd ever been.

Zack peered up at her, wiped his mouth, and gave her a shy, uncertain smile. "Did you . . . ? Did I . . . ?" Amazingly, he flushed crimson. "Was it okay for you?"

Grinning, she reached out and fingered a strand of his hair. "It was awesome and you were fabulous. Why would you doubt it?"

"I'm sort of . . . new at, you know . . ."

Sitting up, she stared at him, processing what he'd said. Holy crap! "You mean, you've never gone down on a woman before?"

He groaned, slapping a hand over his eyes. "More than that. I've never had sex with a woman, period."

"Oh? So you've had sex with a man?"

Snorting a laugh, she ducked the pillow he lobbed at her head.

"Brat," he grumbled. "Go ahead, have fun at my expense."

"Never." Scooting close, she cupped his cheek. "I'd never laugh at you, not to intentionally hurt your feelings."

He nuzzled and kissed her palm. "I know."

The wonderful thread squeezed harder around her heart, nearly strangling it. Good God, how on earth had she snared one of the last sexy male virgins over the age of twenty-one?

"What held you back?" she wondered aloud.

He shrugged. "Plenty of opportunity, little motivation.

Call me an idealist, but I wanted being with my lady to mean something. To be special." He gave her an impish smile. "I was right to wait."

"I wish I had, too," she said, suddenly ashamed. "If I had, maybe—"

"Don't. I wouldn't change a single detail about you, baby."

Gazing into his dear face, she still had trouble believing her incredible luck. That all this wouldn't vanish in an instant. She'd found a kind, heroic, affectionate man who'd never made love with anyone else. Had never known a woman's touch.

The female instinct to put her mark on him *now* rose, drowning out all else. Grinning, she tugged at his sweats. "Lose these and lie on your back."

"Cori, you don't have to—"

"Do it, buddy."

"Yes, ma'am."

Rolling onto his back, he shucked the pants and boxers, letting her take charge in sliding them off his legs. Without a word, he spread his thighs, inviting her in. Waited, anticipation glittering in the depths of his vivid blue eyes.

Cori knelt between his thighs as he'd done to her, but with a decidedly wicked plan to up the ante. Not only would she demonstrate what he'd been missing, but if all went well, she'd blow a charred hole through his brain cells.

"Raise your hips." He did, and she tucked a pillow underneath, thinking she might need new ones if he stayed around very long. "There, total access. You're mine, and I'll do anything to you I desire. *Anything*. Understand?"

His brows shot up. "I—"

"Yes or no."

"Y-yes. Christ, Cori—"

"Good. No more talking."

Her gaze swept to his fully aroused, impressive cock. Oh, this was a much better view than the foggy glass shower. His penis was indeed long and thick. A wide helmet for the tip, a weeping slit, the satiny length roped with veins. And at the base . . . lucky, lucky Cori, the man was hung like a bull. Velvety balls nestled beneath, inviting play.

And so she would, until he shouted loud enough to rattle the rafters.

Zack lay sprawled before Cori, unable to believe his day, which started out so horribly, would end with him being leveled by a storm of tastes and sensations he'd only dreamed of.

Her unique flavor lingered on his tongue, and his fingers tingled as he recalled how much he'd loved pleasuring her. He'd wanted only to make her happy, and now it seemed she wanted the same.

I'll do anything to you I desire.

God help him, he hoped so!

Above him, Cori swirled the drops of pre-cum all over the tip of his cock. Honey brown hair framed her face, tumbled past her shoulders to frame full breasts, tipped with dusky rose nipples he couldn't wait to suckle again. But this was her show, and he'd never seen a more desirable woman than his goddess taking what she wanted from him.

Wrapping her fingers around the base of his cock, she lowered her head and took him in her mouth. His breath caught, rendering Cori's order of silence unnecessary. He couldn't have spoken an intelligible word. Groaning, he watched his length disappear between her plump lips. Deeper, wet heat, sucking with delicious pressure. More skillful fingers, manipulating his balls.

"Shit, yeah." He was lost. Never again would his own hand be able to satisfy him. Never anything like this. So damned good. He wasn't a small man, yet she engulfed him to the root. Owning every inch of his fiery cock. Working him into a near frenzy. He couldn't take much more.

Or so he thought.

He was hardly aware of her pausing for a split second to wet one finger. She resumed her attentions, swallowing him whole again. Her free hand crept past his balls, the damp finger tracing along the seam, upward. Parting his ass cheeks to find . . .

"Cori," he croaked on a strangled breath of air.

A low, husky, feminine chuckle drifted to his burning ears. But she didn't stop. The wicked suction on his cock increased, along with the tempo. Her finger massaged his entrance, igniting a blaze of savage lust threatening to incinerate him. He'd heard Julian brag about allowing his women to do this, and of returning the favor. He'd never imagined being the recipient.

And digging the hell out of it.

She pushed inside, and began to slide the digit. Back and forth. Faster and faster, angling the strokes, seeking the fabled magic button all men supposedly possessed, just as highly sexually charged as a woman's clit.

She found the damned spot, too.

"Ahh, God!" Red lights exploded in front of his eyes. His entire body danced as though electrocuted, at her mercy. "Baby, yes! Fuck . . ."

Cum boiled in his balls, shot from the base of his spine.

Pumped on and on, his entire body spasming. Cori drank every drop he had to give, laving his cock with loving ministrations through the residual shocks until he lay spent.

Releasing him, she crawled from between his legs and snuggled into his side. Swamped with confusing emotions, he held her close as she rested her head on his chest, no doubt listening to the gallop of his thundering heart. He was surprised the damned organ hadn't stopped altogether, considering how she'd just rocked his world.

"God, baby, I loved that," he managed, kissing the top of her head. He felt her smile against his chest.

"I sorta guessed."

"Can we do it again?"

"Anytime, fireboy."

"You know, the day we met, I hated when you called me that."

"And now?"

"God, it turns me on."

"Then I'll be sure to use it more often. *Fireboy*."

He laughed. "I hear there's something to be said for recovery time."

Happier than he'd ever been, he stroked her smooth shoulder, pondering where they'd go from here. "What will your rich, fancy brothers think about their baby sister taking up with a broke firefighter?"

He wouldn't allow the mess he was in to spoil this newfound heaven. Somehow, he'd find a way out.

Cori gave him a squeeze. "I moved here to get away from their influence, remember? Anyway, it's really only Joaquin who cares. He's the major pain in the ass."

Joaquin.

Oh, God. No.

He tried to keep his voice casual. Hoping against the odds. "That's kind of an unusual name—Joaquin Shannon."

"No. I never told you, did I? When I moved here, I took my mother's maiden name for a fresh start."

Zack knew what Cori was going to say, and his world crumbled. Hadn't he known deep inside the moment he'd seen Cori ensconced in the home a ruthless bastard had stolen from him?

"My oldest brother is the hotel and casino mogul Joaquin Delacruz."

10

Zack stared into the glowing embers, his arms full of soft, sleeping woman, and wondered how many times a man had to gain the top of the mountain and fall ass over elbows before he quit reaching for the impossible.

Why continue to fight?

Under the throw blanket he'd draped over them, Cori snuggled into his side, cheek resting against his chest. Even breath fanning over his skin, she lay, not so innocent, and trusting him to keep her safe. *His.*

This was "why fight." For this, for Cori, he'd take on Delacruz and his posse of assholes, her unknown enemy, and a team of Black Ops soldiers armed with hand grenades. Yeah, he had it bad, but the fuzzy afterglow of sex wasn't the whole reason. Though the sex *had* been pretty damned amazing.

Not just sex, making love. He didn't require a world of experience to know lovemaking was more than sharing bodies. Their connection was real and when he finally pushed deep inside her, he'd be home at last, where he belonged.

He needed time. To figure out how to deal with Delacruz and protect Cori. Not only from her stalker, but from the knowledge that her brother had all but destroyed

Zack's life . . . and Cori had directly benefited from his own downfall.

If Cori found out, it might drive a wedge between them. She'd feel awful, maybe even guilty, about a situation that wasn't her fault. He couldn't lose her.

Delacruz had no idea where Zack had disappeared to, and this was certainly the last place he'd look. For now, Zack must keep it that way. His gut churned to imagine what a powerful bastard like Delacruz would do to the man he'd already threatened, who owed him the better part of three quarters of a million dollars, when he found out Zack was sleeping with his sister.

And falling for her. Hard.

Whatever happened, nothing would get solved tonight. Glancing at the fire, he was satisfied it had burned down enough not to pose a hazard. He shifted around, gathering Cori and the blanket into his arms, and pushed to his feet. She stirred against him, raising sleepy eyes to his.

"Put me down. You're going to hurt your back."

"Shh, go back to sleep."

"Too heavy."

"Baby, I may be the FAO, but I'm trained to haul a body down ten flights of stairs in a four-alarm blaze if I have to," he informed her, heading for the landing. "I absolutely can carry you to bed."

"Mmm." Settling, she wound her arms around his neck.

Pleased to get no further argument, he bore her upstairs to the room across from his and laid her gently on the bed. After some tugging, he covered and tucked her in, smiling ruefully as she curled onto her side and went right back to dreamland.

Admit it, Knight. You wanted to be invited to stay.

But she hadn't asked him, and he'd never intrude on her privacy, despite the encouraging development between them. Some days being a nice guy sucked.

Downstairs, he retrieved his clothes, pulling on the lipstick-kiss boxers with a snort. Maybe he'd bronze them for posterity. For sure, he'd never look at them the same way again.

After dressing in his sweats and T-shirt, he padded into the kitchen to use the phone, flipping on the dim light over the sink. He doubted Cori would mind; plus he needed to let an officer on the team know how to reach him in case of an emergency. Since the truce with Tanner was a little thin yet, he opted to call Six-Pack, hoping he wasn't interrupting the action between the lieutenant and his curvy blond bride. A glance at the clock revealed the hour wasn't quite ten o'clock, though it seemed later.

Deciding to risk the big man's annoyance, Zack parked his rear against the counter, picked up the handset, and punched in the couple's number. While waiting, he stared out the bare window above the sink, into the night at the brilliant stars. Another view he'd never thought to enjoy again. After the fourth ring, the lieutenant grumbled a less-than-thrilled greeting. The breathy giggling in the background hinted at why.

"Paxton."

"Hey, Six-Pack."

"Zack!" Some rustling ensued, and the lieutenant's upset jacked up a notch. "Where in the holy frickin' hell have you *been*? Eve went by the hospital this afternoon to take you home and you were gone!"

"What?" Damn, Eve was probably pissed. "She was supposed to have Sunday dinner with her mother today."

"She did, but they moved the time up so she could

fetch you, dinglewad. And I'll have you know, she searched for you everywhere." A heavy pause. "She drove out to your old house, my friend. Nobody was home. She called me all in a snit, looking for your butt. What was I supposed to say when you swore me to silence about losing the place?"

"Shit." Zack raked a hand through his hair. "I'm sorry, man. I had no idea she'd planned to give me a lift."

"Evie's your best friend, Zack. What did you think she'd do? Just leave you stranded?"

"No, I just . . . I guess I wasn't thinking. Someone gave me a ride." *Boy, did she ever.*

"To where, for God's sake? I've been calling your apartment all afternoon and got no answer. I don't recognize this number on the caller ID, either."

"You're not going to believe this." Zack sighed. "I'm back at my house, at least for the time being. Only it's not mine anymore. The place belongs to my new . . . friend. She's the lady we pulled out of the Explorer on the bridge."

"Are you freaking *kidding* me?" A loud noise banged in Zack's ear, like his friend pounding the phone on the nightstand. When Six-Pack returned, his voice was incredulous. "Hell-oo? Is this squeaky-clean Wonder Boy Zack I'm talking to? Disappearing without a word to anyone and shacking up with the hot chick from the wreck that almost got him *fucking killed*? I'm guessing you took a harder blow to the head than any of us realized. Tell me what the hell is going on, kid."

And wasn't this fun? If Howard was this ticked, he could hardly wait for Eve to carve out his spleen with a blunt instrument. "I will, but I'd rather explain in person."

"Yeah? Can you do it Tuesday afternoon? Kat and I have something we want to bring by."

Zack closed his eyes. His buddies were on shift tomorrow, and they had no clue how badly he wanted to be there. He missed being in the driver's seat to the point he felt as if he'd had a limb removed.

"Sure. Where else would I be?"

"Hey, you'll be well and ready to return in a matter of days," Six-Pack said in a firm tone.

"I know."

"And call Eve, tonight."

Crap. "I will."

"Take care, my friend. See you Tuesday."

Zack said good-bye, punched the END button, and rubbed his tired eyes before blinking them open. Long day. In spite of the earlier nap, he couldn't wait to flop down and crash. He turned, reaching to replace the phone in the cradle.

From somewhere outside, a *crack* rang out, followed a split second later by the tinkling of glass.

A hard kick in his right shoulder sent him crashing into the counter. Knocked off balance, he fell, scattering cookbooks and a stack of mail, sweeping them to the floor. Stunned, he pushed to his hands and knees, trying to make sense of what just happened. Too fast. What . . .

Blood. Dripping onto the linoleum.

Pain. Blossoming in his shoulder. Thick and sickening. *Shot.*

"Oh, God." A shock of fear and adrenaline nearly stopped his heart. "Fuck!"

Dazed, he sat back on his heels and slapped a hand over the wound. Sticky warmth rushed between his fingers, soaking his shirt. A wave of nausea assaulted him, bile rising in his throat. Treating a gunshot victim at a scene in no way prepared a guy for being on the receiving end.

The phone. There, next to the pile of cookbooks. He snatched the handset and punched 911, hands shaking so violently he almost dropped it.

A dispatcher asked him to state his emergency, so darned pleasant he might've laughed if he weren't dangerously close to throwing up.

"I've been shot," he gasped. "Jesus Christ."

Voice changing to tight and clipped, she asked for the pertinent details, of which he had few, including having no idea who'd done the deed or why. He gave her his name and address through a dense haze. Shit, he was dizzy.

"Mr. Knight, stay on the line with me, okay?"

"Can't . . . Cori's upstairs."

He had to get to her.

"Mr. Knight?"

The phone slipped from his hand.

Cori awoke with a start, frowning into the shadows of her room. "Zack?"

She groped the bed beside her, but he wasn't there. Had she been dreaming, or had she heard a gunshot echoing across the hills in the darkness? Something else, too. A noise like breaking glass. She strained, but heard nothing else.

The mind could do strange things to a person, confusing dreams with reality. Probably nothing. She wouldn't get any more sleep until she'd checked on Zack and the house, though. Cool air kissed her skin as she slid out of bed, reminding her of her nakedness. Quickly, she pawed through the dresser drawers, found a pair of panties and a large T-shirt, and yanked them on.

Padding across the hall, she peered into Zack's room

first, surprised to see his bed empty. Maybe he'd stayed up to watch TV. As she walked out, however, there were no soft, canned sounds of a program, no glow of the screen coming from the living room.

Starting down the stairs, she called out. "Zack?" At that moment he staggered out of the kitchen, and she huffed an exaggerated breath. "There you are. I thought I heard—"

"Cori," he rasped, clutching his shoulder. "Stay away from the windows."

Her smile died. A dark, wet stain was spreading over his shirt. His fingers were crimson, his face white.

Her feet were flying down the stairs before she even realized she'd moved. "You're bleeding! What happened?"

"Shot. I called the police."

"Oh, my God!"

Meeting Zack halfway across the living room, she caught him as he stumbled. His arm went around her and she hugged his left side, steadying him.

He waved a hand. "Let's go into the foyer. We'll be away from the windows there."

They closed the remaining distance and she helped ease him to sit on the first stair. Her brain whirled with questions, but her single priority right now was to check his wound. She started to sit next to him, and he shook his head.

"This side of me," he said, indicating the place next to the inside wall.

She complied, opening her mouth to question him when his actions struck her. He'd placed his body between her and the living room—and possible danger. Again.

"It's okay; the curtains are drawn."

"Don't care."

He slumped against the railing and her heart skipped. His pallor had gone gray and a fine sheen of moisture beaded above his lip. She pressed her fingers to his forehead and as she'd expected, his skin felt clammy.

"Let's get your shirt off so I can examine the wound."

"Not quite as fun as the last time you ordered my clothes off, huh?" His laugh ended on a strangled wheeze.

"Do me a favor and don't give up your day job to be a comedian, okay?" Lifting the edge of his shirt, she began to work it up.

His handsome face contorted in agony as he pulled his arm out of the sleeve. "Joking might keep me from passing out."

"Under the circumstances, you're allowed. This looks pretty nasty."

It did, too. Puckered, torn flesh edged the bloodied furrow in the top of his shoulder, and bits of his shirt were stuck in the mess. Rivulets of blood streaked down his chest. She prayed the wound appeared worse than it was.

"Gee, thanks. Seems we're going to have to work on your bedside manner, Nurse Ratched."

"Call me that again, and I'll stick my finger in there and twist. Slowly." He croaked a short chuckle at the retort, and she let their banter soothe the worst of her terror as she examined both the entry and exit wound.

"You'll be fine. I know it hurts like the inferno of hell, but the bullet caught all skin. You've got an ugly scratch, that's all."

"Will it need stitches?" He angled his head, trying to see.

"The gauge is too wide. Not enough flesh. We'll let

your buddies clean and bandage this, but at least you won't have to take a ride. You okay?"

"Just feeling a little green."

So was she. Three inches to the left and it would've severed his spine between his shoulders. A slightly different angle, an inch or two lower, it would've blown out his heart.

Someone had tried to murder Zack. Almost succeeded.

His eyes drifted closed and despite her assurances, keeping him talking would lessen her worry.

"What were you doing in the kitchen?"

"Talking to Six-Pack on the phone," he murmured without opening his eyes. "Had to let someone know where I'm staying. Turned to hang up. Shot came through the window over the sink."

So he'd been facing the shooter originally. Who'd probably had the center of Zack's chest in the crosshairs.

"All right. Listen, I'm going to get a washcloth and towel. I'll be right back." She started to rise, and her wrist was caught in his iron grip. His serious gaze pinned hers.

"Be careful and stay low."

His tone brooked no argument, not that she'd intended to give him one. Being independent and being stupid were two different things. Giving him a quick nod, she hurried upstairs, pulled on a pair of jeans. Last, she grabbed a washcloth, wet and wrung it, then a towel.

In less than a minute, she was leaping down the stairs two at a time, toward the figure hunched at the bottom. "Zack?"

"Hmm?" He was drifting, lashes fanning his cheeks like black lace.

"Sorry; this is going to sting."

Cori cleaned his wound as best as she was able with

the damp cloth, turning it red. Finished, she laid it on the step and pressed the towel to his torn flesh. He moaned and she talked to him softly, the way people do when they want desperately to sound reassuring and know it's a total load of crap.

Because the picture beginning to gel was a terrifying one. For whatever reason, somebody had targeted her in a campaign to make her afraid. Now Zack was in the bastard's way, and the would-be assassin couldn't have made his displeasure clearer.

Well, the cops had to believe her now.

If they didn't . . .

God help us both.

For the third time in one night, the chirping of the phone committed the felony of coitus interruptus, punishable by a lingering death.

Lieutenant Howard Paxton glared at the offending instrument, his luscious blond wife's snorts of merry laughter ringing in his ears.

"Sonofabitch."

Kat giggled. "It's not going to stop, sweetie."

"Is the damned answering machine broken?"

"I think so."

"I'm buying us a new one." Grumbling, he rolled off his new wife and snatched the phone, his trademark calm strained to the max. "What?"

"Lieutenant Paxton?"

Howard sat up, already tense. He didn't recognize the voice on the other end, but he knew when a tone didn't bode well. "Speaking."

"Lieutenant, this is Captain Lance Holliday from Station Two."

He slid out of bed, already reaching for his jeans. "You got a four-alarm on your hands?" He glanced to the bed, where Kat clutched the sheet to her bosom, wide-eyed, humor evaporated.

"No, sir. Nothing like that. But I thought you'd want to know we responded to a disturbing call tonight. One of your boys has been hurt."

"Which one?" God, please not Sean. If he'd been drinking again—

"Your FAO, Zack Knight."

He froze, trying to assimilate. "What? I just talked to him an hour ago. Was it an accident? A fall or something?"

"Shooting. Some lunatic scoped him with a rifle. Bullet came in through the kitchen window."

He felt the blood drain from his face. The memory of his own ordeal was still much too fresh. "Sweet Christ, someone shot Zack," he said to Kat, zipping his jeans and reaching for his discarded shirt. Her hand went over her mouth as he addressed Holliday again. "How bad?"

"Grazed his shoulder. We cleaned and bandaged the wound, and he didn't require transport." A weighty pause. "Knight got lucky. Cops said attempted murder, as if there was any doubt. If your man hadn't moved when he did, well, he'd be dead. As it is, he's resting at home, but I thought you'd want to know."

"Thanks, Captain. I appreciate the call." He hung up and tossed the phone onto the nightstand. His wife was out of bed, grabbing for clothes. "You don't have to go, honey. He got clipped in the shoulder, so he'll be all right."

"I know, but I want to, Howard. You know how I feel about Zack."

He did. Knight had been the first of his team members she'd met, and Boy Wonder had a special place in her heart. Hell, he felt the same way, not that he'd go around spouting off like a Hallmark commercial.

A world without Zack in it would be a pretty awful place.

He damned well intended to find out why someone had attempted to take him out . . . and what sort of trouble this lady friend had brought down on Zack's head.

"Mr. Knight, you're positive you don't have any idea why somebody would want to shoot you?"

Zack stared at the grizzled detective—Bernie, if he recalled through his drug-induced trip—and wondered if the man was hard of hearing, or whether cynicism was a job requirement. "Not unless it had something to do with that body I helped bury last week."

Six-Pack, Kat, and Cori worked to hide grins. Eve was not amused.

Neither was Dick Tracy. "Under the circumstances, you might try to take the situation a little more seriously."

O-kay. Must be the painkiller loosening his normally civil tongue, because he'd had his fill of this little pinhead. He struggled to sit up on the sofa and fixed the man with what he hoped to be a lethal glare.

"No, sir," he said coldly, as his friends goggled in amazement. "That would be *your* job. In the past week, I've survived drowning and being shot. Ms. Shannon barely escaped the bridge accident with her life after someone shot out her tire. Since then, she's been followed on numerous occasions and terrorized at her own home.

Stalked, Detective Bernie. You do know the definition of stalking, don't you?"

The detective sputtered, his face reddening, and Zack went in for the kill.

"Then you also know almost ninety percent of stalkers are men, and of the women being targeted, some eighty percent either know their stalker intimately or have had some sort of contact with him. A vast number of these women meet with a sad fate because local law enforcement didn't do a goddamned thing to help them. Is that serious enough for you, Bernie? Because if it isn't, here's one more factoid."

"Zack," Howard warned.

Zack seethed with anger, ignoring his friend's voice of reason. "Start with Ms. Shannon's badass brother Joaquin Delacruz of Atlantic City, and her deceased husband. Leave no stone unturned as to who'd want to hurt her, and find this sonofabitch. Find him, Bernie, because if you don't, I will. And if I locate him first, there won't be any need for a trial."

"Shit," the lieutenant muttered.

The ladies' eyes were round, Cori's face pale.

"You shouldn't have said that to me," Detective Bernie hissed, mouth tight with barely suppressed rage. "Especially in front of witnesses."

"With all due respect, I don't give a fuck. Scribble that down in your little notebook, and be sure you spell my name right."

Casting a humiliated glare around the room, the detective stalked out the front door, leaving an uncomfortable vacuum of silence in his wake.

Eve broke it after a few seconds, giving a low whistle.

"Wow, buddy. Where'd the baditude come from? For a minute, you sounded exactly like Sean."

"Funny, I'm not as bothered by the comparison as I would've been a week ago."

"I've never heard you hand anyone their ass before," Eve said, frowning at him.

"Never had a week like this one before. Or maybe it's the awesome drugs." He gave Cori a hopeful look, gesturing to his pill bottle. "Do I have any refills?"

"Nope, sorry. Those will have to be enough, handsome."

"Oh. Guess I'll have to keep getting my warm fuzzies from you, huh?"

Cori blushed as Eve's eyebrows shot up. Eve's sharp gaze bounced between them, then narrowed as she got the drift.

Whoops. Note to self. Apologize to Evie.

Cori squeezed his hand. "I'm going to go upstairs and see if we have enough bandages. We might need to run to town."

She was giving them time alone, and he appreciated it. After she'd gone, Zack held up a hand to forestall his friends' third degree.

"Don't even start with me. I can't handle any more tonight." Turning his head, he appealed to his fuming best friend. "Evie, I'm really sorry about this afternoon. I had no idea you were picking me up. Please don't be mad at me."

"Mad? *Mad?*" She slapped a hand to her cheek, looking unsure whether to hug him or strangle him. "I was insane with fear for days, positive you were going to die. We all were. Now someone's trying to kill you the very same night you run off with that—that *woman*, and no-body knows where the hell you are or what's going on!"

"She's not 'that woman,'" he said calmly. "Her name is Cori, and she helped me out of a tight spot."

"Any one of us would've done the same if you'd given us the chance, Zack," she replied, sounding hurt. "We can't be there for you if you won't clue us in. You're keeping secrets from me, from all of your friends, and what? You're sharing them with *her*?"

Eve rarely dropped the tough-chick facade, and to see her genuinely wounded over his keeping her out of the loop ripped at his guts.

"It's not like that, I swear. I've had some heavy-duty problems these past few weeks, but I wanted to deal with them myself. Howard knows some of it," he admitted, waving a hand at the lieutenant, who nodded. "Cori now knows part of it, too, but nobody's heard the whole story. I guess I just thought . . ."

Kat spoke up with quiet understanding. "You wanted to handle your situation on your own, without burdening anyone. You thought you could, but it's grown too huge."

"God, yeah." He sighed, knowing he had to level with Eve, at least about some of the story. "Here's the part Six-Pack knows, and only because I had to ask for time off to deal with it. Remember when I took those two days off the week Howard was almost killed?"

Eve rolled her eyes. "Like I could forget? Sean stayed pissed for weeks, even threw it in your face the day you almost drowned."

"What he doesn't know is I didn't have a choice. I . . . I lost my house, Evie. That week, I had to clear out."

He'd stunned her. She gaped at him, letting out a soft

sound of distress, her expression of pity and confusion exactly what he'd wanted to avoid. Moving to his side, she lowered herself onto the sofa beside him, laying a hand on his arm.

"But you're still here. I don't understand."

"I'm getting to that part."

"Why didn't you tell me?"

"I was *ashamed*," he whispered, throat tight. "I didn't want anyone to know, even you."

She lifted her chin, piercing him with pale eyes, communicating her disappointment eloquently without voicing what a complete jackass he was. "You should at least tell Sean. He'll lighten up on you once he understands—"

"No, you're wrong. The captain's curled up at the bottom of a bottle and doesn't give a shit about our personal lives. Let's not go there—I've already said too much."

Sean and Six-Pack were tight, went way back. Zack hadn't missed the big man's flinch at his harsh words, and regretted speaking them.

"You're the one who's wrong. He does care, but we'll drop it for now." Sadness flashed across her angular face as it always did when the subject of Sean came up, but it was quickly masked by determination. "What does Cori know?"

"She gave me a ride to my apartment and was there when I found out I'd been evicted. The manager sold all my possessions while I was hospitalized to cover back rent, so Cori offered me a place to stay. I know," he said, cutting off another round of protests from Eve. "I could've asked you and I would have, except Cori needs me. Someone's scaring her and I needed to crash, so it's an even trade."

"Not quite," she bit off. "The bastard didn't try to murder *her* tonight. You're in his sights, buddy, and forgive me for saying I don't want you smack in the middle of this."

"I know. Please try to understand."

"Spill the rest and maybe I can. How did you wind up losing everything?"

He looked away. "How does anyone? I'm broke. I'm not ready to get into the particulars, all right? It's complicated." And dangerous. Delacruz was a ruthless man whose sister had gone to great lengths to vacate the loving family embrace. Zack had experienced the billionaire's long, unforgiving reach, and wondered how far the bastard would go to rein Cori in. Far enough to frighten her into returning to Atlantic City? And to murder the man living with her if necessary?

No, Zack absolutely could not let his friends know about his connection to Delacruz. However, there was one matter he had to clear up before Eve left. "I phoned Six-Pack earlier and told him this, and I was planning to call you, too. You need to know Cori bought my house. She has no clue it was mine, and we're going to keep it that way. She's blameless in this, and I don't want her upset more than she has been. We clear?"

Howard and Kat murmured their agreement, though they were obviously concerned. Eve hesitated, managing a nod, but visibly skeptical. Good enough.

He tried a smile, but it wouldn't materialize. "Go home, guys. I appreciate you all coming, but you'll be cursing me when you're dragging your butts in to work in a few hours."

"Never, my friend," Six-Pack rumbled, clamping a gentle hand on his good shoulder. "We're here whenever you need us. Just do us all a favor and watch your back."

"I will. You and Kat still coming by on Tuesday?"

"Yep." Six-Pack's brown eyes twinkled. "Eve, too, if she wants to come along. It's a surprise."

"Ooh, I love surprises," Eve said, finally breaking into a smile. "Count me in."

After a round of careful hugs from the women, the trio filed out, leaving Zack alone with terrible reality.

Someone tried to murder me. If I hadn't turned . . .

"Okay, we need more bandages and tape. No way will the one you're wearing last all night." Cori took the seat Eve had vacated, and touched his arm. "Are you really all right? The truth."

He opened his mouth and started to lie. Looking into her beautiful face, stark with worry, he couldn't. "Shaken," he admitted. "And, sure, scared. I'd be an idiot if I wasn't. But I'm not going to run, and if that's what the bastard thinks, then he'll have to improve his aim."

The minute the stupid statement left his mouth, he realized his mistake. Cori's face blanched white, her tawny eyes rounding to huge circles.

"Oh, Zack. What are we doing? You can't stay here with me. It's too risky."

"Uh-uh. The only way you'll make me go is to physically throw me out, and I'm bigger than you."

"But—"

"Forget it, baby."

Zack watched as Cori's relief won over her fear by a narrow margin. She didn't want him involved any more than his friends did, but she needed him in a way that touched his soul—as a woman needs a man. He'd die before giving her up.

"So, bandages," he said, pushing to his feet. God, he was tired. And having second thoughts about venturing out. "Are you sure there isn't something else in the house we can use?"

She shook her head. "That one's already soaked and it needs to be changed regularly. The police are still outside searching the area and the shooter is long gone, so now's the best time to go. Besides, are we going to be held hostage in our own home?"

Our home. His mood lightened somewhat. "Where to?"

"There's a twenty-four-hour drugstore in town, right before the square. I'll drive."

Zack heaved a lungful of crisp night air and silently thanked God he was alive to enjoy it. Cori walked beside him, linking her arm through his as they headed for her car.

"Maybe we can find some ice cream, too," she said.

"Sounds good." Whatever helped her work through her case of nerves was all right by him. A drive might take the edge off for both of them.

He slid into the passenger's seat, easing back gingerly, gritting his teeth at the dull throb in his shoulder. The nice buzz from the painkiller was already wearing off, but it would be hours before he could take another. Damn.

Cori pulled onto the two-lane highway and Zack contemplated whether to drop the subject of her tormentor for tonight. Then again, people often revealed more when their defenses were lowered. He cut a look at Cori, studying her profile in the darkness.

"You told the police you have no idea who might be responsible for all of this. But, baby, I have to ask you . . . what about your husband's death? Joaquin killing him had to be sensational news on the East Coast. What if—"

"There's nothing more to tell," she said, voice sharp

and tight. Upset. "Alex died, my brother was acquitted, and that was the end of it."

A ripple went through him, a chill in his marrow. Cori was lying. Or not revealing the whole truth. Yeah, she was covering, but for whom? About what?

She was on the brink. Instinctively, he knew if he pushed, he could pry the truth from her. And afterward, she'd withdraw from him. Maybe permanently. No, he'd be patient and let her open up on her own. He wasn't innocent in the secret-keeping department and when it finally came down to spilling their guts to each other, his were going to cause her pain. Their budding closeness needed time to find solid footing before that particular session of show-and-tell.

If only he could shake the conviction that her past had a lot more to do with the current situation than she wanted to admit.

They picked up the necessary items at the drugstore, then found an all-night burger place and ordered two chocolate shakes to go. Funny how the cold, sweet treat could make the worst day seem a little rosier.

Cori flipped on the radio, tapping her hands on the steering wheel to the pumping beat of Christina Aguilera. Not exactly his thing—he preferred smooth contemporary or classic rock—but he didn't mind since the music helped lessen the tension with every mile.

Zack downed half his shake before his eyelids got heavy. He didn't realize he'd fallen asleep until a gentle tug roused him from a deep, dark abyss. He blinked, the stubborn cobwebs clinging to his consciousness as he tried to get his bearings.

"We're home, sleepyhead," Cori murmured.

He sat up too fast and a sharp pain lanced his shoulder. "Ahh, crap."

"Easy. Let me come around and help you."

"I've got it." Grabbing his shake and the small drug-store bag, he opened his door. Before he could protest, she was on his side of the car, reaching for his good arm. In spite of the dull throbbing, his lips turned up. Truly, it was simpler to let his beautiful nurse fuss over him. He'd be a dumbass to complain.

"I've got to order a new garage-door opener," she said, shivering as they rounded the vehicle. Their footsteps crunched on the gravel and the cold night was eerily still, the police gone. "I don't like getting out of the car in the dark, especially now."

"I'll look into it tomorrow. There must be some paperwork with information, or a number on the unit we can use to order—"

Halfway to the front door, Zack halted in his tracks and gaped at the front of the house. "I'll be goddamned."

"What . . . oh, no." She swayed in shock, clinging to his arm, her only lifeline in the tidal waves crashing over their heads. "Oh, Zack, look what he's done!"

The front of her house was trashed. A complete, total wreck. Every one of the windows was smashed and spray paint marred the wooden siding and front door in swoops and whirls. As they approached the bottom of the steps, more destruction became visible.

Although empty of flowers for the winter, pots had been broken, the dirt and shards scattered over the porch. The sorry bastard had even taken something heavy—perhaps a hammer—and destroyed many of the vertical slats holding up the porch railing.

In the center of the disaster, letters had been sprayed in all caps on the front door amid the scribbles. Since the porch light had been shattered along with most everything else, Zack would have to move closer to read the message.

"Watch your step." Ordering her to remain behind wouldn't work, so he didn't bother. They took the steps together, dodging glass and shards of pottery until the ugly missive came into focus.

YOU WILL PAY.

Cori sucked in a sharp breath. "Oh, God. Why is he doing this?"

Turning to face her, Zack folded her into his arms. Held her as tightly as possible despite his injury. "I don't know, baby. But if the police can't get to the bottom of this, we will. I promise."

She burrowed her face into his chest, wrapped her arms around his waist. He drew his coat around her, needing her close to his body, desperate to shelter her from an enemy he didn't know how to fight.

The trembling started first, racking her from head to toe. Then her shoulders began to shake. Her muffled sobs tore at his heart, her fear and anger his own.

"Let it out," he whispered, stroking her hair. "I'm here."

A few short minutes of destruction would take hours of backbreaking work to fix. Cori's sense of peace and security would take much longer.

Impotent rage washed his vision in red.

Show your face, asshole. Take on a man instead of a defenseless woman and see what happens.

Zack burned for their nemesis to come out and play.

And when you do, you're one dead motherfucker.

11

Cori's head bobbed through her Monday classes as she fought to stay awake. At this point, she'd given up actually trying to process her instructor's lecture and decided instead to strive for not slipping into a coma.

A lofty endeavor after last night's sinister attacks. Following a second visit by the city's finest, Zack had covered the shattered front windows with tarps, while she swept the downstairs free of glass. Then he sent her to bed and settled in a living room chair under a blanket with a baseball bat on his lap. She'd tossed for what little remained of the night, worried to death about him. He'd still been there this morning, eyes red-rimmed, watching TV and drinking coffee to stay awake and on guard.

Brave, wonderful man. She'd made him promise to try to get some sleep today, but first he'd insisted on making phone calls to find someone to replace the windows, and to the garage-door company. When she left, he'd been sweeping debris from the porch, dark circles smudged under his eyes. A can of brown house paint he must've found in the shop sat nearby, evidence that he'd get little rest today despite his assurances.

On the way home, Cori stopped and picked them up a large supreme pizza, figuring neither of them would have the energy to cook. The rich aroma drove her nuts until she finally turned down the driveway and parked.

She shouldered her purse and got out, pizza box in hand, squinting into the bright afternoon sun. Zack stood at the top of a tall ladder at the corner of the house by the garage, good arm over his head, working diligently on screwing a pair of lights under the eave of the roof. The other arm was curled against his stomach, and she knew his shoulder must be sore.

"Ohh, stubborn, foolish man!" Stalking to the bottom of the ladder, she glared up at him. She would *not* be distracted by how nicely his jeans cupped his tight ass, or how the muscles of his back flexed under the light blue T-shirt as he labored. "What in the hell do you think you're doing?"

"Finishing these lights, beautiful," he called over his good shoulder. "Almost done."

"Well, I can see that! You're going to fall, Mr. Genius. And dammit, it's only fifty degrees today and you're not wearing a jacket."

"I got hot and had to take it off."

"No matter what their IQ states, all men are brain damaged," she muttered. Zack just chuckled. "If you've hurt yourself, you're not getting any pizza."

Lowering his arm, he winced, favoring his shoulder, then turned and grinned down at her. "Pizza? I'm done!"

Screwdriver in hand, he descended the ladder and greeted her with a spine-tingling kiss, leaving her breathless and thinking of munching on him instead.

"I missed you," he said, flicking the tip of her nose with one finger.

"Really? Couldn't have guessed."

"You're supposed to say you missed me, too."

"I missed you all day. Worried about you."

With good reason. If Zack looked exhausted yesterday, this afternoon he resembled death warmed over. His eyes were bloodshot from little sleep; his jaw was dark with stubble. His ebony hair stuck out in every direction, as though the spiky strands had been styled with a blender.

And even so, she'd never seen anyone more gorgeous.

He took the box from her hands and they started for the porch. Cori noted the sparkling new windows and the fresh paint obliterating all traces of last night's vandalism, and a lump of gratitude formed in her throat.

"Thank you for taking care of all this. I'll settle the bill with the glass people, and pay you for the lights and paint job."

"You're letting me stay here, so it's the least I can do. Besides, I get paid next Friday."

"But—"

"Cori, let me do this for you."

The flat line of his mouth, the stiff set of his spine, and the proud tilt of his head made her relent. He really wanted to feel useful, to assist her in any way he could. Something told her Zack hadn't felt useful in a very long time, and that refusing would hurt him terribly.

"Then my triple thanks. Maybe I can repay you some *other* way?" He shot her a sharp look and she raised her eyebrows, which earned her a laugh.

"Baby, I'm just a guy. What do you think?"

"That we'd better eat our pizza before we get into trouble."

They dug in, then carried their plates and drinks to the breakfast nook. It hadn't escaped Cori's attention that the bullet hole in the wall had been filled with Spackle, the blood cleaned from the floor.

"Did you get any rest today at all?"

"I really didn't do much, just directed the workers around. Slapped on a coat of paint, put up the motion-sensitive security lights on each corner of the house—my friend Clay brought those out. Tomorrow the glass guys are replacing the window over the kitchen sink, since they didn't have the right size with them, and I'll work on repairing the porch slats." He hefted a slice of pizza. "God, this smells good. I'm starving. How was your day?"

"Nice deflection of my question." He was hunched over his plate, elbows on the table, and she suspected the position was the only thing propping him upright. The outline of the bandage on his shoulder was visible under his shirt, and she knew he had to be in some pain, but wouldn't admit it.

"You're going to bed early. Alone," she added at the hopeful gleam in his blue eyes.

"So much for my repayment."

"Don't pout. You couldn't win an arm-wrestling match against me at the moment, much less anything more . . . stimulating."

"Rain check?"

"I'm counting on it."

He grinned and they resumed eating while she bored him with details of her day and nursing classes. Neither of them wanted to acknowledge the onset of evening and their fear of a repeat of last night. Even more frightening, they were both so tired she worried they'd sleep right through the monster breaking in to harm them—or worse.

After they finished eating, Cori ordered Zack to the living room to relax, and put the leftover pizza in the fridge.

Just as she started to join him, the phone on the counter rang. She glanced at the caller ID and barely stifled a moan of aggravation as she picked up the receiver.

"Hello?"

"Hey, beautiful! It's Tony."

Cori bristled. "Beautiful" was Zack's pet name for her, and she didn't like the endearment oozing from Tony's oh-so-elegant lips.

"Hi, Tony. What's up?"

"Just making sure we're still on for coffee after your class tomorrow. It's only been three days and I've missed seeing you around," he said smoothly, a hint of seduction in his voice.

Cori's hand tightened on the phone. Damn, she'd totally forgotten. She certainly didn't want to encourage him after their ill-advised kiss the other day, and was far from comfortable trying to extricate herself from this mess of her own making with Zack in the next room.

"Um, that's really sweet of you to say. Unfortunately, I'm going to have to cancel for tomorrow."

"Oh? How come?" His tone cooled.

None of your biz. "I'm dealing with some personal issues," she said, putting some chill into her response. "This week is bad. In fact, I don't know when I'll have time for my usual coffee break."

There. Any man with half a brain could interpret the clear message to back off.

"Dinner tomorrow night, then?"

Any man except, apparently, for Tony.

"I'm sorry, but I'm afraid not. Listen, Tony . . ." She sighed, hating the icky task of giving any guy, even one as self-absorbed as Tony, the brush-off. But honesty was only fair to everyone. "I'm seeing someone. He's really special, and I'm not going to risk messing up what we've got going for a hot fling. And you know as well as I do that's all there would be between you and me."

A heavy silence. "I'm sorry you feel that way, Cori. Perhaps I can change your mind about us."

A statement, almost as though he were talking to himself, not a heartfelt question. Weird. It sort of gave her the creeps and she was more convinced than ever she'd done the right thing. "No, you can't. Good luck finding your someone special, okay? Good-bye, Tony."

She hung up, blowing a strand of hair from her eyes. "Thank God that's done."

"Wow, I'm glad I'm not Tony."

Startled, she spun to see Zack leaning lazily against the kitchen entry with his good shoulder. "Eavesdropping is rude, fireboy."

"But informative." His lips curved in a smug grin. "I'm special, huh?"

"And nosy."

"Nope, just cautious." He stalked toward her, all lean-hipped grace in motion. "A man has to protect what's his."

Goose bumps broke out on her arms and she crossed them over her chest. Not a trace of exhaustion showed in his feral expression, and the way he moved . . . God, he was downright sexy. "Careful, your alpha is showing."

Reaching her, he curled one finger under her chin and tipped her face to his. His mouth took hers, tongue sweeping inside. Bold, demanding. She uncrossed her arms, sliding her palms up his chest. She loved this confident side of him, taking charge, so much potent male.

He reached around her, cupping her rear in his hands.

Spreading his legs, he pulled her close, nestling her intimately against the pole in his jeans. Igniting a blaze only he could douse.

"Complaints?" he breathed against her lips.

"Not one."

"Let's go upstairs."

"Oh, honey. Maybe we should wait until you're better—"

"Corrine Shannon," he said quietly, looking deeply into her eyes, "I've been waiting my whole life. For *you*."

Right then, she melted into a puddle at his feet. Sweet heaven, her man could give lessons in gallantry to every single one of his gender she'd ever known.

"Ditto," she managed around the grapefruit stuck in her throat. Because there weren't adequate words to express what she felt at the moment and even if there were, she wouldn't have been able to voice them without bursting into tears.

He held out his hand in invitation and she took it, hyperaware of what this simple act of acceptance and trust meant to them. The contact sizzled from their linked fingers along her nerve endings, tightening her nipples and sending a jolt of desire through her body. She'd never wanted a man as much as she wanted Zack.

Beside her, he was throwing off heat like a furnace as they went upstairs. At the door to her room he tugged on her hand, giving her a half smile and bringing it to his lips to brush a light kiss behind her knuckles.

"Go ahead and give me about five minutes to clean up," he said. "I smell like paint and sweat."

She craved his naked body next to hers so badly she didn't really care, but she sensed the nervousness he'd hidden so well. A hint of vulnerability, as though he

wanted everything to be perfect for their first time actually
making love—his first to slide deep inside a woman.

"I'll be waiting, hot stuff."

He grinned, ducking his head. "Yes, ma'am."

Good Lord, she could eat him with a spoon.

Fortunately, the hands Mother Nature blessed her with
would do just fine.

Zack wasn't sure how he kept his cool as he took the
world's shortest shower. He was Mr. Suave on the outside, fat nerd boy on the inside. Some things never really
changed, but Cori saw only the man who desired her
above all others, not the dumpy kid who couldn't have
scored a date with Ugly Betty. In his book, that rated
number one on his list of impossible miracles.

Angling the showerhead down and turning his left side
into the thin spray, he managed to wash without wetting
the bandage. Mostly. Finished, he shut off the water and
toweled dry, torn whether to take a painkiller for his burning shoulder or stay awake to please his lady. Frankly, he
preferred not to be comatose for their big night.

He wrapped the towel around his hips as best as he
could, considering the tent his erection made in the front.
Next he fetched the box of condoms from the drawer in
the nightstand—another of Clay's deliveries at Zack's
request. He wished he had his Mustang so he could've
gone to buy them himself. As it was, the good-natured
ribbing he'd taken from B-shift's FAO was worth making
Cori happy.

Fortifying himself, he strode for Cori's room, squelch-
ing his nerves with an effort. She wanted him, and they'd
already been intimate. He was a grown man with no reason to fear having what he'd dreamed of for so long.

A woman who accepted him completely . . . and might just come to love him.

He stopped inside the doorway, mouth watering at the sight of Cori lounging naked on her bed against a mound of plump pillows. Long legs stretched out and parted slightly, honey brown hair falling around her face and full breasts, lips curved upward, she looked very sexy and feline. Waiting to devour the canary.

She crooked a finger, motioning him forward. "I see you brought the team uniform."

"What? Oh, these." He walked to the side of the bed and laid the box on the nightstand. "Presumptuous of me?"

"Smart and considerate," she corrected. "Though we don't need them if you'd prefer to go natural."

"W-we don't?" Jeez, little Zack took that news happily, jerking behind the confines of the towel.

"You've never been with anyone, and it's been ages for me. My most recent tests were clean as always, and I'm on the pill. It's your call."

He grinned. "I feel like I've won the lottery."

She sat up and scooted to the side of the bed, grabbing his towel at the waist. "Yeah? Then hang on and I'll make you feel like the president, too. Whoops, bad analogy."

With a yank, she divested him of the towel and tossed it away. His shaft bobbed near her lips, curved and eager. Leaning forward, she wrapped her fingers around the base and gave the flushed head an experimental lick, gazing up at him, expectant.

"Tell me what you'd like for me to do, Zack."

"Oh, God." His balls drew up and pre-cum wept from the slit of his cock. He fumbled at voicing such wicked thoughts aloud.

"Come on, fireboy. Tell Cori what you need." Another lick, just on the tip.

"Suck me," he whispered. "Please."

She shook her head. "Like you mean it."

His heart was going to explode. "Suck me." His low request, tempered with steel, crackled in the air between them as he buried one hand in her hair. Urged her forward. "Take my cock. Do it *now*."

With a hum of satisfaction, she brought the tip between her lips, suckling. Nibbling and licking. She began to work him deeper, one agonizing inch at a time, squeezing the base of his shaft. The other hand stroked up his inner thigh, seeking. He spread his legs wider and she kneaded his heavy sac, the dual stimulation of his balls and cock driving him mad.

"Oh, yeah," he groaned, thrusting his hips toward her. "Swallow me, baby."

He watched as his cock disappeared between her lips, sliding in until he hit the back of her throat. Her soft, hot little tongue laved his skin and she began to move, sucking with delicious pressure. Liquid fire spread outward from his groin through his belly, to his limbs.

Fingers tangled in her hair, he guided her motions, fucking her gorgeous mouth. He loved this element of control, he realized, dominating her, making her *his*. In return, her enjoyment was obvious. She consumed him with relish, driving him to the edge.

His balls tightened, the fluttering low in his belly signaling a swift climax if they didn't slow down. "Stop, baby. I don't want to come yet." She released him, looking very pleased with herself, so damned beautiful his heart ached. He gestured to the middle of the bed. "Get comfortable and let me taste you."

Cori wiggled into place and smiled, letting her thighs fall open. Her slit, pink and wet, the tiny pearl nub peeking from sandy curls, beckoned to him. He crawled between her legs and lowered his head, flicking her clit with his tongue. Her quiet whimper bolstered his confidence another notch and he took the tender flesh between his lips, sucking gently.

"Ohh, Zack! God, yes . . ."

She arched her hips and he gave her what she asked for, eating her clit, licking in rhythmic precision until she bucked, pulling at his hair.

"I need you inside me," she gasped. "Make love to me."

Music for his battered soul. He inched up her body, careful to lever the brunt of his weight off her. Using one hand, he nestled the head of his cock between the lips of her moist opening, then braced his arms on either side of her head, taking his weight on his elbows. He framed her face with shaking hands, overwhelmed by the emotions surging through him. Words couldn't express how much this union meant to him, but he hoped his actions spoke clearly enough.

Her hands skimmed down his back and onward to cup his buttocks. She urged him inside and he sank by slow degrees, moaning in bliss as her heat enveloped his length.

"Cori," he breathed. Every muscle quivered as he slid in to the hilt. Home at last, buried deep in her. "Oh—oh, God, I never knew. . . . Never . . ."

She clutched at him, writhing. "You feel so good. Don't stop."

Bending his head over hers, he began to thrust. Flames licked at his cock, setting his entire body ablaze. "Baby, I'm not going to last long."

"I don't care! Just fuck me, *please*!"

Jesus. That did it. Drove him right over the edge of a rocky precipice. He pumped her with total abandon, making up in enthusiasm what he lacked in technique. His body quickened, control shattered, balls tightening as he lunged once, twice more.

Balls deep, he stiffened with a hoarse shout. His release exploded, a kaleidoscope of colors bursting in his brain as he filled her, on and on. Indescribable ecstasy. Being locked inside her was a lot like dying, but with a much happier conclusion.

Cori's orgasm joined his and she held him close, legs wrapped around his waist. Her sheath spasmed around his cock, wringing the last of his cum until he was draped over her like a blanket, spent and trembling like a racehorse at the finish line.

"We fit perfectly," she said, kissing his cheek.

Raising his head, he looked into her lovely face and brushed a strand of hair from her eyes. "Yes, we do."

"Zack?"

"Hmm?"

"This isn't some fling for me. I . . . care for you."

He wondered if a man could feel so full he burst. "It's the same for me. I think we've got something here worth giving a chance."

She hugged him close and he wanted to say more, but held back. It was too soon. Would he know love if it smacked him in the head? He'd never loved anyone in his entire life, except his "brothers" at Station Five. Not the same.

He slipped out of her and rolled to the side, gathering her into his arms and pillowing her head on his good shoulder. "I could stay like this forever. I wish the whole world would just take a long hike off a short pier."

"Me, too." Turning in his arms, she propped her chin on his chest and touched his bandage gently. "Are you hurting?"

"Some." She gave him a droll stare of clear disbelief. "Okay, it burns like the devil. Gimme more of those Dr. Feelgood moves you've got going and I'll be well in nothing flat."

Cori giggled. "I've graduated from Nurse Ratched to Dr. Feelgood. I must be doing something right."

"Baby, if you did it any better, you'd short-circuit my heart and have to perform CPR on me."

"Anything for my favorite patient."

He laughed. "Kill me to cure me. Sounds kinky."

"A fetish a day keeps the doctor away."

"Oh, God," he groaned, rolling his eyes as she snickered.

Cori snuggled into his side again and he sighed in contentment, unwilling to allow the threats coming at them from all sides to spoil this moment.

Tomorrow, he'd begin figuring out how to fight for what was his—and win.

Zack wiped the sweat off his brow, checking out his repair job on the porch slats. He'd been in the shop all morning cutting new ones to match the old, and by the afternoon they were as good as new. Christ, he'd missed the texture of the boards in his hands, the shrill buzz of his saw, and though fixing the unwanted destruction wasn't the way he'd wanted to sharpen his skills, he was proud of his work. Cori, on the other hand, would probably fuss at him for overexerting himself—right before she kissed his hurts and made them vanish.

That bright prospect inspired an off-key rendition of Mötley Crüe's "Dr. Feelgood," a wheezy tribute at best to Cori's divine talents, as he gathered his tools. Halfway into the second chorus, his impromptu concert was interrupted by the whine of approaching engines. Glancing up from his place on the porch, he saw Six-Pack's massive black Ford F-250 making its way up the winding driveway.

And behind the truck, Zack's silver Mustang. His perfectly unblemished classic wet dream, not a dent in sight.

"What . . . ?"

Tools forgotten, Zack bounded off the porch and waited, shifting from one foot to the other as the vehicles circled and came to a stop in front of the house. Six-Pack and Kat got out of the truck, the lieutenant's expression partially concealed by a pair of dark wraparound shades.

"Hey, man," Six-Pack called. "What in the hell are you doing up and about? Shouldn't you be resting?"

"Nah, I got a good night's sleep. It's just a flesh wound anyway." Closing the distance between them with quick strides, he waved a hand at the Mustang as Eve opened the driver's door and got out. "I can't believe it! Did you guys do this? How—when—"

The lieutenant laughed and clamped Zack's good shoulder. "You didn't even notice the key to your car was missing off your ring, did you? Ernest Tuttle does a fine job with paint and bodywork, doesn't he? Kat and I took it to his shop the day after the bridge accident, and Ernest put a rush on the job."

"But I was supposed to get two estimates for my insurance," he said in confusion. "Did you already deal with them?"

"Didn't have to. Ernest repaired it for free."

Zack gaped at him. "Why?"

"Remember when his and Donnie Wayne's elderly mother had the heart attack last year and I revived her? They said if there was ever anything they could do for us . . ." Six-Pack shrugged. "Ernest was only too happy to help out when he heard what happened to you."

"I—I don't know what to say, except thank you," he said quietly. "I'm a rich SOB to have friends like you guys."

Kat sniffed and Eve cleared her throat, glancing away. Six-Pack's voice was gruff. "Don't start that shit, my friend. I'm gonna be drowning in estrogen all the way home, you feel me? Oh, by the way—here."

Six-Pack reached into the pocket of his jacket and produced a small item. "I went by the impound lot yesterday and found these in Cori's Explorer. Had them fixed at the eye place inside Wal-Mart."

Zack took his wire-rimmed glasses from the lieutenant, shaking his head. "Thanks, man. You did too much, you know that?"

"Figured you hadn't been able to deal with the details yet, so it was the least I could do. I cleaned out the Explorer and brought a sack of Cori's personal stuff—what didn't get washed into the river, anyway. A few CDs, the garage-door opener that was clipped to her sun visor, and some waterlogged papers from the glove compartment. Wasn't much left."

"She'll appreciate this, Six-Pack. So do I." Zack caught the subtle thinning of Eve's lips, her hostile body language at the mention of Cori's name. His best friend's obvious dislike of the woman he'd fallen for bothered him a great deal.

"Good. You can show your gratitude by getting your ass back to work. It's not the same around the station without you. Got any idea when you'll be released to come back?"

"Next week, I hope." He did a quick mental calculation. "I'd like to be back for the Wednesday shift. That gives me another week to heal."

"Don't push yourself too hard. We want you at full speed when you get behind the wheel again."

The lieutenant's words gave him a jolt of profound joy, which he hid behind a mask of calm. "The captain's sentiment or yours?"

"Everyone's, including Sean. You don't know how bad he feels about coming down on you like he did that day," Howard said softly. "And then to have you go out and almost get killed on a call . . . it's really hit him hard, Zack."

"He shouldn't feel responsible. The fault lies with the bastard who's terrorizing Cori."

"He does all the same. He's carrying a helluva load right now and none of us know how to help him." The lieutenant ran a hand through his hair in frustration.

"Yeah, I remember his son's nineteenth birthday is this week." Or would've been. God, the poor soul. If Zack's wife and kids had been wiped out in one tragic quirk of fate, he'd probably have gone insane with grief. Tanner was hanging on by a microscopic thread.

"Praise Jesus, we're on shift Thursday and short-handed, so Sean can't stay home and drink himself to death."

Sorrow flashed across Eve's pretty, bronzed face. Six-Pack wasn't breaking any confidences—for the past year, the whole team had either observed or experienced Tanner's downhill slide in action.

"I don't know, Six-Pack. I'm not sure work is the best place for him to be that day. Not with the team's safety at stake."

For a split second, anger darkened the lieutenant's face at the insinuation that the captain could unwittingly endanger them during a high-risk call. But Zack was right and they all knew it.

Six-Pack nodded. "We'll keep an eye on him."

"I know you will. I should've kept my mouth shut."

"Nope, we're a team, buddy. We watch each other's backs. So, next Wednesday, huh?" he prompted, switching the subject.

"That's my plan."

"If it works out, what do you say we get the gang together next Thursday night at the Waterin' Hole to celebrate your return? I haven't been there since before I met Kat and that tall brunette tried to teach me that trick with her tongue—ow!" Rubbing his arm, he grimaced at his scowling better half and her balled-up fist. "Tying cherry stems, angel, that's all!"

Kat huffed. "Oh, really? Well, your *wife* will teach you interesting tongue exercises this time, big guy. Assuming wives and girlfriends are invited?"

"Of course, sweetheart. I wouldn't dream of going without you." He placated her with a kiss.

Zack grinned at their antics, secretly hoping he had a shot at this sort of special bond with Cori. "Sounds like fun. I'll run it by Cori, but I'll be there for sure."

Life looked a bit rosier, in spite of Joaquin's looming

deadline for Zack to cough up fifty grand. The man had no idea where he was staying. He had Cori, and couldn't wait for next Wednesday. Yet on the heels of that thought, one reminder sobered him.

When he went back on shift for twenty-four hours at a stretch, no one would be home to protect Cori.

He had to find a solution, and soon.

12

Zack had been quiet for the past couple of days. Her new lover lit up like a Christmas tree when she came home in the evenings, and made love to her with gentle passion, but whenever she pretended not to notice, he withdrew into troubled silence. He left her bed and prowled the house after he thought she'd fallen asleep, baseball bat in hand, ever on guard for their nemesis, who hadn't shown again.

He seemed to be chewing on something, too. She often caught him watching her, all tense, as though he was about to broach a serious subject, only to switch gears and put on a smile, starting a conversation about their day. His swinging moods were about to drive her nuts.

With a sigh, Cori stuck a casserole in the oven for dinner, wiped her hands on a towel, then headed for the living room.

"Thirty minutes until—" She broke off at the sight of Zack reclining in the easy chair he'd obviously claimed as his own for the duration, feet up, head lolling to one side. Sound asleep.

Black wisps of bangs fell over his closed eyes, and his glasses had slipped down on his nose. For some reason, the endearing picture caused a strange, wonderful pang in her heart. He appeared so sweet and vulnerable like this, but he was strong, too. And so damned handsome. She wanted to touch him constantly, as though he were a fever she had no desire to cure.

The newspaper was spread open on his lap, the remote control on the chair's armrest, TV blaring about the latest politician who couldn't keep his trousers zipped. A scene cut from the pages of domestic suburbia.

She smiled to herself. She'd fled hundreds of miles to avoid a man taking over her life again, and this one had claimed her TV remote and favorite chair inside a week.

Even more shocking, she didn't mind. Much.

Creeping to the chair, she took the remote and turned down the volume to a less ear-shattering level, then placed it on the table beside him. The absence of noise, or perhaps her presence, caused him to stir.

Blue eyes fluttered open and he stretched, wincing in pain, favoring his wounded shoulder. "Ah, damn . . . Oh, hi, baby." Dazed from his nap, he gave her a lopsided smile.

"Do you need another pain pill? I'll get it for you." She cupped his cheek, enjoying the prickle of his whiskers under her palm.

"No, I'm just a little sore. Besides, those darned things make me drool." He sat up straighter, inhaling a deep breath. "What smells so good?"

"Chicken and rice casserole. It'll be ready in about twenty-five minutes. Hungry?"

His stomach rumbled in answer. "There's your verdict. I'm starving. Can I help you do anything?"

"I've got it covered, but thanks." A man asking such a question was alien to her. Any one of her brothers would donate his left testicle to science before offering to assist a woman with domestic chores.

She left Zack to channel surf while she tossed a salad and set the table. Truly, she didn't mind the Betty Crocker routine because it gave her much-needed time to decompress from the stress of her classes and clinicals. To have a man underfoot in her kitchen would be equivalent to a spaceship landing in her front yard.

Dinner was a quiet affair, Zack eating slowly and appearing more tense than ever, and she cast about for a way to lighten the mood.

"You're doing way too much work around here. I'm going to have to put you on the payroll."

He shrugged. "I like being outside, or woodworking in my—" He broke off, coughing behind his hand. "I mean, *your* shop."

"Good. Someone should get some use out of all those materials and the equipment." Zack only nodded, pushing the rice around his plate, and she eyed him. He looked as if he'd swallowed his tongue. Given her brothers' attitudes, it didn't strike her as unusual for a guy to think of a manly space like the wood shop as "his," and she wondered at his odd reaction to the verbal slip.

"So, are you going to tell me what you're making out there?"

"You said to surprise you, remember?"

She sighed. "So I did."

"I'll bet you're terrible at waiting." A ghost of a smile hovered on his lips.

"The worst. Not even a hint?"

"Hmm, all right. I believe you'll like it."

"Well, I *know* that! You're not good at giving hints at

all." She thought she'd teased him out of his funk, but his humor faded. He stared at his half-consumed meal as though it contained life's secrets, and her patience evaporated. "Okay, out with it. Tell me what crawled up your shorts and died before I lose my mind."

Giving up the pretense, he laid his fork down and studied her, purpose in his blue gaze. "Cori, I'm no cop. What's going on with this stalker is so far out of my depth, I'm flying blind. God knows the police aren't making any progress."

Oh, God! He's had enough and wants to leave. She couldn't blame him, but the image of Zack packing his bag and walking out of her life constricted her lungs. Left her cold and aching inside.

"You don't have to say anything else," she said stiffly, nudging her plate aside. *Don't cry, don't you dare!* "You didn't sign up for lunatic patrol when you came here. Where will you stay?"

"What? I'm not going anywhere." He frowned. "Unless you want me to leave."

"No! I just thought . . . the way you were talking . . ."

"You automatically assumed I'm a coward who'd turn tail and run from trouble? Leave you alone and defenseless?"

Her face heated. "Of course not! Well, okay, I thought you might want to go, but you're not a coward. I just—"

"Forgot that I've made myself completely at home and I'm so happy here, with you, I can't see straight? That I'm sleeping in your bed, making love to you every night?" He arched a black brow. "Guess I'll have to redouble my efforts."

"Point taken," she said, holding up a hand in surrender. "Your *efforts* are quite unparalleled, believe me."

"Thanks, beautiful," he drawled, looking rather pleased with himself. "You're pretty inspirational yourself."

"I have a great muse." His compliment warmed her, easing the last of her fears of his making tracks. "Where were you headed with the subject of the cops, then?"

His expression sobered. "Like I was saying, this is out of my league. Statistics alone say he probably won't give up until he's accomplished whatever his sick goal is. What happens when I go back to work and I'm gone for twenty-four hours at a time? I can't keep you safe. I think we need to call in reinforcements."

"What, like hire security to watch the house?" She shook her head. "He'll just wait for a better opportunity. If he wants to get to us, he eventually will."

A muscle jumped in his jaw. "I know. I'm suggesting we bring in someone who knows how to fight dirty." He paused, looking her square in the eyes. "Someone with resources, who has damned good motivation for moving heaven and earth to find this monster."

"But who—*oh.*" She stiffened, the breath whooshing from her lungs. "Oh, no. You cannot possibly be suggesting what I think you are."

"Joaquin is powerful, Cori. He and your other brothers probably have contacts we can't imagine and don't want to know about. People who can get things done quickly and efficiently. They could ferret out this crazy guy and kick his ass before you lose another night's sleep."

She narrowed her eyes, studying Zack's grim expression, his posture. He wasn't thrilled with his proposal, either. No, the emotion radiating off him was much stronger than reticence. More like dread.

"All true, but you have no idea what you're asking. I can't involve Joaquin in this. I won't."

He spread his hands, the portrait of frustration. "Why not?"

"Are you under the impression that my brother will find the perpetrator and dutifully hand him over to the authorities?"

"Why not?"

She gave a soft, bitter laugh. "No, Zack. Joaquin is a steamroller. If he gets wind of this, he'll mow down everything in his path until he finds his quarry. And when he does, there won't be a need for a trial. You said as much to Detective Bernie, so what makes you believe he'd feel any differently?"

"Dammit, Cori—"

She shoved out of her chair and began to pace. "He could wind up in prison, convicted of murder. You don't know him or care about his welfare, but I do."

"I care about *you*."

"But not my family?"

Stony silence greeted her question. Oh, this was going to get ugly. The burn of anger spread through her chest, rapidly increasing to a boil. She grabbed the back of her chair, knuckles turning white.

"As long as *our* problem is solved, Joaquin can twist in the wind? Is that it?"

Zack stood, as well, dinner forgotten. "Your brother is a grown man who makes his own choices," he said, his voice cool. "Did it ever occur to you that his stay-out-of-jail pass should've expired long ago?"

Her mouth fell open. "Where in the hell is this coming from?" Silence. Zack clamped his lips shut, glaring at her. She closed the short distance between them, stabbing his chest with one finger. "Where do you get off? *Nobody* dumps on my family but *me*! How *dare* you suggest whining to my brother to catch the bad guy when you don't give a shit what might happen to him!"

His eyes hardened to cold blue marbles. "I don't whine to anyone when I need help, but I'm not foolish enough to refuse when it comes to keeping you safe. If that makes me an asshole, fine."

"I don't think you're an asshole," she hissed. "I just don't understand where this attitude toward my brother is coming from. You think he belongs in jail? I know he's no angel and he's made a career out of grinding his opponents to dust, but why would *you* want him to take a fall?"

"You're putting words in my mouth."

"Really? You're judging a man you know nothing about."

"Maybe you ought to take off your blinders and do a little judging of your own."

"What in God's name is that supposed to mean?"

"How much do you really know about your Tony Banning?"

Thrown for a loop, she blinked at him. "He's a rich artist based in Nashville. Paints in oils and watercolor. I can't imagine what he has to do with this *discussion*."

"So you've seen his paintings?"

"Well . . . no. But art isn't one of my interests, so I never asked to see his work."

"If there *is* any. How do you know he's rich?"

"His clothes, his car," she replied, exasperated. "I haven't asked to see his pedigree, for cryin' out loud. Why are you bringing Tony into our argument? He's not my type, a fact I've made perfectly clear to him. He has no bearing on us."

Zack snorted, the chill in his gaze heating with anger.

"Yeah? Tony doesn't seem to agree. He called here three times today while you were either in class or at the hospital—and he *knew* you weren't home."

Fantastic. This went a long way toward explaining Zack's crappy mood. "I guess he's not taking 'no' very well."

"I answered the phone the first time and he made a point to let me know he ran into you at the coffee shop this morning. Said to have you return his call. I didn't pick up after that and he didn't leave a message. He's yanking my chain, and his games are starting to piss me off. Even more, it made me wonder."

"Oh, boy. I'm not going to like this."

He took her hand, his anger tempered with worry. "Baby, what if this creep is your stalker?"

She stared at him, unsettled by the coil of unease gripping her belly at the simple logic. And her failure to ask herself the same question. "Oh, come on. Tony's so enamored of his own reflection, he'd make love to himself if he could contort that far."

"Maybe the slick, wealthy playboy is who you're supposed to see. That's the world you come from, so perhaps he bet on you gravitating to the type of guy you used to find attractive."

"The type of guy he *thinks* I find attractive. I ran far away from that empty life, remember?" She wasn't ready to concede his point on anything at the moment. She was still ticked and confused about his harsh stance regarding Joaquin. The heat of anger too fresh.

"I'm just saying—"

"You know what? I think you're jealous. I think Tony's pushing your buttons and you're letting him. Furthermore, I *know* there's something else eating at you besides the obvious, and your refusal to talk about it is building a wall between us."

Dropping her hand, he looked away. If he was tense before, now he appeared close to imploding. He offered nothing, and the coil in her gut became a greasy ball of fear. Her brothers were masters at keeping secrets, too. Never letting her in. This, in part, had driven her out of their lives.

Turning away, she began to clear the table. Zack lent a hand, but they didn't speak and when they were finished, she simply said, "I'm going to bed."

She mounted the stairs, aware of his gaze boring into her back. His sadness. He didn't follow and she didn't ask him to—though she should. Stupid pride.

Her heart seized at the thought of leaving him alone. Their first real argument had exposed some troubling issues, and she should go back. Talk to him, especially now. Running never solved problems. Falling in love with Zack Knight shouldn't be so damned hard.

In her room, she froze, fingers over her mouth.

I love him. Oh, God, I've fallen in love with Zack.

She sat down hard on the edge of her bed, scrambling to pinpoint exactly when this occurred. She was as stunned as if she'd been bashed in the head with a brick. Such a monumental event deserved its very own *moment*.

A picture solidified in her mind. Zack, leaning over the seat of her Explorer, hand outstretched, blue eyes calm. The vehicle dangling over the edge of hell.

I'm not leaving without you.

He'd been steady, true to his word. He'd nearly died keeping his promise.

Right then, she'd known. Here, at last, was a man of integrity she could spend the rest of her life with.

She wanted to go to Zack and make up. Hold him and make love to him. But the stubborn side of her insisted he owed her an apology, not the other way around. She wouldn't dream of insulting his family—if he had one.

Hating the sudden, terrible rift between them, she donned her oldest flannel pajamas, crawled into bed, and pulled the covers over her head. Their warmth didn't dispel the emptiness of the space where he loved to spoon against her back, curling around her like her own sexy blanket.

As she drifted into fitful sleep, the irony of attempting to pry into his secrets nagged at her conscience. She had no right to poke at ragged wounds best left to heal. No right to judge.

Not when she'd carry the most soul-destroying of secrets to her grave.

Zack flew along the curvy highway through Sugarland, letting the horses run. Seemed like ages since he'd been behind the wheel of his pride and joy, though not much more than a week had passed.

God, it felt great to get out again. To just drive, even if he had nowhere in particular to go other than Wal-Mart—not exactly the hub of spectacular thrills, but just his speed at the moment. He wasn't up to doing much more than puttering around his—Cori's—place. And sinking himself between her sweet thighs.

Except for last night's Big Freeze. Boy, he'd fucked up. He'd insulted her low-life brother and hurt her feelings with his silence, and he couldn't even tell her why. Not without hurting her more than she'd thought possible.

God, he'd *already* hurt her. He *had* to tell her the truth. About Joaquin, his father, the money, the blackmail, all of it. Today. Joaquin's deadline was approaching fast. Sooner or later, she'd find out. *And if she hears the whole sordid story from someone else first, she might never forgive me.* Hell, she might not anyway.

Wal-Mart loomed ahead. He turned off the highway into the parking lot, and eased into a lone space at the end of a row. He hated fighting the crowd for a better spot, and didn't want his classic beauty dented after she'd just been repaired.

Removing his seat belt, he slipped his new cell phone from the pocket of his jacket and frowned at it, debating whether to call Cori. She might hang up on him, but the truth was he'd rather face rejection than not hear her voice. Pretty pathetic.

A ball of anxiety knotted his stomach as he speed-dialed her cell phone. Hers was now the first number on his list, and he wondered how hard a time the guys would give him when he returned to work. The thought of returning to that easy camaraderie lessened his apprehension as Cori answered.

"Hello?"

"Hi," he said softly.

"Oh. Hey." Her greeting was brittle, a bit wary.

Damn. "Still mad at me?" Funny, he recalled rolling his eyes not long ago when Six-Pack wheedled his new wife with the same universal guy question that means your dick has been lassoed and hog-tied for life.

"Not anymore."

"Good. I'm glad, even though I deserve it." When she didn't deny it, he pressed on. "Say, I wondered if maybe you had a break coming?"

A pause, and a slow thaw. "What did you have in mind?"

"Lunch? That new diner on the square is supposed to have good salads and burgers."

"Plying me with food, huh?"

"Will it work?"

"I guess we can find out," she said, a trace of warmth creeping into her tone. "In forty-five minutes, I have an hour-and-a-half break before I have to be at the hospital. I finished my test in class, but they need someone to fill in this afternoon. Does that sound good?"

"Fantastic, beautiful. I'll see you soon."

Zack ended the call and heaved a sigh of relief. At least she wasn't cutting him cold. Feeling lighter, he stepped out of the car and headed into the store. Thirty minutes later, he'd replaced the bulk of his wardrobe and added another healthy chunk of change to his already-stressed credit card. Two weeks ago, spending so much would've made him sick. Now he couldn't find it in himself to care.

He had a much more important person than himself to worry about these days.

He loaded the bags into his trunk, then made his way downtown to the quaint family-themed diner with red-checked curtains in the narrow windows. Across the street, the stately old courthouse gracing the center of Sugarland's town square lent the scene a glimpse of vanishing Americana.

His father's last words to him, heavy with exhaustion and defeat, rang in his head as he parked and pushed inside.

Nothing lasts, boy. The sooner you face reality, the better off you'll be.

"Just one?"

He studied the young, cherub-faced waitress. Blond and cheerleader cute, not a day over nineteen if he had his guess. And sporting a dimpled grin while giving him a very interested once-over. She made him feel eighty.

"Two. I'm waiting for someone."

Her smile dimmed. "Right this way."

He trailed her to a booth not far from the door, where she set two plastic menus on the table and hurried off. The tantalizing aroma of home-style cooking teased his nose, and his stomach rumbled. The emptiness in his gut reminded him of what a poor job he'd done taking care of himself before Cori. He'd have to start working out again in order to pass the physical-agility test at the team's next training exercise.

Cori blew through the door in a gust of wind. Zack sucked in a breath, feasting on the sight of her, cheeks rosy from the blustery weather, hair pulled back into a ponytail, little wisps flying around her face. She was dressed more conservatively today in navy blue pants, a cream cable-knit sweater, comfortable shoes, and a navy jacket that hid her knockout figure.

She was the loveliest woman he'd ever seen.

Her expression lit when she spotted him, but her pleasure was quickly replaced by wariness as she approached. Zack slid from the booth and rose to greet her, taking both of her hands in his and brushing a kiss across her soft lips. Nuzzled her cheek.

"I'm sorry," he whispered.

Her golden eyes shone suspiciously bright. "Me, too."

He wrapped her in a bear hug, not giving a particular shit what the other patrons might think. "No, baby. It was my fault."

She squeezed him tighter. "I had no right to try and push you into telling me personal stuff, especially when it doesn't affect our relationship."

"Oh, beautiful, but it does," he admitted hoarsely. "And what I have to tell you will hurt you way more than it has me."

She pulled back, looking into his face, full of concern. "All right. I want to hear everything, but I don't have much time. Let's enjoy our lunch for now. Tonight, we'll have the entire evening to work through this."

He nodded, unable to believe he'd set the wheels in motion, though he didn't see another choice. In attempting to protect her from the truth, he'd done the opposite and she'd been upset just the same.

Cori shrugged off her jacket as they took their seats across from each other and picked up their menus. The waitress swooped in and took their drink orders, then bustled away with a promise to return in a minute.

"You look great," he said, eyeing Cori. "Sexy."

"Oh, sure, grandma shoes and all. You should see me in my killer scrubs. Hand me a bedpan and, ooh, baby, the patients can't get enough of me." She grimaced.

"Huh. It's the fancy doctors I'm worried about. I'd hate to be forced to break some jerk's surgery hand." He gave her a fierce mock scowl and she giggled.

"You'd never lay a finger on anyone." She smiled. "That's what I love about you."

Love. The careless word sucked the common sense from his brain, wrung his heart like a floppy dishrag. Nobody had ever *loved* anything about him. The sentiment had never been part of his world, and it wrapped his soul in sweet light.

Before he could form a brilliant reply, the waitress returned to take their orders. Since they'd been more interested in each other than food, they quickly scanned the selections.

"I'll have the Cobb salad with ranch," Cori said.

"Bacon cheeseburger with fries for me."

After the girl left, Cori gave him an arch look. "Buffy was totally checking you out."

He flushed. "Was not."

"Was so."

"Didn't notice," he said truthfully.

"Hmm. Good thing." A teasing light entered her eyes.

"Why?"

"Because the name tag is pinned to her left boob."

"Oh."

She laughed, a low, husky sound that curled around his balls and squeezed. "It's fun to yank your chain, fireboy." She leaned forward, brimming with mischief. "The waitress isn't wearing a name tag, though she *was* imagining you as dessert."

"You have a mean streak, Ms. Shannon. That's what I love about *you*." He paused. "You . . . balance me."

There. He let her chew on that, and her obvious pleasure shone on her face.

"What a sweet thing to say."

"It's true."

"You're too good to me." Her lips twitched. "You could let *your* mean streak out every now and then, you know. Might be fun."

One part of him agreed, and gave the idea full approval. "Any chance you can get out of your rotation this afternoon?"

"I wish! But hold that thought, handsome. I might be able to leave early."

Whatever reply he started to make died as he glanced past Cori. A tall man with flowing, shoulder-length blond hair was striding toward their booth with purpose, his cool gaze fixed on Zack. A pretty boy in designer jeans, a dark sweater, and an expensive-looking black leather jacket. Their eyes locked, a clash of crossed swords before battle. Zack's spine stiffened, his male combative instincts instantly roused and flooding every limb. He knew without being told exactly who was bearing down on them.

Reaching their table, the man threw Zack what could only be described as a smirk before pasting a delighted smile on his smarmy mug and addressing Cori.

"Cori, sweetheart! What a coincidence. I was just going to grab a bite and here you are." The bastard leaned over and bussed Cori's cheek. "Mind if I join you?"

Coincidence, my ass. Zack's lip curled.

Not waiting to hear whether they minded, their uninvited guest shoved himself into the booth beside Zack, leaving him no choice but to move over or make a scene. He gritted his teeth, a slow burn sizzling in his gut like battery acid. The man had usurped his place across from Cori, relegating him to the corner as though he were a nuisance. Just now, he didn't feel a bit like the guy Cori admired because he supposedly wouldn't harm a soul. For her sake, he made a silent vow not to plant his fist in the prissy sonofabitch's face.

"Zack, this is Tony Banning. Tony, this is my boyfriend, Zack Knight. Zack's a firefighter here in town," she said, her tone making it clear how proud she was of the fact. She also scooted over in her seat, repositioning herself in front of Zack.

Boyfriend. A spurt of male satisfaction stroked his ego. Unfortunately, Banning killed the buzz by opening his mouth.

"A firefighter," he mused, sparing a glance at Zack as

though he were an interesting bug before returning his attention to Cori. The boyfriend claim he dismissed altogether. "Well, I suppose that's a worthy profession if you aren't good at anything else and don't have an education. Some of us have to be the worker bees, don't we?"

Goddamned condescending prick. A snarl threatened to erupt from his chest. This guy was no different from the bullies he used to put up with every day as a kid. He itched to rip out Banning's lungs, but his hands were tied now just as they had been back then.

The temperature in Cori's voice plunged several degrees. "If a calling to save lives makes us unimportant little 'worker bees,' then I guess Zack and I are in good company together." She gave a short laugh and went on while Banning sputtered. "I always find it amazing how many people with attitudes like yours find themselves in the ER with their heads busted, expecting us to fix the results of their ignorance."

Banning, who had meant for his slur to be directed only at Zack, scrambled to redeem himself. "My apologies, darling. I didn't mean to offend! Of course your profession is vital and I didn't mean to imply otherwise. My God, you'll have nearly as much training as a doctor, unlike certain blue-collar jobs."

Jobs like Zack's. The slight ate at his control, pushed him to his limit. He told himself it wasn't as if he hadn't turned the other cheek before, on numerous occasions. Told himself nobody's opinion mattered except Cori's. That lording his intelligence over a sleaze like Banning was mean-spirited and wrong. That he needn't stoop to the bastard's level.

The pep talk didn't succeed.

"So, Banning," he interjected, surprised by how level

he sounded, "Cori tells me you're an artist. Where did you study?"

The other man glanced at Zack as though he'd forgotten his presence, but Zack saw it for the mask it was. An affected pose of indifference.

The glint of malice in Banning's eyes gave the man away. The emotion flashed and vanished quickly, leaving his expression placid when Zack knew he was anything but. His nemesis fought his rage the same as Zack, and they hummed with the barely suppressed desire to tear at each other like a pair of junkyard dogs.

"Tulane," the man said smoothly.

"Really? Not Memphis College of Art or someplace actually known as an *art* school?"

There. A flicker of uncertainty.

Banning shrugged. "I studied law. Found the field stifling to my creative expression, so I decided to paint instead."

He's lying. "I see. Nothing like a bored, spoiled artist to make the world a better place. What type of paintings?" At the man's stare, Zack gave him a crocodile smile. Yeah, he was getting warmed up. "Landscape, portraits, still or real life?"

"Real life," Banning said, recovering. "People on crowded streets, on beaches, or in markets, my impression of how people fit into their world, or not."

"So your style is Impressionist, then."

"Well . . . yes."

"Why not Expressionist? Or Americana?"

Banning smoothed an imaginary speck of lint off his jacket. "I enjoy the realistic depictions of artists like Monet."

Good save. Anyone with half a high school education

knew about Monet. "Oh, his work is unparalleled, but he's not my favorite Impressionist artist. You know how I love that Kandinsky of yours, right, beautiful?" Zack met Cori's gaze with a smile, telegraphing the silent message. She might not know about Kandinsky, but she caught the ruse, brightened, and agreed wholeheartedly.

"Oh, yes! My print alone cost a fortune. I wish I could afford an original."

Her enthusiasm seemed to appease Banning. He shot her a sly grin, chest puffing out.

"I'll have to show you mine sometime," he bragged. "I acquired a floral at Sotheby's for a song."

Swish. Zack struggled to keep from nailing the fraud, though God knew he wanted to, badly. He could be simply a rich, horny player out to impress Cori with his imaginary artist persona, in which case flattening him in front of her would be most gratifying.

Or Banning could be an attempted murderer. Zack didn't dare tip his hand before he got the chance to clue in Detective Bernie about this guy. Maybe he was off base, but then again—

"What do you think, Zack?"

He blinked at Cori. Her pointed look and tight smile said, *Bail me out of this conversation!* Before he could cover his lapse, the waitress appeared with their orders, placing them on the table with a rather friendly greeting for the newcomer.

"Oh, hi! May I take your order?" From the body language, what she really meant was, *May I take your clothes off?*

Banning leaned back in the seat, giving the girl a blatant once-over and apparently preparing to make himself at home.

Like hell. Zack cut him off. "Our buddy here was just leaving."

The girl faltered, picking up on the tension. "Oh. In that case, can I show you to a table?"

A muscle in Banning's jaw jumped, irritation flashing in his dark eyes. "No, thank you. I really do need to dash." He pushed from the booth, smirking at Cori. "See you around soon, darling."

"She's not your *darling*, asshole. Not in this life, or the next."

This time, Banning didn't bother to disguise his hatred. "Yeah? Good thing you only—" Snapping his mouth shut, he stalked toward the exit.

Zack narrowed his gaze on the man's retreating back. What had the shithead been about to say?

Cori calmly picked up her fork and speared some of her salad. "Let me guess. Kandinsky isn't an Impressionist."

"I'll do you one better. If your psycho admirer is really an artist named Tony Banning, I'll stock my entire drawer with pink happy-face boxers."

13

The cell phone in Lionel's pocket buzzed like a pesky mosquito, interrupting his concentration and raising his blood pressure to dangerous levels. Wrapping his fingers around the instrument, he fantasized it was the caller's neck. Flesh yielding as the man's face turned blue, eyes bulging and lifeless.

He flipped open the phone. "Yes?"

"Tell me you've made progress."

"I've made progress."

"Don't be a stupid fuck," his partner snapped. "You wouldn't even know about the money if it weren't for me. Do I need to catch a flight?"

Oh, *hell* no. "I'm handling the situation."

"Are you?" The man sounded skeptical, with good reason. "In the way we'd planned?"

"There's been a complication—a boyfriend. I'm working on removing him. The plan has changed, but I'll get the information."

"And you were going to inform me of this, when?" he bit off, obviously seething.

"Does it matter as long as the end result is the same? Relax. I'll be lounging on a beach on a tropical island and you'll get your cut before your hard-on fizzles."

"I'd better. I don't have to remind you how long my reach is, do I, *partner*?"

Not goddamned long enough, prick.

"No."

"Excellent. I'll give you two more weeks to bring our project to a satisfactory conclusion. I'll expect good news."

The man ended the call with a click and Lionel closed his phone, anger rapidly replaced by savage determination. "You're gonna grow old waiting for that call, *partner*."

Knight was home and Cori's rental car had just started up the drive. All he needed now was a window of opportunity to act. He cursed fate for sending her home early, before he had a chance to dispose of Knight.

But the result would be identical.

"I won't need two weeks, you maggot."

By then, Lionel would be living the high life in a warm climate under yet another assumed name, enjoying his final—and biggest—score. As for Cori and her firefighter, he owed them both a lesson in pain and suffering.

When they'd outlived their usefulness, well, this area of Tennessee was covered with miles of virgin forest, hills, and valleys, and a multitude of cave systems stretching forever. Their bones could molder for a century or more before anyone ran across them.

"She can be *your* darling in the next life, loser. I'll take the real reward."

Maybe before Cori died, he'd tell her why.

That she'd been sold out by her own flesh and blood.

Chuckling at his own cleverness, he settled in to wait.

Cori walked into the kitchen from the garage, tossing her purse and keys onto the counter. "Zack?"

No answer. She hadn't seen him puttering outside, either, and she hoped the stubborn man was resting for a change. Whew, she was parched. She dug a bottled water from the fridge, twisted off the top, and took several long swallows, then headed upstairs to find her guy.

Hovering in his doorway, she peeked into his room, noting the polo shirt he'd worn to lunch laid neatly on the bed. His jeans and a green long-sleeved T-shirt were piled on the floor, streaked with dirt, along with his socks and underwear. She moved inside and saw the bathroom door standing open, the light on inside. The herbal aroma of soap teased her nose.

As she crept closer to the bathroom and peered inside, her mouth watered. Zack was fresh from the shower, black hair damp, drying off his chest, abs, and legs with brisk strokes. His half-erect cock showed his mind was on activities other than painting or sleeping, which suited her fine.

"My, my, a naked man in my house," she drawled, sauntering in to join him. He jumped in surprise. "Whatever shall I do?"

Zack slung the towel over the shower stall, turned, and in two steps had her crushed against his chest, mouth descending on hers. His kiss was far from gentle, his tongue sweeping inside, demanding. His mouth punished hers, taking possession.

Desire flared to life, pooling between her legs. Her clit throbbed and ached, her entire body gone feverish. Chill bumps raced over her skin as his palms skimmed under the top of her green nurse's scrubs, up her belly to cup her breasts. His fingers plucked at her nipples through the fabric of her bra, impatient.

Oh, yes. She couldn't wait, either. He ground against

her mound, his erection heavy and hard, making his intent clear. Spiraling them both toward a total loss of control that both exhilarated and frightened her. She'd never seen this commanding side of her lover, and wondered whether he was as shocked.

Pulling back, he took the bottled water from her and flung it away. Then he untied her drawstring pants, dragging them down along with her panties, and off. His movements were hurried, fevered.

"I want you *now*," he rasped, backing her against the bathroom wall. "And you're *mine*. Nobody else's. Do you understand?"

"Y-yes." Lord, she was going to incinerate. Heat rushed between her thighs and her nipples hardened to points.

"Know what I'm going to do to you? I'm going to fuck you, baby." He pressed close, fingers brushing through the curls at the apex of her thighs. He parted her slit, found the moisture gathered there, and spread it around. Rubbing, readying her.

She arched into him. "Oh, God! Zack—"

"Yeah, I'm going to fuck you right here. Just like this," he said, blue eyes glittering with sexual heat. A man who wasn't planning to take no for an answer. He cupped her buttocks in his hands and lifted, bracing her back against the wall. "Hang on to me."

"But your wound—"

"Shhh."

"Zack, I—"

He guided the broad head of his cock to her center, pressed between her greedy lips. She clung to his neck, careful to avoid the gauze on his shoulder, trembling with need. He entered her in one smooth thrust, burying himself balls-deep with a tortured groan.

"Ahh, yes!" Lost, he threw back his head. Began to pump his hips, the slick length of him stroking her channel and clit. "Just like this . . . love fucking you . . ."

"Please," she begged. "More. Faster, harder!"

With a moan, he angled his thrusts, lunging deep and hard, pistoning into her. Increasing the tempo, setting her on fire. She gave herself over to him as she'd never done to anyone, just let herself be swept away by this dark and primal passion. The total abandon carrying them to the edge.

And beyond.

"Yes, yes, yes!" she cried in time to his plunging cock. Owning her. Branding her as *his*. He pounded her into the wall and she was vaguely aware of a hanging picture being upset and knocked askew.

Flesh slapped in noisy rhythm, background music to the storm raging over them both. She felt her body unraveling, lightning shooting from her sex to her womb, and on to her limbs. His body quickened, and he gazed into her eyes, expression fierce.

"Oh!" Her orgasm exploded and she burst into zillions of shards of wicked joy.

His exultant shout joined hers and he filled her in a hot rush, his cock jerking until he collapsed against her, spent and quivering from exertion. After a moment, he slipped from inside her as she unlocked her legs from his waist, lowering her feet carefully to the floor.

Lord, he'd taken her half dressed. Glowing from head to toe, she shot him a grin. "Aren't you full of fun surprises?"

He laid his forehead on hers. "God, Cori, I'm so sorry. I don't know what got into me."

"Well, I don't, either. But when the spirit moves you again, let me know so I can get naked!"

He shook his head, shamefaced. "I can't believe I treated you like that. Hell, I didn't fully undress you, or even take time to make sure you were pleased. I—I've never been so thoughtless and crude." He hesitated, and when he spoke, his voice was crestfallen. "I was selfish. That was all about me, and you deserved better."

"No, Zack, I loved—"

"But what if you hadn't? I didn't give you the chance to refuse, did I?" He snatched the towel and held it in front of his wilting erection.

"I wouldn't have said no to you!"

"Don't you see? It didn't matter to me right then."

"You are *so* full of horseshit."

Quickly, he wiped off the evidence of their tryst and brushed past her. "I'm going to be in the shop for a while."

Great. Now he'd go sulk where she wasn't supposed to trespass because of the secret project he was working on for her. How damned convenient. Women did *not* have the market cornered on the "retreat and pout" method of avoiding confrontation, despite popular rumor.

Watching him dress, she crossed her arms over her breasts, trying not to feel insulted by his not giving her credit to think for herself. He was young, she reminded herself, and inexperienced not only with sex but more important, with the deeper emotions brought about by intimacy.

And she'd lay money he was still smarting over the encounter with Tony—if that was the creep's name. Zack had probably stewed all afternoon, worked himself into a frenzy. She'd happened to catch the brunt of the most basic male reaction.

A supremely pissed man marking his territory.

She sure wasn't complaining. Her lover had some seriously sexy moves, whatever the catalyst. However, she refrained from giving him an analysis of his motivations, figuring he wouldn't appreciate it right now.

He jammed his feet into his sneakers, pushed on his glasses, and grabbed his jacket off the back of a chair. "I'll be back in a bit, okay?"

"Sure."

At least he stopped to plant a gentle kiss on her lips before disappearing out the door. The man was a roiling ocean of turmoil. He had yet to reveal what he'd promised to talk about when she got home, and this mysterious subject obviously was part of the problem, as well.

Battling dejection, she retrieved her bottled water from the floor, padded to her own bathroom, and took a quick shower. Afterward, she felt marginally refreshed and optimistic. Zack would spill his guts when he returned and when he did, he'd feel so much lighter. They'd deal with whatever was bothering him and everything would be fine.

She pulled on a pair of gray sweats and a clingy white baby-doll T-shirt, and went downstairs in search of something a tad stronger than water. A bottle of chardonnay squatted on the shelf behind the milk, just waiting to take the edge off a day like this one.

Five minutes later, Cori was sipping a cool glass of wine and swaying to Norah Jones drifting from the stereo in the living room, when the doorbell rang. Frowning, she used the remote to turn down the volume, and went to look through the peephole.

Her hackles went straight up, every female cell in her

body on the defense as she opened the door to greet her visitor.

"Hey," she said warily. "This is a surprise."

Zack lost himself in the tactile pleasure of cutting the treated boards, the deafening whine of his table saw. The pungent smell of raw wood, the satisfaction that he was creating something to last for decades.

For Cori.

Why did he have to lose control like that? He'd screwed up. He knew no woman could fake such intense passion, knew she'd loved the hell out of his taking charge. But who was the guy who'd fucked her senseless against the bathroom wall? Problem was, he had no clue.

This shit was all new to him. The intense feelings, sharing, developing a relationship.

Falling in love.

Insane jealousy.

The fear that he wasn't good enough for Cori, and never would be.

He didn't know himself. Today, he hated the emotions scraping him bloody inside. The sooner he told her the truth, the better. Hell, she might not even believe what he told her about Joaquin. Might go so far as to throw him out. He'd be alone, like before—

No, he corrected himself. Much worse than before. Because he'd tasted what it meant to belong to a woman, for her to belong to him. He'd felt the first stirrings of real hope he'd ever had in his life that *maybe* someone might love him in return.

Made no difference. He had no right to postpone their talk any longer.

He tripped the OFF switch with his foot. His earplugs

filtered the worst of the noise, and with the machine winding down, he couldn't hear a thing. Pushing his safety goggles on top of his head, he inspected his work, then laid the board aside.

Without warning, a prickle teased the back of his neck. The weird sensation of another presence. Close. Turning, he caught movement from the corner of his eye.

Just as a two-by-four swung toward his face. Pain detonated in his skull and his knees buckled. He hit the concrete floor, tasted sawdust in his mouth. Blood.

Cori! God, neither of them had anticipated an attack in broad daylight. He had to stay conscious. Had to get up and stop this bastard . . . With an effort born of desperation, he pushed to his hands and knees.

Another blow to his head shattered his hold on consciousness, spun him into darkness. He was vaguely aware of shuffling footsteps. A strange hissing noise.

And then the light in his brain winked out.

Lionel stood panting, glaring down at the prone man on the shop floor. Not dead, but Knight would be in minutes. Shit, if he'd known killing would give him such a hard-on, he'd have done it years ago.

How to finish him? He glanced to the saw and thought it might be poetic to cut Knight's throat with his own blades. But that was messy and he didn't want to be covered in blood when he left. Same reason he didn't use his gun—taking a man out with a rifle and a scope was different from walking up, shooting him in the head, and getting his brains all over you.

Casting about, his attention fell on the ancient gas heater on the floor a few feet away. Cheery flames danced inside, warding off the chill in the shop.

Perfect. After the shooting, the authorities would question whether Knight's death was an accident, but what could they prove? For all they knew, he'd become dizzy, hit his head, and fallen unconscious, succumbing to his fate.

Lionel performed his task, smiling. Hurrying, he exited the shop and peered around the corner, toward the house.

"What the fuck?"

Impotent rage blinded him, boiled in his veins. The slut had a visitor! He could try to jump them, but he had no idea how many people had arrived or whether they were male or female. Sonofabitch! He'd have to wait until the guests left, or come back later.

He looked back at Knight and some of the anger calmed. At least he'd removed this obstacle.

One down, one to go.

Cori showed Eve Marshall into the living room, instantly on guard but determined to be polite to Zack's friend. From the woman's stiff posture and combatant, pale gaze, Cori knew she hadn't been imagining the chill in Eve's attitude toward her since they'd met.

Not a comforting realization. Cori instinctively knew this woman would make anyone a formidable enemy—or the most loyal friend. There was a confidence in her stride, a proud tilt to her head, and a glitter in that odd gaze hinting Eve had fought tooth and nail for every good thing in her life. And to keep them, she'd gladly kick ass and take names again.

Cori faced Eve, wishing the woman didn't look so damned *together*, her trim, athletic build flattered by dark jeans, snazzy boots, and a black leather blazer. Dark, curly hair with reddish highlights framed her striking, bronzed face and tumbled unbound to her shoulders.

"This is a nice surprise," Cori said in a friendly tone. "Can I get you a glass of wine?"

"No, thanks. I'm not staying long." Eve's hand clutched her purse strap in a death grip, betraying her agitation.

Oh, boy. Whatever this is about, it's just what I needed today. "In that case, I'll call Zack in from the shop. I know he'll be thrilled to see you." She turned to go, but Eve's flat voice halted her.

"Actually, I'm glad he's busy. I'd like to speak with you first."

Bristling, Cori faced Eve, setting her glass of wine on the coffee table. "Sounds dire. Look, if this is about the shooting, I don't know what to say to make you feel more comfortable about Zack's safety—"

"That's not why I'm here. I'm worried about the attempt, of course, but I'm also concerned about his mental well-being." Eve took a step closer, eyes narrowing. "Zack has a big heart and if you broke it, sister, I'd take that personally."

Cori crossed her arms over her chest, anger starting to bubble. "So you do have feelings for him. Well, I'm sorry he doesn't reciprocate them, but that doesn't give you the right to barge in here and make ultimatums."

Eve laughed, not a happy sound. "I don't have a thing for Zack, not like you mean. He's my best friend, my *brother*. We look out for each other, and that includes serving notice if I think he's being taken for a ride."

Cori stared at her. "Am I supposed to decipher that? If you're making an accusation, then come out with it."

"You really don't know," she mused, frowning. "Zack still hasn't told you."

"Told me *what*? I have no idea what you're talking about." She gestured in the air with frustration. "We've done nothing but support each other from the day we met! He's a wonderful man, and I don't care that he's fallen on financial hard times."

"Really? Even if *you're* the one responsible?" Eve fired back harshly, vibrating with outrage.

Cori's mouth fell open. Clearly, the woman had lost it. "That's completely ridiculous. Since I met Zack, he hasn't had a penny for me to take." Shoot, that sounded awful when she'd only been trying to defend herself, but Eve interrupted before she could explain.

"Of course he didn't," Eve hissed, advancing on her. "You've got every damned thing he loved in the palm of your hand! Take a good look around you—tell me what you see."

"I don't . . ." A suspicion began to form. One too horrible to be true.

Eve stopped less than a foot away, well inside her personal space. "Sure, you do. You're a smart lady. Work it out."

A series of recollections flooded her mind, unwelcome.

Zack, his temper exploding in the hospital, the phone in pieces.

Standing in the foyer when he first arrived here. Pale and shell-shocked.

How he'd known where items in the kitchen were located without being told.

His slip at the dinner table, almost calling the shop his.

The shop he obviously loved and knew his way around very well.

"No," Cori whispered. "Zack would've said something to me."

"And what exactly should he have told you? That while he was living off peanut butter, you were happily nesting in the house he'd labored with his own two hands to make into a home?"

The blood left her head in a dizzying rush, and she clapped her hand over her mouth. No wonder Zack wouldn't talk to her. He'd been protecting her—again. And she'd raked him over the coals for his trouble. "I . . . It can't be true."

"Zack has serious class, always thinking of others before himself. He didn't want any of us to know. But you—" Eve jabbed a finger at the center of Cori's chest. "I have difficulty believing you had no idea this was Zack's home when you purchased it. How could you *not* know?"

"I didn't have any idea," she insisted, shaking her head. "The house was a gift from my brother. . . . Oh, no."

Eve's dark brows furrowed. "What?"

Oh, sweet heaven. In an instant, she understood. The nice, tidy world she thought she'd created was now turned upside down, tainted by her brother's cruel manipulations.

But that was nothing compared with what he'd done to Zack.

The shame was almost beyond bearing. "My brother did this to him. Zack must've ended up owing him money, but how? Joaquin lives outside Atlantic City and he's only visited me twice since I moved to Sugarland. How would they have met?"

"So, you honestly don't know what the hell happened?" she pressed.

"Of course not! I—I care for Zack a great deal, and I'd

never intentionally hurt him. Believe whatever you want, but I'm telling the truth."

Eve paused, then nodded. "All right. Zack insisted you had no part in whatever trouble he's in, but I had to hear it from you."

"You believe me?"

"I do," she said, the ice thawing. "I know sincerity when I hear it. We're just all stumped by how an intelligent man like Zack got into such a bad fix."

"I propose we get some answers. He's struggled alone with this long enough, don't you agree?"

"Absolutely. He's going to give us some answers whether he wants to or not." Reaching out, she squeezed Cori's hand. "For what it's worth, I apologize. When it comes to people I care about, I tend to go overboard, and Zack's special. We're cool?"

Cori smiled. "Yes, he is. And we're cool."

I'm going to cut off Joaquin's highly valued testicles. He's going to scream like a little girl for what he's done.

They headed outside together, and Eve wasted no time getting right to the point. "You love Zack."

"I'm not very good at hiding my emotions, am I?"

"No more than I am."

"Not at all, then." They shared a quiet laugh, and Cori decided to probe a bit. "What about you? Got a terrific man in your life?"

Eve's face grew pensive. Wistful. "Hardly. I tend to make rotten choices. Divorced the first one after I caught him screwing one of my good friends. The second is nursing his own broken heart and doesn't know I exist—as a woman anyway."

"I'm sorry. I didn't mean to pry."

"No, it's fine. I sort of brought up the subject."

Cori sympathized with her pain. Nobody knew about poor choices better than she did.

They reached the shop and Cori halted outside the door, which was open the barest crack. "He made me promise to knock," she explained. "He's working on a surprise for me."

"Oh? The boy's got it bad, huh?"

Cori grinned. "I hope so." Raising a fist, she rapped on the door. "Hey, Zack? Eve's here. Can we come in?"

They stood for a few seconds, but no response drifted from inside. There was only the rustle of the breeze in the bare branches nearby. No shrill racket from his saw, hammering, or grinding of the tool he called a planer.

"Zack, we've got company!"

All was silent. A strange expression settled on Eve's face. "What's that smell?"

She sniffed the air. "I don't—wait. Is that . . . gas?"

With a vicious curse, Eve burst through the entrance to the shop, slamming the door hard against the inside wall. Cori rushed in on her heels, overwhelmed by the noxious odor of gas hanging in the shop. Thick and deadly.

"Zack!" Cori yelled.

"Over here!"

Eve rounded a table saw and squatted between the large piece of machinery and the workbench. Cori skidded to a halt behind her, gasping at the sight of Zack lying prone on the floor. Blood trickled from under his hairline, down his left temple, and across his nose.

She dropped to kneel beside him, shaking his shoulder. "Oh, my God! Honey, wake up." He didn't move.

"Help me get him outside." Eve rolled him onto his back, grabbed him in a hold under his arms. "Get his feet."

Cori lifted him by the ankles and together they maneuvered him toward the door. The fumes were awful, already making her and Eve cough. Terror gripped her lungs. How long had Zack been lying there, helpless?

They carried him a safe distance from the shop before lowering him gently to the grass in front of the house. Cori marveled at the upper-body strength required for a female firefighter to be able to rescue a man Zack's size, and thanked God the woman had stopped by this afternoon. If she hadn't—

"He's breathing, but his pulse is too slow and his color isn't good," Eve said urgently. She glanced at Cori. "Call 911 while I run and turn off the gas."

Cori bolted inside, heart in her mouth, grabbed the phone, and punched in the numbers without breaking stride as she hurried back outside. The dispatcher's calm tone did little to soothe Cori's fear as she related the pertinent information. She cupped Zack's chalk white cheek, trailed a finger over his blue lips. His inky lashes didn't so much as flutter.

Cori hung up with the assurance that the paramedics were en route. "Don't you die on me," she ordered him, voice breaking. "Don't you dare."

She laid a hand on his chest, relieved to find his heartbeat a slow, steady thud under her palm. Pushing the panic down, she reached for her nurse's training. The rational part of her brain knew he should revive after breathing fresh air—if it weren't for the head injury, which was now the main concern. His hair was slick and wet with blood, and he lay far too still.

Eve returned, dropping to kneel beside Zack. "Gas is off."

"The paramedics are on the way." Cori gently parted

the short strands of Zack's hair, trying to get a better look at the wound, but there was too much blood. She sat up, frustrated, wiping her fingers in the grass. "I don't believe this was an accident."

"Me, either. Even if he lost consciousness from the gas, I don't see how he'd have hit his head at the temple."

Cori nodded, feeling sick. "I agree. Nobody would turn their head directly to the side as they fell, especially if they were dizzy."

Another attack. Five more minutes and Zack would've been dead. Eve's stopping by saved not only Zack's life, but her own, as well. Whoever had done this wanted her new lover removed in order to get to her.

Why? For the money she'd inherited? Revenge? Or had she picked up a deranged admirer who believed Zack was usurping his place?

Another idea occurred to her, more frightening than the others. What if the attacks on Zack had nothing to do with her stalker? Oh, God, what if Joaquin was behind the attempts on Zack's life? Maybe he'd learned the man who owed him money was living with his sister.

Would Joaquin kill Zack with so little provocation? She'd like to think not, that she knew her brother.

But she also knew the extremes a human being would go to when pushed too far.

Zack stirred, turning his head with a moan. A beautiful sound. His lashes swept up and he blinked, quickly closing his eyes again as a strangled rasp emerged from his throat.

"Too bright . . . Christ, my head."

Cori took his hand, cautious relief making her limbs so weak she was glad to be kneeling. "You're going to be fine, honey. Try to stay awake, all right?"

"Okay."

"Zack, do you remember what happened?" Eve asked.

"Hmm?"

"Your head, sweetie," Cori prompted. "How did you hit it?"

"Don't know," he whispered. "Where . . . ?"

"You're outside. Eve and I carried you from the shop after we found you unconscious. Do you remember feeling dizzy?" Cori doubted he'd recall much at this point, but keeping him conscious was important.

"Dizzy?"

She and Eve exchanged a worried look. His brains were scrambled eggs. "Zack, open your eyes and look at me," Cori said. "Can you do that?"

He blinked up at her, groaning miserably. Cori pried open one of his eyelids, peered into the eyes, and frowned. "His pupils are dilated."

"Concussion," Eve put in.

"Yeah, a nasty one." She sat back on her heels, studying him. "But his color's returning."

"Thank God. You hear that, old friend? You'll be chasing Cori around the house again in no time." She nudged his shoulder. "Zack?"

He'd lapsed into unconsciousness once more. Cori gazed at the nearly healed bruises from the blow to his face less than two weeks ago, and her stomach pitched. "He got lucky before, and another head injury scares me, even if it is on the opposite side."

"He'll be fine." But Eve's voice betrayed her fear and echoed Cori's own.

Twice he had been attacked, and survived.

Cori couldn't shake the feeling that the third time he might not be so lucky.

14

Zack squeezed his eyes shut, wishing the bed would stop rolling like a ship on a stormy sea. The noises and chatter from the ER outside his cubicle sounded canned and distorted, like a program on an old television set. Nausea had run his stomach through a blender, and sickness clawed at the back of his throat. He lay as still as possible, willing himself not to vomit again. If he did, they'd keep him overnight, regardless of whether his CAT scan came back clear.

A soft rustle alerted him to someone entering the room. He sensed Cori before she spoke, felt their connection. The woman he loved.

And had failed.

"Zack, are you awake?"

He turned his head toward her, the slight movement spearing his brain with waves of agony. "Not by choice," he rasped.

"I know," she murmured. Cool fingers smoothed his brow. "Your scan showed a concussion, but no serious brain injury. The doctor is leaning toward letting you go home. Are you still sick at your stomach? Dizzy?"

"If I say yes, do I have to stay?"

"Doesn't work that way, handsome. Be honest."

He sighed. "I feel just like I did when I rode the Tilt-A-Whirl at the state fair right after eating four corn dogs."

"I asked, didn't I? Give me some warning and I'll grab the container," she said, indicating a graduated cylinder on the table.

He remembered getting sick in the ambulance—on one of his colleagues, no less—and felt too awful to be embarrassed about it. As a paramedic, he'd done his best to ease his patients' suffering, and he was glad. These past two weeks had taught him a valuable lesson.

Being the patient sucked.

A new voice disturbed the silence. "Is he up to talking with the detective yet?"

Feminine. Cori's friend. What was her name?

Shea. The cutie with curly brown hair, sweet little thing. She'd been taking good care of him. Almost as good as Cori.

"Send him in," he said. "Let's get it over with."

Cori laid a hand on his arm. "Want me to stay?"

"Please."

"You got it."

Detective Bernie peppered him with the expected questions, though there wasn't much for Zack to tell him. He'd sensed an odd prickle on the back of his neck and turned to see a board swinging toward his head. Then lights out, period. Seemed like they weren't any closer to a break. Until Bernie cocked his head and dropped his bombshell.

"Checked into the fellow you called me about earlier today, Tony Banning."

"You didn't say anything to me," Cori muttered, shifting in her chair.

"I didn't have a chance." Zack tried to focus on the detective, no easy feat with his brains about to spill out his ears. "What did you learn?"

"Seems no artist named Tony Banning has ever had a showing at any of the reputable galleries in Nashville, at least not that I could find. In fact, there's no Tony Banning matching his description who's registered with a driver's license in the state of Tennessee." The detective paused, looking very pleased with himself, as if he'd been the one to sniff out Banning in the first place. He arched a grizzled brow at Cori.

"Your peacock artist friend is an impostor."

Sipping a mug of rich coffee, Cori paused in the doorway to her bedroom and watched Zack sleep. *Our bedroom*, she corrected herself. She hoped he felt the same.

Especially since, for all practical purposes, she'd taken it from him. However unknowingly. Guilt knifed her breast and she pushed the unwelcome emotion aside to deal with later. Much later.

Her lover was sprawled on his stomach, hugging his pillow, drawstring pajamas slung low on his hips. The cotton material contoured the firm globes of his ass, proving he wore nothing underneath and elevating the plain sleepwear to super-sexy status in her eyes.

His black hair was tousled, spiking in every direction like an endearing little boy's. However, the bunch of his biceps and the smooth expanse of his back, the indention of his spine leading to the curve of his rear and his mile-long legs, were all man.

Suddenly he stretched like a lean cat and rolled to his back, a low rumble sounding in his chest. His blue eyes found her and he held out a hand in a silent invitation she couldn't refuse. She joined him, placing her mug on the nightstand and sitting carefully at his side.

"Hey, beautiful," he rasped, taking her hand and kissing each finger.

"Hey, yourself. Stupid question, but how do you feel?"

Reaching up, he gingerly touched his head. "Sore, but the headache's better."

She brushed his hand away and felt the swollen area for herself. "Liar. The two whacks you sustained are one big knot and your pupils are still enlarged. Want to try again?"

"The hazards of living with a nurse," he complained, the softness in his expression belying his words. "I won't run any laps today, for sure."

"News flash, you're going to be mostly horizontal for a couple of days. Don't even try to argue with me, or you'll be sorry."

"Yes, ma'am." He stroked her arm, sending shivers along her skin. "Why aren't you in class?"

"Today's Saturday, sugar lump."

"Oh. Damn, my brain is mush." He frowned. "You missed another dancing gig last night because of me."

"No, because of the bastard who almost killed you." She shook her head. "I don't care about the dancing. You're the most important person in my life, Zack. Everyone else can wait."

He stared at her, suspicious moisture shining in his eyes. "How do you do that?"

"What?"

"Make me feel like the luckiest guy who ever lived?"

Another wave of remorse battered her conscience, filled her mouth like bitter acid. The secrets had gone on long enough. "I don't know how you can possibly feel anything except anger and contempt around me."

He looked startled. "What do you mean?"

"You know," she said quietly, caressing his dear face with her knuckles. "Tell me how Joaquin managed to wrest your home from you, and don't spare me the details."

Zack was grateful to be lying down. *God, no.* The bottom dropped out of his stomach and the room spun. This was a certified nightmare, worse than losing his possessions in the first place. The hurt on Cori's face. The terrible, misplaced guilt on her part he'd been praying to avoid.

What could he say? "Who told you? Six-Pack?" Immediately, he dismissed the notion. The lieutenant would never have broken his confidence. Eve, with her no-bullshit attitude and fiercely protective nature, was the more likely candidate.

"Doesn't matter. The point is, *you* should have."

"Oh, right. I was really going to dump your brother's role in my problems on you after the heartwarming family portrait you painted at dinner the other night."

"What *is* his role? How did the two of you meet?"

"We didn't. I should back up." Zack pushed to a sitting position, ignoring the stab of pain in his skull. This wasn't a conversation he wanted to have at all, much less lying down.

"My father was a compulsive gambler, an addict. As a kid, I didn't understand why we'd eat steak one week, beans and franks the next. His horrible mood swings, why his criticism of me would change from bearable to a blade cutting me to the bone in a flash."

"He used you as a whipping boy for his own failings."

"I'd figured out that much by around age thirteen, just not why. I thought there must've been something wrong with me and if I could fix it, he'd love me the way other fathers did their sons. By the time I graduated high school, I'd learned nothing I ever did would please him and I'd gotten wise to his gambling addiction. I came to terms with the knowledge I'd never be able to fix either of those things, and followed my own path. I moved on, and he resented the hell out of it."

"Oh, Zack."

He tilted her chin up with one finger. "No sad faces. Remember what I told you about kismet? If you're honest and true to your vision, life works out the way it's supposed to."

Tears welled in her amber eyes. "I'm amazed you have such a great attitude after everything you've been through."

"Actually, I was ready to throw in the towel, but a special lady reminded me how fortunate I am," he said softly. The droplets spilled down her cheeks and he brushed them away with his thumbs. "Hey, what's with the waterworks? This story has a happy ending, right?"

"But you lost everything." She sniffed, leaning into his touch.

"I gained so much more than I lost, baby." He pulled her into the circle of his arms, relishing her warmth snuggled against him. "Besides, haven't you learned material things can't truly satisfy a person deep inside?"

She hugged him hard and he felt her sigh against his neck. "You're right. I just wish my family wasn't responsible for what happened to you."

He pulled back and shook his head. "My father deserves that rap. He owed your brother three-quarters of a million dollars in gambling debts. After he had the stroke last year, Joaquin eventually discovered his condition would never improve and came after *me* for the money."

"So you sold him your home," she whispered, her expression stricken.

"For one dollar. Emptied my savings, too." No use withholding the truth. "I haven't made a dent in the debt and don't have another dime to pay Joaquin, but he seems to believe otherwise, and he's very persistent."

Her lips thinned, anger bubbling to the surface. "You don't owe him the money, Zack. He can't legally make you pay."

He smiled at her naïveté. "You fled Joaquin's household at the first opportunity, remember? What part of 'fight fair' do you think he employed in regard to recovering a serious chunk of change? He didn't ask nicely or threaten to sic his lawyers on me, honey."

Cori faltered. "Wh-what did he threaten?"

His chest tightened and his head swam. God, he hated this. "My life, more than once. Oh, he was careful to keep his meaning subtle, but crystal clear. I went to the authorities, who basically shrugged because the debt is legal and Joaquin hadn't followed through with breaking me in half. Ironic, huh? Like a dead man can file a complaint. When I'd given your brother all I had, he began making comments about my father being helpless and unprotected in his nursing home."

"Oh, God." She hung her head, silent for a long moment. When she met his gaze again, she sat up straighter. "The terror tactics Joaquin used to recover his money were despicable, but as cold as he is, my brother would never resort to murder. I know him, and even he wouldn't cross that line."

"Joaquin killed your husband," he reminded her gently. "You told me yourself."

Cori's face leached to parchment white. "That was a split-second decision, a matter of life or death—mine versus my husband's."

"But he *did* kill." Her lips worked, but no sound emerged. He'd never seen such stark, haunted desolation on anyone's face, and his heart lurched. "I'm so sorry. I don't mean to cause you pain. I was only trying to point out how out of my depth I am with a man like your brother. I don't know how to fight by his rules, and I'm . . . tired, sweetheart."

Ready to explode, in truth. If she had any clue how close to the edge he was, how fed up with being ground under yet another bastard's shoe, how his blood boiled with the need to vent his rage once and for all . . . hell, she'd run from him faster and farther than she had Joaquin.

She thought him gentle and kind. Her protector. What a joke. He wasn't the man she'd placed on a pedestal, and the knowledge frightened him.

"I'll call my brother," she said, breaking into his dark thoughts. "I'll make him leave you alone and if he doesn't—"

"No, you absolutely won't." He winced at his harsh tone.

She scowled at him. "Why not? I can have this settled and put behind us in two minutes!"

"Then why don't I just let you castrate me with a butter knife, too? I can handle your brother myself."

"Nice, fireboy." She huffed a short, pissed-off laugh. "Real nice. Yeah, from where I'm sitting, you've done a lovely job of *handling* him so far."

"Goddammit—"

"Curse at me and I'll demonstrate all the ways a nurse can make you scream besides slicing off your balls." Pushing out of his arms, she slid off the bed and stood glaring down at him. "Men are stupid."

With that accurate assessment, she stalked from the room. Fan-fucking-tastic. He'd hurt her feelings because his ego wouldn't let her run interference.

Unreasonable panic seized his lungs. An awful feeling, almost a premonition, of living on borrowed time. That every second counted and he shouldn't waste a single one arguing with Cori. He needed her in his arms, completing the lost half of his soul.

Zack leapt from the bed and was instantly rewarded with waves of nausea twisting his gut, agony spearing his head. Black spots peppered his vision and began to spread like an ink stain. The floor rocked under his bare feet and his knees buckled.

"Oh, no!" Capable hands turned him onto his back, patted his cheek. "What on earth were you trying to do?"

Blinking, he tried to focus on Cori's face as the dark, fuzzy veil lifted from his own. "I'm sorry," he said hoarsely. "You offered to help and I acted like a prick."

"Jeez, you're almost as impossible as me. Let's get you back into bed."

She steadied him as he pushed up, wobbled a couple of steps, and collapsed onto the mattress with a moan. Resuming her place at his side, she rubbed circles on his chest. Felt damned good.

"Still mad at me?" he ventured, peering at her.

"I'm not angry with you, just frustrated in general. I hate arguing and I'm sorry I got pissy. I'd like to give Joaquin a knot to match yours, though."

"I wouldn't argue there."

"You know, I'd considered he might be behind the attacks on you," she said thoughtfully. "I wondered if he'd try to frighten me into going home and seeking sanctuary in his protection, putting me effectively under his control again. But this isn't his style, Zack. If he ever did come after you physically, he'd be up-front about it. Totally in-your-face. Same with me."

"Yeah, I get the same impression. Which leaves us with your fake artist as a weak suspect and no frigging motive."

"Um, not exactly." Flushing, she dropped her gaze.

"What? The suspect or the motive?"

"The motive. Although it probably isn't related—"

"Corrine." Dammit, this must be bad for her to have kept it from him and the police.

"I sort of . . . inherited a lot of money when my husband died."

"Shit." He swiped a hand down his face. "How much?"

"Fifty million," she whispered.

He bolted upright in shock, causing a fresh onslaught of sickness. "Son of a fucking bitch! And you didn't believe this was important enough to mention?"

Her mouth trembled. "Don't yell at me."

"I'm not yelling!" Okay, he was. *Calm down; you're upsetting her.* But fuckin' A, he was rattled. Taking a deep breath, he closed his fingers around hers, forcing the return of his sanity. "Baby, why would you hide a huge detail like that from the cops?"

From me, he wanted to say, but her financial status was none of his business. He might be many things, but a hypocrite wasn't one of them. Her safety was, however, his primary concern. He absolutely would not negotiate that point.

"Cops ask questions. They dig into matters that aren't their business."

"And sometimes the digging produces the bad guy."

"In a pitifully low percentage of cases, yes."

He frowned. "What are you afraid they'll discover?"

"That the money is dirty, maybe," she said quietly. "I was stunned when the lawyer read his will. There's no way Alex earned millions doing honest work. Why do you think I danced to finish my schooling, accepted Joaquin's so-called gift when he gave me your house? I want no part of money my husband lied and cheated to acquire."

"I admire your integrity, beautiful. If the wealth bothers you, why not get rid of it?" Whether it was ill-gotten or not, a tiny part of him shrieked in protest at the suggestion.

"I do, in a sense. I have charities I donate to each year. I figured it may as well do some good for people in need."

"That's certainly better than the cash disappearing into a black hole if the government seized it," he agreed. "I'm proud of you, beautiful. What concerns me is who else knows you have the money."

"Nobody except my brothers, and they wouldn't tell."

Given his conflict with Joaquin, Zack wasn't so sure, but thought it wise to keep his trap shut. Instead, he asked, "Where's the money?"

"Switzerland. I have a numbered account with all sorts of high-tech safeguards. Paranoid, huh?"

"Cautious. You're a rich woman, baby. Many would go to great extremes to take what's yours." Another idea occurred to him. "What about your ex's family? Any sour grapes over you inheriting?"

She shrugged. "He didn't talk about his family much

and nobody came out of the woodwork to challenge his will. I was his sole beneficiary."

Zack didn't know why this should bother him, but it did. No one stepping forward had to be good, right?

But it wasn't. He didn't like it, for no reason except the weird vibe singing in his veins, the tension in his shoulders. *Someone* should've vehemently protested the man's young wife ending up a millionaire.

Perhaps that someone hadn't wanted to tip his hand too soon. Cori's nemesis had preferred to wait, bide his time.

And found Zack standing squarely between him and the big payoff.

"Should I call Joaquin in on this, give him the whole story?" Cori didn't look happy with her own suggestion.

Neither was he, but for entirely different reasons. Whom did they dare trust with their lives?

"Not yet. But there's something else he can do, if you'll ask him for a discreet favor. Have him dig for Tony Banning's real identity."

Her brows shot up. "Sure, I'll just tell him my creepy pursuer is an impostor and he'll obediently stay home and out of my business while investigating the man."

"Right. That's why you'll lie and tell him Banning is after your friend Shea. You're very worried about her."

She laughed. "You have a devious mind under your gentlemanly exterior, handsome."

"When the occasion warrants."

"It's also a brilliant mind, which reminds me that you could use your genius noodle to hack into wanted-criminal databases or whatever and ferret out Banning yourself," she said thoughtfully.

"I could, but not without landing the FBI on your doorstep. They won't be as forgiving of a federal offense as they were when I was a kid. Your brother, however, can pull strings, circumvent authority without raising an alarm."

"Good point." She sighed in resignation. "I'll give him a call about Banning, if you're sure."

Christ, the traits he loathed most about Joaquin Delacruz might well be the ones that saved their asses now—or quite the opposite. *God, please let me be making the right decisions.*

If Delacruz was behind everything, Zack had just sealed their fates.

"No, beautiful. I'm not sure of anything . . . except you."

15

Zack walked through the big, open garage door of the bay, pulse thrumming a tattoo in his throat. Nervous excitement supercharged his body, spring-loading his muscles. Restless energy flooded every limb, demanding an outlet, but his steps slowed instead.

Swallowing hard, he stopped next to the driver's door of Engine 171. Ran his hand lovingly over the gleaming red paint, the gold Sugarland Fire Department logo. Savored the moment.

This was his home away from home. He had been born to this life, and had nearly lost it forever. Still might lose it if he and the captain couldn't mend fences. He couldn't envision starting over at another station, perhaps in a different city. Station Five was where he belonged, the guys here his brothers in the truest sense.

"Hey, dude! 'Bout time you frickin' deigned to haul your sorry ass back here!"

Grinning, Zack spun around just in time to be slammed by Tommy Skyler, who yanked him into an enthusiastic bear hug and slapped his back hard enough to sting. Zack returned the embrace, laughing, thinking the kid reminded him of an overeager Labrador puppy with the biggest wide-open heart of anyone he'd ever known.

"He wasn't on vacation, numb nuts." This from Six-Pack, who was trailed by Eve, Salvatore, and Tanner. "Good to have you in commission again, bro. Three weeks is a long damned time."

"Seems a helluva lot longer." Because of the nasty concussion, his return had been postponed by another week, their gathering at the Waterin' Hole rescheduled for Saturday night. He'd missed half of January and the first week of February.

Skyler released him and the others followed suit with the same exuberant greeting, practically squeezing him in half. Even Salvatore joined in the celebration. Everyone did, except Tanner.

The captain stood apart from the rest, his green gaze watchful, revealing none of his thoughts. After the others had taken turns welcoming Zack, their attention naturally shifted to Tanner. Waiting.

The happy chatter quieted as the captain stepped into the semicircle of the group. Halting a few feet from Zack, he reached inside his jacket, removed a key ring, and tossed it to him without a word.

Zack caught the ring one-handed, snatching it from the air. Opening his palm, he stared at the keys to the quint. Emotion stole his voice and he willed himself not to make a scene in front of the whole team.

Closing the remaining distance, Tanner slowly stuck out his hand. A peace offering, a new beginning.

Zack hesitated and for an instant, remorse flashed across the captain's stern features. A kernel of humanity as he stood exposed and humbled before his team. Extending his apology the only way he knew how.

Zack gripped his hand, noting the slight relaxing of the lines around Tanner's mouth. A lessening of tension and something suspiciously close to warmth in his eyes.

"It's good to have you back," he said.

And proceeded to render everyone speechless by pulling Zack into a brief, manly hug. The man who hadn't reached out to another soul in more than a year did so now without a single qualm.

"Thanks, Cap. I'm ready to get to work."

Tanner let go and retreated a step, giving Zack a critical once-over. "Good, you've put on some weight. Lungs clear? Concussion healed?"

Zack smiled. "I'm fine. The doctor gave me the green light, remember?"

"The doctor's life doesn't literally depend on the physical strength of the man standing next to him." His lips curved up in a rare ghost of a smile. "For what it's worth, we're all damned glad to have you standing next to us."

After clapping Zack on the shoulder, he turned and walked off, his lean-hipped stride carrying him inside.

"He looks better," Zack said. "Almost like his old self."

"Some days," Skyler replied, unusually serious. "But I gotta wonder if we'll ever have him back."

"Is he still drinking, Howard?" Zack asked quietly. All eyes swung to the lieutenant for the answer any one of them could've given, but he was their anchor. Solid and steady. They trusted him implicitly, looked to him for guidance in matters affecting everyone.

"Yeah." He sighed, running a hand through his spiky, two-toned brown hair. "He's mixing whiskey and prescription drugs, going through a fifth every two days we're off shift. I check on him when I can, but it's not enough. Something has to give or he's going to kill himself."

"Or someone else," Eve said, her expression wretched.

Salvatore broke his silence tentatively, as though unsure he should offer his observation. "Lately, I've noticed . . ."

Six-Pack nodded. "Go on. We're not talking trash about Sean. This is important."

"Watch his hands," Salvatore murmured. "They'll be shaking by midafternoon."

The lieutenant blew out a ragged breath. "Withdrawal. Shit. If he shows at the Waterin' Hole Saturday night, we'll have to keep an eye on him."

Skyler blinked. "Shit, he'll bash our heads together for getting in his biz. What can we really do?"

"Stage an intervention," Zack suggested. "Tough love. Encourage him to get sober, then work through his grief."

"Man, I don't see him going for that," Salvatore put in, shaking his head.

Zack glanced around the worried group. "Maybe not, but what other option does he have? If he doesn't, he's going to die. Howard?"

The lieutenant stood quiet for a long moment, staring out at the cold, cloudy morning. Muscles in his jaw working, brown eyes bleak. "I'll make some calls, find out the right way to hold an intervention. Then we'll pick a day next week and do it. I don't think he's got long before he hits bottom."

"I'll be there," Zack said, hoping it was true. *Provided I haven't been iced by Joaquin's hit man by then.* Despite Cori's adamant claim, he didn't believe for a minute the man wouldn't take him out if it benefited him to do so. Jesus.

The others chimed in their agreement just as three loud tones over the intercom system alerted them to an incoming call. A three-alarm fire at an apartment building had begun as a domestic dispute—two words heralding the most dangerous of situations for all involved.

Adrenaline zinged through Zack's blood as he and the others jogged for the locker area in the bay. With quick and efficient movements, he bunked out in his pants and heavy coat, the same ones he'd been wearing on the bridge. They'd been cleaned and bore no trace of his ordeal, and to his relief, their familiar weight was a comfort rather than a source of unreasonable fear. Last, he slapped on a fire hat that replaced the one lost to the river, and sprinted for the quint.

Hauling himself into the seat, he started the engine and gripped the wheel. Waited as everyone took their places, then eased the quint out of the bay, hitting the lights and sirens. God, he'd missed this. Not people's lives being placed in danger—*never* that—but commanding the two-ton piece of machinery. Fulfilling his role in the universe as few were qualified to do, each day a new challenge.

Today being no exception. As Zack neared the perimeter of the police barricade at the end of a residential street, saw the carpet of flashing lights and the SWAT team taking up positions around the complex, his blood chilled.

Beside him, Tanner muttered a terse, "What the fuck?"

Yeah, that pretty much summed up the circus. Black smoke billowed from the second floor of the building, which meant residents possibly trapped on the upper floor. Yet the police weren't allowing the fire department to approach, as evidenced by the engine company from Station Two crouched on the north side of the building, taking cover behind their vehicles.

Zack slowed to a stop and rolled down his window to get instructions from an officer working the barricade. "What's going down?"

The burly cop leaned forward, hand on the butt of his pistol. "Got a man on his second-floor balcony over there holding a gun to his wife's head. Motherfucker set fire to the unit, blocked entry to the apartment. The flames are spreading to the surrounding units, but it's not safe to approach. Got folks trapped on the third floor; fire's blocking the stairwell. Can't get to them because the asshole's shooting at everyone who twitches."

"A total clusterfuck," Skyler groaned from the back.

Zack couldn't agree more. "Where do you want us?"

The cop waved a hand toward the company from Station Two. "North end, with them. Stay low until you get the all clear."

"No shit," Zack muttered as he drove toward their colleagues. He parked behind the other engine, and Six-Pack wheeled their ambulance in beside the first. Everyone bailed out and Tanner stalked over to speak with Captain Lance Holliday.

The normally easygoing Holliday appeared supremely hacked as he greeted Tanner, raking his fingers through his thick auburn hair, jaw clenched, eyes flashing.

"We don't get in there now, we might as well bend over for the press," Holliday snapped, jerking a thumb toward the news-hungry crowd amassing against the police line.

Pushing back his hat, Tanner gave a slight nod. "Damned if you do . . ." He let the statement hang, his meaning clear.

This wasn't going to end well. The only real question was how much damage would be done on all fronts.

Zack followed the captains' gaze to a balcony near the opposite end of the complex, about sixty yards from where the engine companies were parked. Too damned close. Through the smoke, he could barely make out a man wearing a light-colored shirt. The man's movements were erratic as he bobbed back and forth, holding a smaller person in front of him, presumably the estranged wife.

Zack jogged over to join Holliday and Tanner. He waved a hand at the burning structure. "Will they let us enter around back where this nut can't see what we're doing?"

"Us" being a collective term. The Rapid Intervention Crew worked outside, ready to intervene if a firefighter inside found himself in trouble. The FAO, who was not part of the RIC crew, never left the engine unless there was a major disaster requiring the mobilization of every single firefighter, which was rare. In his years at the Sugarland FD, Zack had never known such a situation to occur.

Holliday nodded. "We're trying to get clearance. What the fuck is taking—" His radio crackled and a police sergeant whose name Zack didn't catch relayed the green light.

"All right, let's go," Holliday shouted, waving an arm at the entire assembly. "Let's move this party to the other side of the building, work it from there."

Firefighters scrambled onto the ladder truck and quint, while Salvatore and another man moved the two ambulances to a side street, accessible but a healthy distance from the danger. Zack followed the other FAO, and they parked with the hostage drama safely on the opposite side of the building. Safe being relative. They still had the fire and trapped residents to deal with, and God knew a crazed gunman was unpredictable at best.

Zack supposed he ought to be comforted by the SWAT snipers surrounding them, prepared to shoot to kill. Somehow, he wasn't.

He noted the location of a nearby fire hydrant, then quickly attached the preconnected hoses and flipped the gauges. Approaching sirens heralded the arrival of a third engine company, an eerie wail that sometimes reminded Zack of the cry of a woman. The sound died out front and in moments, a new team of firefighters skirted the building at a fast clip, two of them carrying a tall ladder.

Three ladders were erected next to balconies holding frightened residents, and none too soon. Flames shot from second-story windows in a burst of shattered glass, licking upward to consume and destroy. Children screamed, mothers and fathers trying in vain to calm them. An elderly couple clung to each other, and one man, half dressed in a business suit, yelled into a cell phone, his fear palpable.

Four men turned two hoses on the blaze through the windows, while three teams, including one consisting of Paxton, Skyler, and Salvatore, entered the complex to battle the flames from the inside. The others manned the ladders, one rescuer positioned at the top, one at the bottom, assisting the residents. They streamed downward like ants, kept from blind panic in large part due to the calm of their rescuers.

The elderly couple made slow progress, the woman first, her hesitant steps guided by the firefighter who'd climbed the ladder below her. On the other two balconies, the able-bodied children shimmied to freedom, followed by a mother carrying an infant, the men last.

When everyone had been extracted and whisked from the scene to be tended as needed, a search ensued for any people remaining in the building. Best-case scenario, there weren't any more, because anyone left was most likely either unconscious or dead from smoke inhalation.

Holliday and Tanner kept abreast of the hostage situation via a pair of uniformed cops hovering nearby. Zack caught snatches and what he heard wasn't good. The guy hadn't surrendered and was completely irrational. He'd either kill his wife or—

A single gunshot cracked the air like a whip, causing everyone to jump and scan the complex for an imminent threat. The pairs of men working the hoses briefly shut off the nozzles, prepared to dive for cover if necessary.

An exchange over one of the police officers' radios broke the tension. "Suspect down! Can you get a visual on him?"

"Negative . . . whoa, the woman's comin' right over the ledge! Somebody get a ladder to her before she falls."

"Got her covered. Down she goes." A frazzled silence. "Okay, they're bringing her around back to get checked out."

"Around back?"

"So the missus doesn't see them working the crime scene around her husband's body," came the terse reply.

"Copy that."

A ripple of relief went through Zack and, he was sure, the others, as well. Activity resumed and in a moment, two firefighters rounded the corner of the building, supporting the shaken woman, who stumbled between them. Tanner struck out to meet the group.

Movement from a second-story balcony caught Zack's eye. It crossed his mind that another resident was in need of rescue, someone their efforts hadn't reached. A man in a light-colored shirt stepped into view, bringing up his arm. To wave, Zack thought, just as the glint of metal flashed in the man's hand.

The man who would sooner kill his wife than allow her to escape.

Oh, God!

"Gun!" he yelled, racing for Tanner and the unsuspecting group. "Get down! Get down!"

Their gazes swung toward Zack, reflecting surprise and confusion, but disaster struck before his warning registered. A series of pops shattered the air. One of the firefighters helping the woman jerked and went down, hitting the asphalt hard, where he lay unmoving. His partner shoved the screaming woman to the ground, covering her body with his.

Tanner whirled and Zack yelled at him again as more pops sounded.

From nowhere, Eve barreled into Tanner like a star linebacker, hurling them both to the ground. Bullets peppered the asphalt around Zack and he got horizontal, fast. "Shit!"

He hadn't survived all the crap of the past few weeks to be taken out by some crazed, abusive husband. Out of sheer reflex, or maybe stupidity, he raised his head to see where the gunman was pointing. Belatedly, he wished he hadn't.

A rifle shot rang out and the man's head snapped. A dark hole appeared in his forehead and for the space of two heartbeats, Zack could've sworn the guy looked surprised to have been beaten.

And then the gunman folded like a puppet with its strings cut, disappeared from view.

Now it was over.

For some.

Sobbing reached his ears. The woman's. And an anguished moan, ripped from the depths of a man's gut. An unmistakable sound of anger and terrible knowledge.

Zack pushed to his feet, spotted Tanner and Eve disentangling themselves, staring at each other. He was so relieved—and wretched with guilt because of it—that the moan hadn't come from Tanner. That Eve, his best friend, was all right. The captain gave her a fleeting smile and stood, saying something Zack couldn't hear and offering her a hand. After a brief hesitation, she grasped it and returned Tanner's half smile as he hauled her up.

Nearby, the second firefighter knelt over his fallen friend. He shrugged off his coat and suspenders, ripped off his regulation shirt, and used it as a compress against the bloody gunshot wound in the other man's chest.

"Come on, Randall," he entreated. "Stay with me."

Zack spun to call for more assistance, but it wasn't necessary. Firefighters streamed toward the group, medical equipment and a gurney in tow. He glanced again at the gravely injured man attempting to speak with blood bubbling at his pale lips, and knew.

So did Randall.

"Tell . . . tell my wife . . ." He never got to finish.

Tears streamed unchecked down his partner's grief-stricken face. "I will, buddy. I promise."

Zack watched the young firefighter's eyes glaze as the last breath rattled from his body. Helpless rage consumed him, choked his throat. His gaze narrowed at the balcony where the gunman lay. *It's not enough. Will never be sufficient justice for a good man's wife and family.*

A promising life gone at the whim of an asshole. One

more bully who'd never answer for his crimes. Who wouldn't face judgment on earth. Had probably gone to hell laughing.

Zack wished with all his soul that he'd been the one to pull the trigger. Put that hole in the bastard's forehead. The direction of his thoughts startled him, but the next realization shocked him to his toes.

No, he'd give anything to have tortured the man. Ripped the murderer apart with his bare hands. Slowly, painfully, his heart a dead thing inside him while the hunter became the prey. Screamed in agony and horror as he saw the tables turned and knew he'd pay.

And pay.

Until he drew his last, bloody breath.

Exactly like Randall.

Walking away from the awful tragedy, he wondered what Cori would think about that. What she would say if she knew the man she'd allowed into her bed wasn't much better than the dead man on the balcony.

Little better than the husband who'd abused her for years. Because if he harbored any doubts before, he had none now.

If their unseen nemesis touched Cori, he'd die begging for mercy.

"Okay, I saw the news coverage. Ready to talk about it?"

Cori set aside her coffee mug and studied Zack in concern. Yesterday, the moment she'd seen a recap of the horrifying spectacle on the television in the nurses' lounge, she'd left a message on Zack's cell phone. One that had gone unreturned for several hours. And when he'd finally called, he'd steered the conversation firmly toward Cori and her safety. He'd needed reassurance of her plans to stay with Shea overnight while he was on shift, etc. She understood why, but he couldn't divert her forever.

He appeared bone tired, which was to be expected after his first shift in the better part of a month—especially after the tragedy of losing one of his own. He tossed his wallet and keys onto the kitchen counter as he'd no doubt done hundreds of times before, dark emotion bleeding through the weariness.

"It's over and I'm fine. How was staying at Shea's last night? Is the arrangement gonna work out?"

"It was a regular slumber party. We stayed up too late, watched an old movie, and ate junk food. Don't change the subject."

He shrugged off his jacket, hung it on the back of a breakfast-nook chair, and crossed the short distance between them, pulling her into his arms. With a sigh, she snuggled against him, resting her cheek on his chest. His heartbeat drummed a steady rhythm in her ear, slow and comforting. God, she could've lost him yesterday on what should've been a routine job manning the quint. Her hold on him tightened.

"Will it always be like this?"

To his credit, he didn't avoid or pretend to misunderstand the question. "That call was a fluke, beautiful. Ninety-seven percent of our calls involve traffic accidents, medical emergencies in the home, and a variation of all sorts of weird situations people get themselves into. Nothing too dangerous given the odds, so don't worry, all right?"

She gave a shaky laugh. "My brainy numbers guy. Must be why I . . ." *Take the plunge. Say it, chicken!* She drew back, tipped her face to his. "Why I love you."

Blue eyes widened behind his glasses. His mouth fell open, his dumbfounded expression so comical she might've laughed if she weren't suddenly afraid of his response.

The slow, sexy smile spreading across his handsome face stole her breath.

"I'm sure I misheard. Say it again."

"I love you, Zack Knight." Reaching up, she brushed a lock of black hair from his eyes. "After yesterday, I wasn't going to wait any longer to tell you."

Framing her face with shaking hands, he lowered his lips to hers. Brushed them in sensual contact before slipping his tongue inside. He stroked behind her teeth, deepened the kiss. Hot, urgent, yet sweet. All Zack. Pouring his feelings into a simple touch, his body straining against hers, arousal searing her through their clothing.

He broke the kiss, gazed into her eyes.

"I love you, too," he whispered. "So much it hurts."

Joy filled her to bursting, but she couldn't resist teasing to lighten the overwhelming moment. "I can tell."

A corner of his mouth quirked. "Not exactly what I meant, but now that you bring it up . . . does my nurse have a remedy for my pain?"

"I believe I have a little something."

Taking his hand, she led him upstairs to their room. And proceeded to do something she hadn't dared before.

Be extraordinarily late to class.

They undressed, savoring each other without touching at first. She loved the way his muscles rippled as he tugged off his navy polo, his lean and sinewy strength. The small scar on his shoulder from the bullet was red, but healed. A smattering of crisp black hair trailed from his chest to his stomach, where it formed a beeline straight to the nest at his groin.

He stepped out of his pants and kicked them aside, facing her in all his naked glory. His penis jutted, seeking sanctuary in her heat, flushed and thick.

She discarded her bra, wriggled out of her panties, never taking her hungry eyes off him. "You're beautiful," she said.

"My line, but thank you." Stepping close, he linked his fingers with hers, erection branding her belly. "You're stunning."

Cutting off her reply, he backed her into the bed, pushed her gently onto the mattress. Levering himself over her, he settled himself between her thighs and reached for his glasses.

"No, leave them on."

"They'll get in the way."

"Just this once? Please?" She waggled her brows. "I think they're sexy."

"Jesus."

But he did as she asked, his playful grin switching to feral male hunger as he positioned the head of his cock between the slick lips of her sex.

She cupped the firm globes of his ass and arched her hips, pulling him inside an inch or two. "Please, I need you."

With a groan, he slid his length deep, filling her. All the way, skin to skin, sparking delicious tremors throughout her nervous system. Stretching her to the limit, a perfect fit.

Bracing his arms on either side of her head, he began to move. A slow, languorous retreat to the very edge, his tip barely inside, then forward again. Impaling her inch by burning inch until seated to the balls.

Out, a long slide. In.

Decadent, unraveling her control.

"Ohh, God. Zack, yes!"

"Like that, beautiful?"

"Yes! Don't stop. . . ."

He kept up the torture until she writhed underneath him, nearly mindless with ecstasy. His cock was so hot, claiming her as his. His muscles played under her fingertips, sweat dampening his back, his chest. His pungent male scent, his wicked lovemaking, drove her wild.

"Faster, harder," she panted, wrapping her legs around his waist.

Tightening around her, he increased the tempo of his thrusts, her wish his command. He plunged deep and hard, holding nothing back.

Cori clung to him, completely swept away. Nothing mattered except his body inside hers, giving and taking. Making love to her, as he'd never done with anyone else.

Mine.

Her body incinerated, her orgasm erupting like a blowtorch. She stiffened with a cry, convulsing around him as he rode her.

"That's it, Cori. Gorgeous. Let yourself go for me. . . . Ah, fuck!"

Plunging deep, he began to spasm. The warm rush of his cum flowed into her womb as he held her close.

"I love you," he rasped. "God, I love you."

"Love you, too."

They floated back to earth in a satisfied haze, unwilling to move. She enjoyed his weight pressing on her body.

"You don't know how much I needed you. I missed you." He pressed an affectionate kiss into her hair.

"Oh, I think I have a good idea." Grinning, she wiggled her hips, emphasizing his being still buried inside her. "I missed you, hot stuff. You know, our schedules stink. I hate going out the door just as you're getting home."

"You could always quit, stay home, and be my love slave. It's your fault I'm ruined anyway."

Her inner feline purred at the reminder. This man was hers alone. To know he'd never been with another woman was a heady drug. "Oh? How, pray tell, have I managed to lead this paragon of innocence astray?"

In answer, he stroked her wet passage with his softening cock. "Like this."

"Then who's the love slave, fireboy?"

He gave a fake put-upon sigh. "Okay, it's me. But now it's my queen's duty to make sure her concubine is petted. Often. Having your very own sex slave is a big responsibility, you know."

"Yes, I do," she deadpanned, wiggling again.

"If you don't stop that, I'm going to keep you in bed all day."

"Your point?"

He paused, gazing down at her in amusement. "Do you know when I first fell in love with you?"

"No, when?" she asked, intrigued.

"When you got out of your SUV looking hotter than a firecracker and madder than hell, and you said, 'Don't they *stop* at red lights where you're from, Forrest Gump?'"

Her face heated in embarrassment and she covered her eyes with one hand. "Oh, my God! I'd forgotten all about it! I can't believe I said something so bitchy to you."

He laughed and kissed her nose. "You knocked my socks off, baby. Well, what about you?"

She peeked at him through her fingers. "What about me?"

Finally, he moved off and to the side of her, but slung one thigh possessively over hers. "Impossible woman. When did you fall in love with me?"

She studied his earnest face, the long sweep of his dark lashes framing those incredible blue eyes, and felt her throat burn with sudden emotion.

"That's easy. On the bridge, when you reached for my hand and said you weren't leaving without me, and meant every word." She traced his lips, heart swelling with love. "In that moment, you became the light in my darkness, in more ways than you ever could've imagined. And somehow I knew I'd love you forever."

In an instant, she found herself sprawled on top of him, crushed against his chest. His husky voice rumbled under her ear.

"Christ, what you do to me. You're going to be late, you realize."

"Horribly late," she agreed happily.

With an exaggerated growl, Zack rolled her underneath him and proceeded to make good on his promise.

16

Every muscle in Cori's body vibrated with the afterglow of morning sex . . . which had become midmorning, then afternoon sex. Whatever punishment her instructor devised would be worth the price—if she ever discovered Cori had lied about being sick.

"Do I have to ask what you're smiling about?" From the driver's seat of the Mustang, Zack cut a glance at her, grinning like a fool.

"Same thing you are, Mighty Phallus."

Zack burst out laughing so hard he choked, swerving and almost driving them right off I-49 and into a deep gully. "Good God," he gasped, struggling for composure. "You can't say stuff like that while I'm driving."

"Hmm. If you're going to run off the road, I can at least make it worth our while."

"Mercy, woman. I couldn't make Junior perform again if you stripped naked right this minute."

"Tonight?"

He shot her an incredulous look. "You're not serious."

"You're young, with the stamina of a porn star. Great recovery time, too."

"Gee, thanks. I think. And you've dated *how* many porn stars?"

"Beside the point." He scowled and she giggled. "You fell for that one."

He rolled his eyes but relaxed, appearing rather pleased. "Back to the subject of my stamina?"

"You're such a guy. Anyway, I've got a plan for this evening. One to guarantee Junior's avid participation."

"Yeah? I'm all ears," he said, curious.

"Nope, it's a surprise. Just get plenty of rest."

"Not fair."

She smirked. "You'll sing a different tune tonight."

They enjoyed the rest of the ride into Sugarland in companionable silence. All too soon, Zack pulled up to the ER's entrance and took her hand, pressing her palm to his lips. Then he leaned close and gave her a sweet, lingering kiss that made her want to tell him to turn around and take her home.

"Miss you already, beautiful."

"Well, the bright side is the rest of the day won't be as long now. Since you seduced me and all."

"Turnabout's fair play." His blue eyes danced with mischief.

"Don't forget it."

"Not a chance. I'll pick you up around six."

Reluctantly, she got out and blew him a kiss. She watched him drive away, heart full and deliriously happy for the first time in her life.

When his car disappeared around the corner, she went inside, footsteps springy despite her being at work. The challenge of the ER was normally one she looked forward to, but compared with wild bunny sex with the man she loved?

No contest.

"Wow, that's some expression on your pretty face, darling. Too bad it's not for me."

Startled, Cori searched for the location of Banning's voice. The man, half hidden by a ficus tree, detached himself from a wall in the ER's waiting room.

Cold enveloped her, and she couldn't keep the hostility from showing if she tried. Didn't really care to, either. This snake needed to get her message, loud and clear.

"Hello, Tony. Or whatever your name is."

Caught totally off guard, he faltered. "What are you talking about?"

Hitching her purse more securely on her shoulder, she glanced around the waiting room. Doctors and nurses hurried to and fro beyond the check-in counter and double doors, reassuring her. Cocking her head, she pinned Banning like a butterfly. "Oh, I think you know. Soon, the Sugarland police are going to know, too."

"You're insane," he sputtered, coloring with anger, fists clenched. "I'm exactly who I told you I am. An artist—"

"Who doesn't know Wassily Kandinsky was considered the first modern abstract painter of the twentieth century. Don't worry. I'm not an artist, either. Who knew?"

He took a step forward, a vein popping in his neck. "Corrine—"

"Careful. I can have five doctors grinding your nose into the tile before you can say 'Miranda rights.' Tell you what. Why don't you fly far away, little man, right back to Transylvania or wherever you winged in from, alrighty?"

"Goddammit—"

"Better make it fast, too," she sneered. "Because the police can't hope to match the resources my brother Joaquin has at his fingertips. He's close to making an ID on you, and when he does, no corner on earth will hide you from him."

Oh, he wanted to throttle her. The desire was etched into the taut line of his furious body. Mask stripped, the airheaded playboy gone, he appeared hard. Lethal.

Without another word, he stormed past her and into the afternoon. She had no doubt whatsoever that if they hadn't been in a public environment, she'd have disappeared without a trace. Shivering, she was immensely glad Zack would return to pick her up later.

She headed through the double doors and into the recesses of the ER, ugly fear treading on the joy of a few minutes before. Try as she might, she couldn't dispel the sinking feeling she'd made a terrible mistake in tipping their hand too soon.

An error that could cost her and Zack their lives.

Zack made productive use of their hours apart, like he did each day their schedules sent them in different directions. Keeping busy seemed to make the time pass quicker, and doing little things around the place for Cori always brought a smile to her beautiful face.

First, he washed her new Explorer she'd purchased in part with the insurance payout on the totaled one. He'd thought she'd want something else, considering, but she insisted the SUV was some sort of good-luck charm. He'd saved her life in the other one, remember? Hard to argue the point.

The remaining hours he spent in the shop working on Cori's Top Secret project—facing the door. Yeah, he resented creeping around their own property like a freaking Navy SEAL, peering into the bushes, trying to spy the enemy, tensed for another attack. He'd even thought about buying a gun, then dismissed the idea. More likely than not, he'd wind up shooting an innocent deer instead.

Still, he managed to enjoy himself and before he knew it, all the lumber was cut, some of it preassembled and ready to haul down the hill to the creek. Surveying his handiwork, he felt a surge of pride swell in his chest. By this weekend, he'd be ready to unveil her surprise—if he could keep his nosy lady from peeking.

After hooking the flatbed trailer to the tail of the tractor, he loaded the lumber and his tools and headed to his destination. He'd chosen the perfect spot for his gift, on the path they'd walked the day he'd arrived, where the trees parted and the trail led up the opposite side of the hill.

He turned off the ignition and decided to leave everything on the trailer while he worked. Hopping down, he got busy dragging boards, maneuvering, and hammering until sweat rolled into his eyes and stuck his shirt to his skin under his jacket. Eventually, the sun began to sink low in the sky and he pushed himself to wrap up for the day. Dark came early this time of year, and he needed to take a shower, go fetch Cori.

Thinking of her was all the motivation he required to call it quits. Throwing his tools in the flatbed, he left everything where it lay and trekked up to the house. Being so far from the main road, he wasn't much worried about thieves absconding with his tractor and lumber. Their stalker was another matter, but Zack knew if the bastard wanted to ruin the project, he'd find a way no matter what.

Shoving the unease aside, he took a quick shower and dressed in a fresh pair of jeans and a striped polo shirt. In fifteen minutes he was on his way to town again, anxious to see his goddess.

At the hospital, Cori wasn't standing outside, so he pulled into a parking space near the ER's entrance to wait. By its nature, her assignment was unpredictable in terms of punching the clock, and she was frequently late. He didn't mind, but after twenty minutes he started to get antsy, pulse leaping in anticipation with each swing of the door.

At the half-hour mark, he was about to go inside and ask for her when she hurried outside. Spotting him, she headed for the car, shaking her head in apology and blowing a strand of hair from her face. Her ponytail was escaping the scrunchie thing and she looked harassed. Tired.

Zack got out to meet her. "Hey, you." He pulled her into his arms.

"I'm so glad you're here," she said, hugging him fiercely.

"Bad afternoon?" Boy, she was strung tight, her entire body vibrating. And not in pleasure, the way he'd left her.

"A car accident resulting in minor injuries, a child attacked by a dog. The usual."

"What, then?"

Releasing him, she bit her lip, expression guilty. "I screwed up."

He frowned. "What, did you get written up or something?"

"No." She gestured to the Mustang. "Why don't we get in? My feet are killing me."

"Sure, baby." He opened the passenger's door for her, helped her in, then went around to his own side and settled into his seat. "All right, spill."

"Please don't be mad."

Uh-oh. Never a great conversation starter.

Patting her hand, he tried an encouraging smile. "I won't, promise."

"Don't be too hasty. Tony was waiting for me when I got here."

"Sonofabitch. Did he touch you?" *If he did, I'll have to cut off his hands and let him bleed out.*

"He didn't get the chance. I sort of . . . blurted that we know he's a fake."

"Ah, crap. Corrine—"

"I'm sorry, but he made me so damned angry! I just wanted him to leave us alone! I thought he might even leave town for good if he knew we're on to him." She crossed her arms under her breasts as she defended herself.

"You honestly think he will?"

The fight left her in a whoosh. "Not really. You should've seen his face when I dropped the bombshell that he's being investigated. Right then, he wanted to kill me."

"I'll see him dead first." At Cori's astonished and frightened stare, he instantly regretted saying the words aloud. He didn't want to remind her of the other men in her past life—men she'd kicked to the curb without a backward glance. "I can't apologize for how I feel, baby."

She nodded, rubbing her arms. "I don't expect you to. He scared me, and I'd defend myself if necessary, however possible. Only one other man has ever looked through me that way."

Her husband. Again, the chill slithered along his skin. Somehow, the two men must be connected.

"Sweetheart, you're sure there's nothing familiar about this man? Maybe he worked with your husband, or the two of you met him at a party? Perhaps his appearance was altered, as well."

She considered this for a long moment, then sighed in defeat. "Nothing. I swear I've never met him before."

"Well, he showed his true colors, so that's something. We'll just have to be careful for the next few days, keep our eyes open."

And hope the cops or Joaquin figured out the con man's real identity before he made his move.

Which would be soon, now that he'd been tipped off.

"I'm sorry, Zack."

Her woebegone expression twisted his heart. "Forget it, beautiful. We'll deal with this like we have everything else. Hungry?"

"Starving," she said, obviously grateful for a change of topic.

"Want to stop on the way home for takeout?"

"Sounds fabulous. Chinese?"

"You got it."

Zack stopped at a restaurant in a strip mall on the way out of town, running in to pick up broccoli beef for himself, sweet-and-sour chicken for Cori. The aroma made his mouth water during the drive . . . but not as much as her hint of a seductive surprise for later.

Horn dog, he admonished himself. *You wore her out; then she had a terrible afternoon. Give her a break.*

They ate at the coffee table in the living room in front of a cheery fire he built in the fireplace. Talked of inconsequential topics, relaxed, and savored each other's company.

He entertained her with stories of humorous calls Station Five had answered. One in particular stood out in his memory.

"So, we get to the elderly man's house and he says, 'The voice won't stop talking to me.' We're thinking, *Great, this guy is senile*, but Six-Pack asks what this voice is saying. The old man says, 'I don't know, I don't know.' We're all puzzled and Six-Pack asks, 'You don't know what it's saying?' and the old man gets upset and yells, 'That's what it's saying! *I don't know, I don't know!* '"

Cori giggled and speared another piece of chicken. "Was he really hearing a voice?"

"Yep. We're searching the guy's house when Tommy and Eve start laughing, trying to get control because they don't want the poor man to think they're laughing at *him*. We all go take a look and they're standing in the hallway. Tommy's pointing to a smoke alarm on the ceiling, and the thing is saying, *Battery low, battery low*."

He loved the sound of her throaty laugh, the firelight illuminating her tiger eyes and golden skin, setting her hair ablaze. Loved everything about her.

"You don't look hungry for food anymore," she said, lips curling into a wicked smile.

"Can you blame me? I warned you early on that you might wish you'd let this sleeping dog lie, remember?"

"Oh, I certainly do, and you were wrong. I'm going to have fun proving it, too. Right now." She rose and gestured to their Styrofoam take-out boxes. "Finished?"

"With the food? Oh, *yeah*."

"Eager, are we? Let me get rid of these. Then I'm going upstairs to put on something more . . . appropriate. When I return, I expect to find you standing in front of the fire. Naked." She waltzed into the kitchen to toss their scraps.

Damn! His crotch tightened to the point of strangulation. When she came out again, he waved a hand at himself. "Junior and I want to lodge a complaint about us getting naked while you stay dressed."

Stepping close, she ran a hand down his chest. Slowly. "Are you or are you not my love slave who's oozing with that marvelous stamina we discussed?"

"Shit," he breathed, cock jerking behind his zipper. "One love slave, at your service."

Tossing him a saucy wink, she flounced up the stairs. He gazed after her butt swinging to and fro for a moment before he shook himself from his stupor and headed up after her. In the guest bathroom he'd been using, he brushed his teeth, then spent a minute studying his reflection in the mirror.

Not bad. A little geeky, maybe, a naked love slave wearing glasses, but Cori preferred them. That settled any question of removing them for what Tommy called better *coolage*.

He grinned at himself. *I don't have to be cool. Cori loves me the way I am.*

Shucking his clothes, he tossed them on the guest bed he hadn't used in weeks. He felt ridiculous jogging down the stairs, erect penis waving like a banner, but his discomfort evaporated as he wondered what she had planned.

For several minutes, he gazed into the fire and tried to envision sexy scenarios, but a vivid imagination wasn't his strong suit. Or maybe he was simply naive. Whatever the case, in his wildest fantasies, he couldn't have predicted her scheme.

"My, my. What a fine backside. And it's all mine."

Turning his back to the fireplace, he gaped in awe. Cori was dressed as a harem girl. Or an Arabian princess. Yes, that was it. His woman was pure, stunning royalty.

Skeins of diaphanous sapphire material flowed along her arms and down her long legs to her bare, pretty feet. Lustrous honey brown hair fell past her shoulders. Scarves were draped around her slender neck and hung past the glittering bra, emphasizing the gorgeous swell of generous breasts, to her navel. Her innie had been adorned with a matching blue jewel. Jesus, he wanted to trace it with his tongue. And lower, to the triangle of material barely covering her sex in front.

"Like what you see?"

"God, yes," he croaked, taking a step toward her.

"No, stay right where you are. Don't move."

Padding to the stereo, Cori turned it on and selected a station playing slow, bluesy instrumental music reminding him of whiskey and sex. Fists clenched, he waited in torment.

He didn't have to squirm for long. She walked to the dining room, and returned with one of the straight-backed chairs from the table. Placing it in front of him, she gestured to it.

"Sit," she ordered, the command hot and sultry as the middle of August. "You're my captive audience. Literally."

He did as told. Hardly registered the cold wooden seat pressing on his ass and balls. Something told him they wouldn't be cold for long.

"What now?"

"Do you want to go wherever I take you, my sexy slave?"

"Do you have to ask?"

She gave the erection throbbing between his legs an arch look. "I suppose not. All right. From here on out, don't speak, just . . . feel. Forget who we are and let yourself slide away."

The easiest order he'd ever received, since he could do nothing *except* feel. When she began to move to the music, he couldn't have said a word anyway. All speech deserted him as she raised her arms over her head, swaying. Her hips undulated in time to the lazy beat. She watched him, her movements a perfect mime of making love.

She was performing one of her exotic dances for him, he realized suddenly. In a way he fervently prayed she'd done for nobody else. In the next instant he no longer cared. She wasn't a dancer; she was his princess. He existed solely to satisfy her however she desired.

Mesmerized, he stared as she removed one of the scarves from around her neck. Twirled and swished it in the air, creating fascinating patterns. Ramping up the anticipation.

Next, she danced to him, taking her sweet time. At his side, she draped the scarf around his neck, trailed it down his chest. Goose bumps broke out on his skin at the decadent sensation of the material sliding down to his belly. His aching groin. She bent low, her breasts near his face, close enough to taste if he turned his head to the side. But this was her show, and he was dying to learn what she planned.

"Put your arms behind you and cross your wrists," she said softly in his ear.

He complied, his heart thumping a mad tattoo behind his sternum. Surely she didn't intend—

By God, she did! A protest almost escaped, but he squelched it, unwilling to end their play. He sat in disbelief as she bound his wrists with the scarf, tied them to the back of the chair.

Making a satisfied sound in her throat, she came to stand in front of him again. With a catlike smile, she removed the remaining two scarves and trailed them down his body in the same manner as before, leaving him quivering.

This time, she knelt at his feet. His eyes followed her, and he blinked at the pearly drop of pre-cum beading on the tip of his penis. Christ, he hoped he was able to hold off the explosive orgasm building in his balls. He'd finally experienced the joys of lovemaking, but he'd never been seduced. *Taken.*

"Spread your legs even with the legs of the chair."

The position made him completely vulnerable . . . especially when she tied each of his ankles to the chair's legs. He was spread naked before his lover, hers to do with as she wished. A dark thrill coursed through his veins, drugging him.

He wanted this—to be claimed by her—more than he'd ever wanted anything in his life.

Standing, she surveyed her handiwork, began to sway again to the music. "Gorgeous," she murmured. "A feast to be savored."

Teasing him, she presented him with her back and began to remove the filmy material from her arms and legs. The covering detached easily, leaving her clad in only the bra and the thong. He couldn't peel his eyes from the sparkly string parting the creamy globes of her ass.

Reaching behind her, she undid the clasp of her top, let the straps fall free. Then she untied the strings around her neck, tossed the bra aside. Turned to face him.

Zack sucked in a breath. Silky hair framed her bare, ripe breasts and rosy nipples. This goddess was his. He still had difficulty believing his good fortune.

She approached, knelt between his splayed knees. Leaned forward, licked the bead of cum from the tip of his cock. "Mmm. So good. You like being at my mercy, I see."

She suckled the crown, snatching the air from his lungs. Coherent thought fled and he was truly a slave to her ministrations, his body hers to lick and sample. Her pink little tongue swept along his feverish length, laving every contour. Slim fingers manipulated his balls, drawn and taut with arousal. Then she took him in her mouth, sucking him deep, tormenting the turgid flesh. The sight of her lips stroking his cock almost finished him, and his hips bucked off the seat. A low moan escaped him, a plea without words.

Releasing him, she stood. Swung her legs wide and straddled the chair, her thighs on the outsides of his. The position thrust her breasts to his nose and placed her womanhood dangerously close to his cock.

"And now, for your private lap dance, honey. Relax and enjoy."

Lowering her mound, she squatted over him, allowing his penis to brush along her sex as she writhed in hypnotic rhythm. Just the light contact of heat against slick femininity. Nothing more.

Hands on his shoulders, she threw back her head, causing a shower of honey brown silk to cascade around them both. Held his gaze through half-open lids, an alluring sexual creature who loved the power she held over him.

So did he. His breath sawed in his lungs and he knew he couldn't hold out much longer. He was desperate to be inside her when he came, where he belonged.

She ghosted a kiss over his lips, trailed her fingers down one cheek. "Tell me what you want, slave."

"God, please . . ."

"Say it."

He was lost.

"Fuck me, please!"

Bracing one hand on his shoulder, she guided the tip of his cock to her entrance with the other. She paused with him inside her an inch or so and he thought his heart would burst.

"Watch me fuck you," she said.

"Yes, I . . . ahh, god*damn*!"

A trickle of sweat rolled down his temple. His eyes fastened on her sheath swallowing his pulsing length. Bit by bit, torching him from the inside out. Down, down, until she sat in his lap with him buried inside her.

She began to ride him, up and down, and his mind checked out. He was hers, her toy, her instrument of pleasure. Never anything like this, so dark and sensual. Totally owned by another, never wanting the torture to end.

"Yesss, baby! Fuck me, use me . . . please, don't stop!"

With a throaty moan, she increased the tempo, impaling herself on his rod. Faster, harder, her feminine walls squeezing and stroking him into a frenzy. He thrust to meet her, unable to help himself. Out of control, their bodies slamming together.

She rode him with abandon, rushing them headlong toward the edge. The now-familiar gathering of the impending explosion tingled at the base of his spine, and then . . .

"Oh! Oh, God, baby! Yes!"

He shot deep inside her womb with a hoarse shout, blessed, exquisite release. On and on, his cock milked of every last drop. Arms linked around his neck, she ground against him, shuddering with her own orgasm, incoherent little cries spilling from her lips.

She fell against him and they remained locked together, struggling for air. For how long, he didn't know.

"Jesus Christ," he whispered. "That was . . . incredible."

She gave him a naughty grin. "You liked?"

"Seriously, what do you think?"

"That Junior will never be the same." She wiggled on his lap for emphasis.

"Baby, you blew the top of my head off. Can you see my brains?"

"Nope, just one unbelievably sexy man."

Well, he was far from sexy. He wasn't, however, about to argue. "Promise me something," he said suddenly.

"Anything," she replied without hesitation.

"Swear to me you'll never perform a lap dance for another man again." Even though she'd never allowed a client to touch her, the idea tore him to shreds.

"I'll go one better, fireboy." She leaned in, nibbled along his jaw. "What would you say if I told you I'd retired from exotic dancing . . . except for when I dance for you?"

Had he been standing, his knees would've buckled from sheer relief.

"I'd say that's the best news I've ever heard, beautiful."

"I'll find a way to finish paying for my education, Zack. One that doesn't involve dancing or touching Alex's dirty money." She smiled, her love reaching out to wind tendrils around his soul. "I'd never do anything to hurt you. I love you."

"I love you, too, sweetheart."

"I'll finance."

"*We'll* finance, like the rest of the population does." He

kissed her nose, the only part of her he could reach while
bound hand and foot. "Baby?"

"Hmm?"

"Can I be your love slave more often?"

"Anytime."

He sighed, happiness no longer an intangible ideal forever out of reach.

"That's the *second*-best news I've ever heard."

17

Cori clung to Zack's hand as he pulled her through the Saturday night crowd at the Waterin' Hole. The establishment was ancient and worn, its walls plastered with yellowed framed photographs and local memorabilia such as high school banners and trophies. Probably because the owner had graduated here in Cheatham County, or so Zack claimed. The patrons were working-class, raucous, and here for a good time, the atmosphere friendly.

Still, Cori was nervous about meeting Zack's friends in a social setting, Eve Marshall in particular. Oh, Cori could take her in a fair catfight if that was all it came down to, but a rumble would settle nothing. Not when the woman had the respect of and influence over the guys at Station Five.

Hopefully it wouldn't come to that. She'd like to think the fragile connection they'd begun to develop the day of the attempt on Zack had survived.

"We're about to find out," she muttered. Thank God she'd talked Shea into meeting them here. Zack had a ton of friends. It wasn't as if anyone would notice another body jammed in this place, and having her own girlfriend along would be fun.

Cori spotted Eve as they approached a group of tables along the left wall, up front near the bar. The gang had

commandeered three tables, and Cori recognized the rest
of Zack's buddies one by one. Seeing them in street
clothes and letting their hair down gave her a moment of
weirdness, which she quickly dismissed.

Firefighters at play. Yum.

She might be taken, but she wasn't dead.

The young, drop-dead gorgeous blond, Tommy Skyler,
was flirting with the cute barmaid taking their drink order.
Howard and Kat Paxton were sitting next to him, chatting
with Sean Tanner, Eve Marshall, and a black man Cori
hadn't met. Cori didn't miss the way Sean's green eyes
narrowed at Eve's companion—who was really quite
striking, with a lean frame and an angular face. Interesting. She wondered whether anyone else felt the captain's
vibe, especially Eve.

The only two not engaged in conversation with the
others were the sexy Julian Salvatore and his knockout
date, a Hispanic woman with long hair the color of dark
cinnamon. The pair seemed sort of apart from the rest,
somehow. Julian had an arm slung across the back of the
woman's chair in a familiar manner. While they seemed
comfortable with each other, the same ease didn't appear
to apply to the rest of the group. Julian sat with one ankle
propped casually on his knee, but his body language radiated tension. Unlike his date, he wasn't smiling as he
picked a napkin with his free hand.

"Hey, Zack!"

Howard's booming greeting was met with whoops and
table thumping, followed by claps on their friend's back
and punches in the arm as he and Cori joined them.

The three women, including Eve, smiled and gave Cori
a warm hello, unloading the stress headache waiting to
squeeze her temples. Okay, so it wasn't hugs and air

kisses, but it was a start. At least she wouldn't have to worry about deflecting poison darts all evening.

After the exuberant male thumping ritual died down, she and Zack took seats on the other side of Julian and his lady, across from Tommy. The imp with the pale blue eyes shot Cori a dimpled grin, giving her a thorough once-over, even as he spoke to Zack.

"*Dayam*, Einstein, where'd you find Ms. Booty-licious?"

Cori snorted a short laugh, unsure whether to be offended. Something told her the kid was harmless, just afflicted with a case of diarrhea mouth and raging hormones, like most guys his age. Since Zack took Tommy's comment in stride, she figured she'd guessed right.

"Her name is Cori, and she's the girl we rescued from the bridge accident last month, dipstick."

Tommy's guileless pale eyes widened, and he studied Cori more closely. "Oh, dude! Jeez, I'm sorry. I didn't recognize you. I mean, that day you were all wet and stuff—"

"No problem," Cori interjected. She did *not* need to be reminded of how awful she looked in the emergency room while Zack fought for his life.

"Anyways, it's nice to meetcha. Officially, I mean."

Cori grinned back at Tommy. She couldn't help it. The kid was an open book, and beautiful as a fallen angel. Someone like him should've taken up acting or modeling, and she wondered why he hadn't.

"You remind me of someone," she said to him. Which, of course, caused him to puff out his chest and grace her with a lazy, heavy-lidded look fringed with thick, dusky lashes that might've scorched her underwear had she been ten years younger.

"Most people say I resemble Brad Pitt—you know, before he got old."

Old? She barely managed to stifle a laugh. "No, that's not who I was thinking."

His face fell. "Really?"

"Yeah, let's see. . . . I've got it! You remind me of Robert Redford when he was young."

"Who?" He appeared genuinely baffled.

"Oh, God," Zack groaned. "You are *such* a loser."

Tommy shot him the bird. "Wasn't talking to you, geek."

"Get your own date, pretty boy," Zack returned, putting his arm around her.

"Maybe I will."

Their banter held an affectionate tone Cori suspected was the usual routine with the men. She relaxed even more, beginning to enjoy herself very much.

The barmaid took the rest of their drink orders. Everyone ordered longnecks, except for Julian, who asked for Patrón Silver, and Howard and Cori, who ordered Cokes. No one commented on the lieutenant's abstinence, so Cori guessed he wasn't a drinker.

"Cori, this is my good friend Carmelita Gutierrez," Julian said from beside her. "*Dulce*, this is Zack's beauty, Corrine Shannon."

"Hello," Cori said. Carmelita returned her greeting. She was poised and confident, but not stuffy. Were she and Julian lovers? Hard to tell. Before Cori could speculate further, Eve walked over to introduce her companion to Cori and Zack. From this, and the way the man's dark eyes darted over the group, Cori surmised he hadn't hung with them before.

"Hey, guys, this is Drake Bowers," Eve said, hooking

her arm through his. "He teaches choir at Sugarland High School." Her date smiled, nodding to them.

Drake struck Cori as a polite, shy man. He was also quite good-looking, in spite of the dreads Cori didn't care for on any man. Still, he couldn't hold a candle to the hard, uncompromising Sean Tanner, with his harsh features and sad eyes.

Who took a long draw of his beer, skewering the unsuspecting teacher with a gaze sharp enough to cut glass.

Whoa. She hoped never to get on the captain's shit list. Did Eve know Sean was simmering on a low boil?

"Who's up for pool?" Tommy bounded from his seat, pointing to an open table.

Howard rose, towering over everyone else. "I am. Girls against guys?"

"Woo-hoo! Count me in," Kat yelled. "Come on, ladies, who's with me?"

"I'm in," Eve said.

Eve and Kat had a head start on the female bonding, Cori noted. They shared an easy camaraderie, and Kat fit in well with the group. Thinking of her own brothers and their tense, complicated relationship, Cori was blindsided with an attack of wistfulness, but shrugged it off. She had Zack, and Shea, who'd become the sister she'd always wanted.

As if she'd conjured her friend, Shea materialized at her side and hugged her tight. Her curly brown hair fell in unruly waves to her shoulders and tickled Cori's nose.

"Sorry I'm late! I had a terrible time getting away from the ER this evening."

"You're not. We're just getting started."

Her friend took Tommy's vacated seat as another round of introductions ensued. At the other end of the table, Julian started a conversation with Drake, asking him about his high school students, while Sean listened and sipped his beer.

Shea stuck out a hand to Zack. "Hi, I'm Shea Ford. I don't think we've actually met."

Zack glanced at her hand in surprise, then shook it briefly, obviously charmed by her straightforward attitude. "I'm Zack, but I guess Cori's told you about me."

"Every second she's awake." She rolled her eyes and wrinkled her pert, freckled nose. "She's got all sorts of cute pet names for you, like Super—"

Cori swatted at her across the table, gasping. "Ooh, some friend you are, breaking the sacred Girl Code!"

"I don't want to know," Zack said, cheeks reddening.

"I was only going to say Super*brain*."

Zack wasn't biting. "Jesus." He waved a hand, eager to change the subject. "Thanks for letting Cori crash at your apartment while I'm on shift. We owe you."

"No sweat. We've had fun hanging out, but I hope they catch whoever's behind the attacks on you, fast. Shane tells me this Banning creep is a frickin' ghost," she said in disgust.

Zack nodded. "Yeah. It's like the guy doesn't exist. They don't have prints on him and he's probably altered his appearance more than once. They can't even get a physical resemblance from the most-wanted lists."

Cori made a face. "Ugh. Do we have to talk about this tonight?"

Zack took her hand, brought it to his lips. "You're right. I'm sorry, baby. Let's just have fun."

"I'm going to barf," Shea said.

They laughed, and Zack steered the topic toward how Shea met Cori. Shea entertained him with the story of how she had a flat tire on I-49, nobody around for miles and her brother not answering his cell phone. Dubious help came in the form of Cori, having just arrived in Sugarland, SUV loaded with her stuff. Like Shea, she had no clue how to change a tire. But how hard could it be?

One hour later, giggling and covered in grease, they were well on their way to becoming fast friends. They got the flat tire off, but never managed to get the spare on— Shane finally arrived to save the day. By the time he was finished, she'd warmed to Cori as she did to very few people so quickly, and Cori had a place to stay while she went apartment hunting.

The barmaid returned and Shea ordered a glass of white wine. Howard and Tommy sauntered over, and Cori caught the very interested gleam in the younger man's pale eyes as he studied Shea. Howard spoke first.

"Man, the girls kicked our butts. Winners play." Noticing Shea, the lieutenant cocked his head. "Hello, I'm Howard. You look really familiar."

Shea's merry attitude sobered a bit. "My twin brother's a detective. He worked your case a few months ago. Not that Shane blabbed about you or the details, but I read the papers—"

"Your brother is Shane Ford?" Howard gave her a brilliant smile. "Any sister of his is a friend of mine and Kat's."

The server handed Shea her glass of wine and left. Shea looked up at the big man, hesitant. "That's nice of you to say, but . . ." She bit her lip, then sighed. "My brother still has nightmares about your shooting. He blames himself for what happened to you."

Howard looked stunned. "Christ, why? He did everything he could to break the case. Nobody could've predicted what was going down."

"Well, that's my brother. He feels like he failed."

"No way in hell. I'll tell him myself."

"Just don't mention I said anything, if you don't mind."

"I won't," the lieutenant promised. "Thanks for telling me."

Tommy cleared his throat. "Do I get an introduction to the new babe?"

Shea stiffened, and Cori smirked inwardly as she and her friend exchanged a knowing look. Hollywood beautiful or not, Shea had a real problem with exactly Tommy's type: immature, ruled by his libido, and he possessed a vocabulary that included words like "dude" and "babe."

"I'm Shea," she said coolly. She did not, Cori noted, extend her hand, as she'd done to greet Zack.

"Tommy Skyler." His open, infectious grin seemed to have no positive effect on the object of his attentions. He was nothing, however, if not persistent. "Any good at pool?"

She gazed up at him from under her lashes. Took a leisurely sip of her wine. "I hold my own."

Everyone knew she wasn't referring to pool. The line was drawn in the sand. She wasn't the least bit impressed by his boyish charm, and made no bones about it. They all watched, avid spectators as the couple thrust and parried.

"Want to go a round?" His voice, low and sexy, dripped with the double entendre.

"No, thank you."

"Afraid you'll lose?"

She rolled her shoulders back, lifted her chin. "I'm an ER nurse. Very little frightens me."

"Except a simple game of pool."

Touché. In a blinding moment of clarity, Cori knew this man wasn't the dumb pretty boy he let everyone believe. She wondered if Shea noticed, too.

Apparently so. Her friend's lips curved in challenge. "Let's play."

Wolf whistles followed them as Tommy took her hand and led her to another open table. Picking up on her misgivings, Zack squeezed Cori's hand.

"Don't worry; she'll be fine with Tommy."

"She'd better be, or Shane will go Hannibal Lecter on his ass. And it won't be his brains the man will be feeding him."

He hugged her close, planting a sweet kiss on her lips. "I love you."

"Trying to distract me?"

"Is it working?"

Snuggling into his side, she laid her head on his shoulder. "Absolutely. I love you, too."

"God, enough with the mushy crap," Howard grumbled, taking an empty seat.

Zack snickered. "Says Mr. Studly Groom. Still having Kat swab antiseptic on those scratch marks on your back, big guy?"

Howard gave him a toothy smile that looked decidedly dangerous, and flexed his arms, making his biceps and massive chest strain in his T-shirt. "Careful, my friend. I'd hate to have to break you in half just when we got you put together again."

The evening passed quickly, the guys bullshitting one another with gusto. Everyone had fun, even Julian and Carmelita, who eventually loosened up and joined in a few rounds of pool and darts. Everyone except Sean, who stayed too quiet and drank too much . . . and stared at Eve with a mixture of longing, anger, and a load of confusion.

That can't be good. But since she didn't know Zack's friends very well yet, it wasn't her place to voice an opinion.

Squinting one eye shut, Cori aimed a dart at the target a few yards away. She let the little missile fly, and huffed as it buried itself in the wall a good three feet to the right of the target.

"Well, damn! I aimed right at the bull's-eye."

Beside her, Zack laughed and put both arms around her shoulders, giving her a fierce hug. "How about a dart contest? Loser has to strip for the winner when we get home."

"I already gave you a show." Turning, she leered at Zack. "It's your turn."

"Oh, boy. Time to go." He cupped her chin, love shining in his blue eyes. "I've been practicing my act, you know."

Grinning, she pressed against the part of him that liked the suggestion. A lot. "Now you're talking. Take me home and seduce me, handsome."

Quickly, he said their good-byes. The men shook hands with Zack, clapping his back, and the women hugged Cori. She felt incredibly at peace. Shea embraced her last, and Cori frowned in sudden concern.

"I don't like leaving you here."

Flushing, her friend gestured to her new admirer hovering in the background. "Tommy said he'd make sure I got to my car safely. You two go on—I'm having fun."

"You're sure?"

"Yes. I'll call you," she whispered in a conspiratorial voice.

"Details?"

"You bet!"

"Girls," Zack muttered. "Come on, baby."

He put an arm around her shoulders and she leaned into him, encircling his trim waist as he steered them toward the exit. They stepped into the brisk February night, and the clean air, the smell of the nearby Cumberland River, shocked her senses like a slap after the dingy atmosphere of the pool joint.

She breathed in a lungful of cool air, and caught a whiff of Zack's spicy cologne, as well. He was warm, strong, and solid against her side. Hers.

Suddenly there was nothing she wanted more in the world than his body covering hers. Around and inside her, making sweet love to her all night long. No scarves or props. They'd make their own music, together.

"Zack?"

"Hmm?"

"When do I get my surprise? The one you've been working on?"

She could practically feel his radiant smile as he answered. "In the morning, when the sun comes up."

"Why do I have to wait? And why so early?"

He chuckled. "You'll see, beautiful."

"Good. Because I have a surprise for you, too."

"Give me a hint?"

"No way."

They headed around the side of the building toward the far end of the parking lot, shoes crunching on the gravel. Anticipation of getting him home and in bed hurried her steps.

"Going to a fire?" he teased.

"Nope, that's your job. Mine is to get you naked as soon as possible."

"If you don't fall asleep first."

"Ha! You just wait—"

Coming to an abrupt halt, he removed his arm from her shoulder and took her hand. Tugged as though in warning. "Hang on a sec."

Blinking, she glanced around the parking lot crowded with vehicles. "What's wrong?"

"It's too dark out here."

"It's after midnight, silly."

"That's not what I mean." He stayed put, scanning the lot.

Every muscle in his body seemed spring-loaded. Alert. His intensity made her nervous, and the prickle at her nape sent a trill of fear down her spine.

"Zack, where's your car?"

He pointed into the shadows. "Right over there."

"Where—oh, I see it, barely." She shuddered, yanking at him, anxious to be gone. "Come on."

"No, wait." After a brief silence, he pointed to the side of the building, then to the three poles spread at intervals throughout the lot. "The lights are out. *All* of them."

"Power outage?"

"Broken."

She saw it then. The shards of glass glittering in the moonlight on the walk next to the building. "Zack . . ."

"Okay," he said quietly. "Let's go inside and give the management a heads-up about the lights. We'll wait until some of the others are ready—"

"The waiting game is over," a voice sneered from behind them.

His voice.

They spun together and Zack pushed her behind him, shielding her with his body. Cori looked past him to the man standing just a few feet from them, and clutched at Zack's shirt.

"Oh, God, Zack!" The glint of a gun barrel was trained on the center of Zack's chest, cold and menacing in the man's hand.

Terror injected her blood with ice. She took in the man's form, so familiar . . . and yet not. He was tall and lithe, but the long blond hair was history. Instead, dark locks were shorn close to his head, lending his face a much rougher, sinister appearance.

"Figured it out yet, darling? Do you know who I am?"

His *voice*. It wasn't quite right, and neither was his facial structure. A few adjustments to the nose, forehead, and cheekbones and she'd almost believe . . .

"No," she whispered in horror. "You can't be."

"Who can't I be, Corrine?" He laughed, enjoying this. "Satan himself? Your worst nightmare risen from the bowels of hell?"

If she hadn't been hanging on to Zack, she would've fallen. Her knees turned to water, her heart ready to explode.

"Alex."

Zack sucked in a sharp breath, and let it out on a vicious curse, keeping her firmly behind him. "Stay the fuck away from her, asshole."

"Oh, I don't think so. Cori dearest has something belonging to me." Alex waved the gun, leering in the darkness.

"And unless she's ready to see her lover die, she's got about fifty million and one reasons to cooperate. Turn around and start walking."

18

Zack kept Cori in front of him as they walked toward the very back of the parking lot, their captor behind him. Rage and fear roiled in his stomach, and he was sick with the need to kill this sonofabitch before he hurt her.

He didn't believe for one second this man was her deceased husband risen from the dead. She'd spent time with him as Tony. She would've known. A mannerism, a phrase. He couldn't have hidden forever behind a new face. Plastic surgery covered the skin, not the rotten soul underneath.

She was shocked and afraid. When her mind cleared, she'd realize this man wasn't Alex. But who the fuck was he?

Someone who not only desired her fifty million but clearly believed he had the *right* to the fortune. That alone made him extremely dangerous.

As they reached the edge of the lot, the man's order broke the silence. "Keep going to the tree line, to the van parked there."

Once he got them in the vehicle and away from here, their chances of survival dropped dramatically. Those grim figures danced in Zack's brain, but he shoved them away. One split second. All he needed to go for the gun, tackle "Alex," and allow Cori to run back to the bar for help. The man couldn't possibly keep an eye on both of them, especially in the dark.

But as they reached the old van, their situation plunged to a new low. The bastard had thought out his plan well. Skirting his captives, he laid the keys to the van on the hood and backed away.

"Cori, you'll drive," he snapped. "I'll ride in the front passenger seat. But first, I want your boyfriend to open the side door and buckle himself into one of the middle seats."

Damn, he'd covered almost every angle. *But maybe I can attack him from behind. Get the gun or strangle his sorry ass.*

It might work. He climbed into the old bucket seat directly behind the passenger's spot and buckled his seat belt, tensed and ready for an opportunity to strike. The gun was trained on Cori now, to ensure his cooperation as she and Alex climbed in.

At the man's nod, Cori started the van. Zack was working on the best method of attack when Alex turned in his seat, his grin feral and ominous in the overhead light inside the vehicle.

"Here, lover boy. Catch."

Something light bounced off Zack's chest and landed in his lap. Puzzled, he looked down—to see a syringe filled with clear liquid. His blood ran cold and he scrambled to come up with a way out of this. He'd stick it in their captor instead—

"I'd put a bullet between your eyes before you finished

your swing," the man broke into his thoughts, pointing the muzzle at Zack's head. "Inject the drug into your vein, my friend. Every drop."

"No."

"What's in the needle won't kill you, but the bullet will. Do you want your sweetie to see your brains splatter all over the interior of the van, all over her? To endure this very long night with your death on her conscience?"

Oh, sweet Jesus. Help us. "You're going to kill us both anyway."

"True, but if you choose to die now, I suppose I should tell you what I'll do to her after you're dead. After she transfers the money to my account, I'll ride her. Hard. All night long. She'll scream underneath me, but you won't know, will you? She'll cry and beg for mercy—"

"Shut the fuck up." Zack's fist closed around the syringe. Rage shredded his soul and he fought for reason. Control. This man wanted him alive to play him and Cori against each other. It sucked, but he had no choice. Playing along might buy them some time.

Hands amazingly steady, he uncapped the needle.

"Zack, no," Cori begged. "Please don't!"

He didn't look at her as he extended his arm. Pressed the tip of the needle into a bluish vein at the crook of his elbow. Pushed the unknown substance into his bloodstream, every last bit.

Fire and ice zipped through his system, stealing his breath. He gasped, his heart accelerating. His body went limp and the syringe slipped from his deadened fingers.

Alex leered, pure evil. "Of course, I might have lied."

No! God help me. . . . Cori . . .

His vision grayed and went black.

The last sound he heard was Cori's frantic cries chasing him into oblivion.

Cori watched, horrified, as Zack's eyes closed. His arm flopped to hang beside him, the syringe on the van's floor at his fingertips.

I might have lied.

"Zack? Zack!" A scream welled in her chest, erupted from the core of her being. She faced Alex, wild fear ripping her apart. "Is he dead? Because if he is, I don't care what happens to me! Your precious money can rot for all I care, you filthy animal!"

The open-handed slap on her cheek snapped her head back, made her see stars. Brought her to her senses. She had to *think*.

No, he wouldn't have killed Zack yet. He needed her cooperation to get the money.

"May I check his pulse?" It galled her to ask, but thankfully, he consented.

"No sudden moves."

She nodded, biting off a smart-ass retort. Twisting, she reached for Zack's dangling arm, taking his wrist between her fingers. There. Relief flooded her, and she carefully shifted his arm, putting his hand in his lap, before turning to grip the steering wheel.

"Where to?"

"Good girl. Drive to the road and take a right."

Cori followed his directions, praying Shea or one of Zack's friends would exit the bar and see the van leaving. No one did.

Disheartened, she drove out of town, doubt clawing at hope with every mile. About twenty minutes into the drive, he directed her to turn left onto a bumpy county road. Deeper into the hills they penetrated, leaving civilization behind, the skeletal branches of the winter forest like bony fingers beckoning her and Zack to their graves.

At last, he directed her to a driveway leading to a log cabin set back in the woods, modest though not run-down. A light glowed in one window.

Will we leave here alive?

An image of Alex burying their bodies in the earth somewhere in the hills beyond gripped her with fear, and she shoved it aside. *Calm. He won't kill you until he gets the money.*

Which was why she'd not give in.

"Get out, nice and slow. You and I are going to go inside."

"Wh-what about Zack?"

"Shut up and you'll find out."

Cori got out and stumbled on shaking legs to the front of the van. Alex met her, keeping the gun trained in her direction. He waggled the weapon toward the house, so she walked. Across the uneven yard and onto the front porch, hating that she had to leave Zack even for a few minutes. Then again, maybe he'd wake up and escape. Get to the highway, flag down a car.

Right. The drug had probably leveled him for hours.

"Inside."

He flung open the door and she walked in ahead of him. Looked like he'd been living here, using the cabin as his home base. The furniture was a bit sparse, but the place was actually sort of nice.

If it hadn't been inhabited by a jackal.

The carpeted living room boasted a flat-screen television and a sofa. Strangely, the sofa had been moved from its position in front of the TV, off to one side; she noted the four dents where the legs had been. In the center of the room, a single chair had been placed.

One wall was mostly taken up by a stone fireplace, while another was home to the desk and laptop computer. It was here that the vile bastard would attempt to force her to transfer the fortune from her account to his.

As evidenced by the handcuff dangling from a chain, which was connected to a bolt in the wall next to the desk.

She almost laughed. Almost. If he had any clue she didn't know how to transfer the funds electronically, how to circumvent the maze of online security safeguards, they'd already be dead.

Thank God I called Joaquin and confessed everything before we left for the bar. How he would locate them was a long shot she didn't care to think about.

"Sit in the computer chair and hold out your wrist."

She did, avoiding eye contact, trying not to flinch as the cuff tightened with a series of metallic clicks.

Alex smiled. "Lost some of your attitude, huh? Wait until you see what I have in mind for your boyfriend."

She glared at him, holding her silence as he laughed and went out the front door again. The second he was gone, she jumped from the chair and ran to the bolt, twisting and yanking in a futile effort to loosen it.

Nothing doing. The eye was screwed deep into the log, so tight a tool such as pliers would be required to remove it. "Shit!"

Heavy tread on the steps sent her diving for the chair again. A series of thumps sounded on the porch. She was sitting again as Alex pushed the door open, walking backward, dragging Zack by the feet. Anger boiled in her gut. The thumps had probably been Zack's head bumping up the porch steps, and God knew he couldn't take any more blows to his skull.

Their captor wrestled Zack into a sitting position. Working quickly, he removed one of several sections of rope he'd carried around his neck and used it to bind Zack's shoulders and torso to the back of the chair. Next, he wrenched Zack's arms around the chair's back and tied them, then secured his ankles to the legs. The rope bit into his skin, partially because of his weight sagging against the bindings.

Cori willed herself not to cry. His face was pale, breathing shallow. His glasses were gone. He'd come to, and then what? Things would only get worse. She didn't see how they'd be able to break free of this monster. Zack might wish he'd died after all.

Stop it! He'd be so incredibly upset to hear her thoughts. They'd find a way out of this. They had no choice.

"Now we wait for the prince to awaken. Sit tight, Cori, dear," he said, raking a hand through his cropped brown hair.

Alex disappeared into what she assumed was the kitchen from the swooshing noise of what sounded like a fridge and him rummaging around.

Like a bolt, the truth hit her.

Alex had never raked his hand through his hair. And he'd never, ever lifted a finger to do things for himself!

No, he'd have led her into the kitchen and beaten her as he forced her to fix him something to eat, then thrown it on the floor and ground it under his heel while shouting that her offering wasn't fit for a dog.

Whoever this piece of feces was, he wasn't her dead husband.

But for some reason, this man was content to let her assume. He was more patient and cunning than Alex had ever been.

And those traits, she knew, made him ten times as deadly.

Zack came awake by slow degrees. He hurt. All over. His mouth was as dry as cotton and his head pounded. Why?

He flexed his back and arms, tried to stretch his cramped muscles. Couldn't move. What the hell?

"Zack, honey?"

Cori. Her voice nearby, thin with worry. Where was she?

He licked his lips, tried to swallow. God, he was parched. Thirsty. He tried to open his eyes, but his lids felt glued shut. He hadn't drunk that much last night, had he?

Wait. His ass was sore, too. He was sitting on something hard, uncomfortable. Upright. He wiggled his wrists and feet.

Ropes. *Ropes?*

Last night.

A gun.

Their kidnapping flooded his memory in an awful rush. Bitter panic and nausea pushed bile to the back of his throat and he fought down the sickness. His eyes opened and the room whirled, fuzzy.

"Cori," he rasped. "Where—"

"She's here," the hated voice interrupted. Footsteps, coming closer. "Glad you joined the party. The bitch refused to cooperate until she saw you weren't dead yet."

Zack concentrated on the blurry form standing in front of him. His vision was better, yet remained somewhat unfocused. His glasses. Missing. Which bugged him, because he had trouble seeing Cori's face clearly. If he had to die like this, tied like an animal, he wanted to take the image of her lovely face with him.

More practically, he needed to be able to read her expressions. Oh, the fear in her huge, golden eyes was telegraphed plain enough. What he hoped to relay and catch in return were those subtle nuances their kidnapper might miss between them.

"Hey, baby. This isn't nearly as much fun as last time I was tied to a chair." There. A brave, tremulous smile. Holding her gaze, he thought, *Help me stall him.* Then he asked, "How long have I been out?"

"A couple of hours—"

"Shut up!" The man spun, his arm shooting out. A resounding crack echoed in the room as he slapped Cori's face. Hard. "What information either of you need to know, I'll tell it!"

"Noo!" Zack bucked in the chair, straining against the cords.

Cori's tongue flicked out, capturing a smear of blood on her lower lip. Strands of hair hung loose over her eyes, which were glaring at the man with pure hatred, almost as potent as the red tide choking Zack.

You are so fucking dead.

"Untie me and try that, motherfucker."

Their kidnapper turned his attention to Zack once more, apparently amused. "You wish. Comfy?" He chuckled, glancing at Cori. "You're going to log in to your overseas account, or you're going to watch me take your lover boy apart, piece by piece."

Cori's wide, frightened eyes collided with Zack's, and he gave an almost imperceptible shake of his head. Even if she knew how to make a transfer, there was no way she'd be able to empty the account of fifty million without assistance and verification from her bank's representative.

And if she somehow managed the transaction, they were both dead.

"You're not her ex-husband," Zack said, hoping to distract him. "Who are you?"

"I never said I was." Flexing his fingers, he waged a visible battle against gloating. And lost. "She assumed, probably because of the family resemblance. I suppose I should thank you for your part in my brother's demise. I'm Lionel Gunter. Small world, isn't it, my dear sister-in-law?"

Cori's jaw dropped. "Alex never mentioned a brother. None of his family came forward after his death or even attended his funeral."

"Despite the fact that I was the one who clued in my worthless brother about the advantages of marrying into the Delacruz hotel dynasty, I wasn't named in his will, sweet thing," he spat. "Even if I hadn't been in prison, why would I go to his goddamned funeral?"

"To spit on his grave?" Zack suggested. *Keep his attention from Cori.*

Lionel grinned. Zack longed to rearrange his face.

"Under different circumstances, I might've liked you, Knight."

"You'll excuse me if I don't find that much of a compliment."

"Take it however you prefer. I don't care. I'll have the fortune that should've gone to me, not some cheap whore Alex was married to for, what? Five minutes?"

Cori's expression hardened. "I already told you, Joaquin is looking for you. When he finds you, kiss your ass good-bye."

"Oh, he'll find me, all right. I'm counting on it." The bastard let this sink in, smug. Unconcerned.

"He'll kill you," Cori said, voice wavering. Uncertain.

"Will he? Did you honestly believe I didn't have a partner in my endeavors?"

Cori's face blanched chalk white. "Joaquin? He'd never betray me. *Never.* You're lying."

"Am I? Let me share something," he said, reaching out to caress her cheek. "In a few hours, your brothers will arrive here to save the day, as it were. One of them is my partner, the one who informed me of your husband's untimely death and the mastermind of this entire scheme . . . and he will die with the others. I don't share well. Being played is a bitch, huh? Guess which brother, Corrine, my love."

Before Zack could protest, get her attention somehow, she reacted. Her bravado folded and she spat full in his smirking face.

For one heart-stopping moment, Zack thought Lionel would hit her. Sheer instinct caused him to surge, the bindings cutting his wrists and ankles, his need to come between them, to protect her, a physical agony.

Slowly, Lionel withdrew from her. Wiped his nose and cheek. Jaw clenched, he doubled his fist. Turned to face Zack.

Relief warred with dread. This was it, then. The monster intended to beat the shit out of him to keep her in line. Play on her emotions. Zack knew he'd hang on, however bad it got. He'd endure anything, for Cori.

But could *she* hold out?

The first punch connected with his jaw as Cori cried out, snapped his head to the side, wrenched his neck. So powerful he saw stars. Blood filled his mouth, ran down his chin.

"You hit like a girl," he goaded, spitting blood in the direction of the man's shoes. Too bad he missed.

The next blow took him in the stomach, dead center. Waves of nausea battered him and he struggled not to throw up. The third punch caught his ribs on the left side. Another, and another. Stomach, ribs. He doubled over as far as he could, absorbing the blows, tensing the muscles in his abdomen. Grateful his kidneys weren't exposed to the brutality.

Body shots, he'd survive. For a few hours anyway. Unless a rib shattered and punctured a lung. Or his heart. Otherwise, it would take a long time for the bastard to kill him this way. The shithead might even break his hand in the process.

One could dream.

"Stop," Cori begged. "Please!"

Lionel glanced at her, eyes cold. "Transfer the money."

The laptop screen waited behind her, luminous. She hesitated, looking to Zack for guidance. Desperate, unsure what to do. He curled a lip at Lionel.

"She's not doing it. Go fuck yourself."

"She will."

Lionel redoubled his efforts, keeping the blows concentrated on Zack's stomach. Breaking him down, knowing his prey couldn't hold out forever.

He punched, again and again. Zack hung forward in his bonds, gagging. Choking. Dry heaves twisted his gut, but there was nothing to expel. At least he'd been spared that indignity.

He'd lost count of the blows when Lionel took a break.

Zack lifted his head. Smiled. Blood and spittle dribbled from his lips.

"Go easy, huh? I can't afford any more sick days."

Lionel laughed. "By God, you have balls." He sauntered into the kitchen and came right out again—holding a large butcher knife in one hand. "I'm going to hate cutting them off."

Cori gasped. Zack didn't look at her. His wide gaze was fixed to the wicked, eight-inch blade. Lionel stepped between his spread knees, grabbed the neck of Zack's polo shirt, stretching the material. Positioning the blade at the vee, he cut in a swift downward stroke, bisecting the material with a rending tear.

On reflex, Zack glanced down at himself as his captor parted the shirt, pushed the loose flaps back and over his shoulders. A line of crimson slashed his belly and he watched the liquid bead in numb fascination. The tip of the knife was so sharp, he hadn't felt the cut, which was just beginning to sting.

Shallow. He'd seen much worse on stabbing victims before. No big deal, nothing more than a head game his tormentor was employing to get off.

Except the bastard was just getting warmed up.

Lionel placed the razor-sharp blade behind Zack's ear, ran it along the vulnerable skin in an arc to his throat. There was no pain as the wet warmth trickled down his neck, his chest. The sting came after, but he ignored it. Kept his expression impassive, eyes locked on his tormentor's, unwavering.

"Log in to your account," Lionel said softly to Cori, not taking his gaze from Zack's.

"No, beautiful. Don't."

The knife skimmed to his chest. Made another cut,

across one pectoral. Then the other. Blood ran, and Cori stifled a low sob.

"Please, stop," she pleaded. "I'll try to log in."

This got Lionel's attention, and he glared at her over his shoulder. "Try? What the fuck does that mean?"

"I—I have to remember my account number. It's really long and I'm n-not sure if I've got it right."

That's my girl. Zack knew her voice by now, heard the false conciliatory tone she was using to appease him. She was lying to stall him, buy them time.

Staring past Lionel, he met her solemn gaze, saw the flash of mutiny their kidnapper missed. She turned to the keyboard and he silently cheered her on, sent her love he hoped she could feel wrapping around her.

Her fingers clicked on the keys. Hesitated, backspaced. Continued, filling in a series of letters and numbers on two lines. Hit Enter.

Access Denied.

"Try again, dammit."

Casting a furtive glance over her shoulder at Lionel, she started over. Every now and then, she paused. Pretended to think hard about which combination to use. Entered.

Access Denied.

"I'm trying! I'll get it right!"

"You'd better," he hissed.

With the third failed attempt, she and Zack knew he'd been pushed too far.

"You slut," he snarled, jerking her chin up. "I'll show you the consequences of fucking with me."

Striding to the fireplace, he laid the knife on the mantel. Slid a heavy iron poker from its stand. His gaze fell on Zack and an evil smile curved his lips.

"No," she whispered. "Please, I remember now. I'll log in and—"

"Let this be a lesson to ensure you'll think twice before yanking my chain."

Fear stole Zack's speech. His body went cold and he could do nothing. Say nothing as the man came to stand in front of him, the iron rod hanging loosely at his side.

"I'm going to break you apart," the monster said, matter-of-fact.

Ah, shit.

Then he swung the poker like a batter hitting a home run out of the park. Zack's side exploded in white-hot agony.

"Ahhhh!" His yell mingled with Cori's scream. With the rushing noise in his ears.

He swore he felt the ribs shatter. Actually rip from their moorings to do untold internal damage. He struggled to draw breath, to—

A second blow sent his stomach into his backbone. The pain was unbearable, like nothing he'd ever been dealt. He hung his head and retched, then began coughing. Harsh, gasping, an ominous rattle in his chest. The flecks of crimson came next, splattering his jeans.

Coughing up blood. Bad, very bad.

The clock was ticking now, winding down.

Think of something, anything. Or you're a dead man.

Vaguely, he became aware of Cori sobbing. Begging for Lionel to stop. The poker landed on the floor, discarded.

"You're done fucking with me, I assume?"

"Y-yes. I swear. I know how to log in."

"Get started, or your boyfriend won't survive the next round."

More clicking. A satisfied grunt from Lionel. Zack raised his head, tried hard to focus his swimming vision. A page was up on the laptop screen, though he couldn't read the information from here.

"Now what?" Lionel demanded, waving a hand at the screen.

Cori worked for a few minutes, clicking on icons and typing in what Zack assumed to be a transfer request. Finally, she shook her head and sniffed, wiping her face.

"It's blocking me. I can't transfer that kind of money online, and my rep won't be in now. It's evening overseas." Cori looked up at Lionel, halting his tirade before he started.

"But I know who *can* get us in."

"You'd better know, because I don't have goddamned time for this!"

Cori shot Zack a meaningful look, and his admiration for her grew tenfold, if that were possible. He smiled at her through the agony clawing at his body, and nodded.

"Zack can do it. He has a genius IQ, and he's a skilled hacker."

Lionel shifted his stance, obviously not certain whether to be relieved or pissed. "And you're imparting this news *now*? Why should I believe you?"

Cori shrugged. "Whether you do or not is up to you. But Zack told me he once hacked the FBI's classified files—at age twelve. If anyone can make you a rich man in a short period of time, he can."

Lionel fell silent, debating. Zack watched him sift through his options, knowing what he'd decide. What choice did the man have?

"All right," he snapped at Zack. "I'll let you up. You sit in her place and get the job done, or I cut her throat."

Their captor retrieved the knife from the fireplace mantel, then went to Zack and sliced his bonds. Freed his wrists, then his ankles. Zack rubbed his hands and arms, sore and tingling from lack of circulation.

He stood slowly, unsteady on his feet. Racked by pain, he stumbled to the chair and lowered himself into it. Hunched over the keyboard, buffered by Cori's presence at his side.

Placing his fingers on the keys, he called upon skills he hadn't utilized in years. The part of himself he'd left behind long ago in favor of his dreams.

He'd wanted only to live an ordinary life.

Now he was being forced to perform an extraordinary act.

And he had a plan.

Zack sent a prayer heavenward that he and Cori would survive once Lionel discovered exactly what he'd done with fifty million dollars.

19

Minutes became a half hour. An hour? He didn't know.

Sweat rolled down Zack's face. Dizziness swamped his brain, and fatigue weakened his limbs. As he was immersed in code encryption, time ceased to have meaning. In the periphery, he was aware of Cori sitting on the floor by his feet. Lionel had finally given up and dragged over a kitchen chair to sit just behind his right shoulder.

Little else registered. Especially when he cracked the first level of the security system, and received clearance to proceed.

"I'll be goddamned," their captor blurted.

Zack didn't answer. His sights were set on his goal, and nothing would stop him.

Jesus, he was chilled. Not good. He needed to get to an emergency room, which wasn't happening in the foreseeable future.

Maybe not until it was too late.

He blocked thoughts of bleeding to death internally and redoubled his efforts. Patterns and combinations. Nothing to it, just like a mouse running through a maze to get to the cheese.

Another level. Lionel swore again, impressed.

You think that was cool, fuckhead? Wait for it.

So close. He had to concentrate not to pass out. What he'd give to lie down on the floor and sleep forever. His fingers flew, the numbers flashing across the screen in a blur.

And then he was in. For a few seconds he sat staring at the screen, almost unable to comprehend.

"Sonofabitch," Lionel breathed. "You did it."

Cori pushed to her feet, laid a hand on Zack's left shoulder, the chain attached to her wrist jingling.

"Yeah," Zack replied, wiping sweat from his eyes. His hands shook. "I need your account number and password."

The man slid a scrap of paper onto the desk next to his right arm. *Here we go.*

Pretending to read the information Lionel provided, he began to type in a series of letters and numbers. Fast. One line, then the other. Praying as he'd never done before that the bastard didn't note the discrepancy.

His fingers hovered over the Enter key.

A king's ransom, one keystroke from cyber oblivion.

He depressed the key, and sat back in the chair. *Transaction Complete.*

Lionel whooped, shooting from his seat. Danced around the living room, spiked an imaginary football.

Zack stared at the screen, exhausted. Cori squeezed his shoulder, lending her support even if she wasn't quite sure what he'd done or how they'd get out of this alive.

Zack's lips curved into a wicked smile. "Hide-and-seek," he rasped, breath rattling in his chest.

"Oh, my God," Cori said, stunned.

Lionel's victory dance came to an abrupt halt. "What'd you say?" Spinning, he grabbed the knife and stalked to Zack, hauled him out of the chair by his arm.

Fine by him. He'd just as soon be standing for what came next. "Hide-and-seek, the extreme version. I just hid fifty million dollars somewhere in cyberspace, and I'm the only one who knows where." He laughed at the man's poleaxed expression, coughed up more blood. Zack almost felt sorry for the poor fuck.

Almost.

He couldn't resist the coup de grâce. "If you live to be a hundred, you'll never find the money. Never fuck with a geek, asshole."

A roar of rage erupted from Lionel and he launched himself at Zack, swinging the knife. Out for blood.

"Look out!" Cori yelled.

Zack grabbed his arm, but the other man had the advantage and they bounced off the desk, crashed to the floor. They rolled, each delivering kicks and punches, each struggling to gain control of the knife. A glint of metal shone on the floor nearby, and he realized his nemesis had lost the gun. Probably fell from the waistband of his pants.

The weapon wouldn't do Zack any good lying several feet away. He had to wrest the knife from Lionel.

The front door splintered, louder than a shotgun blast, banging against the inside wall. Rolling with Lionel, punching the man in the gut with his free hand, he glanced up to see three dark-haired men rush into the house, guns drawn.

Cori's brothers.

And then she was screaming because, God help them, the third brother had the one in the lead dead in his sights. Preparing to gun down his own brother.

"Joaquin, behind you! Rafael, noo!" Cori clasped her hands over her ears.

Joaquin spun as Rafael's bullet took him in the shoulder. He went down shooting, his handsome face a grimace of anguish.

Christ! Zack's attention strayed to Cori's wide, beautiful eyes. Her grief was a mirror of Joaquin's as she twisted in her cuff, desperate to be free.

It was the split second of distraction that cost Zack.

Lionel wrenched his wrist from Zack's hold and plunged the blade between his ribs. "That's right. Die," he gloated. "Go to hell thinking about your bitch's legs open for me."

Pain washed over him. Tired. Oh, God.

Then he saw Cori straining to get to him, fighting off her remaining brother, even though he was trying to unlock her cuff. Tears streamed down her face.

She'd endured too much. Lost too much.

Exhaustion was swept aside in a red haze of rage. Strength born of vengeance flooded every cell in his body. Lionel drew back his arm to deliver another strike with the knife.

The sonofabitch never got the chance. Heaving with his lower body, Zack flipped and rolled them both. Caught Lionel's wrist and slammed it to the floor until he heard bone crack. The man howled and the knife fell useless to the floor.

Zack knocked it aside and something inside him snapped. Broke, like a dry twig. Poison flooded his soul and he poured all his hatred into his fists.

Done. He was done being the fucking whipping boy. The victim. Nobody would mess with him or his woman again. Ever.

He was a machine. The satisfying crunch of bone met his fist. Over and over. He existed to deliver justice for every wrong he'd suffered. For every time he'd had to scrape himself off the floor. For every person a dirtbag like this one had beaten down.

"You thought you'd take Cori's money?"

No more.

"Zack!"

"Her life?" he shouted.

Never again.

"Honey, no!"

Die, motherfucker.

Hands caught his arm, pulled him backward. Totally consumed, he lunged for the fallen man.

"Zack, stop! You're killing him! *You're killing him!*" Arms wrapped around him, and her sweet voice reached him through the rage. "If you kill this man, you'll regret it for the rest of your life. Don't do this. You're not like him."

Not like him.

Zack blinked. Looked around him. Joaquin was on his cell phone, barking into it for help, one hand pressed to the wound at his shoulder. Rafael lay nearby, unmoving. Dead? The third brother crouched next to Lionel, mouth in a grim line.

"Honey, it's going to be okay," Cori soothed, holding him close, stroking his hair. "*You're* going to be okay."

Would he?

Dazed, he finally turned his stare to Lionel, who lay unmoving in front of him. The man's face was unrecognizable. A mask of blood and gore.

Zack lifted his shaking hands, held them up. They were covered in blood—and it wasn't all his own. "My God . . . what have I done? Cori?"

"Shh, it's okay."

You're not like him.

But he was. He'd killed a man.

And nothing would be okay. Ever.

A buzzing sensation filled his head. Adrenaline and madness spent, he was hollow. Just a shell of nothing.

He felt himself toppling over. Cori eased him to the floor, on his back. He tried to focus on her face, but couldn't. Three forms hovered over him. They became a blur as his vision went white, then gray.

"He's in bad shape, Joaquin," the third brother said. "How long for the paramedics?"

"At least thirty minutes. They can't get a chopper in here. Fuck."

Christ, he didn't have half an hour.

Cori took his cold hand, held it to her cheek. "Talk to me, handsome. Stay with me."

"I love . . . you."

But he no longer had the right. He'd lost everything that mattered when he'd become the type of man he hated.

A black veil covered his eyes, Cori's musical voice receding down a long, dark tunnel.

Until it disappeared altogether.

Blood. Everywhere.

All over Zack, saturating his jeans and torn shirt.

Her brother Manny handed her a thick towel. Peeling aside the flap of Zack's torn shirt, she pressed the towel hard into the knife wound on his side. For all the good it did. They were too far out of town, help too many minutes away.

"Stay with me," she repeated. "I can't lose you now. Not after all we've been through."

"You won't, Sis." Joaquin squeezed her shoulder. "We're going to drive Knight out of here, meet the paramedics at the highway. Save some time."

"You're hurt, too." She sniffed. The tears kept coming.

"I'll keep."

"What about—about . . . ?"

His voice hardened to ice. "Rafael's dead, the traitorous snake. I should've known something was up with our dear half brother. His accomplice is hanging on, barely. With any luck, he'll follow his partner to hell."

Cori shook her head, unable to take her eyes off Zack's white face. "Lionel can't die. Zack will never forgive himself."

She'd never forget the look on Zack's face when he gazed at Lionel's unconscious body, realized what he'd done. The light in his blue eyes was extinguished, her kind, gentle lover replaced by a stranger.

"Then he won't die." That was Joaquin. All the world black-and-white. Never any gray, no give-and-take. No mercy.

Well, he'd see the shades of gray soon enough.

"You and I will talk," she promised, tone as uncompromising as his. "Or rather, I'll talk and you'll listen."

Expression unyielding, he nodded. With Manny's help, he carefully lifted Zack and carried him out to the Mercedes they'd probably rented at the airport. Laid him in the backseat.

"Manny, stay here and deal with the sheriff's department," he said to his younger brother. "I'll call when we get to the hospital."

"Tell them to call Detective Bernie with the Sugarland PD. He can fill them in," Cori added.

Concern clouded his face. "No worries. Dealing with

cops is what I do best." He glanced at Zack bleeding all over the leather seat. "Better hurry."

Cori held out her hand for the keys. "I'll drive. We won't get there if you pass out at the wheel."

They met the county ambulance about a mile out on the highway, cutting precious minutes off the drive to Sugarland. The trip would still take too damned long, but there was no help for it. The nearest clinic out here wasn't equipped for major trauma, the paramedics said.

The worst part was having to watch them speed away with Zack, and not knowing what would happen. If he—

No. He had to survive. He *would*.

If he didn't, she'd want to die, too. But she'd have to go on, somehow. She'd have no choice.

He'd left her with one very good reason to live.

Cori was curled up in a corner of the ER's waiting room when Joaquin emerged from inside, his release papers in hand. He hadn't wanted her inside with him, stubborn, arrogant jerk. Bandages were visible under his loosely buttoned white dress shirt, his suit jacket draped over the injured shoulder without his arm in the sleeve. She'd known they wouldn't be able to keep him overnight. What the great Joaquin Delacruz wanted, he got.

Well, not always.

He might have gotten himself shot playing the hero, but that act alone in no way made up for his ruining Zack.

The man she loved, who was fighting for his life.

The father of their child.

Joaquin came to stand before her, proud and arrogant as ever, though a hint of sorrow shone in his dark eyes before he masked the emotion. "You're going to make me grovel, aren't you?"

"Not to me. Zack is the one you'll apologize to, if he'll listen." *If he can.*

"The debt was legal, Corrine. Darius Knight owed me three quarters of a million dollars. If I let everyone who owes me slide—"

"I don't care," she said coldly. "Threats are beneath you, brother mine, no matter how veiled. And especially when you insinuate you'll hurt a helpless old man in a nursing home who's little more than an infant. That makes you a monster, same as Rafael and Lionel. Same as Alex."

Unconsciously, he rubbed a hand over his heart. He stared at her a long moment. "What do you want me to do?"

"Make this right with Zack. Wipe out the debt, and restore his finances. Or we're done. You'll never hold your niece or nephew in your arms, and that would be a shame."

Not exactly the joyous announcement she'd envisioned.

"I'll be damned." This time, the flicker of pain was real, and he didn't bother to hide it. "You remind me of Mother more and more every day," he said softly. "You've grown a backbone of steel, Corrine Shannon Delacruz."

"I learned from the best."

Admiration shone in his eyes. "Consider it done."

"I never thought otherwise."

Heaving a tired sigh, he lowered himself to the seat beside her. "Any news about Knight?"

"He's in surgery. Two broken ribs, some internal bleeding. He's lost a lot of blood." Her voice broke on the last.

Never one to stand for tears, Joaquin draped his good arm around her in an awkward attempt at comforting his sister. "He'll be fine. Only a weak or stupid man would leave behind a woman such as you."

In spite of herself, she gave a watery laugh. "Always black-and-white."

"Does he know the truth about Alex?"

"No, but I guess he'll have to now, won't he?" she whispered.

"Not if you don't want him to. Though knowing might help him to deal with what's happened," he said, surprising her with a rare moment of concern for someone outside the family.

She nodded, moving the subject along. She didn't want to talk about the night of Alex's death. "So, Rafael contacted Lionel and they schemed together."

"I'm sorry, love. I never dreamed he'd turn against family."

"It wasn't your fault." She knew he'd never believe that. Joaquin was as tough on himself as he was on everyone in his midst.

"Does Knight know about the baby?" he asked suddenly.

"No. I was going to tell him this morning. He had a surprise to show me, something he's been working on, and I was going to tell him. . . ."

Her throat constricted to the size of a pinhole. Burned and ached. She refused to cry anymore because Zack would live.

Hours crept by. Detective Bernie came, peppered her

and her brother with questions. After imparting the news that Lionel Gunter would survive to stand trial, he left.

Just before noon, Dr. Chu appeared, looking tired, but pleased. "Cori, Zack is stable. He gave us quite a scare, but he's going to be all right."

She buried her face in her hands. Drew a shuddering breath and raised her gaze to Chu's. "Thank God. When can I see him?"

"Won't be long. He's being settled into ICU. Someone will come to get you."

Unable to put it off any longer, she located Eve's number in a phone book she borrowed from the receptionist and called her from a hospital courtesy phone. Despite her assurances, Zack's best friend was beside herself with worry. Eve promised to call the others, and after thanking her, Cori hung up.

Manny finally showed, and how he got to the hospital, Cori was too frazzled to ask. She was merely grateful for her brothers' presence, even Joaquin's, their hard-ass attitudes welcome comfort to her battered soul.

A nurse arrived and offered to take her to Zack. She leapt to her feet, anxious to see for herself that he'd survive. At the door to his cubicle, the nurse gave her an encouraging smile and disappeared.

Cori tiptoed in, unsure why she was being quiet. He was lying like a wax figure, face pale, lashes fanned against his cheeks. God, he looked dead.

She pulled up a chair and parked by his side, curling her fingers around his. "I'm here," she said, hoping he heard her on some level. "I'm not going anywhere. Just rest, okay? I love you."

He didn't move, not so much as a flicker behind his lids. But she was a patient woman. He'd be all right.

Their lives would soon be normal. Their own, free of trouble. They'd be happy.

As soon as he was better.

Cori strode to the ICU, eager to see Zack. A call at home from Dr. Chu early this morning gave her the wonderful news she'd been waiting for: Zack was awake. He'd had a restful night, dosed on drugs as he was, and now he was sitting up a bit.

Damn, she'd wanted to be there when he awoke, but she'd had to go home. Get a few hours' sleep, shower, and change clothes. Manny had flown home in the private jet last night to hold the fort in Atlantic City while Joaquin stayed on, using the guest bedroom Zack had abandoned shortly after arrival. He planned to honor her wishes and talk to Zack, today if possible.

Approaching his cube in ICU, she felt guilty relief that his team was on shift today. She'd quickly come to adore them, but being around them en masse when they were out of their minds with terror was draining. Dealing with her own fear had been taxing enough.

Fixing a cheerful smile on her face, she gave a light knock, then walked inside. "Hey, handsome. You know, if you keep coming back, the hospital might have to assign you a mailbox. I was telling Dr. Chu . . ."

Cautiously, she approached his bed. His face was turned away from her and he was staring at the wall. His blank, hollow expression frightened her as much as his bleeding half to death on the way here.

"Are you okay?" he asked, voice barely audible.

Sitting next to him, she squeezed his hand. "I'm just fine. And so are you, honey. We made it. We're both okay."

"Are we?"

Two simple words. They sent a chill down her spine, and her heart kicked painfully in her chest. "Of course we are. Rafael is dead," she said quietly. "He was conspiring with Lionel, who's going to recover. He's in police custody and he'll go to prison as soon as he's released."

Zack closed his eyes. "No thanks to me."

Oh, God. This was what she'd been afraid of. "Honey, you can't blame yourself. Anybody would've reacted—"

"Don't. Please."

Silence. A hard, tight nugget formed in her chest.

"Don't shut me out, Zack. We can work through this."

The despair in his voice ripped at her. "I almost killed a man. I *wanted* him to die."

"No, I don't believe—"

"Believe it," he said harshly. "I'm a firefighter and paramedic. I'm supposed to be a healer, a man who saves lives. But I would've killed him if you hadn't stopped me. I'm no better than him."

"That's not true!" She had to make him understand. "You're a good man, and you only wanted to protect me!"

"I crossed the line. I'm no good to you, or anyone."

"Zack—"

"I need for you to go," he said, voice breaking.

"Wh-what? No!"

"Please, just give me some time."

"For what? To push me away?" she cried. "To disappear from my life? Is that what you want?"

"I don't know what I want."

He was lying. He loved her. She knew it to the depths of her soul, but the words still broke her heart. This wasn't the joyful reunion, the happy-ever-after she'd imagined.

Zack was hurting, his sense of failure hanging over him like a shroud. He, a kind and gentle man, had lost control. He *had* nearly killed Lionel Gunter, and he needed time.

Away from me.

Acute loss speared her middle, but she stiffened her spine with resolve. She'd give him the space he required.

But not forever.

Bending, she placed a kiss on his cheek and stood. "I love you and I'm here for you, always. You know where to find me. Call, and I'll come."

With all the dignity of the most stoic Delacruz, she sailed from the room.

She didn't break down until she was well down the hallway, where he'd never hear her cry.

Zack managed to keep it together long enough for the door to click behind Cori. Then the tears slid down his face, hot and bitter. One senseless, base act, and he'd lost the only person who'd ever mattered.

The only woman he'd ever loved.

His father had been right. He was worthless. So much for aspiring to noble causes, for showing the old man he'd follow his own path, his dreams. For letting himself believe, for one moment, he could find happiness on his own terms.

Most little boys get over playing with fire trucks. I never did.

That part of his life was over. He wasn't a man anyone could be proud of. He'd failed himself, the team, and, most of all, Cori.

You're not like him.

He drifted on a sea of pain medication and misery.

When the door to his room suddenly opened, he hurriedly wiped the dampness from his face.

"Knight?"

He turned his head at the deep, unfamiliar voice, and stared in surprise. Of all the people he expected to see at his bedside, Joaquin Delacruz wasn't one of them.

"Come for a friendly visit, or to put a bullet in my brain? Because if you're here for the rest of your money, I don't have it and I won't. Not now, or next week. Not ever."

The man ran a hand through his longish, perfectly styled black hair, and sighed. "That's why I'm here, but not the way you think. I'm here to thank you for saving my sister's life, more than once."

"Thank me . . ."

"Yes."

Unbelievable. "I don't need or want your fucking thanks. I love Cori."

The devil arched a black brow. "Really? Oh, yes, your great love is why she nearly mowed me down in the lobby, sobbing her heart out."

His chest tightened. "Is that why you're here?"

"No. If you're a big enough imbecile to screw things up with her, she's better off without you." Delacruz shifted his stance, drawing his jacket more securely over his injured shoulder. "I've come to tell you I've forgiven your father's debt. The slate is clean, as it were."

Zack gazed at Delacruz. Weeks ago, he'd have given anything to hear those words. Now? "Fuck you."

"Let's get one thing clear—I'm doing this for my sister, not for you. She's the one bright spot in my existence, Knight, and I'll forever be grateful she's safe. So, whether you like it or not, it's a matter of principle to me. The debt has been canceled out, and your funds have been restored to your savings, with interest. There's just one more thing."

"What?" he managed.

"The title to your house. Cori signed it back over to you," he said. "Now I imagine she's wondering where she stands."

"Cori belongs there. The house is hers as much as it is mine," he said. The idea of her moving out numbed him to the core. Scared him on a primal level, inspired fear he'd never known.

Pure terror that he'd arrive home to find her gone.

For good.

And yet, how could he expect her to stay? She deserved better than a man who'd almost committed murder.

"Tell her to stay. If anyone leaves, it'll be me."

Delacruz's expression went arctic. "Tell her yourself." He turned and strode for the door, then paused, tossing the parting shot over his shoulder. "She told me you're some sort of genius. I think you're a very stupid coward."

Cori's brother closed the door quietly behind him.

20

Cori went to see Zack one more time, two days later. She'd attended her classes, checking her cell phone every half hour. She had done her ER rotations, resisted the wild urge to catch the elevator up to the regular room he'd been moved to and see him. She'd pumped Dr. Chu for information, kept her ears open. He was recovering well.

But he hadn't called.

She was losing him, and didn't know what else to do except try again. The visit had been a mistake.

Their conversation was so stilted and sad, she'd left after ten minutes. And spent twenty more sobbing in the ladies' room.

No more. She couldn't fight this battle here. He'd have to work through the trauma of what he'd done, and he'd either let her help him or not. One thing for certain, he'd not be able to hide forever. He was getting well, and he'd have to come home, eventually.

Then what? She refused to dwell on the worst possible outcome.

So it came as something of a shock the following Saturday, one week after their kidnapping, when Sean Tanner called her at home. Tucking the receiver under her ear, she paused in the act of drying dishes, scrambling to think why Zack's captain would phone.

"Hello, Sean. What can I do for you?" No sooner had the question left her mouth than a horrible scenario formed. "Is something wrong with Zack? Has he relapsed?" Please, no—

"Cori, I don't know how to say this," he began, voice heavy with regret.

The mug in her hands slipped and clattered into the sink. "Oh, God. What's wrong?"

"Zack was just here."

"He's been released?" Anguish lanced her, the hurt unbearable. He hadn't bothered to call.

"Yeah, just a little while ago." Sean blew out a breath on the other end, sounding tired. Defeated. "He turned in his resignation."

The world tilted. "Wh-what?"

"He quit without notice. Of course, I'm not about to accept it. I'm hoping you can run interference, talk some sense into him."

Pulling out a breakfast-nook chair, she sat before she fell down. "He *loves* his job, Sean. He told me himself that he never wanted to do anything else."

"He's dealing with some tough shit. He's been through a lot. You both have. Listen, just . . . try, okay? He's headed your way. One of the B-shift guys is giving him a ride."

"All right. I'll do my best."

"Zack's a good man, Cori. Don't let him go."

"It may not be up to me, Sean."

She hung up and laid the phone on the table. Stared blindly at the wall.

Zack was coming home. And he hadn't cared to let her know.

The man she loved was coming to tell her good-bye.

Zack slapped the hood of Clay Montana's truck, waved so long, and shuffled slowly up the front-porch steps. Even though he was doped to the gills, his taped ribs and the healing knife wound were killing him.

But not nearly as much as the hole in his heart.

Sean had probably called her right away. She must hate him by now. Which was for the best. Right?

The front door wasn't locked. He stepped inside, and she rose from the sofa. Stood silently, returning his gaze.

She looked tired. Too thin; dark circles under her lovely eyes. Apparently, she hadn't been eating or sleeping. Worst of all was the devastation etched on her face. She wiped her palms on her jeans, then crossed her arms under her breasts. Uncertain, hesitant as she'd never been with him before.

I've done this to her, to us. I don't deserve her.

"Welcome home," she said.

"I'm here to pack."

A spasm of pain ruined what little composure remained. "You're leaving. Just like that, even though we love each other."

"It's not enough." No, that wasn't quite right. "*I'm* not enough."

"What do you mean?"

His throat burned. "All my life, I've fallen short of the mark. I should've been more, made better choices. For a while, I let myself believe I'd risen above the loser everyone thought me to be."

Shaking her head, she took a few steps toward him. "You're not a loser. You're the man I love. Nothing will ever change that, no matter how far you run."

He gave her a sad smile. "You once told me one of the things you loved most about me was that I settle my problems with my brain, not my fists. I let you down."

Spreading her hands, she closed the distance between them. "No, you didn't! You're kind and brilliant, and—"

"I almost killed a man, Cori. With my *bare hands*! How could you love me now? I'm not what you wanted."

Shamed, he hung his head, hands fisted at his sides. He swallowed hard once, twice, but couldn't stop the tear that escaped to roll down his stubbled cheek. Or the next.

Her palm was warm on his face and he turned into her touch, a small sound of agony emerging despite his efforts.

"Everyone makes mistakes, and sometimes people are pushed beyond their limits," she said softly. "Tell me, would you love me any less if I'd been the one to beat Lionel to a pulp? If I'd taken the fireplace poker and brained him?"

A tiny kernel of hope formed in his chest. For the first time in days, a ray of light.

"No, of course not. But you didn't."

"I would have. And it wouldn't have been nearly as bad as what I've done in the past."

That brought his head up and he searched her face. Read the sorrow in her eyes, the regret. "I don't understand."

"I lied to you, Zack. From the beginning, about something very important. Given the circumstances, it might change the way you feel about me."

"You're wrong. Nothing ever could." Fear gripping his gut, he cupped her cheeks in both hands. "What is it?"

"The night my husband nearly beat me to death . . ."

"You can tell me anything, baby."

"Joaquin didn't shoot Alex. I did."

"Oh, my God." What she must've gone through. The fear, the guilt.

"I *did* kill a man. In self-defense, but he's just as dead. The enormity of taking a life never really goes away, though it was him or me. My brother took the blame to protect me from the press, from speculation. And I let him. Do you hate me now?" she whispered. "Do you love me any less?"

He pulled her into his arms, gathered her close to his heart. "God, no. How could you ever think that?"

"Then how can you love *yourself* any less?"

The truth, every word.

The kernel bloomed, unfurled. She snuggled against his chest, tears dampening his T-shirt, and he knew he'd never let this woman go. "I love you, Cori Shannon."

"Please don't go."

"Try and make me." He nuzzled her hair, inhaled her scent. "I'm so sorry for putting you through hell this week."

"I'm a woman. I'll save it up and pay you back later."

He chuckled, and winced at the pain in his ribs. "Damn, don't make me laugh."

"You shouldn't be out of the hospital, stubborn man."

"I'll get more nursing care right here in your arms."

"Mmm, true."

"I wish I could make love to you."

"We have plenty of time."

Winding her arms around his neck, she gave him a soul-searing kiss. Her tongue delved into his mouth, licking him into a state of bliss. Pulling back, she cocked her head at him. "What did you really do with the fifty million?"

"Pretty much what I told Lionel. I created another account and hid the money. I can put it back anytime, though Detective Bernie said the Feds might make some noise."

She bit her lip. "Can they do anything? I paid my taxes, and the account is overseas. Plus, you were under duress."

"Probably not. Don't worry, beautiful." A sudden, awful thought occurred to him. "Damn! I quit my job."

"No, you didn't. Tanner called me, and he's not accepting your resignation."

"Thank God."

"All right. Let's change the subject." She grinned. "I believe you owe me a surprise, fireboy."

Happiness filled him to overflowing. This morning, he was convinced he'd never hear her call him that again. "You haven't peeked?"

"Nope. I promised I wouldn't, and I haven't."

"Come here." Taking her by the hand, he led her through the house to the door leading out onto the deck. "Close your eyes."

She squeezed them shut. He slid open the glass, led her through. "How far are we going?"

"A little ways. Don't worry. I won't let you fall." Carefully, he led her down the hill to the creek. The going was slow and truthfully, it would've been easier just to let her open her eyes and see his gift, but being there together was important to him. Symbolic, somehow. He led her onto the wooden planks and positioned her at the rail, facing the creek trickling under their feet. Took her hand.

Her fingers grabbed the rail. "What . . . ?"

"I hope you like it."

"You know I will. Now?"

"Okay, open them."

She did, her gaze widening. And took in his gift, dappled with sunshine, arching gracefully under the trees. He watched the pure, unadulterated joy flood her face.

"You . . . Oh, God, you built me a bridge! Zack, it's gorgeous!" She launched herself into his arms and he caught her with an *oomph* as she smothered him with kisses. "Oh, I'm sorry! Your ribs!"

"Hey, that's all right," he teased. "I'll build you a few more if I get this reaction."

She kissed him again, lingering this time until he was hard against her belly. Throbbing.

"Thank you," she said, raking her fingers through his hair. "I love it."

"You're welcome. I love you. Can't have my baby falling into the creek anymore, can I?"

"Nope." She paused, a strange light in her eyes. Taking his hand, she pressed his palm flat against her tummy. "Neither one of your babies."

He stared at her, struck stupid. "What?"

"Surprise, Daddy. Whoopsy-daisy, the pill isn't always one-hundred percent effective."

He couldn't have been more shocked had she smacked him in the head with a shovel. Hands shaking, he framed her sweet face. "Y-you're pregnant?"

"How do you feel about that? Still want to go pack?"

God in heaven, he'd nearly left her. Nearly walked out of her life, not knowing about their baby.

His child.

Overwhelmed, humbled, he sank to his knees in front of her. Took her hands in his, and did his best to put his feelings into words.

"You're my heart and soul, Corrine Shannon. As long as I have you by my side, believing in me, I can do anything. I love you, and I love our baby," he said hoarsely. "Will you do me the honor of becoming my wife?"

"Oh!" Dropping to her knees in front of him, she threw herself into his arms, almost knocking him over. "Yes! Yes, I'll marry you!"

His ribs screamed in protest, but he didn't care. All that mattered was the woman in his arms. "Then I'm the luckiest guy on the planet."

"And don't you forget it." She kissed him soundly, a promise, he hoped, of the evening to come.

"Keep that up and I'll let you have your wicked way with me. If you're *very* gentle."

"No ropes or scarves?"

He laughed, shaking his head at her cute little pout. "Not tonight. This time, it's just you and me."

"Welcome home, handsome."

"I wouldn't be anywhere else, beautiful. Just here, with you."

Forever.

Turn the page for a special preview
of the next book in the
Firefighters of Station Five series,

HIDDEN FIRE

Coming from Signet Eclipse in December 2009

Julian Salvatore sprayed a steady stream of water at Station Five's ambulance, rinsing off the soapsuds and gyrating to "Life in the Fast Lane" blaring from the radio just inside the bay.

Nothing like the Eagles to make a boring task bearable.

Using the nozzle as a microphone, he lip-synched a little Don Henley, punctuating the heavy downbeat with blasts to the bubbles. Watching them slide away. Thinking, yeah, he could relate. He enjoyed life a bit too fast, a lot too naughty.

Too bad he was on shift. He craved some action, and not the type to be found here, working with five guys he couldn't quite call pals. He conjured an image of feminine curves, toned thighs. Long, white-blond hair draped over his chest, violet eyes holding him captive while their slick bodies moved in time to the pounding music—

Which abruptly lowered several notches, poofing his fantasy to dust.

"Jeez, man. You selling tickets?"

Julian glanced toward the door to the bay. Zack Knight, A-shift's fire apparatus operator, straightened and turned away from the portable radio, cell phone to one ear. Knight leaned against the grille of the big quint, cooing into the phone like a frickin' turtle dove.

". . . you know I don't care, beautiful," Knight was saying, face glowing with happiness. "Whatever color you want me to stain it is fine."

Yep, totally whipped.

Rolling his eyes, Julian made an exaggerated gagging noise. Knight shot him the finger and a big grin, and Julian couldn't resist smiling back as he shut off the water. So, the geek had grown a big, steely pair after all. Love must do weird shit to a guy.

He wouldn't know. Nor did he care to.

"Salvatore!"

He started, stifling a curse and the urge to grab his chest. *Cristo*, the captain had a way of lying low, then leaping out of nowhere to lop off an unsuspecting victim's head like some sort of damned ninja assassin.

Julian turned, pasting on his most innocent expression—a stretch, even on his best day. "Hey, Cap. What's shakin'?"

Sean Tanner got in his personal space, vibrating with anger from head to toe. He rested his hands on his narrow hips, green eyes snapping. Hoo-yah, this was gonna be a scream.

"I'm going to say this once. Knock that crap off before you wind up with a formal complaint in your file."

Julian stared back. What the hell? "Am I supposed to know what you're talking about?"

"The tampon prank was funny the first time, although inappropriate. You're lucky Eve didn't make an issue of it before, but this? Stringing them across the ladies' room door is going too far."

Knight closed his cell phone, slid it into his pants pocket, and watched with interest. Julian laughed. He couldn't help it.

"Man, you need to lighten up. Eve's cool and you *know* she dishes out as much as she takes."

Tanner's face hardened. "Nevertheless, your prepubescent shit is getting old. I'm about fed up—"

Julian's humor fled. "Why don't you look into the mirror, *amigo*, say that three times, and see if you land in Kansas? You're not the only one who's fed up."

Color flooded Tanner's cheeks as he sputtered. "What the fuck do you mean by that?"

"Want me to spell it out? Fine. You haven't been doing a perfect job yourself, but you don't hesitate to stalk around here shouting and bitching at everyone who doesn't meet your impossible standards." Julian shook his head. "You know what? Forget it. I'm not doing this. The point is, I'm not the one who pulled the stunt, I don't have a clue who did, and frankly, sir, I don't give a flying rat's ass. If you'll excuse me, I have work to finish."

For the first time in his career, Julian gave his back to a superior. And it hurt a helluva lot more than he'd have thought.

Because in that moment, in a startling burst of clarity, he realized he'd lost all respect for his captain.

Everyone went through rough times, Tanner's rougher than most. But the captain wasn't the only one who'd faced total devastation and lived to tell, even if he hadn't wanted to.

Oh, no. Not going there. Grabbing an old towel, he shoved the memory into its tamperproof compartment and began to dry the ambulance. He longed to get in Tanner's grill, set him straight. Tell the uptight bastard he didn't have the market cornered on pain and suffering. Tell him—

"Damn, you should've seen his expression," Knight remarked quietly, coming to stand beside him.

"He's gone?" Julian wasn't about to give Tanner the satisfaction of looking.

"After he gave about two seconds' thought to ripping your head off, yeah." Knight paused, blinking behind his wire-rimmed glasses. "You shocked him. I mean, I've gotten pretty good at not letting him get to me, but nobody stands up to him like that except Six-Pack."

Julian started on the windshield, keeping his voice low. "Has the intervention been scheduled?"

"I was on my way out to talk to you about it when Cori phoned. Six-Pack needs to meet with all of us first so we're on the same page. Everyone else is free Friday afternoon. Work for you?"

"I've got a date later, but sure. I'll be there."

Knight clapped him on the shoulder, then wandered off. Julian tried to imagine Tanner's reaction when he realized what they'd planned, and winced. No man wanted to listen to the people closest to him air his problem in a public forum. He had a feeling this giant group hug was going to backfire something awful. For the record, he'd warned them.

Still, something had to be done before Sean drank himself to death.

Three loud, high tones over the intercom system scattered his thoughts. The pleasantly creepy computerized voice announced a kitchen fire at one of Sugarland's few high-end restaurants.

Pitching the towel into the bay, he sprinted for his gear, almost relieved for the distraction.

Almost. If he'd learned anything in all his years as a firefighter, complacence on the job was usually followed by unmitigated disaster.

He might get a dark thrill out of tempting fate, but he wasn't stupid.

Julian grabbed a hose and jogged for the rear entry of the restaurant, Tommy Skyler at his back. Displaced diners milled around the front and side of the building, and Julian spared them a glance as he and Skyler approached the kitchen door.

Most of them appeared to have departed, but a few onlookers watched the proceedings with avid interest. As always, his roving eye zeroed in on the women, some dressed business casual, but a couple in classy power suits. Including a tall, willowy blonde who seemed to be staring right at him.

Recognition zapped him like touching a live circuit, charged his libido. He stopped so abruptly, Skyler plowed into his back with a curse.

Grace McKenna.

Five feet eleven delectable inches of cream-your-boxer-briefs temptation. The violet-eyed beauty of his lusty fantasies, the Ice Princess who'd ignored every one of his advances.

And Six-Pack's off-limits sister-in-law.

He couldn't have Grace.

Which, of course, only made him want her more.

"What're you doing, man? Go, go!" Skyler yelled.

Shaking it off and breaking eye contact, he ran. What *was* he doing? A split second of inattention on the job could get a firefighter killed. He wasn't ready to die today, and certainly not over a woman.

A woman who wouldn't suffer a moment of remorse if something bad *did* happen to him.

Focus. The kitchen was almost fully engulfed in flames, but he and Skyler managed to wrestle the blaze under control without too much difficulty. The stove provided the worst problem, covered in grease and equipped with a vat for frying, but was quickly subdued by Eve with chemical foam.

The heat was a nasty bitch, though, boiling his skin through the heavy protective clothing. He'd reek of smoke and sweat and he hoped they had a long enough reprieve from the calls to sneak a shower later.

Through the kitchen entry into the restaurant's dining room, he saw Eve join Six-Pack to do a walk-through of the premises. Six-Pack gave him a thumbs-up for an all clear, so they had to concentrate on only the kitchen area and make sure no hot spots remained.

Leaving their buddies to handle that part, Julian and Skyler shut off the hose and exited the way they'd come in. Skyler took charge of helping Knight put the hose away, and as Julian removed his mask to let it dangle around his neck, he observed that the younger man had really started to mature in the past couple of months. When had that happened?

He shook his head with a rueful laugh. Yeah, he was such an expert on maturity.

Then he didn't have time to think about Skyler anymore because, *Dios mío*, Grace was striding toward him purposefully, lovely expression cool and composed as ever. If he didn't know better, she might have been marching forward to serve him with a subpoena. After months of her ignoring his phone calls, he couldn't imagine what on earth she had to say to him.

But it couldn't be good.

And here he was caught off guard and out of his groove. With her crisp blouse under her tailored suit jacket and her hair in an elegant twist at her nape, the woman looked as if she'd just stepped out of the pages of *Vogue*. An equally sharp-dressed man—her lunch date?—trailed in her wake while Julian was a stinky, sooty old gym sock. Shit. Feeling self-conscious and hating it, he raked his fingers through his wet hair, pasting on a grin.

"*Querida*, you picked a fine time to accept my dinner invitation. As you can see, I'm a bit underdressed."

Grace stopped in front of him, huge eyes softening the merest fraction. "I had to stay and make certain you were all right," she said, her soft, melodic voice edged with a tiny hint of concern.

Just like that, his knees went weak. His heart thudded madly in his chest and for once in his life, he could think of nothing clever to say. The armor of his wit deserted him, leaving him naked and squirming.

"I . . . I'm fine, Grace."

"And Howard?" She squinted toward the smoldering restaurant, worry for her sister's husband plain.

"We're good. Just another day in the jungle. How have you been?" *Why haven't you acknowledged my existence?*

Clutching her purse, she favored him with a polite smile that seized his lungs. "Busy. Half the population needs an attorney."

"And they're all innocent, I'm sure."

"Of course. Those are the only ones I defend." As though suddenly reminded of her lunch date, she glanced to the man standing behind her and waved him forward. "Oh! Gentlemen, I apologize. Derek, this is an acquaintance of mine, Julian Salvatore. He works with my sister's husband. Julian, this is Derek Vines."

The name slammed into him, a double shot to the head and gut. His gaze swung toward the man's good-looking face. Fifteen years older, but the same face that haunted his nightmares. One he'd never thought to see again in this lifetime, or the next.

He couldn't breathe. Was being held underwater. Vision graying at the edges.

Drowning.

"Julian? Are you all right?"

He blinked at Grace, fighting to breathe, the fog clearing some. He'd never fainted and he wasn't about to now, in front of her.

In front of the man who'd nearly destroyed him.

This must be cosmic punishment for his most terrible mistake, and the promiscuous life he'd led since. Hadn't he suffered enough simply struggling each day to rise above the past?

"Julian?" She turned to Vines. "Get one of the others—"

"No!" He gave her what he prayed was a reassuring smile, when what he needed to do was find a restroom and be sick. "No, I'm fine. It's just . . . all of this clothing and gear is hotter than hell. Vines, nice to meet you," he said.

Because that was how a normal person greeted another. A normal guy would shake the man's hand, too, but he couldn't bring himself to do it. Not even under torture.

Before Vines could open his mouth, Julian took Grace's arm. "I need to speak with you in private."

Vines wore a puzzled frown, not a spark of recognition in his eyes. Thank God. Julian steered Grace toward the back of the ambulance, aware of the captain's disapproving scowl and the other guys' curious stares. He ignored them all, getting right to the point.

"What the fuck are you doing with a slimeball like Derek Vines?"

Score. That damned irritating chilly sophistication slipped several notches, and she gaped at him, bristling. "Derek Vines is my client, not that it's any of your business."

"Really? You called him *Derek*, not Mr. Vines," he pointed out, struggling to remain calm. And losing.

"Derek is a family acquaintance, which is *also* none of your business. If you'll excuse me—"

"Cut that asshole loose. Trust me on this."

"Let go of my arm," she hissed, jerking the limb in question.

Blinking, he uncurled his fingers from her sleeve. He hadn't realized he'd grabbed her. "I'm sorry. But please listen," he entreated, injecting his voice with all the sincerity he possessed. Where Vines was concerned, it wasn't difficult. "Vines is extremely dangerous, Grace. You have no idea."

She obviously wanted to leave, but hesitated, anger tempered by curiosity. "How would you know this?"

Oh, God. "Just . . . trust me."

"Not good enough. I don't know you."

"Yeah? Well, you don't know Vines, either, or you'd never have accepted him as a client. You only defend the innocent?" He gave a bitter laugh and wiped a hand down his grimy face. "Jesus Christ, Grace. Even you can't be right in every case, about every person, and you're not right about him."

"How so? Throw me a bone, Salvatore, or I walk."

Salvatore. The bastard is "Derek" and I'm "Salvatore." Great.

What could he tell her when he was shaking apart inside, trying to keep from hitting his knees?

"Derek's from San Antonio, Texas, same as me and my family. Suffice it to say his whole family is trouble for everyone unfortunate enough to cross their paths. Do some research."

"All right," she said, nodding slightly. "I can do that much."

"Then drop the bastard like yesterday's bad garbage, because that's what he is."

Anger animated her face again, and he knew he'd never seen a more gorgeous woman. Sucked to have her fury directed at him, but better for her to be aware of the viper in her midst.

"Thank you for the information, however vague, but I'll be the one to decide which clients to take on." A strange expression clouded the anger for a second as she held his gaze; then it vanished. "Good-bye, Julian."

Good-bye. At least she'd used his first name again. Wasn't that a positive sign?

And she'd never actually turned him down, had she?

"Why haven't you just said *no*?" he blurted, inwardly cursing himself for an idiot.

Grace paused, looking over her shoulder, violet eyes cool as ever. The irritation was gone, a ghost of a smile hovering on those plump lips. "Perhaps I just haven't said *yes*."

Jaw clenched, he watched her walk away, small, round butt swinging in her tight skirt. *Damn her* for stringing him along.

A hand clamped hard on his shoulder. "Oh, boy. Our Latin lover's got it bad." Six-Pack stepped in front of him, shaking his head. "I've tried to tell you, forget about her. Grace is as elusive as the wind."

"You're just afraid I'll break your precious sister-in-law's heart."

The lieutenant's expression sobered. "Not anymore, my friend. I'm afraid she'll break yours."

Six-Pack strode away and Julian watched, relieved, as Grace and Derek Vines left in separate cars. Even if she wasn't his business, he cared for her safety. She was representing a monster, and he couldn't make her understand.

Not unless he told her everything.

And that was *never* going to happen.

ABOUT THE AUTHOR

Jo Davis spent sixteen years in the public school trenches before she left teaching to pursue her dreams of becoming a full-time writer. An active member of Romance Writers of America, she's been a Golden Heart Award finalist for Best Romantic Suspense. She lives in Texas with her husband and two children. Visit her Web site at www.jodavis.net.